Divine Appointments

**Center Point
Large Print**

Also by Charlene Ann Baumbich
And available from Center Point Large Print:

Snowglobe Connections Series
Stray Affections

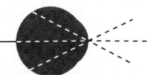

Divine Appointments

A Snowglobe Connections Novel

CHARLENE ANN
BAUMBICH

CENTER POINT PUBLISHING
THORNDIKE, MAINE

This Center Point Large Print edition is published in the year 2010 by arrangement with WaterBrook Press, an imprint of The Crown Publishing Group, a division of Random House, Inc.

All Scripture quotations are taken from the New American Standard Bible®.
© Copyright The Lockman Foundation 1960, 1962, 1963, 1968, 1971, 1972, 1973, 1975, 1977, 1995.
Used by permission. (www.Lockman.org).
The characters and events in this book are fictional, and any resemblance to actual persons or events is coincidental.
The text of this Large Print edition is unabridged.
In other aspects, this book may vary from the original edition.
Printed in the United States of America on permanent paper.
Set in 16-point Times New Roman type.

ISBN: 978-1-60285-903-6

Library of Congress Cataloging-in-Publication Data

Baumbich, Charlene Ann, 1945–
   Divine appointments / Charlene Ann Baumbich. — Center Point large print ed.
      p. cm.
   Originally published: Colorado Springs, Colo. : WaterBrook Press, 2010.
   ISBN 978-1-60285-903-6 (library binding : alk. paper)
   1. Single women—Fiction. 2. Businesswomen—Fiction.
   3. Self-actualization (Psychology) in women—Fiction. 4. Large type books. I. Title.
   PS3602.A963D58 2010b
   813´.6—dc22
                                                    2010022604

To Bridget Ann and Colleen Ann

May encouragement rise to meet you,
May friends be always at your side.
May the moon light your spirit.
May rainbows curl softly in your smiles.

May lush be the colors of your joy,
May intimacy be easy and right,
May pure be the love you desire,
May grace be the gift you receive.

Until we hug again,
May God hold you in his heart.

I love you,
Grannie B

Blessed is the man who trusts in the LORD
And whose trust is the LORD.
For he will be like a tree planted by the water,
That extends its roots by a stream
And will not fear when the heat comes;
But its leaves will be green,
And it will not be anxious in a year of drought
Nor cease to yield fruit.

JEREMIAH 17:7-8

Part One

One

Attempting to release the stifling heat from her body, Josie threw back the covers and heaved a sigh. Stuck in her languid, sweltering, hot-flashing body, she rolled out of bed, shucked off her damp pajamas, and dragged herself down the hall. Within a few moments, she stood in her kitchen, eyes closed, head stuck in her freezer.

Who would believe that at 2 a.m. on a below-freezing February morning in Chicago, I'd be standing here like this? Up until a minute ago, certainly not her. Hoping she was trapped in a nightmare, she willed herself to open her eyes. *Wake up!* But instead of pulling out of a deep slumber, she looked straight into the swirling curls of mist flowing over a low-cal frozen dinner four inches from her lips.

While waving freezer air toward her sweaty armpits, she surveyed the items before her. Healthy everything. *See, I* am *sane. So what has led me to such a preposterous moment?* But she knew. Same as always, her course of action was set as a result of last night's Internet research.

Research: her instinctive course of action against the unknown.

In an attempt to find something—anything— short of hormone-replacement therapy to help her through what she hoped was a brief perimenopausal stage, she'd clicked from one medical and holistic site to the next. One set of survey results reported that some women stuck their heads in the freezer for relief. Her initial reaction upon reading that finding had been, Not in a million years. But when this tsunami of a hot flash rolled into her forty-seven-year-old body, the idea rose to the forefront, and desperation led her straight to the kitchen. Much to her surprise, the bizarre procedure seemed to help. Or had the flash simply begun to subside already?

Always analyzing, Josie. Give it a rest. Who cares why? You feel better, and that's the goal, she thought, her eyes landing on a small container of frozen yogurt tucked behind a bag of broccoli. But as she reached for it, a chill quaked her body. She closed the freezer door, crossed her arms over her bare chest, and quickly padded back toward her bedroom. Once the hot flash retreated, the reality of the cool temperature in her condo set in.

Even though she had no need to pinch pennies, she still tried to look after her dollars. The first thing she did when she moved into a new dwelling—an annual event—was swap out the thermostat for the latest and best energy-efficient model. During the winter, she programmed it to sixty-five during weekdays, then up to sixty-eight in the early evenings after she got home from work, and down to sixty-two at night. Summers, well . . . When the flashes began last July, she often found herself lowering the temperature a notch no matter what she'd programmed.

In the faint red glow of her bedside clock, she opened her dresser drawer and withdrew a powder blue cotton pajama set with three-quarter-length sleeves. Counting the set of pajamas still on the floor, and in keeping with her lifelong motto to simplify, it was one of four identical sets, all pastel blue, all worn year round. Shivering, she scooped the soiled pj's off the floor and scurried to the master bathroom. She turned on the light, ran warm water on a washcloth, and wiped her face and neck and then behind her ears. She gulped a glass of water, slipped on the clean pajamas, and smeared a dab of night cream over her cheeks, then laid the damp items over the top of the hamper to dry. "No sense risking mildew," she heard her Grandmother Nancy say.

Grandmother Nancy had dealt with bountiful piles of laundry produced by seven children. "It doesn't take long for damp things to sprout moldy wings," she used to say in a singsongy voice. Josie smiled at the memory of one of her many sayings.

Once back in bed, she drew the flannel sheets up to her nose. "Freezer to flannel? Come on, body!" she chided, tired, yet now wide awake. Although occasional daytime hot flashes were annoying and embarrassing, the sleep deprivation these rampant night sweats caused was wearing her out. The last time she looked at the clock, it said 3:15 a.m.

Next thing she knew, her alarm was ringing. Five-thirty. Time to get up and work out.

To further boost her morning cardio workout and burn off the few M&M's she'd nabbed from the small art deco bowl near her key hook, Josie walked down her building's five flights of stairs. Anxious to gulp a blast of fresh air, she stepped out onto the sidewalk while tossing a "Good morning, Howard," over her shoulder to the doorman. She sucked in her breath. The wind blustered, causing her to pull her scarf a little tighter around her neck.

When she'd contracted for the job in Chicago, she told the Realtor that proximity to her labor was primary. This move's goal: as often as possible, leave the car behind. Despite the cold, she felt a renewed surge of gratefulness for that freedom. The last two years, both her Houston and Raleigh locations had kept her sitting in traffic too many hours a day. She needed exercise and more scenery than the exhaust pipe of the car in front of her. She set a brisk pace down the sidewalk, only slowing after she skidded on a small patch of ice and nearly lost her footing.

When Josie was growing up, her mother constantly asked her why she moved so quickly. "Where's the fire? Walk like a lady, Josie." She'd heard it a thousand times. But in all ways, Josie was a mover. She almost always walked a different route to work. Residing just under a mile from her current job, she'd explored nearly every city block between it and her condo—within the boundaries of reason and safety—by foot. But today after chugging only two blocks, and even though she'd pulled her scarf up twice, the tip of her nose was nearly numb. In these freezing conditions, she decided walking didn't make sense, not with "L" stops only a short distance from both ends of her journey.

Before her virgin ride last summer, Josie had made sure to memorize and follow the "L" safety instructions posted on the Internet. She learned where to locate both radio and call buttons in the cars and on the platforms and programmed emergency numbers into her cell phone. She stayed alert, toted her handbag and briefcase cross-body style, and kept her transit card handy so she didn't have to rummage for it.

Immediately after swiping her card, she tucked it back into the slot in her handbag she reserved solely for that purpose. She zipped the bag closed and settled comfortably into her seat. Riding the "L" was second nature now. Relaxing, really. *So simple,* she thought, as she leaned back and recalled her first "L" adventure. She'd studied the maps and made sense of the different color-coded lines, and she possessed a steel-trap memory.

During that first ride, her every move was calculated to make it appear as if she'd been riding the elevated system for years.

A big man stood just a few feet from Josie—the type of guy that might inspire caution in "L" riders. Although she couldn't see his face, he reminded her of one of the people she'd encountered at a previous job.

In Atlanta, Josie had been in charge of notifying the employees being laid off, not a task regularly included in her consulting work. The first employee to receive her dismissal notice was Roger Elmquist, a physically daunting bruiser of a man.

"Roger," Josie said the day she let him go, "I need to see you in my office, please."

"Yes, ma'am." He was always polite. Large in stature but quiet in voice. Good at his job, but his position was being eliminated. Bottom line. End of story.

Once she closed the door and asked him to take a seat, she got right to the point. "Roger, I'm sure you are aware that your company is streamlining operations. Sometimes through no fault of an employee—and such is the case with you—a position with a company becomes obsolete. I've called you in here to let you know that, unfortunately, this is your last day on the job."

Roger looked at her as if he did not understand English. Josie had heard rumors of his penchant

16

for karaoke, but she couldn't picture the man in front of her at the mike.

"Human Resources has arranged for you to receive job counseling. I'm sure they'll help you find just the right match for your skill set." She stood and held out her hand. "Good luck, sir."

Roger remained seated, eyebrows knit together. He stared at her outstretched palm.

"Roger?"

He blinked, then looked up at her.

"Roger, they're waiting for you in HR. You're a good worker, and management here is giving you a great recommendation. I'm sure you'll land on your feet."

After a very long pause, Roger stood. He appeared shorter, smaller, his shoulders slumped. Without saying a word, he left.

The next day, Roger's itsy-bitsy wife stormed into the building, wanting to see Josie. Josie could hear her yelling clear through the glass in the reception area.

"What do you mean I *can't* see her? She *crushed* my Roger! He can't even lift his head off the pillow this morning. What kind of a monster— what kind of a company—doesn't give notice, or warning, and just upends a man like that? Do any of you even care that six years ago he tried to take his own life, he was so despairing? Of *course* not! All you know is your own power and greed!"

When she threatened to storm the place if Josie

did not have the common decency to look her in the face and explain exactly why her Roger was treated that way, Josie started toward her office door. *Some people,* she thought, *need a strong word about simmering down.*

"Is that her?" the woman yelled, noticing Josie through the door. "I swear, if my Roger slides back into depression, I am going to hold you personally accountable!"

Before Josie even reached for the handle, a security officer appeared. First he tried to reason with the woman, explain that she needed to calm down. She made the mistake of drawing back her arm as if she was going to strike him. He grabbed her wrist and said, "Come with me. It's time you leave before you get yourself in real trouble here."

"Any trouble, sir," she said, speaking through clenched teeth, "has been brought about by this company's lack of common decency." At that, the fight seemed to drain out of her, and she began to cry. She cried so hard they nearly had to carry her out. "You've sapped the life out of my Roger," she said, sniffing. "You have no idea how hard he worked to build himself back up as a man after he lost his last job. And now you've gone and robbed him of his dignity again."

Decency. Dignity. The words twirled in Josie's head as she scanned passengers in her car.

That older woman to her right . . . *Hmm. Might*

be on her way to a cleaning job. Or maybe to visit a sick sister in the hospital. Yes, that's it. She wore a tired sadness around her eyes. Likely a widow, which gave her something in common with Josie. Although Josie had never married, she understood the responsibilities and nuances of an oldish woman living alone. What they probably didn't have in common was that Josie liked it that way.

Josie's body jerked slightly to the left. She glanced at the floor as a stream of murky winter-boot water shifted in the opposite direction.

How quickly life ebbs and flows when you're off to the next station.

Her eyes shifted to a stately man wearing a plaid neck scarf. He somewhat resembled Victor. Tall. Lean. Strong jaw. Powerful presence. She studied his shoes, his haircut, his fingernails. This guy was richer than Victor, she thought. Likely a CEO. They briefly made eye contact, which she had not meant to happen, and he nodded at her. She nodded back, then averted her eyes. She was glad when he stood to get off at the next stop. After he departed, she swiveled and watched him walk down the platform. He even moved like Victor. Erect, shoulders squared, chin tucked to chest, military cadence. She leaned back to see around a couple of heads, unable to take her eyes off him, wondering what Victor was up to lately. If one person on this earth moved faster than she did, it was Victor.

She recalled the day she'd finally caught Victor on the phone to ask his opinion about a high-paying corporate job dangling in front of her. She wasn't surprised by his answer.

"Pick something that keeps you in the lifestyle to which you are accustomed: fluid. It's a big, wonderful country we live in, Jo. You're a strong woman. Make sure you can always call your own shots. Why be another corporate clone?"

Who wouldn't *heed the voice of such a powerful father?* She'd called her father Victor for so long that sometimes it seemed easy to forget he *was* her father, not just Victor Brooks, military lifer, man of convictions with the power to influence.

She watched the stranger until he disappeared when the train took off again. *Movin' on.* Within forty-eight hours of Victor's call-your-own-shots pep talk, she had begun the process of incorporating and setting up shop as an independent systems analyst and consultant. Two weeks into her well-planned flurry of self-promotion, her sterling résumé and focus on the world of corporate insurance landed her first major client. *Interesting, how the course of a life can take shape during such short encounters, like how a passing stranger can jog such memories.* It seemed so very long ago that she flew to Denver to seal the deal and sign a year's lease on an apartment. One year was how long she estimated that first contracted job would last. In fact, she finished three months ahead of schedule, which gave her the opportunity to take a class and score another software certification.

You've come a long way, baby, she thought as she recalled the worn, uneven floorboards and the banging water pipes in that first apartment, which was the last dwelling place she rented. From that day forward, she bought. With every annual move, she upsized her income as well as the value of her condo or town home. Shrewd research and negotiating skills proved each real estate investment a more luxurious accommodation than the last. She smiled at the satisfying fruits of her diligence.

But as the elevated train car rounded the last bend before her stop, she watched the skyline change and wondered if her next move, due to take place in only four months, might be the end of that grand roll. Not long after she'd signed on here in Chicago, the housing market tanked. It would be interesting to see where she landed next and what kind of hit she'd have to take. Then again, in some areas, housing was selling so far below market value that she still might make out. Seemed lots of folks were already looking for 2009 to end, and they weren't even six weeks in. But wouldn't it be just like her to land on her feet in the midst of an economic downturn? Victor would be proud.

The train lurched to a stop. Josie stepped out of

the car and was once again reminded why she'd ridden today. The wind howled down the raised "L" platform. She hiked up her briefcase strap and held a gloved hand over her nose. A man frantically ran up the stairs toward her, coat flapping open, as if he'd been sitting at the table and just noticed he was late. *Could be on his way to a shareholders' meeting. Likely runs late every day, a habit his wife finally gave up trying to change.* When they passed each other, she got a whiff of his cologne. Cheap. Too strong. *Maybe he's having an affair, and they woke up late.*

She trudged down the slushy sidewalk, trying to expel the remnants of that guy's fragrance from her sensory memory. It brought to mind a VP in Augusta she'd once invited in for drinks after a dinner date. He'd scrutinized her surroundings over the top of his wineglass.

"A bit stark," he'd said, shifting his eyes to hers. "Don't you think? I bet you'll be happy to settle down one day, finally personalize a place and make it your own. I can't imagine moving every year. What we put up with to make a decent living, right?"

She'd replied with a flat no, and that was the end of him. How she'd made such an error in judgment, she could not imagine.

She entered her work building, pulled her scarf from around her neck, and hopped on the elevator, which had just landed. *Moving on and up has definite advantages,* she thought, even though as a military child, it had at first been difficult to keep moving away from new friendships. But she'd soon realized that all that moving also offered its perks, and she'd quickly learned how to take advantage of them. Endlessly able to start over, she'd reinvent herself, try on new personas. The more moves, the better she became at leaving her old self and longings behind. At one base, she played the shy child, while keeping her nose stuck in a book. At the next, she was the tireless sojourner, off exploring and blazing new trails. "Follow me!" she'd shout. But whatever persona she tried on, she made sure to keep an emotional distance from those brave enough to attempt to make friends with her. *Funny thing to ruminate on now,* she mused, since at the moment she was pressed against the back wall of the elevator while two more people squished their way inside.

Well, I was who I was, and I am who I am, she thought when she exited the elevator at her floor. She opened her coat and involuntarily shook like a dog trying to expel a spider off its back. She detested cramped elevator rides.

Hopefully, she thought as she removed her boots, swapping them for heels, *the next place is warmer than Chicago.*

Two

Marsha Maggiano clamped down on the little edge of fingernail between her teeth and gave her head a jerk. The nail ripped so low in the quick she winced. She spit the ragged nail slice into her hand and tossed it in the garbage can, then splayed her fingers in front of her and stared at them. Not a normal fingernail left. The fervor of today's mastication might actually tie the record-low shape of her nails right after her divorce last year.

Marsha looked up just in time to see that analyst woman, the one who'd been lurking around for several months, walking toward her, notebook in hand, writing as fast as she could while staring directly at Marsha. How could she last on those heels all day, especially at the pace she kept?

That analyst She-Cat, Marsha thought, had the most uncanny way of catching her with her hands off her keyboard. To her, Ms. Josie Victor Brooks seemed to move like a dangerous robot, a feline robot even, eyes slicing this way and that, just waiting for the weakest links to reveal their vulnerability. Marsha heard it joked about in the lunchroom that Ms. Brooks had eyes not only in the back of her head but in her ears as well. Kind of a creepy thought, really, eyeballs floating around in ear canals. Marsha liked the concept enough that when she first heard it, she immediately withdrew her Moleskine notebook from her handbag and wrote it on the "Character attributes" page.

Marsha glued her eyes to her computer monitor and banged her sore fingertips on her keyboard. Still, her mind reeled off character names. Firing Matrix or possibly—*hmm*—Peeping Perpetrator. *Good one!* It struck her as hysterical to imagine that the uptight Josie, who had been hired to come in and "fix" what did not at all seem broken, could actually spy on people through a fog of earwax. But then Marsha always laughed at the most inappropriate times—in church or at a funeral. Or when something was extremely sad. Or when she was scared, like now.

Hmm. Why is she talking to Barb, but still staring at me? Right! Because with that eye in her ear, she's actually spying on Barb too. A chuckle escaped Marsha's lips, which she quickly covered with a cough. At least she hoped she had. Either way, she loved it when she cracked herself up.

Barb, the department head, was also a good friend of Marsha's. They'd met on the job fifteen years before, the day Marsha started at Diamond Mutual. Barb had not only taken Marsha to lunch her first day, but had also taken her under her wing, just as she did with every new employee, showing her the ropes and encouraging her to be patient with herself. Since the day they met, the two of them had always sat near each other.

Marsha tried not to pay attention as Beastie Babe—*Oooh! Yes!*—sidled up behind her. She was glad she'd thought to quickly switch computer screens. She'd opened a little notebook window to type all the clever character nicknames popping into her creative head, which she'd later transfer to her Moleskine. *Good thing I had that spreadsheet open too!* She clicked on one of the menu items and added a formula to a column. By the time she completed that task, Josie had moved toward the next desk, still burning words into her notebook. Marsha could hardly wait for break time when she and Barb could debrief about her . . . *encounter of the dragon kind. Oh, man! The muse is with me today!*

Marsha felt a twinge of guilt for thinking and saying such terrible things, applying such a plethora of cruel nicknames to someone she didn't really know. But the writing was on the wall. Word had spread that when the new system was actualized, almost everyone in her department would lose their jobs, thanks to Hatchet Hand. But then, that was the Brooks woman's job, to come in and "upgrade" the system, make Marsha's department more efficient—which meant irrelevant, which meant Marsha would soon be culling help-wanted ads rather than spending her evenings working on the great American horror novel, or sci-fi adventure, or murder mystery, or whatever genre it turned out to be in the end.

Moments after Josie finally left the area, Barb walked over to Marsha's desk. She wore a big smile. "You crack me up, you know that?" Barb said. "I wish you could see yourself in action. It was all I could do to keep from busting out laughing when Our Ms. Brooks came around and I saw your 'I am sooo busy' face." They both giggled.

Lyle Waters, Diamond Mutual's VP of operations, strode in. Several times lately he'd appeared right after Josie left an area. Marsha wondered if he might be checking for fallout.

"Ladies," he said, nodding to each of them, "it's good to hear laughter in this department again. I know with changes in the wind, everyone's been a little uptight. Just last night I heard another tickler on the news about how laughter is a healthy way to combat stress."

"Barb is so good for us, Mr. Waters, for *all* of us," Marsha said, her eyes roaming the department. Just that morning Barb had held a brief meeting to thank everyone for their diligence under pressure.

"Yes, that she is." Lyle nodded. "That's exactly why we've kept her all these years."

"Back to work," Barb said, turning toward her desk. "Enough about me."

"Yes, back to work for me, too," Lyle said. "I

was just making a pass through, checking the climate. Good to know at least *one* department is still running on sunshine."

Marsha watched Barb resettle herself at her desk. She'd meant what she said: she was so grateful for Barb. Glancing down the hall, she noticed Lyle stopping to chat with Frank. Lyle put his hand on Frank's shoulder and nodded, taking in Frank's every word. If Marsha were writing romance, her leading man would be very similar to Mr. Lyle Waters. Kind. Handsome. Thoughtful. He'd have a name like Lance Looker, or maybe Lawrence O'Loverly, or . . .

Nah. Stick to murder, fantasy, sci-fi, or action adventure. You stink at love anyway.

Lyle sat in his office across the desk from Josie. She'd knocked twice and opened the door, expecting them to get right down to business. When she noticed he was on a call, she started to back out, but he wagged his finger toward himself and then pointed at the chair for her to sit. In return, she pointed her finger at her wristwatch and raised her eyebrows. Yes, he had her down for 2 o'clock, so he repeated his finger-wagging gestures. Reluctantly, she closed the door behind her and took a seat.

While he listened to his call, he watched Josie shuffle through a few pages in her notebook. She was obviously annoyed. But he couldn't just hang up on his surprise 1:45 conference call that should have ended by now, not when it was with two members of the board of directors explaining that another member had suddenly resigned over some "unconquerable discord." They didn't say what discord, but the repercussive fallout was evident in their voices. "We've always trusted and supported you, Lyle, and didn't want you to hear about his resignation through the grapevine or in a memo." They said they'd keep him informed, then finally said their good-byes.

"Sorry to keep you waiting," he said to Josie. He looked at his watch, as did she. It was barely 2:02.

"Yes, well, I don't have long. Busy day." Her voice was curt.

While she started in on her briefing, Lyle quickly jotted down a couple of key words from his conference call that had triggered his intuitive sensibilities. *Trust. Support.* Two words that in and of themselves were good, but they'd sounded too carefully chosen. He set down his pen and gave Josie his full attention.

She opened her mouth to speculate, as she put it—although most of her speculations were actually calculated conclusions—as to which line of computer code involving the something or other might hold the error causing one of their greater issues.

"Can you break that down? Slower, please," he

said, when he realized she awaited his response. Though still slightly unnerved and distracted by the call, he also could never quite size this woman up. Every work day for eight entire months, he'd studied her. He was a good people reader, but she was a mystery and unlike anyone he'd ever met. Unintentionally and unaware she was doing it, she extracted a dichotomy of emotional responses from him with every encounter.

Two days after she started, he was convinced she was truly a genius at her job, just as her references had said. But he also suspected she might be a somewhat scary, cold-hearted loser in her personal life, despite her physical beauty. But then, out of nowhere, she'd say something so remarkable that the surprise of it knocked his assumptions completely off kilter. Something like, "I once saw the Grateful Dead in concert." No way could he picture her as a Deadhead. Or "I like what Obama said about . . ." when he could have sworn she was a die-hard Republican.

The real scale tipper came the day she happened to be standing next to him when he received a call from his sister and learned that his mother had taken severely ill. Josie divulged that she'd spent a few sessions with a therapist shortly after her mother died.

"Too much guilt and grief to sort it out on my own. It had been so long since I'd been home for a visit, and I assumed her hospitalization was just another of her bad spells. If your mother is ill," Josie'd said, her tone of voice a mix of authority, kindness, and guilt, "don't second-guess. Just go!"

He took her advice, made an airline reservation, and left that evening. Between bouts of fretting about his mom during the flight, he found himself revisiting the moment that Ms. Brooks admitted there was a time in her life when she needed help—that she needed anything from anyone.

Amazing.

As Josie flipped through her notes, Lyle studied her perfectly oval, groomed fingernails. *So feminine.* Slowly, methodically, tenderly, almost, she repeated the technical issue and the cause and response for her summations. But when she shifted gears to read the list of employees she recommended be let go, there wasn't a hint of softness about her. She peeled further back through her notebook, glanced at her list, and named three more names. She sounded so certain, so unemotional, so *casual,* as if she neither felt a thing she said nor cared about how anyone would fare after a job loss. She could just as easily be reading her grocery list.

"Ashley Storm, Ted Frazier, and Barb DeWitt."

The last name caught Lyle up short. Barb DeWitt? She'd been with the company for nearly twenty years, nine years longer than he had. She'd been the head of the data entry department for the last seven years, and there were good reasons for that. Barb was one of the most likable people in the whole company. She took charge of her department and settled the hysterical buzz the day it was announced an outside consultant and systems analyst would soon be among them.

Although he was aware before his firm contracted Josie Brooks that Barb's entire department would likely be the first to go once the new system was fully operational—new equipment installed and all the bugs worked out of the software—Lyle figured those who served in supervisory capacities would still be utilized somewhere. But according to Josie, who continued talking while he reeled from the reality of the depth of the cuts, Barb's skill set would no longer be a compatible match.

Not for the first time, Josie explained to him that it would be more cost-effective to hire a couple of entry level employees already trained in the new systems rather than to invest in "old school, we've always done it this way" attitudes. "Besides, she's likely ready to retire soon anyway." Josie sounded like she herself would never think of doing such a thing.

"You sure we're not opening ourselves to an age discrimination case?" Lyle asked. "The CEO sent me a cautionary e-mail."

"Look," Josie said, closing her notebook. "I get paid to make recommendations and upgrade systems. I don't think about who's young or old or make your final decisions. You can offer selective buyout packages if you're concerned, but I'm sure you already know the financial limitations of that. If it's Barb you're worried about, she would likely be happy to accept a fair offer, especially if you help cover insurance. She seems like a reasonable person. But then that's not my area of expertise or advisement. Those types of decisions are up to Diamond Mutual." She stared at him, impatience skirting her eyes.

"You're right, of course." He would not mention, though it was certainly on his mind, that when, at age sixty-two, his mom lost her job in a corporate "rearrangement," he'd encouraged her to file an age discrimination case.

Lyle studied the deep blue of Josie's eyes and unsuccessfully tried not to check out the swing of her fanny, as his dad used to say about Doris Day, as she headed toward the door.

"Josie," he said, causing her to stop and turn. "For the record, I am grateful for your expertise." He stood and walked toward her. "And thank you for your patience when you arrived today. Just to make things clear," he said, now standing in front of her, "I don't want you to think I take your time for granted any more than I want you to believe I'm *incapable* of making my own corporate decisions." He flashed her a playful grin, which she did not reciprocate. Did the woman even have a sense of humor? "You are good at what you do, which is why I both ask for and value your opinions." He meant every word.

All she offered in return was a slight nod of her head. Although he reached for the door handle, she beat him to it. Why did he have the distinct feeling she'd rolled her eyes as she closed the door behind her?

"Whew!" was all he could say when she was gone.

After arriving home from work, Josie shed her winter wear, recalling flashes of people doing the same thing as she passed by their office windows during her "L" ride this morning. *We come and we go.* She walked to the bedroom, hung up her work clothes and donned one of her three comfy gray sweat suits.

Rummaging through the fridge, she decided she owed it to herself to leisurely prepare a stir-fry concoction using some of her fresh vegetables and a block of tofu. No rice or noodles this time. Just wholesome crunchy goodness, an unusual blend of spices, and maybe a few cashew nuts thrown in for good measure. One by one, she lined up the veggies on the counter and surveyed their beautiful range of colors, then rearranged the lineup in descending color order.

Yes, it was time to unwind. Create. Brighten her world. Ongoing trouble with a code, people in data processing all but laughing in her face, a slight headache that set in the minute she left Lyle's office . . . *No wonder the employees all adore him,* she thought as she fixed herself a tall glass of water. *What a brown-noser.*

She downed several hefty gulps of water, screwed the lid back on, and set the bottle out of spilling range. After placing two lightweight chopping mats on the countertop, she went straight to methodical work on an onion. She drained the block of tofu, sliced a stalk of celery on the diagonal, smashed a couple of garlic cloves, then cut a few very thin wedges of Chinese cabbage. Next she snipped a small pile of fresh lemon grass with her kitchen scissors and grabbed a handful of fresh bean sprouts from the fridge. She took out her stove-top wok and set the bottle of peanut oil nearby. After cutting perfect squares of tofu and surveying her mounds, she decided to rummage for at least one more color. "Perfect," she said, when she spied the eggplant.

She was glad she'd made a stop at a nearby market yesterday. As was often the case when she went to the market, she remembered a conversation with her Grandmother Nancy. Shortly after Josie's mother died, Josie made an uncommon spur-of-the-moment trip to visit her grandmother before she accumulated one *more* irreversible regret. Thank goodness she did; shortly afterward, Grandmother Nancy was gone too.

35

"All your gadding about, Jo-Jo." Grandmother Nancy had pushed a hair behind her grown granddaughter's ear, a hair already perfectly in place. "I understand that you can't help but have a little wanderlust in your blood. After all," she said, smiling, "you are your father's daughter, and he sure didn't stay put the moment he could fly. No sir. That boy was chompin' at the bit to get out of here. But when good homegrown tomatoes come into season, can you even buy one when you're stuck in the middle of those cement cities?"

Josie laughed. "You'd be surprised at the wonderful produce I can buy in the city, and from all over the world! Just last week I made a Thai dinner with some wonderfully fresh and fragrant vegetables and a few spices I bet you've never even heard of. I wish you'd take me up on my offer to fly you out for a short visit. We could spend a whole *day* going from one market to the next. You'd love it. You'd find *twenty* kinds of tomatoes!"

"Early Girls and beefsteaks are enough *kinds* of tomatoes for me. Fresh off the vine, there's nothing like them. I'm a homebody, Jo-Jo. Besides, who would bring in my mail if I just up and disappeared? Who would be here to baby-sit my wily passel of grandkids and great-grands if I just took off?" Grandmother Nancy said, smiling, her eyes flashing their wonderful twinkle. Her grandmother adored nothing more than just being there—for everyone. Having lived with a husband, seven children, and countless pets, she once said she could never imagine living Josie's life. "I'd feel like a kite without a tail, sailing a sky way too quiet for me."

On the other hand, there was Victor. "Why get stuck in the same place for the rest of your life, Jo?" he'd counseled when Josie first began charting a course for her career. "Think about it: what does your grandmother really know of the world?"

Victor loved his mother, but he often talked about her as if she were an old fuddy-duddy. In fact, Josie believed Grandmother Nancy was quite in vogue for her age, at least among her small-town peers. But Josie understood why, after his childhood, which he referred to as "stifled by quaintness," a phrase he always followed with a dramatic yawn, Victor enlisted in the army. He was the oldest of seven children in a family perpetually scraping the bottom of funds, and the military seemed Victor's only practical and affordable way out of town. And yet, no matter how much he derided his hometown, he also knew he'd fight for the rights of the families within it, so enlistment was not only doable, but a good fit for his inborn sense of independence and scrappiness. A military lifer, he'd witnessed his share of the world and change—and death.

And who, Grandmother Nancy, would get Diamond Mutual running leaner and meaner if I lived like dad, always having to go where someone else told me to go? Or if I lived like you, never leaving town?

Josie rummaged through the vegetable bin in the fridge one more time and decided to add a handful of pea pods. As the gas burner sparked to life, flashes of her day's encounter with Lyle shot unbidden to the forefront of her mind. That he was not ready for their meeting and then didn't give her his full attention right away after he hung up was, in her opinion, unprofessional. She poured peanut oil into the pan and let it heat a moment. *His seeming indecision followed by a well-timed compliment and a quirky grin?* The oil sizzled when she tossed in the tofu, which she stirred with aggression. She removed the tofu and stir-fried the rest of the ingredients, adding a few spices along the way. After tasting one of the pea pods for flavor, she decided to grate a little ginger into the mix. Before rinsing the grater, she put her nose to it and inhaled.

Smells better than any *man's cologne.*

Although it wasn't her best meal—it needed more . . . something—it was tasty and healthy. She eyeballed the M&M's. *No. Not even a little caffeine this time of day.* She'd read that caffeine exacerbated hot flashes, which, when she did indulge, was another reason to limit herself to

38

only a few at a time. She straightened up the kitchen, then forced herself to put in a load of laundry. She'd have to stay up later than she'd like, but piles of laundry—all things left undone—weighed her down.

That was why this whole job thing was getting to her. She'd never been this far into one job without having locked in the next. She'd spoken on the phone with Donovan, her only sibling, about just this the other night, after he'd asked her where she'd be moving next.

"It's disconcerting, Donovan. For the first time ever, I have this gnawing question about meeting the contracted deadline, enough that it's kept me from pursuing a next place."

"You've put out feelers though, right? I'm sure you've got *something* in the works."

"Only halfhearted attempts. A few months into this job, before I realized how bad things were going to get, I checked out a couple of possibilities in Minnesota, but they were too small. Not enough challenge. Since then, every time I experience another setback or surprise at this venue, I have to rein in my aggressive tendencies to think that far ahead again. I know you've always wondered why I go through the hassles of buying and selling every year, but aside from the monetary gains, another upside is that I'm free from the pressure of yearly leases. Can you imagine if I had to deal with *having* to move or signing another year's lease again any time I ran behind or got done early?"

"Wait. Rewind. Did I just hear you say you reined in your aggressive tendencies? Is this really my sister? We must have a bad connection. You think it's on your end or mine here in Paris?" He laughed.

"Very funny. Seriously, Donovan, you know I don't rely on emotions or gut hunches."

"Yep," he said after another chuckle. " 'Until you prove it to me, it doesn't exist.' Do you know how many times you said that to me when we were growing up?"

"Fair enough. And for the most part, I still believe that. But Donovan, I keep sensing something about this current job's circumstances that demands a constant time buffer or reevaluation or . . . It's making me crazy."

"If anyone can figure it out, you can, Sis," Donovan said. "You always do."

Yes, she'd thought after they'd hung up, on herself she could ultimately rely. But still, she was currently struggling into the second week of solving something she initially thought would take a few hours. The project felt close to hopelessly behind. She'd put in many late nights attempting to ward off the possibility that she might have to seek an extension on her contract, something that, until now, simply was not acceptable.

You just need to relax, Josie. She finally let herself sink into the couch, the remotes to both the television and stereo, which was on, within reach and a small glass of sherry in her hand. *Donovan is right. If there is one thing I do really well, it's figure things out.* To shore up a minor dip in her resolve, she ran through a personal list of affirmations.

- She made companies better. Always.
- She was excellent at her job.
- She made smart real-estate decisions.
- She maintained her living quarters exactly the way she liked them: sparse. Just a few expensive and meaningful objects of art.
- Always on the move, she'd learned to travel light. Aside from her mattress, for two of her relocations, she'd rented furniture, which not only saved money but gave her the opportunity to "try on" new decorating styles.

When the timing is right, you'll figure everything out and be smart enough to trust it.

A few years ago, she'd even sold her mother's heavy, dark dining room furniture—the only reason she'd kept a storage shed—happily unburdening herself of the last of her anchors. "Maybe one day you'll settle down and start a family," her mom had said, just before anyone knew she was dying. "I'd like to think my grandkids will one day sit around their great grandmother's dining room table. At least someone in the family will finally enjoy it!" Madeline, Josie's mother, had inherited the set from her mother, a farm wife in West Virginia. A military wife, Madeline kept it in storage her entire lifetime, hoping that one day they would settle in one place. But it wasn't in her husband's genes to do so. Josie had decided she wasn't going to die with it in storage too.

There was no sense in holding on to dreams that were not hers. You move on and cut your losses.

Three

Just when Josie felt fully relaxed, shoulders falling away from her earlobes, her cell phone rang. She checked her watch. Nine o'clock. At first she didn't recognize the name on the caller ID. Then the Minnesota area code brought the caller into clarity. It was Cassandra Higgins, the woman whose nose she'd broken back in September. She'd only met her that one time.

Josie had flown into Minneapolis and rented a car for the two-hour trek to her interviews. She'd stopped at the fairgrounds on the way back to the airport, only because she'd read about the Collectors Convention in the paper, it was a beautiful day, and she was running extremely early. Even though she wasn't a fan of dust or "geegaws," as her Grandmother Nancy called them, seeing the fairground buildings up ahead reminded her how excited her grandmother got about the county fair. She'd write about it at length in her weekly letters, describe the preserves she made to enter in open class, and beg her father to let their little Jo-Jo come for a visit, which only worked out once during fair season. Even though it was dusty and stifling hot, what a great time they'd had! Without giving it another thought, Josie put on her blinker and entered the fairgrounds. But my, oh my. All that junk. And then that terrible incident.

Josie hadn't carried her giant Gucci bag, the cause of the accidental nose breaking, since. When she'd slung the massive bag over her shoulder and pivoted—the bag heavy with a snowglobe she'd purchased from a gypsylike vendor on a misguided whim—it hit Cassandra in the head, twice: once on the first pivot and again when she turned to see what she'd hit.

Since their embarrassing encounter, Cassandra had called only one other time. It was a strange call. Pretty nonsensical, really—no different from their entire nose-breaking debacle. During that call, Cassandra asked Josie a curious question about another snowglobe from the same vendor she'd all but grabbed out of Josie's hands. She and Cassandra had only shared one e-mail exchange since then too. Cassandra wanted Josie to know that she'd seen a doctor, and that yes, her nose was broken, but there was no need for Josie to worry or pay.

Now, five months since the incident, Josie stared at the caller ID, hoping Cassandra didn't turn out to be the kind who suddenly claimed whiplash. While lowering the volume on the stereo, she chastised herself for not having her attorney draw up medical release papers.

"Josie Brooks here."

"Josie, it's Cassandra Higgins from Minnesota. Remember me?"

"How could I forget? It's not every day I break someone's nose." Josie chuckled. *Keep it friendly, and cut to the chase.* "I assume you're all healed now?"

"Yes ma'am. Aside from a very slight bend in my nose—so slight the average person would never notice—my nose is fine. No physical repercussions. In fact, my life couldn't be better, and I owe it in part to you, which is what I called to tell you. To *thank* you. The kids are in bed, and I was just sitting here scratching Sarah behind the ears—she's our new Border collie—and thinking how grateful I am to you for surrendering that snowglobe you were holding when I so rudely pronounced I was about to buy it. I won't bother you with the details. I'd never be able to explain what I don't fully understand anyway. Let me just say that the day that mystifying snowglobe came

44

into my life, things began to change for the better, and in quite mysterious ways."

Josie set her glass of sherry down and uprighted herself on the couch. "I don't understand," she said, impatience slipping into her tone. "There's nothing to thank me for. I broke your nose!"

Cassandra chuckled. "Look, that was an accident. The whole . . . Oh, it's all inexplicable. I probably shouldn't have called. I just wanted you to know that your generosity in handing the snowglobe over is what set the extraordinary changes in my life rolling, so thank you."

"I don't know what to say."

"No need to say anything. I hope I haven't upset you."

"It was nice to hear from you," Josie said. *Lie.*

"Good-bye."

Josie tossed her phone on the end of the couch and shook her head. Some people were just too strange to even try to figure out. She decided that if she ever saw Cassandra's name or number on the caller ID again, she wouldn't answer.

She cranked the stereo volume back up, rearranged the throw pillows, and resumed her partial recline on the couch. After her second sip of sherry, she couldn't help casting her eyes toward the hutch, to the snowglobe she had purchased. Such a surreal and atypical day, breaking a nose *and* buying a geegaw. Feeling a bit of a chill, she pulled the throw over her legs,

45

closed her eyes, and allowed the memory of it to wash over her.

Just before her happenstance meeting with Cassandra, she'd been walking along thinking how thirsty she was. Hoping to spot a fresh-lemonade stand, she fixed her eyes down the aisle in front of her and a flash of light, refracting off a snowglobe on a nearby vendor's table, nearly blinded her. She closed her eyes and looked away for a moment. When she reopened them, they landed directly on a globe with an uncommonly peaceful scene of a meadow with a creek running through it. A large tree grew near the shoreline. The creek looked so refreshing. When she looked closer, the water appeared to actually be running in the creek.

She chalked up the odd vision to the aftermath of the momentary blinding, like accidentally looking at the sun and not being able to see anything correctly for a while. She blinked a few times and stepped closer. The creek *was* running! Although the snowglobe looked quite old, she thought it must be a retro knockoff with a battery in it.

She stared at it, thinking how utterly quenching and soothing the creek looked, imagining herself palming a drink of water to her dry lips, sinking her toes into the cool bank, listening to the happy babbling noise. She wasn't sure how long she stood frozen while her mind wandered from one glorious scenario in the creek to the next, but finally she picked up the snowglobe and examined the bottom to see what made it work, to analyze how someone could build a snowglobe that could make water appear to be running inside water. *Hmm.* No windup knob. No on-off switch. Nothing other than a symbol or trademark stamp or something. When she uprighted the globe, the snow was the only thing moving. It gently landed on the lush summer scene, an oddity in itself, if she got right down to it.

"Would you like me to wrap that for you?" the vendor asked.

"No. I was just looking." She started to set it down.

"That Bakelite base likely means it's a real oldie. Had a bunch of vendors here before I opened this morning trying to buy it from me. That's when I knew the forty bucks I'm asking is probably too little."

"Forty dollars? You can't be serious." Josie couldn't imagine anyone paying that kind of money for a cheap knickknack. She took one more look at the creek. Nothing.

The man standing next to her said to the vendor, "I'll take it." He reached for the snowglobe, two twenty-dollar bills in his hand.

She started to hand it over, but the vendor grabbed her wrist, almost causing her to drop the globe and scream.

"Sir," the vendor said to the man offering him the bills, although he continued staring straight at Josie, "the pretty lady here has not made up her mind yet, have you, miss?"

She pulled her arm back to make him let go of her wrist, which he did. The action positioned the globe right in front of her eyes. The creek water was running again! The next thing she knew, she heard herself saying that she had made up her mind, and she reached for her wallet.

What a con artist that guy was. Better than your average carny huckster. Her Grandmother Nancy used to marvel at their skills at the fair. "They could sell you your own right hand." Yes, he'd duped her good. How he managed to make the water appear to be running, she'd never know. But not only did he get her forty bucks, she injured someone with the dumb thing after she put it in her big Gucci bag. Obviously, he'd duped that Cassandra woman too. As Josie walked away from the vendor with her new purchase secured, she'd stopped and picked up a globe with dogs in it, thinking her nephew might like it. That's when Cassandra had pounced and said *she* was buying that globe.

Mysterious? Mystifying? Come on, she thought, taking another sip of her sherry.

Once Josie got her creekside globe home, she never saw the water run again. She set her glass on the end table and stared at it. It was nothing more than a hideous reminder of her moment of weakness, an embarrassment to her better judgment, and an affront to both her taste and décor. If Cassandra's call accomplished anything productive, it was to set her conviction to get rid of it.

Next stop, Salvation Army.

Four

Unable to sleep, Marsha decided to put her fretful energy into her novel. She needed to focus on her writing while she still had a paycheck to subsidize her authorly development. She'd come late to the writing game and quite by a back door.

Fighting a deep depression and a mixed sense of abandonment, loneliness, and betrayal six months after her forty-fourth birthday and a painful divorce, Marsha went to see her doctor. The ex had already married "that blonde hussy"; her daughter, Gina, was busy with a new family of her own; her son, Anthony, left for college; and rumors of impending changes in her workplace had taken their toll. She'd hoped to receive a brain-numbing prescription.

Instead, Doctor Pliter recommended she write her emotions in a journal. "Do not judge yourself. Don't try to be literate, careful, or kind—which I know you always do," the doc told Marsha. "Just write what you feel. Let it all out. The page is a good listener. Check back with me in two weeks. If you feel no improvement, we'll consider alternatives, but I have a sneaking suspicion that just letting *out* some of what's bottled up inside you will help."

On the way home from that doctor appointment, Marsha pulled into the parking lot of her local bookstore. She couldn't even enter the store until she'd sat in the car and cried for five minutes. Then she blew her nose and determined to spend whatever amount of time and money it took to buy herself the most user-friendly, leather-bound journal she could find. Maybe a red one. Something fiery to help her get in touch with her anger, her rage—maybe even her vengefulness.

Marsha was raised with the ongoing reminder that "blessed are the peacemakers." Of course she'd *felt* anger, but letting it out was a no-no in her quiet household. It was quite the shock when she first visited her ex's big Italian family and saw how they freely argued with such passion and volume. It often caused her to shrink into herself. Her mother would definitely not approve of such earthy and uncontrolled exchanges. Nonetheless, she'd also heard her mother say that "doctor knows best."

Never once had she yelled at her husband, not even after she learned of his multiple affairs. Maybe the doctor was right; it was time to do something about it.

Mission bound, it took her only five minutes to find the perfect notebook. Not only was it red, it was a shade of blood red. It had a hand-hewn slice-of-bone button with a sinewy leather strap to wind around the button for "security." *All the better to flail you with, my dear ex,* she heard in her head the moment she fingered it.

As soon as she returned to the car, she took the journal out of the bag and kissed it. "I promise you," she said to her new friend, tears springing forth again, "to be nothing but honest. You listen. I'll write. I hope the words of my anger don't get so heated that you spontaneously combust from the pure passion of it all!" She paused. "Holy cow! You're already working!" she said before kissing it again.

She stopped at Barb's house on her way home. She needed someone to hold her accountable. Not by ever—*ever*—reading what she wrote, but by occasionally asking if she was, indeed, writing.

"You know," Barb said, "it's not my journal, but if I were you, my first sentence might be something like, *'The lying cheating bastard!'* That ought to get the ball rolling."

Marsha's mouth flew open. In all their years of friendship, she'd never heard Barb curse. The emotional shock was so powerful that she burst out laughing until she sobbed. Barb wrapped her arms around Marsha and patted her back until she quieted.

When Marsha got home, that was exactly the first line she wrote in her flaming red journal—and with red ink to boot. She lifted her pen from the paper to study the words, but like a magnet, the notebook drew her hand back until she wrote more. It was as if someone uncorked a crowded bottle of words that took flight across the page, determined to speak their own truth.

Marsha was stunned. She had no idea she had so many thoughts and emotions tangled and buried inside her in such a deep web. She felt as if she'd finally discovered the loose end of a knotted torment, then word by word, pulled the thoughts into order so that she could know her own mind.

That first night, she wrote nearly fifteen pages. She wrote and wrote until her hand cramped and her tears ran dry. Her wrist and fingers were so sore she could barely manage her data input at work the next day. By night four of writing, she understood that the power of setting words to paper worked better for her than any drug ever would or could.

After her two weeks of trial writing, she went back to see Doctor Pliter, whom she nearly knocked over with a hug. Marsha assured the doctor she had no *idea* what she'd unleashed. She reported she'd already signed up for a writing workshop through the community college.

After getting Cs in English throughout her grammar and high school days, it was nearly impossible to believe that writing was not only therapeutic but fun. *Take that, Mrs. Brock, you stuffy old English teacher!* she huffed to herself, then wrote exactly those words in her journal. As the words poured forth, Marsha recalled countless episodes of the dismissive teacher carrying on about classmate Erma Franken, the teacher's pet of the century. Next came four blazing paragraphs about Erma Franken.

It wasn't long before the idea of writing fiction struck a match in her heart. Horror or maybe a murder mystery or sci-fi or at the very least, haunted fantasy. Maybe all of them rolled into one.

What she loved about the freedom of writing "out there" on her computer was that she could take all her emotions and channel them into story lines having everything to do with her, and yet seemingly nothing. She could be as free and honest, and as gruesome, vindictive, angry, or filled with rage as she needed, all while letting the emotions and words flow straight into *Helmoot, the Reaper Rephotsirch*, which was the current working title for her WIP—work in progress—as she learned to refer to it in her workshop. She loved spelling it *WHIP* since that was what she was doing: whipping all evildoers into submission with her words. The more times she said her title aloud and tried different fonts for visual effect, the more she could hear it coming out of the announcer's mouth on the six-o'clock news. "And tonight, coming in at number one on *The New York Times* Best Seller List, where it has been for six straight months: *Helmoot, the Reaper Rephotsirch.*" The more she "heard" it on the six-o'clock news, the more she could envision the title on movie theater screens across America, but especially in Chicago, where the real reaper still lived.

"The title was the result of intense scrutinization," she told Barb during one of their girls' nights out. "As you know, my ex-husband's name is *Christopher.*" She said his name as though cranking it through a wringer. "First I thought I'd call it *Christopher the Reaper.* But no, I'd never feel free enough to really let him have it—not in public like that, anyway. You know, when the book releases."

"What about at your writing workshop?"

She thought a minute. "Nah. Not there either. Feels too vulnerable, and I don't really know some of the people *that* well. But it doesn't matter because in the end I decided *Christopher the Reaper* sounded boring anyway."

"Now that I think about it, I see what you mean. So what's the title now?"

"I changed it to *Chris Topher, Reaper at Large.*"

"Oh, I like it!"

"But . . . ," she said, pausing with dramatic flair, "Gina, my wordsmithy daughter, clever and sensitive and literary-loving woman that she is, would likely figure out that I'm actually blasting her dad. I decided the title has to *allude* to the crumb bum but still be unrecognizable as he who is married to the blonde hussy."

Barb howled with laughter. "Maybe *that's* a good title. *He Who Is Married to the Blonde Hussy.*"

"Don't tempt me," Marsha said, wagging her finger. "It struck me to just spell Christopher's name backward." She grabbed a pen out of her purse and wrote his name on a paper napkin. "But R-e-h-p-o-t-s-i-r-h-c," she said, pronouncing each letter, "doesn't look or sound like anything." She turned the napkin to face Barb. "And if I can't pronounce it, how can the folks who have to introduce me at my book signings?"

"Good point."

"So after I juggled the letters for a few days, I came upon R-e-p-h-o-t-s-i-r-c-h, pronounced Ree-pot-search." I presented it at my writing workshop last night and they loved it! They agreed that Rephotsirch sounded archaic and big and evil, kinda like a Tyrannosaurus rex, but a Rephotsirch."

"Brilliant!"

"To add just an extra layer of disguise, I stumbled upon the perfect addition. While I was flipping through the television channels, I came across one of those professional poker games.

When I heard the British announcer refer to Phil Hellmuth, whose last name sounded like *hell* plus *moot* the first time I heard it—which is *perfect* for Christopher—it caught my attention. Then when the announcer explained that Phil Hellmuth had a reputation as the brat of poker, happy bells rang in my head. In order not to get sued by Mr. Hellmuth, I altered his name too. Thus, *Helmoot, the Reaper Rephotsirch* was born."

"You, my dear friend, are a genius!"

"I know," Marsha said, dabbing her mouth with her napkin, making sure the word *Rephotsirch* was turned away from her lips.

She'd already written 152 pages, thinking that an even 300 would be just right. By then, Reaper Rephotsirch, who rained despicable havoc on so many lives, would surely be disempowered, and perhaps disemboweled too. Never again would he wreak his reapy havoc with another living soul, and she would be cleansed of her ferocious unleashed anger, which at times felt so tornadic it scared her.

"T-o-r-n-a-d-i-c," she wrote in her notebook. "Good description."

As frustrating, behind schedule, and mystifying as this Chicago stint could be, Josie still enjoyed going to work every day. Even though she'd again been haunted by night sweats and did not feel completely rested, it was a new day, she loved a challenge, and this one certainly stretched her, which was always good. *Something to be thankful for,* she thought as she walked to work, the tail end of the winter storm having moved out several days ago. By comparison, the toxic corporate atmosphere during her year in Houston made her everyday work life miserable. But she was in it until the job was done and done right, so she tolerated it.

"Gut it out, Jo," her dad told her the day she sprained her ankle before a high school track meet—and countless other times in her life. "Same as me, you're not there to make friends or to win a popularity contest. You're there to do your job."

Houston had been a worst-case scenario. The moment she set foot in the offices, several layers of employees rallied to protect their jobs and soon became uncooperative, making her assessment three times more difficult. They covered for each other, presented false information, and did not even try to hide the fact that they despised her presence. By the end of her first week, it was clear the hostile attitudes trickled down from top management. A domineering and micromanaging director of operations set the tone. Even though he was among those who interviewed her for the position, it quickly became evident he was worried about his position and had likely voted against the decision to hire her—a *fe*male, as she once overheard him refer to her. He spent his days finger pointing and describing everyone's incompetence, including "those knuckleheads" up the ladder. Compared to Lyle . . . Well, there was no comparing him to Lyle, who was utterly taxing in his own sappy and bleeding-heart kind of way.

Breaking with the stream of scurrying walkers, Josie sidestepped toward a window display of Coach handbags. Though she intended to study the bags, her attention was snagged by the window reflection of a man, the guy with the navy blue scarf who'd been behind her the last several blocks. He was one of *those* kinds: an overt letch. He had stood beside her when pedestrian traffic stopped for the light, then lagged behind when the light changed. The whole time he followed her, she felt his eyes burning into her. Now, in the glass, she watched as he thoroughly, brazenly, checked her out, from the back and then in the window. Then—*Oh, puke!*—he winked.

After waiting until the moron was far ahead of her, she hiked the strap of her massive briefcase further up on her shoulder and merged back into the quickly flowing pedestrian stream. She'd worked with more than a few of his type throughout the years. *No matter where I go in the country, people are the same. I hope that slithering Houston director of operations is still job hunting.*

In the end, she had recommended to his

superiors that for the overall health of the company, he needed to go. She withheld the personal commentary as to how he'd likely cause them a sexual harassment suit if he stayed. They were lucky she was leaving; she'd have made sure of it. So although this Chicago job was puzzling and behind schedule and the guy she reported to seemed to live in la-la land—she could read in his eyes that the recent ax list just about gave him the vapors—she was glad it wasn't another Houston.

And yet, as she paused to shift her briefcase to the other shoulder, an uncommon flicker of loneliness tugged at her heart. She'd determined to walk it off this morning, but here it was again.

It struck first at the end of yesterday's workday. Barb and Marsha had stepped into the elevator together, unaware that Josie was behind a row of tall gentlemen standing behind them.

"Crazy day, huh?" Barb said.

"To be sure." Josie caught a glimpse of Marsha rotating her shoulders, as if to shrug the day off. "But I bet we set a department record for data input. I was typing so fast, I think my fingers were actually smoking at one point."

Josie smiled. It had become clear over the last eight months that Marsha was a character.

"Ah, nothing like a department peaking just when systems are about to change," Barb said.

"Oh? Hear something specific?"

"No. I just figure it's time. I have a sixth sense for big changes right around the corner."

"I noticed you had a serious encounter of the dragon kind with Ms. Hatchet Hand right after lunch," Marsha said. "You two were talking awfully softly. Try as I might to eavesdrop, no such luck."

Barb *tsked.* "She was just asking me about a couple of programs. I told her to talk to you. Did she?"

Josie realized they were talking about her. *Encounter of the dragon kind?* She shook her head. *Hatchet Hand?* Over the years she'd no doubt been called worse. Actually, this was kind of funny.

"No. Maybe tomorrow. But enough about work. Where should we go for dinner? I'm starving."

"It's your turn to pick. I can't wait to hear how your reaper story is coming along."

The elevator doors opened, and the crowd of people poured off. Josie found herself hanging back, fussing with her scarf and gloves until the two of them were out of the building.

It wasn't like she *could* go for drinks or dinner with the girls after work and swap stories about her day, or that she even wanted to, really. She was at Diamond Mutual for a reason. Personal distance needed to be maintained. It was just that before her mother died, she'd give *her* a call on the rare occasions when she did feel a little too isolated. Chat about her day. Find out what her mom made for dinner or discuss whatever book either of them was reading.

Her mom once asked her how *she* unwound after work, aside from calling her. "You know I love hearing from you, so don't misunderstand my question or ever stop calling. It's just that I hope you've made some friends this time, Josie."

"I cook; I read; I research; I listen to music. Mostly the same things I did as a child. I'm not the only single person in the world. I love my freedom, Mother. You know that."

"Yes, but you're *always* by yourself. Don't you get lonesome?"

"You did just fine all those years Dad wasn't around," Josie said, suddenly sounding defensive, if not accusatory. She pulled herself together. "I'm sorry. I don't mean to sound like I'm snapping at you. But seriously, Mother, I'm fine."

The phone line was quiet for a spell.

"Yes, your father was gone a lot. But I had you and your brother, and I always made friends on the base. Spouses in the same boat share a lot in common. We kept each other sane. It's good to be able to talk with somebody who *understands* your life."

"It's different for me, Mother. Different boundaries apply. I'm perfectly happy with my lifestyle choices, and I love my job. Please don't worry. I'm just fine. I love you for caring, though. Thank you."

Josie realized she'd walked two blocks in a daze. *I still miss you, Mother.* Who could she chat with to ward off this crazy bout of . . . whatever? If she called her brother again so soon, he'd worry something was wrong. They didn't talk that often. And who knew where Victor was these days? Without her mother holding the fort down, he hardly bothered to come home.

She switched her briefcase, which suddenly felt like the weight of the world, back to its original shoulder. *There. That's better.* She had a good life with a good job and only a few blocks to go until she got to it. *Stand back. An encounter of the dragon kind, coming at you!*

Efficiency. That was what she got paid for. Not friendships or folly, but scrutinization, recommendation, and success. Upgrade and streamline. Analyze, study, research, imagine, conclude. Question if her first set of assumptions still fit the growing broader picture. Think outside the box and strategize. Consider the latest products and software to get the job done most efficiently. Make her staff cutback recommendations.

Simplify and improve. Whether in her personal or professional life, that's what Josie Victor Brooks had long ago determined she was about.

As she kept cadence with the rest of the walkers, she reminded herself that her mottos were still good ones. She would *not* buy another handbag until she was ready to get rid of the one she already owned. No matter how heavy her briefcase, the black leather handbag she carried was just starting to feel like the buttery soft leather of her Grandmother Nancy's old coin purse, which Josie kept tucked in her mother's slim jewelry box on top of her dresser.

The first thing she saw when she opened that jewelry box to retrieve one of her small pairs of earrings or swap out her wristwatch—or to simply inhale a memory—was a picture of her mother and grandmother together. Her mother couldn't have been more than sixteen when the picture was snapped. So many hopes and dreams in those eyes. "I'm sorry about the dining room set, Mom," she whispered the day she got rid of it. "But I have to find some dreams of my own."

The realization that she had no dreams took her by surprise. But then, she had her work, and that was enough.

Josie began to march along in left-right military cadence, as if reciting a poem with measured line breaks.

Simpli-fy. / Im-prove. / Toss in a-dose of / creative-thinking. / Throw back your-shoulders. / Use your-mind. / Keep-moving.

She silently repeated the words to the strike of her footsteps until there was absolutely no doubt they were good and right and true. Just the way Victor taught her.

Five

H ey, Sis," Lyle said into the phone. He turned
it on speaker while he unwrapped a couple
of pork chops he'd picked up at the butcher's on
his way home. "How's it going in OKC?" He and
his sister, Noreen, spoke at least once a week,
usually twice.

"Fair to middling."

"You sound like Mom."

"I wish. She didn't have a very good day yesterday. For that matter, neither did I." Noreen sighed.

"How so?"

"Regarding me or Mom?"

"Take your pick. Just start with one issue, and
move on to the next. That's the way I got through
my crisis management at work today." He pulled
a stool up to the counter and perched on it. The
pork chops could sit for a moment.

"Maybe you should go first then."

"Okay," he said, grinning.

"Shameless male ego talking, but go ahead.
First big brother, then Mom, then me. The agenda
is officially set," she said.

"So as not to wear you out, I'll limit my turn to
one incident. Let's see. You've heard me talk
about Frank, right? The mail clerk?"

"The quirky older gentleman?"

"Exactly. Quirky and a gossip. He's been

spreading speculations as gospel again. Everyone's on edge enough, what with Josie Brooks and two new tech people lurking over everyone's shoulders. Three different managers, one of them Barb, came to my office asking about ridiculous scenarios. 'No,' I told them, 'the company has not been sold. No, we are not on the edge of bankruptcy.'"

"And the root of these untruthful rumors is Frank?"

"Always."

"What makes him dream stuff like this up?"

"Who knows. He's always putting two and two together and getting seven. I guess he thrives on the attention it gets him."

"Why is he still there?"

"You'd have to know Frank to understand the answer."

"So how do you handle him?" Noreen asked. "I mean, how do you settle everyone down? Is the guy ever held accountable?"

"There is only one person in the company who can handle Frank, and I'm smart enough to let her do that." Lyle's stomach rumbled. He slid off the stool and put his heavy skillet on the stove.

"Let me guess," she said. "Barb." When he talked about business, Barb's name often came up. After so many years, Noreen felt like she personally knew many of the people he worked with.

"She was the third one in my office today.

Although she seemed a little concerned about the rumors, all I had to say was, 'Frank.' She told me she'd take care of it. I didn't hear from anyone else after that, so I'm sure she took him to task without ramping him up. I can't imagine Diamond Mutual without her."

"Why would you?"

He decided not to talk about Josie's recommendation. Final decisions hadn't been made yet. "I'm just saying . . . On to Mom, okay?" He poured a little flour into a plate, slid the chops onto the edge of it, and threw the paper in the wastebasket.

"When they changed her bedding today, they found two of her pills. At least the blood pressure mystery is solved."

"How are they gonna keep that from happening again?"

"They said they'll put a note in her file."

"Right. That oughta do it," he said sarcastically.

"They said when they bring her pill cup—and you *know* how many meds are in that thing— they'll stand right there while she takes them, one at a time. So far when changes are made, they stick to their word, so I'm trusting them—until they give me reason not to. Nathan's visiting her on his way home from classes today. Mom could use more familiar stimulation. Sometimes I'm afraid we're losing her . . ."

Nathan, Lyle's nephew, was the kind of young

man who gave Lyle hope for the future. "He's a good kid. And you? How you holding up?"

"I'm making it. Robert's cooking dinner tonight. From the sounds of the paper and the clatter of pans, you're eating in tonight too."

"I have a taste for braised pork chops, and there isn't a place around that makes them to my satisfaction. Picked up a couple of green apples to slice and simmer on top."

"Yum."

"I better concentrate here. Tell Robert and the kids I said hello. Talk to you soon."

He dredged the chops with a thin layer of flour mixed with salt, pepper, and a little paprika, then began the browning process. *Smells good already.* Some frozen corn jazzed up with a coarse pepper blend and a sautéed green pepper, a couple of potatoes—pared, cooked in the microwave, and mashed—a little white gravy with the drippings . . . *Yum, indeed.*

Gray Saturday afternoon. Four-mile walk complete. Laundry done.

Josie decided to entertain herself by driving around a few ethnic neighborhoods to study the architectural style of row houses. Earlier in the week she'd picked up a book about Chicago architecture and found it quite interesting, so she did some research, charted a safe route, and headed out.

Such an interesting lifestyle, houses so close together like this. She slowed down and watched an elderly woman grab her husband's arm and give him a kiss as he walked out the door. The woman wore a robe and a pink curler attached to one side of her head. By the time her husband chugged to his car and began fumbling in his bulky winter-coat pocket for his keys, Josie was right next to him. He was older than he looked from a distance and appeared fragile and tired. But when he looked up at her, he smiled.

No wonder your wife has stayed with you so long. Such tender twinkling eyes, like Grandmother Nancy's. A sudden pang of loneliness ruffled her otherwise happy feathers. *It must be nice to grow old with someone.*

When she could no longer see the man in her rearview mirror, she speculated on the intimate moment she'd witnessed in that doorway. Maybe he was coming out to warm up the car while his wife finished dressing for Saturday night Mass. *But why the kiss? Probably because she was thanking him for being such a gentleman, even after all these years. I bet she's got a pork roast in the Crockpot, bubbling in sauerkraut for after-church dinner. The whole house probably smells like sauerkraut.* Josie'd always enjoyed imagining the details of people's lives. She smiled. *She'll likely cook some dumplings in the broth before she serves it.*

Josie once stumbled upon a cooking show on television and was surprised at how easy dumplings were to make. The chef talked with such love about the fragrances and recipes from her family's history that she made Josie lonesome for . . . what? What *was* the family recipe from her youth that made everyone in her household glad to circle around the table on the rare occasion they were all together?

Meat loaf!

When her dad was around, he was sometimes critical, especially of the temperature and saltiness of things. He'd speak his opinion in short military cadences as if talking to an underling, which usually made Josie's mom raise her eyebrows, at which point he'd apologize for his tone of voice and say something soft and sweet to her. Josie could never figure out why her mother always asked, "How does it taste, Victor?" as if she really wanted to know.

But he never criticized the meat loaf. They all loved the meat loaf.

Josie straightened behind the wheel as she turned the corner, away from the old couple, away from . . . *all that sodium in the sauerkraut. I wonder how you two have lived so long.*

She switched on talk radio. "Experts agree that an economic turnaround is nowhere near." *Exactly.* Times were tough and getting tougher. She listened to the doom-and-gloom program all the way home, grateful for her own job security and a place to live.

The sun set so early in February that when she pulled into the parking garage at five o'clock, it was already pitch black outside. With the wind howling again, Josie also found herself grateful for the luxury of a dedicated space in the parking garage attached to her condo building. She couldn't imagine what it must be like for people in some of the neighborhoods she'd driven through. To have to vie for a spot in front of your own house every night, maybe even end up parking down the block somewhere, getting up before dawn just to shovel yourself out in time for work—to have to scrape off your car or warm it up for someone else? Not the life for her. She was glad to be a creature of luxuries living in a much sought-after location—well, at least when the economy was moving.

She felt badly for her Realtor. Amelia had phoned just last week, wondering if Josie was ready to list her condo yet. When Josie began working with Amelia, she made it clear that the length of her ownership was debatable, that her stays were sometimes shorter than expected, especially if her next job was in a more favorable location than Chicago—although she'd since discovered that the bustle of the city was quite energizing. Amelia's call was exactly the reason Josie worked with her to begin with: Amelia was on the ball. Dedicated. Kept updated tickler files and didn't waste Josie's time the way so many previous Realtors had. She was a careful listener who never tried to talk Josie into something against her wishes.

When she first started buying her residences, Realtors just about drove her nuts—until she figured out how to weed out the Deaf Ones. The first time she heard one of them say, "With a little fixing up . . ." or "It's a real dollhouse," or "It's a few miles farther out than you'd like to be, but . . . ," she knew they hadn't listened to a single unbreakable and specific criteria she'd presented. She never did business with Deaf Ones.

But from the beginning, things had been different with Amelia. While Josie was still in Raleigh, she'd worked with Amelia on the phone, asking dozens of questions, then online with a few virtual walk-throughs Amelia suggested. Amelia wanted Josie to see what she could get for her stated budget, as well as to point out styles that would never do and to note features she deemed exceptionally nice. When Josie flew to Chicago to look at places, Amelia had only three on her list, which at first felt disappointing. But she'd already been to each of them, done her homework, and planned a smart viewing route, one that included a leg of public transportation to give Josie an honest feel for travel time. Josie was pleased to learn that any of the three would serve her, but the second was the winner.

Amelia was a woman after Josie's own heart: assess and deliver.

More than once, Amelia had told Josie, "If you'd ever like to get together for coffee, let me know. I imagine it's difficult to make friends when you're only in the area for such a short time, and in your profession."

"The lifestyle suits me," she'd responded.

But once in a while, when she thought up a story like the one about the fragrance of pork roast and a husband to give a thank-you kiss, and she missed her mother and grandmother lately, and it was Saturday night, and, as usual, Josie had not a thing to do . . . Sure, she always had a stack of trade magazines to read and a book at hand, but she wasn't in the mood to dig deeper into *The Story of Edgar Sawtelle.*

Oh, what the heck.

Josie scrolled through the contacts list on her BlackBerry. Since it was Saturday night, she used the personal number Amelia had given her, saying she only passed it out to those she could trust and whom she personally liked.

"Hello!"

"Amelia! I'm glad I ca—"

"You've reached the voice mail of Amelia Santos. I'm sorry I missed your call. It's important to me. Please leave a message at the sound of the tone, and I'll call you back as soon as I'm able."

Josie was chagrinned she hadn't recognized Amelia's chirpy recorded greeting. She almost hung up, then realized she'd be caught on caller ID as a missed call.That was the problem with spontaneity, which Josie usually didn't believe in for exactly this reason: you often got caught short.

"Amelia. Josie Brooks here. It's Saturday evening, 7 p.m. No, I'm not ready to list my condo yet"—she paused to chuckle in hopes she sounded more casual than she felt—"which is why I used your home number. I thought I'd finally take you up on that cup-of-coffee offer, if you were available. Give me a call on my cell if you have some time after work this week. Or maybe lunch, if you're down in my area? Good-bye."

It wasn't until after she hung up that she noticed the date. February 14. Valentine's Day. *No wonder the couple kissed in the doorway.*

Of course Amelia wasn't home. She was likely out with her fiancé. Probably at a four-star restaurant wearing red and sitting across from . . . *Alfred, she called him.* Josie imagined him wearing the tie Amelia's folks would have given him for Christmas. Corner table. Bottle of Dom Pérignon half empty. Romantic electrical currents passing between them as they raised their glasses and toasted to the future, their love, their hopes, a home brimming with children and laughter. Promises and stability. A home in which they would grow old together, cook pork roast, bathe their grandchildren, and dance by the light of the moon, same as she'd heard Grandmother Nancy say she and her husband did on "oh, so *many* starry-lit country nights."

When Josie snapped to, she realized she was wiping a tear from her cheek and that her cell phone was ringing. She quickly pulled herself together, eyes still too blurry to see the caller ID. A surge of hopeful expectation surged through her. Amelia probably hadn't made it to the phone in time to answer Josie's call.

"Josie Brooks here," she said with a sudden upshift in spirit.

"Oh, I'm sorry. I've reached a wrong number," a male voice said. "But Happy Valentine's Day to you too!"

Click.

Lyle set the receiver back in the cradle. His mom had sounded confused again, confused about the meaning of Valentine's Day. "I thought it was Tuesday," she said. He was glad she was in a long-term care facility now, one both he and his sister felt good about, but still, the pills . . . At least she was safe.

His last visit two months ago left him with a

hurting heart. After her first TIA, the one that sent him for an emergency visit two months before the most recent visit, she'd rallied. But the last ministroke seemed to plunge her in a bad direction. That was when he took a week off and, in a whirlwind of concentrated and exhausting effort, helped his sister get her settled.

He was glad Noreen lived near their mom, although he suffered guilt pangs thinking that the burden of visits and seeing to her daily needs landed, as usual, with the sibling who lived closer. But what was he to do? Noreen assured him she understood, and no doubt that was true. Still, he was glad he'd sent both his mom and his sister a dozen roses for Valentine's Day—a day that would forever be laced with sorrow in his heart. A day he did not wish to revisit . . . again.

Lyle folded the day's newspaper back on itself to reveal the sudoku. After a few minutes of failed fill-ins, he gave in to the reality that some insistent thoughts could not be manipulated by numbers. He kept thinking about the fact that twelve years ago on Valentine's Day, the love of his life, Miriam—the one he did not marry when he should have, the one who begged him to commit, then finally gave up waiting and married another—was killed in a head-on car collision.

He got off the couch and headed for his workout room. Today he'd tackle the NordicTrack Incline Trainer. *Time to climb some mountains, burn off some stress.* But after a few minutes on the machine, his thoughts about Miriam's imprint on his life had not relented. For all those years after their split, it had been one thing to run into her around town, to see her with her son or daughter or husband or the whole family. When that happened, he would smile, make small talk, experience the shadows of pain, but then feel his heart shift gears when he comprehended anew that he sincerely did wish her well. But after he heard about the accident, he could feel only remorse for what might have been—what might not have happened—if he'd just been able to trip his trigger and propose.

Lyle looked at the machine's LED panel and ramped up the incline a few degrees. *Life is an uphill battle,* he mused. Still, in hindsight, he was glad Miriam had a chance to experience what he might never know: the love of her own family and the blessing of children. At close to fifty-four, he thought odds were slim to none he'd find that special someone now and produce a family. He wondered how he'd be as a stepfather, should that opportunity arise. He thought he'd be okay, but you never really knew until you were in the circumstance. Nonetheless, his eyes were always open.

"Patience and faith, Son," his mother used to tell him when she caught him with that look around the corners of his soul, the telltale signs only a mother recognized. But now, after her last stroke, it sometimes took her a few minutes to recognize him as her son—if she could figure it out at all.

He lowered the incline. At this pitch and clip, he'd do himself in. He was huffing and puffing way too early in the workout. He should have warmed up longer and paid more attention. He settled into a comfortable pace and stared out the window, unyielding thoughts barraging him as quick as his steps.

Who would remind him about patience and faith after his mother was gone? His sister was a gem, and they were close, but there were some things only his mother understood about him, especially regarding his sensitivity and passion. Who would continue to convince him they were his best assets rather than his undoing?

"Stop thinking and trust your gut, Son." When he worried too much about too many details—as he'd done with that "missing" marriage proposal— he'd not only wounded the one he loved but lost her. In the end, after Miriam married another, he realized it did not serve him well to overthink, to overprotect, to wait for the perfect moment, until the perfect job was at hand, to wait until it was too late. His mother was right: follow his passions and his gut.

Lord, help me keep my eye on the positive.

He slowed the machine and reduced the incline until it was once again parallel to the floor, then he stopped. He kicked off his gym shoes, shucked off his clothes, and headed for the shower. As he let the warm water run on his head, he opened himself to listening prayer mode. By the time he was done with his shower and into his sweat suit, he knew one thing to be true: try as he might, he could not change the fact that he'd been created by God with vulnerable feelings and deep emotions, sometimes too deep to sort out. He understood that for the most part, his sensitivities and intuition served him well in his career, as long as he kept them balanced with good business.

At the thought of business, Josie Brooks popped into his mind. Cool, calculating, efficient Josie. He bet life would be easier if he were more like her.

Although it was a little self-defeating, especially after a lame workout, he decided to dish himself a big bowl of strawberry ice cream. As he skimmed the ice cream scoop across the top of the container, watching the ice cream curl into a round ball, he thought how wonderful it would be to be able to compartmentalize his life the way Josie seemed capable of doing. Whatever she had, he wished he possessed a bigger dose of it, especially for the task at hand, which was passing down word about who at Diamond Mutual would lose their jobs.

He settled into his lounge chair, bowl of ice cream in hand, and turned on the TV. Surfing through the channels, he landed on a game show.

While the audience clapped and the MC fired questions, his eyes glazed over and his mind drifted back into his analysis.

He was effective in his position mostly because he possessed good communication skills, he was likable and "nice" (a description that made him cringe, since he'd so often heard it applied to hopeless blind dates), he truly cared, he worked hard, he made thoughtful decisions, and it showed. Starting with his first internship in college, he'd heard and read recaps to that effect on every job review since. But what good did those tools do him now?

He slid a scoop of ice cream into his mouth and licked the spoon, wondering how he could separate his emotions from the task and still deliver the terrible news to his employees with integrity and care. A popular beer commercial popped into mind. *How about this? "I love you, man. But you are so fired." Right.*

How about, "You've done a great job the last twenty years, but you've become obsolete, so we have to let you go." Or, "Truly, I care about you. No, I have no idea what you and your family will do for health insurance. Not my problem."

"It's not my fault; it's the fault of Josie Victor Brooks."

He wondered if it might be healthier for people to hate the coldhearted woman who pegged them for dismissal rather than to hear it from the "nice guy." Josie could certainly cut their Diamond Mutual cords without duress.

A cop show was on, and he hadn't even noticed when it started. Sirens, gunshots . . . He decided to turn the TV off. He'd just give in and mull, figure out how he could protect himself from feeling the pain of every single pink slip. *How about, "Your job is over. That's all I have to say on the topic."* But he knew himself too well. He owed it to the intelligence and the honor of his hard-working department heads to at least look them in the eye. And their employees deserved the same sincere look from the people they knew best—their immediate "superiors"—when they received notices.

Trickle-down bad news. This really stinks.

Six

"How ow was your Valentine's weekend?" Barb asked Marsha, as they settled behind their desks Monday morning.

"My daughter and her family sent me a beautiful Valentine's Day card. You know how those Hallmark commercials make me cry?" Marsha waited until Barb nodded. "This card ignited a sob-a-thon. Gina must have browsed through cards for hours. For a while, I thought I might never stop crying, first because the card made me so happy, then because I realized I am so miserable this Valentine's Day. Pity party number 5,762. Poor me with no husband. Then my son called. My son who forgot to send his mother a card? Well, he has a new girlfriend, so what did I expect. To be honest, I'm glad about the girlfriend. Mostly. She seems a little on the wild side, which I try not to think about. But it was great he called, and he made me laugh, the way he always does. Honestly, it's a good thing my Anthony has such a hysterical sense of humor or he probably wouldn't have survived his child-hood. I'd have done him in."

Marsha smiled, recalling an incident from her son's ninth year, a year filled with mischief. She'd arrived home from work to find him sprawled on the kitchen floor, blood on his chest and puddled all around him. She screamed, dropped to her knees beside him, and cradled his head in her lap, wailing all the while, *"Tony! Tony!"* She watched him open his eyes, run his finger through the blood, then lick it off his fingertip, withdrawing it from his mouth with a loud pop. Marsha screamed, and he burst out laughing.

"Mom! Settle down. It's only ketchup. I just wanted to see how sad you'd be if you thought I was dead."

First she cried, she was so happy he wasn't. Next she wanted to kill him for scaring her like that. She yelled at him until they both started laughing, and then she made him clean up not only the ketchup but the entire house. After his dad learned about the incident, he grounded Anthony for a week. "Men don't scare ladies like that, Son, especially not those they live with and love," he'd said, putting his arm around Marsha's waist and pulling her close. Such a warm, protective memory. *What happened to that guy? You ended up inflicting such terrible wounds, Christopher.*

"I know what you mean," Barb said. "My kids all crack me up, especially the boys. But even funnier is watching the oldest two with their kids. Wish my Ted could have lived long enough to see them together. Their youngest looks so much like him."

"Your kids are wonderful," Marsha said. "I enjoy every chance I get to spend with them, which, granted, isn't *that* many. But you know I'll always be partial to your Michelle. That girl has a heart as big as her momma's." Marsha moved her keyboard slightly to the left. "Remember, last summer, that night we spent together with our daughters, strolling Navy Pier, sitting outside and eating peel-and-eat Bubba Gump shrimp, watching the skyline? That was one of the highlights of my entire 2008. We should all do that again this summer."

"I agree. But this time you are *not* getting me on that Ferris wheel! I thought I'd never get my feet back on the ground. Aside from *that,* it was a great evening. Good music, too. As soon as the winter weather breaks, let's talk to the girls and look at our calendars."

"Guess what?" Marsha said as she removed a bunch of papers from her in box and began sorting the papers into piles. "I wrote two entire chapters Saturday night. Not exactly a romantic Valentine's evening, but at least I was productive. I poured every ounce of my sad and mad into the story, nearly killing off the evil Helmoot. But I stifled myself. I can't let me do that, not yet. Not enough pages. I don't want my publishing debut to be a novella."

"Good morning, Josie," Barb said, causing Marsha to look up.

Marsha didn't know how Barb could sound so nice, as if she were speaking to an actual human. But that was Barb, always one to give people— even the enemy—the benefit of the doubt. The day Marsha told Barb that she'd discovered her husband was having extramarital affairs, Barb was clearly and totally in her corner. But a few days later, Barb said she'd started fervently praying—for both Marsha and Christopher.

Marsha was livid. Prayers for her were one thing, but for *him?* Even so, it took Marsha only two days to forget she was mad at Barb. Who could stay mad at *her?*

Nobody.

"Good morning to you, Barb," Josie said. "Have a nice weekend?"

Wow, Marsha thought. *Aren't we Miss Unusually Friendly this morning. Somebody must have had a very special Valentine's weekend.*

"I did have a nice weekend. We were just recapping. And you?"

Josie turned from Barb to Marsha, then back again. She looked like she was about to say something but then changed her mind. "It was fine. I'm actually here to talk to Marsha."

"What can I do for you?" Marsha asked, stacking two of her sorted piles.

Josie rapid-fired a few technical questions. *So much for hearts and flowers,* Marsha thought. She was glad she knew the answers. At least she felt pretty sure she'd given the correct ones. It was hard to tell, the way Josie stared at her before scribbling on her notepad. It felt like a test of some kind.

"Thank you," Josie said, and away she went.

As soon as she was out of earshot, Marsha asked Barb if she thought she passed or failed.

"I'd give you an A-plus. But then I don't have a clue what either of you were talking about."

Sheila, one of Marsha's co-workers, scurried up to Barb's desk.

Such a small little creature Sheila is, Marsha thought. *The way she moves, her twitching nose . . . Maybe I should introduce a gnome or a leprechaun into my book.*

"I can't figure this out," Sheila said, handing

Barb a piece of paper. "I'm sorry I have to bother you again. I just can*not* seem to remember which of those two things comes first. It's so embarrassing."

"No problem," Barb said. "Come around to my side of the desk so you can look at this with me." She opened her lower desk drawer, pulled out a manual, and began flipping through the pages. "Let's see now . . . Yes! Here it is." She pressed the binding to keep the page open. "Here's a series of schematics I bet will help the order of things sink in. It's my experience that some of us are better visual learners than auditory. I'll just bet you're one of them. Go ahead and take the book to your desk. You can return it when you're done."

"Thank you, Barb. I think just seeing them has already helped!"

As soon as Sheila was gone, Marsha said to Barb, "You're incredible, you know that? I don't know another living soul who can make people feel as good about themselves as you do."

"Go on," Barb said, her cheeks turning crimson. "I'm just doing my job."

"The way no one else ever could. Ever."

"Mom," Gina said, seating herself across from Marsha at the kitchen table, "now that Valentine's Day is over, I need to talk to you about something."

"What on earth had to wait until after Valentine's Day? And by the way, thank you again for my beautiful card." Marsha nodded to make sure Gina noticed she'd stuck it to the fridge with a magnet.

"I was thinking about how you always loved Valentine's Day," Gina said, her voice soft and sympathetic. "You still got that heart-shaped Jell-O mold?"

"Yup."

"And heart-shaped cookie press and heart-shaped pizza pan?"

Marsha nodded and gave her daughter a lackluster smile. Christopher used to make such a fuss over her heart-shaped everything. "Maybe you should have them now."

"I don't know. Maybe. I guess missing all that Valentine-shaped stuff is what got me to thinking how tough the whole day had to be for you."

Marsha nodded. "Your card helped. And your brother called."

"The day was kinda tough for me, too—well, as far as Dad was concerned. I mean, I sent him a card and all, but am I supposed to wish *her* a happy Valentine's Day too?"

"Did you?"

"No."

"Good." But as soon as Marsha said it, she noticed a shadow cross her daughter's face. "I meant to say 'Whatever makes you happy, dear.'"

She shot Gina a Cheshire-cat grin, realizing what an obviously insincere and lame attempt she'd made at political correctness. But since she'd begun to let her real emotions out on paper, there was no putting the truth back in the bottle.

"The thing is, Mom, since Easter isn't until April this year, I know it's a little early to bring this up. And I know we've always had Easter at your house. But Rich and I were talking, and we'd like to have Easter at our house this year."

"Wonderful!" Marsha said, giving her hands a clap. "Hey, I'm not going to be one of those parents who insists on forever slaving over every holiday meal." She smiled, actually relieved to switch up tradition, now that tradition no longer existed for their broken family.

"And we want Dad to come too."

"Oh?" This would be a family first. Since the divorce, they'd celebrated holidays and their kids' birthdays separately. It never occurred to Marsha that they could or should do it any other way.

"Dad and his wife," Gina said.

Marsha felt sucker-punched and sat back in her chair with a *thunk.* She started gnawing on her fingernail to keep from blurting, *Not on your life!*

Although she'd seen the hussy from a distance, she'd actually met her only once, which was once too often, and that was by accident. She'd run into Christopher and the hussy at the grocery store. Although she stammered around, as did

Christopher, Marsha acted civil enough. Afterward she wondered why. She should have rammed them both with her grocery cart until she'd knocked them clear into the meat locker. And of course Marsha looked her utter worst that day. *Why,* she chastised herself later, had she gone to the grocery store in her old jeans and a stained sweatshirt? *Why* hadn't she put on some makeup and fixed her hair?

It took her several days to get over the encounter. The woman was a looker, complete with massive fake bazooms, which Marsha later told Barb were so "*obviously* fake and in your face—literally since I'm so short and she's so tall. Men are so *gullible!*" But aside from that, the woman was undeniably beautiful.

A perfectly beautiful husband-nabber. She wondered if aiming those giant bazooms at Christopher was what sealed the deal. But then, one could not take that which could not be had.

"Mom, talk to me," Gina said, leaning forward on her elbows.

Marsha stared at her daughter, who was biting her lip. "The truth is, Gina, I can't answer you right now. I wish I were a bigger person. But I just don't know. This is something I'll have to think long and hard about. I wouldn't want to say yes and then ruin everyone's day. I have to be sure I can handle it and not embarrass everyone."

Marsha saw her daughter's eyes start to mist

over before she quickly blinked away the moisture. "This is even harder than I thought it would be."

"Sweetheart, you just surprised me."

"No, Mom. I mean *all* of it. The whole divorce."

Marsha put her right index finger to her mouth, then immediately retracted it. She needed to stop biting her nails. "I'm sorry you and your brother have to go through this. I'm sorry *I* have to go through it too," she said, an edge of bitterness lacing her voice. She swallowed, fighting back her own tears.

"I gotta get home and make dinner," Gina said, rising from the table. "Think about it and let me know what you decide. I don't need to know right away."

"Gina, at the very least, go ahead and invite your dad and . . ." She couldn't bring herself to say the hussy's name.

"I already did," Gina said, staring at Marsha. "Tony's coming too. Apparently he and Dad have been keeping in better contact lately."

"Oh. Well. Then I guess I'll let you know. It's the best I can do for now."

Gina pursed her lips, cocked her head, shrugged, and left without saying another word.

For a while after Gina was gone, Marsha thought she might be sick. It seemed that every time she found her bearings and could move on with her life—finally live apart from her wounds—she was slam-dunked straight back into misery.

That night she lay in bed and sobbed. She shed a tear for every heart-shaped memory and heartbroken moment she'd shared with Christopher. She tossed and turned and flipped her pillow to the dry side. She moaned, blew her nose, and cried some more. But no matter how many tears she shed, she simply could not talk herself into spending a holiday with the man whose actions had, at this very moment, once again rendered her utterly lost.

Seven

Wednesday. Hump day. April Fools' Day. Usually a day filled with at least a few chuckles around an office. *Call it what you want,* Josie thought, *but people are acting more like it's doomsday. What's wrong with everybody?*

She'd arrived at work exactly when she said she would: two hours later than usual. Yesterday before leaving the office, she'd downloaded a bunch of troublesome code and arranged a private meeting at her condo office with a guy one of her industry associates referred to as a "code genius." Although Diamond Mutual's IT and code gurus were good, this stubborn problem obviously needed a fresh pair of eyes. "When the troops you're commanding can't get the job done on their own, call in the reserves," her dad always said. It proved a fruitful choice, which made her glad. But her tardiness shouldn't have ticked anyone off. If anything, they should have enjoyed their two-hour reprieve from her eyes over their shoulders. Whatever was wrong, it had clearly happened first thing that day, since everything seemed fine yesterday evening.

Who can I ask without making it sound like I'm nailing them for a bad attitude? She had no in-house confidant. That wasn't unusual, but today it would have been nice. Even naturally charming Barb appeared uncommonly gloomy, although she managed a half smile on Josie's first pass through. The IT guys, who were the only ones brave enough to joke with her—although she often did not get their geeky humor—and who she figured would surely be full of April Fools' Day mischief, moved slower than dial-up. One actually glared at her. Even La-La-Lyle bordered on surly.

It was true that a stage-one equipment switchover was about to take place in two departments, which meant hard, careful work and a round of dismissals; but as far as she knew, the announcement hadn't happened yet. But *something* was up. The whole atmosphere smacked of the toxic spirit at her Houston job, so she hoped whatever it was soon passed.

She sat at her desk, tapping her pencil on the file

folder containing the morning's fruitful code yield. In order to stay on task, she decided to ignore the situation and just keep her ears and eyes keenly open, even more so than usual. For the first time in a long while, she'd arrived this morning feeling hopeful about actually making her contractual deadline. She didn't want to put a kink in her own forward momentum by poking around and unwittingly igniting mental combat with someone. Her tactic would be to pour on a dose of "niceness" and plow ahead.

She needn't have calculated a tactic. Within the hour, Lyle called her into his office.

"You've no doubt noticed a change in climate here this morning, but I'm sure the employees, all good people—those who are staying, as well as those receiving their walking papers—won't cause trouble for us."

Us?

"But I think we're likely in for at least a few rocky adjustments."

"Did you make an announcement or already begin escorting people out?" Josie asked.

He looked surprised by her question. "No. It's neither my style nor that of the greater politics of Diamond Mutual to activate without transitional preparations." He paused and worked his jaw. "In terms of personnel dismissals, for me phase one was to communicate with department heads. I called them into my office this morning to give them each an envelope containing first-round lists of people in their charge, since they'll need to do the dirty work."

Josie stifled a judgmental frown. The guy had no spine. Rather than soldier up, he'd passed the buck on . . . *the dirty work? Good grief.*

"As you know, at least so far, Barb DeWitt is the only department head on your list. And as I'm sure you've witnessed, she's *the* most popular employee here at DM." He stopped a moment and straightened his posture.

"Yes, I have noticed that," she said, flatly. *Who wouldn't?*

"From the beginning, everyone figured her department was slated to take the worst hits, so no surprise when her envelope was the largest. I asked them not to look at their lists until the end of the day, when they would have time to take in the breadth of them, which I warned them would likely be more rigorous than imagined. I told them they'd have the rest of the week to prepare pink slips, decide what they want to tell their people."

Josie nodded.

"The board of directors continues to come down hard about bottom lines and upper-level pay scales, and although I put in a good word for Barb, in the end, realistically, not even I could justify her continuation here, not after all the changes are facilitated. Your recommendation was spot on."

Judging by the way he'd pronounced "realistically," Josie thought reality was possibly his least favorite mode of operating.

"As we're both aware," he said, shifting tone and seeming to work hard to keep the *us* in the center of his conversation, "due to the economy, we're no longer just upgrading; we're also officially downsizing. So my meeting this morning was an uncomfortable one and the mere size of the envelopes was a shock for many people. A few outright asked me how many more rounds of cuts there'd be, how we made our decisions—had it all been up to *you*, Ms. Brooks, which I assured them it had not. I told them all final decisions were made by upper management at DM. I'm not a buck-passer." He smiled, obviously thinking he'd clarified a concern of hers.

As if. "You did nothing more than what had to be done," she said flatly.

"*Then* . . . ," he said, pausing a moment and lowering his voice and chin, intimating there was more to the story, "as everyone was leaving my office, I asked Barb to stay. Barb was one of the people who helped make my entry here a smooth one, some eleven years ago. She's one of those positive people . . ." He fiddled with his pen, scribbled on a pad as if to make sure the ink was still working. "She's always been the one to arrange retirement parties, birthday breaks in the lunchroom, baby showers . . . In hindsight, I admit I should have waited to give her notice until after she'd let the others go, but it just felt so deceptive and I respect her too much for that type of end run."

"Lyle, whatever you're trying to tell me, just *tell* me. Your personal relationships with your employees is neither my business nor my concern."

"I am sharing this, Josie," he said, his tone firm, "as a courtesy, simply to help you understand the atmosphere change today. If you know how things came down, you'll be better prepared for any push back or temporary lack of cooperation."

"Go on," she said, crossing her legs and pulling out a pen, hoping he'd finally say something worth writing down.

"When I invited Barb to stay back in my office, the others took note—which was, I admit, my tactical error. To have asked her in front of them. She was, to say the least, pretty stunned by the news that she was being let go too, but she held herself together."

He talks like a sappy woman, Josie thought. *I neither want nor need all these details.*

"I told her about the bonus we're offering her to stay on for two weeks to help see us through the transition, and the buyout package we've put together. She asked me how many others were getting the same deal. I told her only one. She asked if it was Marsha. I told her no, that only trusted department heads were even considered. But since she brought up Marsha, I had to tell her that Marsha would stay."

"Good choice, Marsha." *Now, can we get on with it, please.*

Lyle worked his jaw again. "That's what Barb said too. Good that her best friend Marsha would still have a job. But I could tell Barb was hanging on by a thread."

Better than you are, I bet, she thought.

"I shook her hand, and she gave me a hug."

Oh, for crying out loud. What kind of man shared these types of details? *Oh!* Maybe she'd been a little slow on the uptake. Maybe there was a reason he wasn't married.

"Barb's always looking out for everyone else. She said she understood how difficult it was for me to tell her. How thankful she was to have worked here for so many years, to be trusted enough to help see us through. She said she would pray for me and herself and everyone else."

Josie felt her eyebrows rise, which caused Lyle to frown. "Lyle, do you have something I need to know that I don't already? Barb is nice. I understand. It's difficult to let someone go when you've worked with her for years. The employees are going to be extra upset about her departure, but . . ." She looked at her wristwatch. At this rate, she'd be in Chicago another year, and here she thought she'd arrived that morning with a breakthrough!

"Josie, please just hear me out. Most of the department heads who'd attended the meeting sensed something big was up and managed to hang around the water cooler until the door opened." He shook his head. "Barb is normally a rock, but the fresh emotional impact of her job loss coupled with everyone waiting, *staring,* caught her off guard."

"She had a meltdown in front of everyone?" *Emotional leadership breeds emotional followers. You reap what you sow.*

"Not exactly. She ducked into the ladies' room, but we could all hear her crying. A couple of women went in to check on her. Although she didn't tell them she'd been let go, she later told me the look on her face said it all. Word quickly spread, and now it's a cross between a morgue and a battleground out there," he said, looking toward his door.

He talks like we're hiding in a bunker. "This too shall pass," she said. "Believe me, I've been through it enough times to know that it always does."

Lyle stared at her, as if he wished she, too, would pass, and right this minute. "Although I wanted to let everyone go with a two-week notice—it just seems the *decent* thing to do—after the meeting I received a call from the CEO. He made it clear there would be absolutely *no* notices given, aside from the two department heads we asked to help see us through for the next couple weeks. I was cautioned that when financial worries start taking hold, everyone needs to be viewed as a security risk. *'Data is commodity,'*" he said, drawing air quotes around the words, his voice a mix of defeat, concession, and sarcasm. "We need to work in stealth mode, in waves of different days and different times. As employees are called into an office, others will begin securing their computers and boxing up their belongings. Out the door they'll go, like criminals. I had to *re*summon the department heads and make next week's task clear. No notices. No pink slips."

"You do know that's how it's usually done, right? No warnings or *phase ones,*" she said. "Difficult, yes, but tidier in the end."

He suddenly appeared utterly transparent. Childlike, in a strange way that tugged at her heart. As if he were nine years old and for the good of his family, he had just given away his puppy. Maybe he wasn't gay after all. Maybe, she thought, suddenly hearing her grandmother's voice ring in her head, he was just an "old softie," as her grandmother used to say about her grandfather.

She swallowed, attempting to dampen her dry throat, and a sudden wave of heat flushed her cheeks. She pulled the collar of her blouse away from her neck. Surely *she* wasn't going soft now. The instant she realized she was having a hot flash, she snapped to. *Bedeviling hormones!*

"I'm sure Barb is grateful for the opportunity and her severance package. I assume it was generous."

Lyle did a double take. *"Grateful?"*

"Yes, grateful. Lots of people today get nothing but walking papers. I'm sure you went above and beyond for her, and it sounds like you made that clear. At her age . . ."

"Her *age*," he said, his voice now absent of any melancholy or softness, "is exactly the same as that of my mother when she received her *walking papers*." It was the first time in ten months she'd seen a glint of honest anger in his eyes. "When I speculated with Barb, as you did with me, that perhaps this would come as good news to her, since maybe at sixty-two she was looking forward to retirement, she told me she loved her job and the people she works with—most of whom she now has to help escort out the door. She said she couldn't picture herself *ever* retiring, or being happier anywhere than here at DM. And for the record, Ms. Brooks, my mom never was able to find another job."

He was going to snap that jaw if he clenched it any tighter.

Enough is enough, she thought. She wasn't about to sit there and let him spew misplaced guilt her way. It was Diamond Mutual's choice to streamline and upgrade.

"I can only say this: we move forward from where we are, and this is where we are," she told him. "Thank you for the heads-up. It's tough, but people will live."

With that she left him in her backdraft, every eye on her as she steamed her way toward data entry. She had a job to finish, which couldn't happen too soon.

But first, she would get a diet cola, something to quench her thirst and cool her down.

Barb and Marsha huddled in the parking lot after work. Although people were gathered into several large pockets here and there, the two of them stood alone. They rotated between bouts of crying, hugging, and trying to cheer each other up.

"In all my years at Diamond Mutual," Barb said, "this day was the longest, and certainly the most humiliating."

"You're being too hard on yourself, Barb. There's no way anyone could have walked out of Mr. Waters' office and kept their emotions intact, not after learning they were losing their job. Not after twenty years. *I* am in shock! Just the fact you stuck out the day, got your job done, and are still standing says eons about your character."

"I don't know. I'm ashamed of myself. I couldn't stop crying for the longest time. I feel like I let everyone down. Lyle was just trying to be considerate. I really upset the applecart. Just look at everyone." She nodded here and there. "Stressed out sooner than they need to be."

"Barb, stop it!" Marsha said, her voice firm. "Let me wash a few of your own wise words back over you, okay? 'Life is way too short to fret over being *human.*' How many times have you told me that? Anyone would have done what you did. We're all hanging on by a thread. We've all known the threat's been hanging for a long time. Sure, we've each hoped that in the end, it wouldn't be us. How could we not? And to be perfectly honest, I still can't believe you heard right, that *I'm* staying. That just *can't* be true! You going and me staying?"

"Trust me, it's true. And it's the one thing making any of this bearable, to know that at least *you* don't have to worry about paying your bills. I'll be fine. I have a nest egg. But you younger ones . . ."

"Why you? *Why?* I might just quit in protest."

"Don't you dare even think about such a silly thing!"

They stood in silence for a few moments. The cool evening air started to seep in, causing Barb to shiver.

"Look," Marsha said, "are you gonna be okay to drive home? Maybe you should just hop in my car and come home with me tonight."

"That's sweet of you, but to be honest, I'm exhausted. I just want to crawl into my own bed and go to sleep, give God some time to pull me together. I have to shore myself up for what lies ahead. I have never dreaded anything more in my life."

Marsha searched Barb's swollen eyes. "If you're sure."

Barb nodded.

"You call me if you want to talk, no matter what the hour, okay?"

Again, Barb nodded. They threw their arms around each other for one final hug before heading their separate ways.

Eight

Lyle thought it best to hang around after work, just in case any of the management team stayed late to open their envelopes and then came looking for him. He had plenty of progress reports to pore through.

As it turned out, the place cleared pretty quickly. At 5:45, he looked out his office window and watched as, nearly directly below him, Marsha and Barb embraced. Even though official announcements had not yet been made, he found it difficult to believe Barb hadn't shared Marsha's good shred of news with her. How could she not? He would have.

Where is the justice?

He packed up his briefcase, grabbed his jacket, and headed for the elevator. He was glad Marsha and Barb had each other for moral support. It had been too long since he'd connected, at least in a meaningful way, with a few of his buddies—all of them married except Mason, who was recently divorced and acting like a sex-crazed teenager. "No, thanks," he'd told Mason after he'd called Lyle for the fourth time in the last month to go bar-hopping. Lyle hoped Mason either found someone soon or tired of the dangerous game of one-night stands.

During one of Lyle's mom's more lucid moments, when she'd inquired about his friends, he'd told her about Mason's crazy escapades.

"You know, Son, loneliness is a snaky thing. Mason just thinks he can outrun or outdrink it."

The next time they'd talked, she had no idea who Mason was.

On his walk to the train station, his thoughts swirled. Although it was hard to admit such a thing at his age, the truth was, his mom had always been his ballast. What would he do without her? She was fading so fast. This was one of those rare times when he could use both a good kick in the pants and a boost to his psyche.

Even Frank in the mail room, who had to be seventy-five if he was a day—and never one to withhold his opinion—had pulled Lyle aside near quitting time and tongue-lashed him. "That was a dirty-dog trick you played on Barb, humiliating her in front of everyone like that."

Gheesh, Lyle thought. No wonder everybody knew what was going on: Frank was the most viral mouthpiece at DM, even though he prefaced every tidbit of gossip with, "It's not like me to spread hearsay, but . . ."

When Lyle arrived at the station, he had twenty minutes before the next train departed, so he decided to have a beer. He watched people scurrying this way and that, and his mind wandered back to Frank.

Like Barb, Frank was a strong part of DM's charm, but he wasn't a guy you wanted to mess with. The bigwigs questioned why Frank's name wasn't in the dismissal brief. They had nothing more than tabled departmental employee lists in front of them with the most basic of HR facts: name, age, length of employment, and a few key words from their last three job reviews. Lyle warned them that if they wanted to avoid the age discrimination courts, they better steer clear of Frank. Frank went from department to department pushing his mail cart every morning. He delivered a second mail run at one, and popped in and out of offices all day with special deliveries. He possessed both a direct network to rally the troops and a temper.

"There's enough of a hornet's nest surrounding

Barb's dismissal. Since Frank is also a favorite, for the good of the morale, such that is left, you better keep Frank," he'd told them.

Who will keep Frank in line without Barb? he wondered, as he twirled his coaster. Barb dropped a plate of homemade cookies or bag of red licorice, the old bachelor's favorites, in Frank's cart at least once a week and thanked him for delivering the mail with such dedication. She told him, in her chipper upbeat way, that she hoped the goodies reminded him that sweetness in the form of good words, rather than idle gossip, helped make everyone's days nicer. It was clear to everyone that Frank had a crush on Barb. Kind of cute, really. No wonder Frank was extra mad; not only was he losing the person who plied him with sweets, he was losing his sweetheart as well.

What, exactly, *would* the new normal be after the cuts were over and the new systems were up? And Josie Brooks was gone?

Lyle left his tip on the counter and walked toward his track. What was it about that woman? Aside from the few times Josie Brooks had revealed a softer underbelly, she was one of those people who seemed to make everyone quake in their boots, occasionally including him. It took a certain type to live with numbers and outcomes, firings and constantly moving, and not go insane. Who could survive a job like hers if they personalized everything the way *he* did? Still, she was such a mystery. He boarded the train and climbed up the narrow stairs to the top deck, then pretended to read his newspaper.

This morning, for a while anyway, it seemed like she was affirming him. What had she said? *"You did nothing more than what had to be done."* He was very aware that when she spoke kindly, she was even more attractive.

But somewhere along the course of their conversation, the look on her face appeared close to mocking. Checking her watch? Getting red in the face, then all but storming out? What was *that* about? Rather than appreciate his effort to deliver complete honesty by bringing her up to speed about events during her morning absence—and to share a few personal stories as to why company reaction to the news, especially about Barb, was strong—Josie suddenly acted like *he* was the enemy. He was just trying to get things right with a little human decency and dignity. What was so wrong about that?

On his ride home, a new thought struck him: maybe she was gearing up to turn his name in to the board of directors too—or already had. Maybe she'd actually spent her morning scheming and steering clear in order to keep her hands clean. He could almost hear her now. *Lyle Waters is an indecisive bleeding heart who prolongs the obvious and therefore exacerbates the agony.*

And she would be right. If Miriam were still alive, she could attest to that.

Josie arrived home and vigorously kicked off her boots, sending sidewalk sludge splattering every which way. In order to clear a place in the closet for her coat, which she shucked off like it was on fire, she smashed the clothes against each other so sharply she caused the hangers to screech on the rod.

"The nerve of him!" she spat, as she jabbed a hanger inside her coat sleeves. Then she stormed down the hallway, yanking her sweater over her head as she went. The angry words had been rising up inside her since their meeting this morning, and finally she could let them lose. She quickly changed into a sweat suit, washed off her makeup, and nearly drowned her face in hydrating cream, then slathered herself with lotion. Her entire body seemed to scream for moisture.

In the kitchen, she guzzled an entire bottle of water and opened a second before feeling quenched. She rifled through the mail and tossed some greens with a can of tuna, adding a little olive oil and a sprinkle of slivered almonds. She decided to add fresh cilantro—*where* are *my kitchen scissors anyway?*—then caught herself banging the knife blade against her chopping mat, which was not good for the blade. She tossed in a few slices of onion and ate about half the salad before pushing it aside. She cleared the dishes and hurled herself on the couch, using the remote to turn on the stereo, which she quickly turned off again.

Time for a little self-analysis, Josie Victor Brooks. She fluffed one of the throw pillows under the curve of her neck and wiggled around until she felt mildly comfortable. *What on earth are you so angry about?*

Although she'd managed to pull off a productive day, even in the midst of the silences and glares, her gut had been churning since she'd left Lyle's office. His inefficient and inappropriate managerial "skills" had single-handedly managed to ruin not only her happy day but the entire atmosphere at DM.

Not that next week would be a fun week. No, it was never fun to witness the humiliation, fear, and trepidation on people's faces as they were escorted out of the building. And Lyle was right, they were treated as if they'd been charged with a criminal offense rather than simply being victims of the times. But Lyle's ability to botch one single bit of managerial protocol—was the guy completely out of touch with today's protect-the-data-at-all-costs practices?—certainly unsettled the troops. It was official: Lyle was too soft for his own good.

And his explanation, which seemed more like a confession, as to what had gone wrong? *Ha!* It both sounded and felt like an attempt to defer his blindsiding guilt onto *her*. Then he made it sound like she was in cahoots with anyone and everyone who tried to sift out the seniors.

She put the backs of her hands to her cheeks, which felt on fire. She really was worked up. Or was it just another hot flash? *Good grief, I'm becoming the senior he's trying to rescue!*

She determined to calm down. Apparently highflying emotions triggered the dumb flashes—or was it the other way around? What else could explain that for a moment today, when Lyle had appeared so vulnerable, she was drawn to him, in an uncommon and, if she were to be completely honest with herself, extremely unprofessional way. Indeed, for a brief moment, she—

No. That simply could not happen, especially not with a sap. Work was work. And Lyle was weak. And she'd be leaving soon anyway.

She propped herself up on the couch and gulped more water from the bottle. Following a method she'd once read about, she inhaled deeply to the count of four, then exhaled through her mouth, taking eight beats to do so. She repeated that exercise until she felt her heart rate idling down a notch. *Since when do I let my emotions get the best of me? How did he make me feel more like a heartless hatchet woman than the efficient, kick-butt professional I am? How is it—*

She heard the faint sound of her cell phone ring.

In her storm of an entrance, she'd broken with her usual thoughtful routine and must have left her phone in her handbag, which was . . . *still by the front door?* By the time she got to it, the call had already gone to voice mail. She waited a moment and retrieved the message.

It was Amelia, her Realtor, apologizing and saying that it was hard to believe that in almost two months, after endless bouts of phone tag, one emergency dinner cancellation, and way too many wedding planning evenings, they still hadn't managed to get together. At the sound of Amelia's voice saying, "I was afraid you'd given up. I was *so* glad to hear from you again!" tears from an unknown well sprang into Josie's eyes. "I was hoping you might be available for a spur-of-the-moment late dinner. Oh, well. I'll try again next week." Desparate for company and distraction, Josie thought, *No! I'll call you right back, Amelia! Don't go without me!* "Alfred and I are flying to Maine tomorrow night to spend a long weekend with his folks. More wedding stuff, which is just about to do me in. I'll catch you later."

Josie wiped her nose and sniffed, then pushed the key to return the call as soon as she heard the prompt. This time, *she* went straight to voice mail. Amelia must have made another call. "Amelia, Josie. I didn't get to the phone in time, but I'm here. I'd *love* to go for a late dinner." It didn't matter that she'd already eaten. She could have a bowl of soup, a glass of wine—some welcome conversation. "Call me right back. I've got my phone in my hand."

She raced to her bedroom, threw on some casual clothes, mascara, and blush, and waited. It was as if a new breath of life gratefully switched her emotional gears. Like a child waiting for Santa to arrive, she stared at her phone. It was another ten minutes before it finally rang. Caller ID proved that it was, thank goodness, Amelia.

"Josie. Sorry for the delay. Right after I left your message, Alfred called. He said if I wasn't busy, maybe I could grab a bite with him near Macy's. We have got to finish our gift registry. Our parents have been hounding us—I've been hounding him—and since we're going to see his folks this weekend . . . I didn't think you were home, so I said yes, and he's already on his way. I hope you're not too disappointed. Maybe we can plan something for next week?"

Josie's chin dropped to her chest. No, she wasn't disappointed; she was emotionally deflated.

"Josie? You there?"

"Yes. Yes, I'm here." She fired up her business energy and made herself smile, knowing a smile can be heard in a voice. "No problem, Amelia. To be honest, I already ate a salad earlier. I was going more for the company. Picking out items for a guest registry sounds like a much more delightful way to spend an evening anyway. Next week would be great."

"Well, to be honest with you, picking out items is a pain-ola, especially since it's become evident how very different our tastes run when it comes to so many, *many* things. That's why we're not done yet; we had to take a break for a couple of weeks, so we could each reevaluate what mattered most to us and where we thought we could do better at compromising."

"Wow."

"Wow, indeed."

"How's that going for you?"

"Seriously?"

"Curiously, would be more accurate."

"I cannot live with black towels. Alfred says they don't show the dirt as much, which led to a lengthy discussion about how often he thought towels should be washed, which led to further dialogue about showering in the morning versus showering at night, which . . . You know, let's just say it's going, and leave it at that. Tonight will be a test of sorts. We both had pretty decent days, and it'll be good to get the parents off our backs. However, this is a story to be continued," she said with a chuckle. "I'm hoping we do much better this go-around."

What a hassle it must be to constantly compromise, Josie thought. That was one of the great things about living alone: she got everything her way. Whatever pity party she'd allowed herself to engage in, this conversation helped slam things back into perspective.

"Would you like to pick a date now," she asked Amelia, "or get back to me?"

"Hold on. Let me get my calendar. We've been at this far too long." Josie finally felt her brows unfurrow. Something on the calendar to look forward to. "Okay, how about next Tuesday?"

"Sounds good."

"Would you like to go straight from work? There's a property I've been wanting to scope out for a client, and it's not too far from your building. I could meet you outside your door. We'll hoof it."

Normally, Josie preferred to change clothes and unwind before a leisurely dinner out. But all she said, her voice revealing her genuine enthusiasm, was, "That would be great. See you Tuesday about 5:15 at the entry to Diamond Mutual."

After they hung up, Josie took a few more swigs of her water. What was up with her thirst? Maybe hot flashes dehydrated her. That's what she could do to distract herself tonight: seek more information about menopause.

While she waited for her computer to finish booting, she downed more water. The near urgent thirst again brought to mind the day she bought the snowglobe. She still hadn't gotten rid of it.

She wrote a reminder note on a Post-it and stuck it to the edge of her monitor.

As she clicked from one menopause link to the next, her mind drifted to the odd calls she'd received from Cassandra. *Huh.* This was the first time she'd ever related Cassandra's odd query and mysterious comments to the strange experience with *her* snowglobe. What had Cassandra asked her that first call? Had she seen anything in the globe?

A prickly feeling ran up Josie's arm, but it soon passed. There were two new posts under things women did to endure their hot flashes. She was almost afraid to look. Her last bout left her with her head in the freezer, which, to be honest, hadn't turned out that badly. Maybe she'd leave a comment saying she'd tried it and recommended it.

Are you insane? If anyone does a Google search and finds you talking about putting your head in the freezer, you'll never get hired again.

Nine

Helmoot, the Reaper Rephotsirch,
Chapter 29

What a fool the beautiful Marshalleon had been to ever fall for the evil Helmoot. She should have known better than to think any one human—although Helmoot, the Reaper Rephotsirch, certainly was far from *human*—could cause such devastation and havoc and perpetrate such horrible evilness alone. But now, Marshalleon's naive days were over. Having stepped into her own power, she was the queen avenger.

And she was just beginning.

On a recent dark night, during a secret meeting under a streetlamp, the Great Barbizone reminded Marshalleon of her latent superhuman gift: the gift of Knowitall. All Marshalleon had to do to activate her deeper calling was to rest the pad of her left index finger on the half moon of her right pinky fingernail and utter the words, "Marsha-Marshalleon, Mistress of Magic, Maker of Payback to Reaper Rephotsirch."

And so she did. Instantly, Marshalleon felt the power surge through her like a lightning bolt hitting a hot tin roof. Instantly, she knew: the gift of Knowitall was hers!

The first thing she knew was that NAY! Helmoot, the Reaper Rephotsirch had not been working alone all this time! Helmoot was in fact working in tandem with a *cast* of miserable swine, one even more evil than himself, that being ~~She-Cat Beastie Babe Hatchet Hand~~ Firing Matrix, who brought destruction and heartache to the Land of Sparkling Diamonds. Once the beautiful Marshalleon knew it *all,* she set about preparing her plan for not only revenge but death unto the wicked. If she joined forces with the Great Barbizone, nothing could stop them.

But wouldn't you know it?! Before she could engage in her stealth and cunning actions, the wicked-to-the-core Firing Matrix banished the Great Barbizone from the land.

This was war. This called for . . .

Marsha sat staring at her words, again gnawing on the nail of her ring finger, a finger that never had fluffed back into its original shape after she'd finally removed her too-tight wedding bands. "This called for . . ." What?

Who am I kidding, to think I can write my way to any sort of healing and resolution for this mess?

Why is it that the one person who seems the most connected to God is losing her job, when I, who am often angry at God for allowing so much heartache into my life, will still have mine? Why is it bad things way too often happen to the really good people, and that the rotten unfaithful people like Christopher get the beauties?

She gnawed on a loose piece of skin around her nail as she sat and waited for the beautiful Marshalleon to once again show her the way.

And she waited and she waited and she waited.

Barb felt humiliated, unnerved, defeated, and exhausted. Two o'clock in the morning, and what did she have to show for the five hours she'd lain in bed other than a tear-soaked pillowcase and hours of hashed-over regrets? Not even a twenty-minute bout of arthritic, knee-numbing bedside prayer helped assuage her fretting. She lay on her back, covers tucked up under her chin, eyes wide open, her anxiety-ridden heart still trying to bang its way out of her chest.

After her countless pep talks and winged prayers, *good old spiritual Barb* had fallen short today by causing such a scene. Where was the quietude of her faith? Had she given it away to everyone else's needs?

Twenty years at Diamond Mutual. Didn't it used to be that after twenty-five years of ongoing service, dedicated workers received a gold company watch and a retirement party?

Her mind locked on the passing of the decades. Twenty years of employment that had not only helped pull her out of her grief and hardship, but had also helped put her kids through college and graced her with a new best friend. She originally took the job at Diamond Mutual on account of what happened twenty-one years ago that day, April Fools' Day, the day her husband died.

When his office called to tell her Ted had been rushed to the hospital, she could barely breathe. When she arrived at the hospital and they told her he was gone, in her shock, she just kept repeating, "April Fools', right? Tell me this is just one of his April Fools' jokes!" Ted was like a kid on April Fools' Day, every year managing to pull at least one good foolery, as he called them, over on her. But this was no joke: she had lost the first love of her life.

Eight months after his passing, her financial advisor and longtime family friend told her she'd have to find a job. It still made her stomach hurt to think about the paralyzing horror of that moment. "But what will I do? For eighteen years, I've been a full-time homemaker. Ted and I married right out of high school!"

The financial advisor didn't offer any specific

advice, but he did ask her if she knew how to type, which she did. He said, "What about data entry?" He'd heard some companies offered on-the-job training. The next day, she started scouring the newspaper.

Same as it did this early morning in April, her heart beat so fast twenty years ago that when she showed up at Diamond Mutual for an interview, she thought she might hyperventilate. But no matter; she came out with the job and had been happy there since.

Now she couldn't imagine her life without heading off to DM every workday morning. In so many ways, her job defined her, boosted her self-esteem. *I am a supervisor at Diamond Mutual.* She hadn't realized how much that title—which she'd written on countless forms and so often spoken—validated her. Sure, with the package she'd likely be okay financially; the kids were each on their own now. But mentally, emotionally, having to walk people she loved out of the building?

Maybe she should just go in tomorrow and quit. Or just not go back in at all.

But who would that help? Certainly not those she cared about. And hadn't she told Marsha not to do anything ridiculous? One thing she'd never called herself was a quitter. No, now wasn't the time to start that.

Apart from a few church friends, the dearest

people she knew worked right alongside her. Who, she wondered, aside from immediate family, knew people better than those they spent eight hours a day with, including her boss, Lyle Waters, whom she'd grown to love like a nephew?

She remembered his first day on the job, how he introduced himself to everyone with a genuine smile on his face and an air of humility that instantly made him likable, if not endearing. He always remembered her children's names, ages, and hobbies; asked about her pastor long after his appendicitis; lagged back with her slow ascent the day the elevator was down and they all had to walk up the stairs. He'd been liberal with raises, fair with evaluations, and kind. Always kind.

She so appreciated that he'd talked to her directly today, rather than letting her hear it through the grapevine. Imagine if she'd learned through Frank? She pictured the mail clerk all but jumping out of his worn, black Converse shoes, nearly busting his suspenders with *that* kind of bulletin. Frank would have spouted the news like a fountain. But Lyle . . . she understood what it took for Lyle to tell her she'd be losing her job. He'd verbally affirmed how he'd always valued her gift as a peacemaker and comforter, which is why he wanted her, and especially her, to help get them all through this mess the next couple of weeks. He'd obviously gone out of his way to get her the extra benefits, for which she was extremely grateful.

But here was the crux of her unrest: what had she given him in return for his sensitivity and kindness? There'd been no time between the news and his open door to even pray. Kathryn, an otherwise bubbling person, was speechless when she and another co-worker entered the ladies' room to comfort her. When Barb finally came out of the restroom, she was smothered with hugs from nearly everyone in the room, each murmuring how unfair it was, how terrible that they all had to go through this, how angry they were.

How frightened they were about their livelihoods.

She kept trying to convince them to calm down, to remind them that times were difficult everywhere, that Mr. Waters and Diamond Mutual were just doing what lots of other companies had already done.

That their anger wouldn't get them anywhere.

That it was the fault of no one single person, not even Josie Brooks.

But she didn't sound that convincing, even to herself. She'd been rattled to *her* core, the same as she'd been on April Fools' Day twenty-one years ago.

When Josie Brooks walked through her department, it was all she could do to crack a smile at the woman. She knew Josie had likely recommended her release.

Barb hated the way she felt inside. *I despise you,* she'd caught herself thinking when Josie passed by. Why was human nature so hard to overcome? Marsha was right: she needed to heed her own advice. But no matter how much she told herself it was not Ms. Brooks' fault, that times had changed, deep within she flared with outrage that someone who didn't know a thing about any of them could come in and so casually mess with their lives.

But as Lyle said, all final decisions were made by DM management, and that's who'd hired Josie Brooks to begin with.

Silent prayers flew, and yet Barb's body was so tense she thought she'd crack in half. She turned on her side and whapped her pillow a few times. *Calm me down, Lord!*

The one thing she'd been grateful for today was that when she returned to her desk, it was clear Marsha hadn't yet heard the news, otherwise she'd never have held it together. Marsha had made a funny face behind Josie's back. But when Barb didn't respond, Marsha studied her and asked if she'd been crying. All she could say without breaking into tears again was, "We'll talk about it after work, okay?"

Barb turned on her bedside lamp and sat up. She'd been so self-absorbed that she hadn't even opened her envelope containing the list of those she'd eventually have to usher out. *Might as well get it over with.*

She got out of bed, donned her robe, made herself a cup of chamomile tea, and sat at her kitchen table. Before turning the fat parcel over to undo the clasp, she rested her palms on it.

Sweet Jesus, help me get a grip on myself. Give me Your wisdom. Help me be Your comfort to so many in need and to trust You with the rest of my life, however many days or years remain.

For a while, she could do nothing but sit there and cry.

After she pulled herself together and withdrew the list of names from her envelope, she gasped. So many people with so many problems already in their lives. Throughout the years, she'd become a confidant to several of them. Lillian in Human Resources often kidded her that they should switch jobs. Oh, the stories she'd heard—of spouse abuse and cancer, cheating husbands and wives, and difficult issues with teenagers. So many things to pray about.

And now, she had to add unemployment to all their lists.

Lord, have mercy.

She mentally walked through her department, her mind's eye settling on the sweet family pictures displayed on so many desks. It wasn't just the employees who would be affected.

She decided the best thing she could do was pray for each name on the list. She got out a fresh tablet of stationery and started in. For each name, she wrote a few words of affirmation about the person's best qualities, then a short specific prayer. Maybe she'd send the notes to their homes after they were released or ask Lillian if she could tuck them into their belongings when they were packed up.

At just about four-thirty, her list finally complete, she crawled back into bed, once again reminded that turning her heart toward prayer and helping others was always the best way to help herself. She still had two hours left to catch some sleep before her alarm went off. Today, she would apologize to Lyle for any unnecessary drama she caused, forgive herself, and set about doing her job to the best of her capabilities. She would let people go with dignity, honesty, encouragement, hope, and kindness.

Then she'd rely on God to help her let go of her own job.

Lord, hear my prayers.

Ten

The weekend delivered a little bit of everything for Barb.

During an uncommon Saturday morning breakfast out with Marsha, her friend shared the trials and tribulations of her first writer's block as a novelist.

"Marsha," Barb said, "when the muse returns, please don't let your personal anger spill into the Great Barbizone, lest *she* get so angry she does everyone in—including the beautiful Mashalleon!"

Although it felt good to laugh—wonderfully good—Barb's most productive and fruitful moment arrived via her prayer circle at church on Palm Sunday. She'd asked her prayer circle to please pray for the wisdom and courage to face the day on Monday, and for God to use her as a calm and reassuring presence in what would undoubtedly be a crazed state of turmoil. By the middle of the afternoon, God came through when she was jolted by a brilliant idea.

In a leap of faith, she typed up a flier and ran off several copies at home Sunday night, ready for distribution on Monday.

First thing Monday morning, fingers crossed and prayers flying, she called her friend Beth to check on a location for her brainstorm. *Please, Lord.* Miraculously as it seemed to Barb, Beth said her side room at the bagel shop was unoccupied the whole next week, which would be just long enough to see her plan through. In fact, Beth was so excited about Barb's idea, she not only offered the room for no charge, but said she'd throw in a few day-old bagels to boot.

"Business has been so slow that I could use a good dose of encouragement too, so expect to see me hanging around between customers!"

Next, Barb cleared her brainchild with HR. "Thank you, and go, God!" she said out loud when Lillian gave her the approval to post announcements about the newly formed Encouragement Club.

ENCOURAGEMENT!
ENCOURAGEMENT!
ENCOURAGEMENT!

Whether you're staying at Diamond Mutual or moving on to the next thing in your life, please drop by for one—or all—of the half-hour (keeping it doable!) meetings (prompt start and dismissal) of the newly formed and short-term ENCOURAGEMENT CLUB, which will meet each day next week. Barb DeWitt, one of the folks "moving on," will open the first meeting by sharing a riotous story from her earliest employment, a victorious story about her time here at DM (thanks for the memories!), and a hopeful thought or two about *everyone's* future. She encourages (exactly!) all who attend—and she hopes all do attend—to come prepared to do the same.

WHEN: Next Monday through Friday (April 13-17) TIME: 5:10 p.m. sharp

PLACE: Beth's Bagel Haven (side room), right across the street

REFRESHMENTS: YES—for your body and soul

WHAT TO BRING: Yourself, your stories, a co-worker (please encourage the reluctant), job leads, and a positive attitude. The Encouragement Club is a Negativity-Free Zone. (In other words, no whining.)

She knew dismissals would begin near the end of the day and continue all week, so she quickly posted fliers in the cafeteria and near water coolers throughout the building. She also made sure to tuck one inside the dozen brownies she'd baked for Frank. She couldn't change lives in a mere five days, but together they could lift each other up in the aftermath of a horribly stressful week.

Although Barb still dealt with insecurity attacks about her own future, she knew there was nothing like reaching out to others to get her mind off herself.

"If it's the last thing I ever do on this earth," she told Marsha, "helping us get through this breath-holding mess will have been a worthy last hurrah!"

Humor and counting her blessings, especially through the darkest times, had always helped pull her out of a funk. Surely good doses of laughter and encouragement would deliver hope to the masses too. She and Marsha felt so much better after their Saturday morning guffaws about Barbizone and Marshalleon that Barb was even more aware how laughter jiggles people open and therefore helps them relax, let down their guard, and think more openly and clearly.

The mission of the temporary club was not to force encouragement down people's throats by preaching, counseling, or relying on the clichéd "Don't worry, be happy" mantra. With so many people dealing with baby-sitters, commuter trains, and previous engagements, many might only be able to attend a meeting or two. But that was okay. Capturing a little encouragement was better than none, and Barb believed this could be accomplished through a presented opportunity, proximity, story, shared hope, and as much hearty laughter as they could cram in. The *worst* thing she could do was hamstring their ability to encourage each other by locking them into a boring agenda. Thus, she decided to keep the sessions very brief and kick off the first session of the Encouragement Club by sharing a few details from her first job as a part-time waitress in high school. Something to hopefully get the storytelling ball rolling.

Barb could still hear her mother's ringing

laughter when she'd shared how she watched in horror as an entire shelf of desserts and creamers tilted, spilling its contents onto the floor.

"Why?" her mom had asked.

"I was asked to clean the cooler, and I didn't reinsert the shelf properly. I just panicked, Mom. I couldn't even raise my hands to try to stop it. The aftermath looked like the remains of an explosion at a custard-pie factory."

But that was just the opener: later in the day— her very first day on the job—while putting the finishing touches on an ice-cream sundae, she accidentally squirted whipped cream on a client sitting at the counter. Then she spilled an iced tea in the owner's wife's lap. For her grand finale, she forgot to "carry the two" when tallying the bill for her first table of four. They caught her error at the cash register, but by then, it was too late.

The manager patted her cheek and said, "You're a sweet girl, Barbara Jean, and I'm sure you'll go on to have a great life, but you are just not cut out to be a waitress. I'm sorry, but as of this moment, we're letting you go."

With that, they handed her a few dollars for her efforts, which was far less than the broken dishes from the cooler incident would cost to replace, told her to take her dollar and fifty cents in tips, and bid her a friendly adieu.

Aside from baby-sitting, that was the only job she held until her employment with DM.

It was the perfect plan. She would tell people that story, get them laughing, then briefly extrapolate the message: when job hunting, it's good to know what you are *not* cut out for. She'd simply trust that others would want to share as well, and if not, they'd still be together for some camaraderie and refreshments.

As for Barb's good memories at DM, there were so many it was difficult to narrow the pickings to a select few. She perused what she referred to as her memory portfolio, recalling so many good times. But rather than feeding the bitterness, it was a lovely exercise in cultivating a spirit of gratitude for her years of worthy employment, a helpful hint she hoped to pass along too.

But no matter how hopeful she felt about the Encouragement Club, the day was still filled with foreboding—and that was her fault. She'd let the cat out of the bag that cuts were coming, and soon. Most figured it would be this week; only management knew the bomb would drop today. That is until word spread at three-thirty that the first desk had been packed up.

From that moment on, the air crackled with the jitters. Barb noticed that even the ever-cool Josie Brooks seemed edgy. Still, oddly, a few coworkers admitted to Barb that it felt like a weight would soon be lifted off their shoulders, since not knowing—speculating, fearing, waiting, awfulizing, as many had come to call it—was often more intense than the event itself. For now, all eyes were peeled in every direction, waiting to witness or feel that dreaded tap on the shoulder.

Another week of this in front of us? Lord, hear our prayers!

Many had used the weekend to mentally adjust to their likely dismissal and start scouting the want ads—and to allow their fears to keep them awake at night. Before the day's end, the rumor mill was already packed with new worries. Once all the upgraded systems and switch overs were complete, might there be even more cuts? Who knew when the recession would end and how much deeper the layoff knife could ultimately cut?

At least people in Human Resources were available for counseling. They'd also compiled a list of area job fairs for anyone who wished to stop by and pick one up. By two o'clock, Lillian had to run off more copies.

Barb, dark circles under her eyes, prayed through every breath she drew. Thank God Lyle had removed her from the burden of actually delivering the one-on-one "let go" news to her employees. He said that for her department, he'd "do the deed" himself. She speculated his decision also had to do with the location of his office, which was away from her department and therefore more private.

But still, employees under her care watched as

Barb packed desk after desk. Although she'd begged God to hold back her tears, they still flowed while she packed up precious family mementos.

At least packing gave her a chance to slip her prayer notes into the belongings. She decided not to ask permission first for fear DM would turn her down. She smiled when she realized she'd adopted her own "don't ask, don't tell" policy. She knew it would be against company policy to ask management for home addresses, so this was her only chance to pass on the late-night prayers she wrote at her kitchen table. What could DM do if they found out anyway? Fire her? The thought made her snicker. At least the personal encouragements and written prayers—to those she knew were open to prayer—would already be passed along, and hopefully she'd see some of them at the Encouragement Club next week.

By day's end, she felt nauseated. How could anyone watch so many co-workers disappear like dust and *not* feel ill? Her data entry department looked like a ghost town, with more company cuts to come throughout the rest of the week. She quickened to the truth that people made a workplace special, not titles or prestige, business cards or reputations. Not even Marsha, the only woman who'd be left in her department, was there to lend Barb emotional support. She'd called in sick.

A wave of second-guessing the Encouragement Club set in. So many people gone, the atmosphere so depressing, and yet she'd heard very little feedback on her fliers. Not an ounce of encouragement for the Encouragement Club. Any other day, that might have struck her as funny, but not today.

What had she been thinking? That a few stories and a bit of laughter could save people from despair? That people would even notice the announcements when they were busy watching and waiting for notification? To make matters worse, Frank told her he'd even heard a few grumblings about her idea.

"Some folks said they'd be using every spare ounce of time to look for a new job, and one of your own department workers—and seeing as how you're against gossip, I won't say who, although I'm just saying—was actually telling everyone *not* to attend. She said she'd had enough of DM's misery to last her a lifetime, and she wasn't about to come to some meeting to act like everything is all hunky-dory and fun and games when clearly it is not. Plus, she said you could be too religious for her, and that she could do *without* your prayers, which, she said, certainly hadn't helped the people who were already gone. I'll be attending all the meetings, though," Frank said, giving her a serious nod, "so don't you worry. At least you'll have me."

Great, Barb thought. *Mr. Positive.*

She assured Frank she'd be glad for his presence, which she knew she would, even if he was only one of three attendees, including herself and Marsha, who she hoped didn't bail on her. Taking another leap of faith, Barb assured Frank that those who were supposed to show up would be there. "I've told you before, Frank, God has a plan for each of us. But *please,* if anyone should happen to ask you if I'm staging a sneak attack to make the Encouragement Club *about* preaching and prayer, the answer is absolutely not."

"I already told folks you'd be praying for them. It's what you do!"

"Frank! Of *course* I pray for people; everybody knows that. But I'm not setting up prayer meetings! I'm just offering a chance for group encouragement. If somebody wants to stay afterward and share in private prayer, fine. But that is *not* my mission here, nor is that what the gatherings will be about. What, exactly, have you been telling people?"

Frank looked a little sheepish. Then he grabbed his suspenders and snapped them, one of his many nervous tics, straightened his back, and looked her right in the eyes. "Barb, now you just simmer down. The only thing I've told people is . . ." He glanced up to the ceiling while he nodded, as if he could see exactly what he'd told them, right there in the acoustic tiles.

"The only thing you've told them is *what,* Frank?"

"The only thing I've told them," he said, looking away from her, "is that you make the best brownies on this here planet Earth." He was still nodding when he walked away.

That night Barb stopped by Marsha's on her way home. "I'm glad you're not really sick," Barb told her, "because I need a hug something fierce."

Marsha was happy to oblige, saying the need was mutual.

"It wasn't just the work stress that kept me home," Marsha said. "Since Easter is only a week away, yesterday I finally found the courage to confess to Gina that I cannot bring myself, at least not this year, to sit around an Easter dinner table with Christopher and his wife."

"Ooh. How did that go over?"

Marsha led them both to the couch. After they were seated, Marsha kept her eyes on her hands. "She said my silence on the topic—neither of us had brought it up since she originally invited me in February—had already led her to that conclusion. Honestly," she said, looking into Barb's eyes, "I felt so small. Between that failure and the whole work thing, which I haven't even told her about yet, I just could not face anyone today. I feel so guilty, failing as a mother and keeping my job when you'll no longer be sitting across from me. I have tons of sick days due me anyway, so I figured I'd stay home and try to write my way out of my funk."

"Does this mean you're going to be *alone* on Easter?"

"As it turns out, no," Marsha said, her eyes suddenly filling with tears. "You know, Barb, Gina deserves better parents than she has. If you can believe this double whammy, Christopher called her this morning and cancelled. He and his lovely young wife decided to book a holiday cruise. Oh, Barb, my heart is just breaking for Gina." She buried her face in her hands and wept.

Barb waited till Marsha's tears wound down. "So you're going to her house for Easter then?"

"Can you even believe she invited me after I told her I couldn't sit at a table with her own father?"

"Knowing her, yes, I can. God is good, even when we stink at life. Case in point, let me tell you about my day. They started escorting people out today." Barb shared as many details as she could remember. She now felt free to reveal that Marsha would be the only one left from their whole department.

First Marsha claimed that if that was the case, she *definitely* wasn't going back, but Barb assured her that she had to stay and "represent" for all of them. "Just be grateful and do your best."

She told Marsha that Josie Brooks had watched them all closely enough to know who would fit in with the new ways. The fact that Marsha was a wizard not only at using spreadsheets and databases but at writing HTML code as well, and had, on a continuing basis, attended software classes on her own initiative, meant she would serve the company well.

By the time Barb was done shoring her up, Marsha appeared more settled. It would be tough, Marsha said, but she knew Barb was right, especially when Barb reminded her that to voluntarily remove herself from her job didn't make an ounce of sense in today's economic climate.

Then Barb talked about Frank. "The Encouragement Club is doomed. When Frank doesn't look you in the eye, there is always more to the story."

"Never fear!" Marsha said with a sudden burst of doom-breaking enthusiasm. "I bet Frank snapping his suspenders is what awakened my muse. It was exactly 4:55 today when I felt the beautiful Marshalleon's powers beginning to whir again. By 5:00, I'd added three more pages. And now that Marshalleon has learned about this new issue—and I have ESP ties with her, you know—she'll swiftly handle the likes of Loose-Lip Frankenmunster. Well, at least in the land of *Helmoot, the Reaper Rephotsirch.*"

"You know," Barb said, once their laughter dimmed, "I hope this is one of those times life imitates the inspired art of Marsha Maggiano, rather than art being bound by the constraints of reality." She chuckled again. "I'll make you a deal. You keep writing, and I'll keep praying. Together, we'll be unstoppable!"

Josie's weekend was filled with uncommon failed attempts to stay on task, hot flashes, continued simmering anger, and the gnawing feeling that she was losing her emotional balance. She'd be glad when her job at Diamond Mutual came to an end. Throughout her consultant career, she'd felt nothing more than the satisfaction that comes with a task well thought out and executed. At Diamond Mutual, for the first time, she was acutely aware of the personal upheaval piercing so many lives in the wake of her recommendations. What was it about this job that made such a difference—with everything? Her age? The recession? Hormones?

As she pulled on her pajamas, she thought about how she'd seen it all before. Packed boxes, closed office doors, angry glares. She'd survived the worst of the Atlanta cannings, including the incident involving the police, without so much as an emotional flicker. Sure, the experience made her heart beat a little fast, but people eventually sucked it up, got over themselves, and moved on.

She decided to do a few crunches. She flipped out her yoga mat and began, her mind a whir of memories. At that Atlanta job, letting people go herself was written into her contract. Whatever a corporation paid her for, she did. It wasn't the first time she not only consulted but also served as the hatchet. More commonly, however—as was the case with Diamond Mutual's contract—when it came to specific personnel, she merely assessed and recommended. After sitting through Lyle's tormenting saga regarding Barb, perhaps she should have just done the canning herself.

 . . . *five, six* . . .

Decency. Dignity. The words yawned awake, stirring her pot of emotions.

But this economy was not her fault. Businesses needed to streamline in order to survive, and running lean was prudent. She enjoyed troubleshooting, she was good at her job, and her efforts made a difference for the better. She enjoyed multitasking, assessing, and interacting with other competent and successful businesspeople. So what *was* the difference between all her past job-related triumphs and this sudden emotional teetering?

She could sum it up in three words: Lyle Waters, storyteller.

He just had to go on and on about Barb DeWitt. He had to be the first man she'd ever worked with who had pudding for a heart and a need to share way too many personal details, using words like . . . *dignity* and *decency*.

Finished with her crunches, Josie washed her face with enough vigor to nearly tear her skin.

He just had to bring his mother into the picture. His *mother.* Josie's mother died before she even had a chance to enjoy retirement.

Teeth brushed, she tried to bang out a progress report on her laptop before heading to bed. She couldn't believe she was still huffing and puffing. *How is it that one wimpy man has managed to just about undo me, to ruin my weekend—to even cause me to question my own lack of sympathy and kindness?* she fumed.

She picked up her glass of unsweetened, decaffeinated iced tea. Empty. Again. It wouldn't bode well for a good night's sleep if she filled it; she'd be in the bathroom all night, same as last night. She smacked her lips, willing moisture into her mouth. She saved a copy of her file on a flash drive, which she plunked into her purse, and shut down her computer.

Maybe just a sip or two of water. But when she got to the kitchen, she downed an entire glass of water before she could stop herself and still longed for more. *Absolutely not!* She put her glass in the dishwasher, brushed her teeth again, set her alarm, and went to bed. She lay in the dark, staring at the ceiling. *Tomorrow is Tuesday. One day closer to getting out of here.*

"Tuesday! Dinner with Amelia tomorrow after work," she said into the darkness, a happy note infusing her words. *Something to look forward to. Maybe it's even time to start Amelia looking for a place in . . .*

"You are losing it, Josie. You need to find your next job before you know where to tell someone to shop for housing." She gave herself a light head bang with the heel of her hand. "Obviously it's perfect timing that you're meeting with someone for dinner and conversation tomorrow evening, since you've taken to talking to yourself out loud."

That night, the strangest nightmare visited her sleep. She was swimming in the ocean, trying to drink it before she drowned in it. Just when she saw the safety of the shoreline off in the distance, an old woman wearing a pink curler stepped in front of her—why didn't she sink? why wasn't she drowning?—and blocked her view, causing Josie to burst out crying, her tears only making the water deeper. Large dumplings began floating around her, too large to fit into her mouth but large enough to block it, like a rag clogging a drain pipe.

All that water, yet she was thirsty and unable to swallow.

Just when she felt herself begin to gag, Lyle Waters drove up in a car covered with snow, held out his hand, and asked her to get in.

She startled into wakefulness.

Her heart thumped. Two-thirty. Damp, night-sweat pajamas. Powerful thirst. The details of the nightmare still alive in her body and mind.

But worst of all, Josie was completely incapable of ridding herself of the absurd sense of relief she'd experienced when she grabbed Lyle Waters' hand, as if it were a life jacket.

Eleven

Monday night, Lyle sat at his kitchen table perusing the "career-builder" section in the *Chicago Tribune*, the remains of a frozen turkey dinner pushed off to the side. Although he first considered his exercise in job hunting an amusing diversion from the aftermath of that day's "job reduction" pit, suddenly the prospect of ditching the corporate life and diving headlong back into one of the postcollege job choices he'd felt so passionate about seemed oddly appealing. When he noticed anything that smacked of social services or nonprofits, he folded the paper back on itself and grabbed a pen.

What happened to that gung-ho nonprofit guy? He sure never imagined he'd find himself here in twenty-five years.

He surveyed his kitchen. First-class everything. Nothing fancy, really, but it was well appointed and stocked with the best, including excellent cutlery and expensive stainless steel pots and pans hanging from a chef's rack. He was glad his mother had taught him and his sister to appreciate the art of cooking. From the time they could stand on a chair in the kitchen, she encouraged them to pitch in, taste, stir, experiment. She'd inspired a way of life. He'd much rather stop at a meat market or Whole Foods and buy fresh ingredients than eat fast food or dine out every night.

Cooking alone was relaxing and enjoyable, but cooking with Miriam had elicited one of their great pleasures as a couple. *How many spaghetti sauces did we concoct, salmon trials did we laugh our way through?* To this day, it was hard to believe she was no longer on this earth. That she wasn't happily cooking with someone else. He knew it did him no good to glue himself to regret, but sometimes reminiscing ushered in the vague comfort of memories.

Maybe if he had someone, anyone, to share his culinary enjoyment with tonight . . .

Then again, after this grueling and heart-wrenching day, he felt like all life's pots had been stirred up enough. Tonight, he just needed to sit; thus the frozen dinner.

He circled the column header "Social Services" with his pen. Memories drew him back to those impassioned days when his naive and pure sense of moral duty guided his path. From writing countless grant proposals, to traveling overseas, to packing boxes filled with underwear and shoes, shovels and seeds, he'd tirelessly done it all. Whatever it took, he was devoted to enabling the underserved and unfortunate to help themselves.

He'd been good at what he did, a "born motivator," and had quickly risen to the top of the ranks. Thus began relentless calls from corporate headhunters to lure him away from nonprofits. It was shocking to learn what someone would pay him to do no more than what he was already doing. He and Miriam, whom he'd met at one of the multitudes of fund-raisers he attended, had been dating for about eight months when one of those callers tossed out such a ridiculously high salary that he decided to at least go for an interview. He'd allow himself to check the place out, prove to himself it wasn't possible anyone could make that kind of money for less than he handled now and in fewer hours.

The reality of it shocked him. Even the purest of do-gooders—and he considered himself only moderate under that heading—would be tempted.

"I'd be daft not to take it," he told Miriam as he studied her huge, blue, wading-pool eyes, hoping she would help him resist. But those beautiful eyes revealed excitement, trust, and a yearning for more.

"How could *anyone* afford to start a family on nonprofit pay?" she asked.

And that was that.

They had me hook, line, and sinker, he thought,

feeling suddenly fidgety. How easily he'd been lured away from his passions—or too easily surrendered them.

Yet Miriam—and admittedly, he too—reveled in their newfound financial ability to see more, do more, enjoy more lavish undertakings and vacations. Miriam was raised in a lower-class family. "I'm living a dream, babe. You're moving up the ranks so quickly. I am so proud of you. After our kids—let's say two girls and one boy, okay?—are out on their own, we're going to be so happy in our retirement days, traveling the world, season tickets to the opera, maybe even buy a little place in Florence."

Her dreamy sentiments stuck with him, niggling at him, prodding him to keep moving up the corporate ladder.

Tossing down the pen, he wondered if his inability to pop the question to Miriam had been rooted in unrest with himself. Eleven months into corporate life—where everything hinged on the bottom line rather than the humanity—he began to wonder if he had sold out his soul. Had he surrendered the thing that made him feel most alive?

One thing was for sure: when Lyle worked with the nonprofits, he'd never taken personal shots to the psyche for being a bleeding heart; after all, you *needed* to be a compassionate soul to be drawn into them. But what critical differences had he made in a world of need since he'd become Mr. Corporate?

He folded the paper and tossed it aside. "That is not a fair question," he said aloud.

Yes, it had been a bad day, one pressing in on his conscience. And the downturn in the economy surely had not been kind to the nonprofits, what with severe lags in contributions. But he also knew that on some level, what *everyone* did mattered to the greater world.

Many nonprofits—dare he say most?—wouldn't survive without corporate donations. One of his proudest accomplishments at DM was introducing the board of directors to his favorite nonprofit plights. It felt wonderful to attend fund-raising banquets from the other side of the giving-and-receiving spectrum. To be the one handing out a check, or offering matching grants and donations, and watching the grateful light in the eyes of the recipients when announcements were made. When he revealed the amount of DM's contribution, which was always more than the nonprofit expected, he'd receive a double rush. He still remembered exactly what it felt like to be on that receiving end of corporate generosity.

In his own way, he was still supporting his heart's passions. In his own way, he was still fighting for the underdog. It was possible he'd orchestrated a more prolific financial reward for those charities from the corporate side than he could have provided had he never "crossed over." The insurance industry ultimately served the masses, helped save lives, and made a difference to those who suffered. Sure, there were issues, but overall . . . He planted his elbows on the counter and rested his forehead in his palms.

This whole line of sad-sack thinking about "doing something that truly mattered" was rubbish. He'd remain content where he was. Diamond Mutual was his future until retirement, which grew closer by the day. He could still do good there, grow what he could with what he had.

"Lighten up on yourself, Son," he heard his mother say.

He adjourned to the living room, settled in his lounge chair, and flipped on the TV. He'd done nothing wrong today. Cutbacks and layoffs were a sign of the times. Even though he had to let Barb go, at least he'd been able to spare her the terrible duty of looking people in the eye to do the same. It would have killed her.

He shuffled back into the kitchen. Just before they'd both left work that day, Barb had handed him a sealed envelope, which he'd tucked into his briefcase. Until this moment, he'd forgotten about it. Sitting at the kitchen table, he opened the briefcase, withdrew the envelope, and extracted the contents.

Dear Mr. Waters,

Words cannot express my gratefulness for so very many kindnesses throughout your eleven years with the company. I know I will see you tomorrow and for several more days to come. But in case I don't get a chance to speak out loud the deep gratitude I harbor for Diamond Mutual, and especially your kind leadership and friendship (and your knight-in-shining-armor sweet spirit), please know I will forever give thanks to God for your hand in my life. I know you have always been my boss, but after all these years, you feel more like family to me.

Keep Diamond Mutual the great place it's always been to work. I hope we stay in touch, at least through Christmas cards, so I can know you are well.

Sincerely, respectfully, and with prayers for your continuing good health,
Barbara DeWitt

How was it that something intended to make him feel better instead made him feel so very much worse?

Monday may have been the day of doom and the beginning of the firings, which were thickening in other departments now, but Tuesday was a day of action, especially as the old data entry area was reconfigured and new equipment moved in. What looked good on paper would soon be actualized. *Today,* Josie thought, *the payoff is either close at hand or about to implode on us.*

The two new recruits, both savvy and riding the cutting edge of procedures and equipment, showed up bright and early. Lyle introduced them to Josie and made it clear that they should follow her every command. Although he'd said it with a halfhearted smile, she'd become familiar enough with the intonations of his voice to recognize that it lacked any real amusement. *Whatever.* She was loaded, cocked, and ready for success. *Don't look-back, / stand your-ground, / drive-through, / move-on* she repeated in cadence as she scurried through the building. She'd heard her dad say it a thousand times.

Her earliest recollection of this form of her dad's tutelage took place at a playground situated close to their military-housing unit. It was just before she turned five. Victor was trying to get her to stand up to a couple of older boys who'd decided little girls shouldn't be on the playground.

Where most fathers would have likely stepped in and stood up for their daughters, instead, when Josie puckered up, Victor gently nudged her toward them. He stood behind her whispering, *"Don't look back. Stand your ground. Drive through. Move on."* He repeated it with such poetic and mesmerizing cadence, his voice very close behind her, that she obeyed. Each step she took forward, the firmer and therefore the more encouraging his voice grew. The closer she came to the boys, the more she began to sense—and believe in—her own power, which felt better than the imaginary friend she'd dreamed up and quickly abandoned due to the fact that the friend always hid behind her.

The louder the boys taunted, the firmer came Victor's voice, until finally the boys fled. Looking back, of course they'd no doubt been terrified of whatever look Victor, towering behind her, presented on his face or of what must have sounded like an ominous and eerie threat. But as a child, at that moment, she learned to respect and believe in not only Victor's council but also her own ability to stand her ground. From that day forward, Josie determined that moving toward a challenge was the way to go. Backing down, Victor told her, was simply not acceptable, a benchmark phrase that served her well.

So headlong toward the day's challenges she marched, each step drawing her closer to 5:15 p.m., when she could go to dinner with Amelia and talk and relax and think about anything other than work, Victor, or remnants of the dream of the outstretched hand of Lyle Waters.

Josie stood by the front entrance to Diamond Mutual waiting for Amelia. A few pieces of paper and an empty plastic bag blew by like tumble-weeds, once again reminding her why they called Chicago the Windy City. For the third time since exiting the building, she looked at her wristwatch. Five-seventeen. Amelia was two minutes late.

The rumbling of the "L" momentarily caught her attention. *All those people going who knows where.*

Something knocked Josie sideways, almost sending her over. She gasped and clutched her handbag. A teen girl wearing a bright red jacket and taking very long strides had crashed into her. The girl, who was texting on her cell phone and laughing as she walked, threw an apology over her shoulder. Her almost-a-skirt left her extremely long legs way too exposed in these winds, Josie thought.

Kids have absolutely no manners these days. She's likely sharing what a nerd or geek or loser her boyfriend is. She frowned at her own thought. *Why is the negative always my default thought lately? Maybe he's a stud or a hottie, or whatever today's kids' word of choice is. Maybe he'll be voted most likely to succeed in his high school yearbook and she'll become a systems analyst—although I seriously doubt anyone that provocative and carefree could pull it off.*

Josie had all but missed her own giggly teen-boyfriend years. Out of the handful of guys who'd been brave enough to ask her dad—who proudly sported a reputation for grilling suitors—if she could go on a date, only one had been brave enough to brave *her* again, and then only once. It came back through the grapevine that she was aloof and snobby. In actuality, she'd simply been petrified and therefore nearly silent. She had no idea how to behave on a date, how to play the giddy weak girl who enjoyed the fine art of conversation. She could understand how silence could be interpreted as snobbishness, but there was no sense in trying to clarify. Soon her family would move on anyway.

Soon she would go to college, where strong women like her were accepted and admired.

Soon she would graduate second in her class, earn her master's, start her own business, make lots of money, attract a few men who deemed strong women an asset.

But never past a second date.

And then she'd move on, and on, and on, and then . . .

And then what? What happens after that?

She leaned against the building and sighed.

Twelve

Hey, Josie!" Amelia said, somewhat breathless. She crooked her finger and peeled a few blond strands of hair out of her mouth. Josie had forgotten how striking Amelia was. She wore deep red lipstick that matched her lightweight trench coat, tightly cinched at the waist, accenting her trim figure. "Sorry I'm late. The code I was given wouldn't work on the key box. I waited and waited for a super to arrive, but I finally gave up."

"That's okay. I was just . . ."

"You okay? You look a little distressed."

"I'm fine," Josie said with a halfhearted smile. "Sometimes"—she paused for a moment and rearranged her briefcase and handbag—"one's own mind is a good thing to escape. Thanks for bailing me out."

Amelia laughed. "That's a line I'll soon be quoting. Did you read it somewhere?"

"No. You're the lucky person who just happened to walk up the moment genius struck," Josie said, laughing at herself, something she was unaccustomed to but which felt extremely good.

Amelia guffawed. "I had no idea you were so funny."

"Me either."

"Decide where you want to go for dinner?"

"To be honest—and I sure don't say this very often—I'm tired of making decisions. How about you just start walking, and I'll keep up with you until we get there."

"Sounds like a plan. Any ethnic food group you don't like?" Amelia asked, her eyes briefly flicking over Josie's right shoulder.

"Just don't make me eat olives or liver."

"That I can handle. How long a walk can you handle?"

Amelia's eyes flicked behind Josie again, and Josie turned to see what kept grabbing Amelia's attention.

Lyle! He stood just inside DM's door, looking right at her. She nodded; he nodded back. He probably thought the two of them were talking about him, since they'd simultaneously looked in his direction.

"So?" Amelia said.

"So, what?"

"So are you up for a long walk, or would you rather catch a cab? I have a place in mind."

"The longer, the better. I could use some exercise right now."

"Good. Me too. And it's so nice out."

After eleven blocks, during which their discussions flowed easily from the latest news, to a few department-store window fashions, to how the wedding registry was going, Amelia finally ducked into a quaint little place.

The hostess, who recognized Amelia, asked if they had reservations, to which Amelia responded no. The hostess rifled through the seating chart and asked if the ladies would be joined this evening by Alfred or . . . She raised her eyebrows when she turned to face Josie.

Amelia answered for both of them. "No. Just the two of us tonight, Sonia."

They were assured it would only be a minute or two. By the time they took turns using the restroom, their table was ready.

"They make their own sangría here," Amelia said.

That sounded good, so Josie told the waitress to make it two. Before the wine arrived, she'd already downed her water and half of the refill the attentive server poured. As soon as the waitress walked away, Josie quickly picked up the fruit-laden glass of sangría.

"Let's have a toast," Amelia said, extending her glass toward Josie. "Here's to what comes next."

"Yes," Josie said, a welcome burst of enthusiasm zinging through her. She enjoyed Amelia's casual presence and easy spirit. "That is perfect."

After the clink, they each took a small sip, then spent some time talking about how good it tasted and dissecting why. Right mood. Right fruit garnishment. Right combination of ingredients. Josie decided to Google sangría ingredients when she got home.

"So," Amelia said, "I couldn't help noticing the way that gentleman inside your building so intently studied you. I saw you nod at each other."

Lyle'd intently studied her? Josie felt her cheeks flush. She waited for a prying question from Amelia, but none came. Again, Josie appreciated why Amelia was so good at her job and why she liked her: not overtly nosy, patient, clever, curious, easy conversationalist, good listener. Smart. Very smart.

"Lyle Waters," Josie explained. "He's the VP at Diamond Mutual."

"Hmm. Handsome."

"You think?"

Amelia took another sip of sangría and raised her eyebrows as if to say, *Duh!*

Josie wasn't about to speculate on the looks of Lyle Waters, which she'd not seriously considered, although he wasn't bad looking. "Yesterday was the launch of the big cutbacks, which meant today we could begin facilitating the new plan in the key department." She took two swallows of her sangría, then thought she'd better set the glass down and drink more water first. She was still too thirsty to have the long-stemmed glass in her hand.

A fresh loaf of crusty Italian bread arrived, and they watched as the waitress adeptly poured olive oil into a saucer, then ground fresh parmesan and pepper into it. They each ripped off a slice of the warm bread and synchronized dipping into the olive oil mixture.

"Delicious," Josie said. "If it weren't for my waistline, I think I could live on good crusty bread."

"Agreed. Well, and Alfred, of course," Amelia said with a smile, which looked half sincere and half mischievous.

Josie chuckled. "Of course."

"Who couldn't you live without?"

"What an interesting question. Let me think about that for a moment. Who couldn't I live without?" Josie took another sip of sangría and swirled the fruit in her glass. Then she dipped the rest of her bread into the olive oil and ate it. "I was going to say Victor, but in one way or another, I've already spent a good portion of my life living without him."

Amelia tilted her head.

"Victor is my father. Military man. Often gone for long periods of time, and sometimes emotionally absent when he was home." Josie stared into her glass.

Amelia must have sensed something, for again, she did not speak.

"I've never said that out loud before. In fact, this might be the first time I ever admitted it, even to myself." Josie wiped the corners of her mouth with her napkin. "I'm already living without my mother, who's been gone for a long while now, and my dear grandparents. So I guess the honest answer is no one." She started to pick up her sangría, but diverted again to the water, which she finished.

"Gosh," Amelia finally said, obviously to break the awkward, perhaps sad, silence. "I can't imagine that. I come from this very large, raucous family. So does Alfred. Since he's Italian, his family is even more raucous than mine, which I wouldn't have believed possible until after I met them." She smiled, her eyes revealing the genuine warmth she felt for everyone she'd mentioned. "They're all terribly close. Insanely close, sometimes. You don't have any siblings?"

"Yes. One brother. We stay in touch, and I adore my nephew. We don't get to see each other very often, though. Donovan, that's my brother, and his family have lived in France the last six years. I doubt they'll ever move back to the States. They thrive there. Both he and my sister-in-law are in the arts. They only get back here about once a year."

"You ever go there to visit?"

"Several times, although I can't say France is my favorite."

"Do you mind talking about your personal life? I don't mean to pry," Amelia said.

"I don't think so."

Amelia raised her eyebrows.

"Not many people inquire. Actually," Josie said, running her finger around the top of her sangría glass, "I think it feels rather good, but I'll let you know if I change my mind."

With a sigh, she sat back in her chair. Before she had time to enjoy the sensation of opening up a little more, she felt a hot flash rolling in. She'd read where alcohol was reported by many to set them off. She shucked off her jacket, grateful for the sleeveless blouse she wore beneath it.

"Hot flash?" Amelia asked.

"That obvious?"

"My mom's been having them for about five years. I recognize the flushed cheeks and beads of dew," Amelia said with a chuckle. "That's what my mom calls it."

Her *mother,* Josie thought. It was the first time their age difference really struck her. Amelia was old beyond her years, though, same as Josie had always been. "Did she happen to mention if they made her thirsty?"

"Not that I recall. Have you had your blood sugar tested? Thirst can be a sign of diabetes."

The waitress appeared and asked if they would like to order an appetizer.

"Go ahead," Josie said. "I trust your judgment." She raised her near empty sangría glass as evidence.

Amelia smiled and ordered an antipasto tray which the waitress brought with haste. She asked if the ladies would like to place their order yet. Amelia deferred to Josie, who said she had all evening—when didn't she, she wondered—so it was up to Amelia. Gratefully, Amelia made it clear they were on the slow track this evening.

"They're not busy, so we don't need to feel guilty about taking up a table. I'm a big tipper anyway," she said, a practice with which Josie agreed, as long as service was good.

After they enjoyed some of the antipasto in

silence, Josie asked Amelia if she and Alfred were set for housing after the wedding. Since their phone conversation about the gift registry, Josie had grown more curious about them as a couple.

"Interesting question," Amelia said, smiling and mimicking Josie's tone of voice when she'd used that response earlier. Josie waited for a further offering on the topic, but it didn't come. Instead Amelia asked Josie if the progress at her work meant she was ready to think about listing yet.

"Another two weeks will tell. If we don't run into any major server, network, or software issues—or employee disasters—I might seriously start casting around for my next job. I have to line that up first before I think about selling. Finding my next job usually doesn't take me long, although I have to admit that referrals and inquiries are coming in slower since the economy's taking such a hit."

"I'll keep your place in my back-burner listings then. Real estate is moving pretty slowly right now, but you never know. You sure don't want to find a hot buyer before you have a place to go."

"Exactly."

"Any geographic locations in mind? An area you haven't lived yet that captures your attention?"

"City living has grown on me this trip," Josie said, thinking about how much of this city she had not yet enjoyed. "After my last two locations, I was about to give up on city dwelling, but maybe

. . . oh, I don't know. I've never taken a job in New York City. What about you? Do you and Alfred think you'll stick around Chicago? For that matter, are you both even from Chicago?"

Amelia stared at Josie, as if pondering something. Josie realized she'd unwittingly steered Amelia back toward an area she'd already once avoided.

"I'm sorry if I'm getting too personal." *Time to back off the sangría, maybe?*

"It's not that. It's just—remember how I told you Alfred and I were learning how many things we felt differently about? As it turns out, a strong sense of place is another one of them. He was born and raised in Chicago and can't imagine ever living anywhere else. Me? I came from a little farming town in Iowa, and I'd rather raise a family someplace like that than in Chicago. Although my folks moved to Florida and the home I was raised in was razed to make room for a shopping mall, I still picture myself one day in a small farmhouse near a quaint little town with a gaggle of kids, a sweet little church . . ."

"Sounds like you want to live my grand-mother's dream for me. How are you and Alfred working out that kind of disparity?" Josie couldn't imagine ever having to compromise on something that big.

"For now, we'll stay put in Chicago. When we get ready to start a family, say in another three years or so, we'll see where we are then. What about you? Where do you actually call home?"

Josie swirled the remaining bits of her sangría before downing it. "Wherever I am," she said resolutely, clinking her glass with Amelia's.

"Interesting. For both of us."

"Isn't it."

"Yes," Amelia said, finishing her sangría too. "One more?"

"Go right ahead," Josie said, feeling the end of her nose, which served as her barometer for alcohol. Slightly tingly; she'd always been a lightweight drinker, which was fine with her. "I need to study the menu first and eat something. Maybe for dessert. We'll see."

"Good idea, although they do have the best Irish coffee here, which is pretty funny for an Italian place."

The rest of the evening went just as smoothly as the beginning. Since the restaurant was in the opposite direction from her condo, Josie decided it was too far and too late to walk home, so she hailed a cab. By the time the cabbie dropped her at the door, it was going on nine. She couldn't remember when she'd felt more relaxed. The glass of sangría had helped set the festive mood for the evening, but without adding one more drop of liquor—they decided to split an order of cannolis for dessert instead—she'd remained just as unwound.

Perhaps working a little harder to make friends earlier in her life would have been a smart idea. It surprised her to realize how good opening up felt, their friendly and easy exchange extracting a few surprising realities out of her, like Victor's lack of emotional presence in her life. Already, she could not imagine losing contact with Amelia, not even after she moved. Before parting, they'd arranged a dinner date for next Tuesday. She readied herself for early bed and crawled between the covers with a happy sigh.

Not long after she closed her eyes, she heard the sounds of running water. She waited, listening, and decided the toilet tank in her master bathroom was still filling. But the sound persisted long past the time it took to fill the tank. She got out of bed and checked the toilet and the faucet. No water running in either.

From where she stood at the sink, the sound seemed to come from down the hall, so she checked the kitchen. Nothing. The laundry room. Nothing. She stood in the middle of her living room, ears wide open, the only light coming from her bedroom down the hallway.

Oddly, the water sounded loudest right where she stood. Perhaps a pipe in the wall? Mindful of her steps in the low light, she carefully moved toward what now sounded more like a babbling brook.

When she stepped near the curio cabinet and the

sound deepened, goose bumps sprouted. *Surely not.* She groped until she found the switch on a nearby table lamp. The moment she turned it on, she saw the source.

"No!" The water in the creek within the snowglobe was running! The bubbling noise was so loud it sounded as if it played through her stereo speakers.

She stood staring, the refreshing vision and sounds of the water instantly igniting her thirst again. Her lips felt parched, and for the life of her, she could not swallow. Her heart raced, and she broke into a fit of trembling, but she could not look away. As if the snowglobe held the gift of life in the vastest of deserts, the creek water within beckoned her to touch, to taste, to see how it refreshed.

Her body felt on fire.

Slowly, she reached toward the globe, the water now running more rapidly, the sound intensifying. When her fingers reached the glass, they passed right through and landed in the middle of the stream. The instant relief of the cool water ran up her arm, over her shoulder, up her neck, around the curve of her chin, and through her parted lips. She gasped, then sighed, then cried with relief as the waters poured into her, quenching not only a physical thirst, but her deepest unknown and unrequited longings.

Thirteen

Do you realize I'm just four days from the abyss of not knowing what comes next?"

Barb admitted to Marsha, whom she saw only a few times a day now, that receiving full pay for no work made her feel guilty. Marsha, who was living through her own dramatic changes—a new boss, a new work area, new computer, new software, new procedures manual, and the lack of any familiar faces within view—told Barb that she'd more than earned her pay just by showing up.

"Catching an occasional glimpse of your smile," Marsha said, "is the only thing seeing me through right now. I don't know how I'm going to survive after this week without you here as my touchstone to sanity. Mr. Jed McCormick seems about as humorless as Josie Brooks, but at least the Firing Matrix will leave before long. Me and the Jedster Jungleman? Marshalleon and I are both stuck with him." She winked at Barb, who laughed.

Earlier that same day, Lyle professed to Barb that her calming presence was worth twice the pay she received for her two weeks of "steadying the ship." In fact, he said they couldn't have paid her enough for the familiar encouragement she radiated. *If he only knew how I sometimes feel inside, he would never say such a thing.*

But her prayer group reminded her that the work of the Holy Spirit was a mystery and a miracle, and that she should not underestimate what could happen when she was doing nothing more than living in her faith. When she felt queasy, useless, and inadequate, that was the thought she resurrected, and it never failed to calm her to know that it didn't need to be her power that accomplished anything.

Now, if only she could remember that perspective—which seemed an impossible task on this, her very last Monday at Diamond Mutual. Barb was so full of emotions she could barely sort them out. Not only was this the first day the Encouragement Club would meet, but her children wondered if they should throw her a retirement party.

"I don't feel *that* kind of happy," she told them, "and I'm not ready to retire, so don't even think about it."

She tried to rest in the prayers of others that she would make wise decisions for her future. But the thought of not coming to work at Diamond Mutual next week terrorized her. She was glad for the stressful distraction of the Encouragement Club, even if it failed. At least it gave her something else to think about.

Mr. McCormick, the new department head in charge of the web-based system—or, as Marsha had put it, "whatever they're calling that which replaced data entry"—was already in place; Mr. McCormick was responsible for all things official, which even included opening the mail. Occasionally he showed up in Barb's makeshift area, one that would clearly be dismantled the moment she walked out the door Friday. He'd asked her a question or two, but for the most part, she already felt like a lame duck without so much as a wading pond to distract her.

Even though Frank no longer delivered mail to Barb, he still stopped by a few times a day. It was clear to both of them he was looking after her, which Barb felt was really sweet.

"The meeting is still on for tonight, right?" he asked when he popped by Barb's desk Monday morning. Barb nodded. "The new guy who started today asked me about the Encouragement Club. Asked me if it was really open to everyone, as in *everyone*. Said folks in new job positions needed encouragement too. I said, 'I do not know, but I will ask the chairwoman and get back to you.'"

"New employees? At the Encouragement Club meeting?" The idea of new employees attending had never crossed her mind. Her knee-jerk reaction was not positive. Resentment seemed a good possibility. "*Who* asked you?"

"Now Ms. DeWitt, that would surely be gossiping, wouldn't it?" he chided with a devilish smile.

"I don't think so, Frank, not if you're just relaying a direct question from one person to another. That's not gossip; that's just being a good messenger. But if you're teasing me or playing mind games"—she'd begun to expect it from him—"that would just be mean."

"*Buzzzzz* Blinker."

"*Buzzzzz* Blinker?"

"*Buzzzzz* Blinker."

For a moment, Barb wondered if she was talking to Marsha about one of her characters. "Is that code for something, Frank?"

"No ma'am. It's a name. Buzz Blinker, but he sometimes likes to *buzz* the *z*'s."

"Frank, you're making that up. Did Marsha put you up to this?"

"Marsha? I haven't even talked to her today. No ma'am, I am not making this up. That's how he introduced himself during the handshake."

"What department?"

"You didn't read the all-company memo they circulated this morning?"

"Seems I'm already off that list."

"You didn't see one of the notices posted in the cafeteria or near the water coolers, right next to your memos about the Encouragement Club?"

"Frank, it's not even ten-thirty, so no, I haven't been to the cafeteria. And I brought a thermos of coffee today."

"He's the new vice president."

"Of what?"

"Of Diamond Mutual." Frank studied her face rather intently.

"Oh! Did Mr. Waters finally get that much deserved promotion?" she asked, her face lighting up.

Frank grabbed his suspenders, pulled them out, then gently maneuvered them back to his chest without snapping them. He swallowed and puckered his lips, shuffled his feet, crossed his arms over his chest, all the while looking increasingly uncomfortable. "You haven't heard yet, have you?"

"Frank, just get to it. You're scaring me."

"Mr. Waters has been replaced. Apparently they walked him out after everyone left last Friday. And Good Friday to boot. Nothing good about that!"

Barb was utterly speechless. She could not process what she was hearing, and at the same time did not want to believe it. A shadow crossed her face, and her eyes began to well. "No. Do not tell me this, Frank."

Frank leaned toward her, as if he were going to hug her, but stopped just short. "I'm sorry, Barb. I know how fond you were of him—how fond we all were, but . . ."

"Do *not* speak of Lyle Waters in the past tense, Frank. You're making it sound like he died!"

"Of course not," he said, moving back a step. "He's just been replaced, lost his job, like so many others. Like *you.*"

The conversation slammed her back into perspective: Nobody was dead. Unemployment was not death—although she'd been thinking a lot lately about what it would be like to one day be with Jesus.

"I'm sorry to have to break this to you, Barb. Truly I am."

Here stood the king of gossip, yet every inch of his face revealed that this was one piece of information he had not wanted to spread, not to Barb. He knew how much she liked Mr. Waters. Everyone did.

"Thank you, Frank. I would have found out sooner or later. I'm just so terribly sorry," she said, her voice quaking.

"He was good to all of us."

"Barb, I could use your help with something." The demanding voice of Josie Brooks jolted them. She strode up next to Barb, clipboard in hand, her typical air of impatience swirling around her.

Barb stared at Josie. She wondered if she'd heard any of the conversation—or if she'd been responsible for Lyle's firing.

"Thank you, Frank," Barb said, momentarily diverting her attention to—Frank's back. He was already scooting off, his Converse sneakers a blur, likely feeling the same way she did about the presence of Josie Brooks.

Barb was going to miss the odd old coot, which was how Frank often referred to himself.

Josie tapped her clipboard with her pen.

"How can I help you?" Barb heard herself ask, when really she wanted to run to the restroom and cry. Again. She'd rather do anything than help the person who might be responsible for Lyle's departure.

"Branford asked about this company policy," Josie said, pointing to a few scrawled lines on her clipboard. "It's something I really know nothing about. Since it seems to involve an area of your old department, I was hoping you could shed some light on this for me."

Barb glanced at the notes, finding it a) hard to focus, b) difficult to decipher the scrawl, which did not look to be Josie's, with which she'd become familiar, and c) fighting back an intense anger.

"I'm sorry, Ms. Brooks, but I doubt it. I've never worked with a *Branford* before. I can't make heads or tails of the writing. Maybe you can give me some more information?" She knew her voice was tight, but so was her throat.

Josie took a deep breath. *Likely to keep herself from yelling at me,* Barb thought. "Branford Blinker, your new VP."

"Branford Blinker, as in *Buzzzzz* Blinker?" She hadn't meant to roll the *z*'s. It just happened.

Josie looked surprised. "Yes."

"I haven't met him yet. Is that his handwriting? Perhaps if you could decipher the notes?"

"Certainly." Josie brought the clipboard a little closer to her face. "Maybe," she said, with what appeared to be a tired smile crossing her face. "Maybe Branford went to medical school before getting into management." She chuckled, which Barb thought bizarre. She'd never heard Josie Brooks chuckle before. "I'll have to get back to you."

"I'll be right here," Barb said. Hiding in her invisible corner. As if she had anyplace else to go until five o'clock sharp, when she'd hightail it out the door to set up the coffeepot and the trays of cookies for the first meeting of the Encouragement Club. She hoped it didn't turn into the Hostility Club, should *Buzzzzz* Blinker or Jed McCormick or anyone else new to the staff show up. That was, if anyone showed up—besides Frank and Marsha, who'd promised they'd be there.

Someone who called himself *Buzzzzz* Blinker was her new vice president? No way. *Thank You, Jesus, that I'm almost out of here.*

I'm sorry. I know that's not nice. I haven't even met the man yet.

Lord, hear my prayers—whatever they're supposed to be. But please don't let me show up at the first meeting of the Encouragement *Club with a bitter heart! Give me courage, and encouragement, please.*

Amen.

P.S. If it's in Your will, please let Lyle show up. Who might need encouragement more than him?

Lyle looked at the clock. Four-fifteen. He just had time to make the commute to the first meeting of the Encouragement Club. But did he really want to go? *Should* he go? After all, he'd been one of the people who brought down the employment ax. As much as he could use the encouragement, he wasn't sure he had any left to give—or that he deserved to receive any.

Or was the only thing keeping him from attending the meeting his pride, since he'd been let go himself?

Last Friday, he was blindsided by the proverbial closing-time tap on *his* shoulder. He'd never felt more humiliated than when he realized someone was packing up his belongings while he sat in the president's office facing Stan Kubic and two board members, listening to the same thing he'd told Barb a week previous and then her employees a few days later. Stan, who'd only been in his position for two years, was obviously extremely uncomfortable about his task. Lyle knew the feeling. The board members simply served as witnesses.

That strange conference call popped into his

head. The one advising him a member of the board had suddenly left over "unconquerable discord." The discord must have been over him! *No wonder he said they'd always trusted and supported me.*

"Diamond Mutual is heading in a new direction," Stan said.

This cannot be happening to me, Lyle thought. *There is some misunderstanding.*

"You've helped us launch that new direction, but now we feel we need fresh eyes, fresh insights, fresh visions to help us take that next step forward."

"I can't tell if I'm being honorably discharged, flat-out fired, if you're unhappy with what I've done here—"

"If you're worried about work performance recommendations," Stan said, cutting him off, "don't be. We will speak kindly and positively about your years of service here. But to set the record straight—and for your own personal corporate growth—it has come to our attention that tough times take tough actions and tough leadership. You are a people person, Lyle. A people pleaser, if you will, with the power to motivate. For years that has served everyone well here at DM. But right now, we need a stronger hand at the helm."

Lyle had no idea what that meant. None whatsoever. *Perhaps,* he thought, *they also need a new president who is a better communicator,* but he kept it to himself. "I'm still trying to understand. Am I being let go because of poor job performance?"

"I wouldn't put it that way, Lyle."

"How, exactly, *would* you put it, Stan?" Ire rose within Lyle. It didn't happen often, but when it did, he could be more tenacious—fiercer, perhaps—than most would expect.

"There is no need to make this more difficult than it already is, Lyle."

"There *is* a need for me to know, *exactly,* under what terms and terminology I am being forced to take my leave! Never once in all my years here have I received anything but a positive review."

"Okay. Paperwork will say the company is heading in a new direction, and it believes you are not the right match. That's it."

Lyle shook his head. He wondered if that statement came out of the mouth of Josie Victor Brooks. "Was this a recommendation that came after the new plan was facilitated or during or—?"

"If you're asking who made the decision, the board was unanimous."

Although that still was not an answer to his multiplying questions—after all, the board considered her recommendations—there was simply no point in pushing it further. He was done, and that was clear. And security was there to escort him out of the building.

Fourteen

Josie couldn't decide if she was living in her glory days or at the bottom of a pit, or if sometime during the last week she'd become a character in a hilarious cartoon strip. Nothing added up in the right columns.

She sat at her desk at Diamond Mutual staring at her laptop screen, but nothing was in focus. Her mind raced. Things that should have made her happy, like the creek finally running in the snowglobe for which she'd paid forty bucks, and the absence of Lyle Waters at Diamond Mutual, instead left her confused, sad, and dazed. Things that went against the grain of her lifelong mantra to stay independent, like never getting attached to anyone, were proven wrong once she started cultivating a warm and welcome friendship with Amelia. The two of them had already spoken on the phone three times since their dinner and both expressed happy anticipation of tomorrow night's dinner as well.

Some bizarre incidents, such as whatever happened with the snowglobe, were dreamlike in her memory, all gray and confusing around the edges; while other incidents, like Branford Blinker coming at her with an outstretched hand, introducing himself as "My-friends-call-me-*Buzzzzzz,* so why don't you," were so colorful and bizarre and cartoonish they were just as hard to believe.

And yet, in real time, Buzz walked toward her again, bright green shirt, neon blue tie, and another sheet of paper in his outstretched hands, likely full of questions she could not decipher and agendas which usually had nothing to do with her. What a time waster this guy seemed to be. Who on earth interviewed him? What did they think they were getting?

What possible good fruits could her efforts and hard work ultimately bear if this man was now in charge of them?

Throughout her career, she'd seen too many of his type. All sales talk and friendly up-front banter. All can-do, have-done, will-accomplish attitude convincing others that "I am your man." Until things started unraveling and the truth began to reveal itself. Smoke and mirrors, bravado, and forcefulness eventually faded away, and when they did, all that was left was the naked truth: the person in question was just one more person who had it all wrong about himself. Or herself.

Josie's breath caught in her throat, which went suddenly dry.

Was it possible she could just have described herself ?

Barb decided to leave work fifteen minutes early just to pull herself together before the meeting.

Hearing about Lyle, even though she'd held back tears all day, seemed to lift a weight off her shoulders. His absence made her departure feel easier. *Yes, it* is *time to move on. It couldn't be more clear.* While she shot up a quick prayer for Lyle, she also thanked God for this rather back-door but welcome gift.

She scurried to her car to retrieve her two giant baskets of Encouragement Club supplies, but as soon as she unlocked her car, she jumped in, slammed the door, and broke out in tears. After a few moments of cathartic sobbing, she decided she'd allow herself to cry for only two more minutes. Then she had to turn her efforts toward encouraging others. What kind of encouragement would she be if her face looked like a puffer fish? She had to coordinate this initial setup with Beth. She had cookies to set out, a coffeepot to get percolating, an agenda, such that it was, to review—and more praying to do.

When she looked at her watch, the thought that she could, in exactly two minutes, instantly turn off her tears—as if they were a sprinkler attached to an on-off switch—struck her as so funny that she laughed while she thrashed through her handbag for a tissue to blow her nose.

Frank tapped on her window, causing her to squeal.

Thank you, Lord, for the comfort of friends, she thought, after her heart stopped racing.

Barb looked at her watch again. It still wasn't 5. Frank never left early. He must have been a mind reader, for instantly he said, "What are they going to do? Fire me? They wouldn't dare. But if they did, to be honest, I wouldn't even care. I've got places to see, things to do, lovely ladies to serve. How can I help you, Barb?" He gave a dramatic sweep of his arm and a bow so low he teetered off balance for a moment.

Together they carried the laden baskets across the busy street. "Talk about a timely encouragement. Thank you, Frank," Barb said. "You are my knight in shining armor today."

Frank blushed.

When they arrived at Beth's Bagel Haven, Beth greeted them with the best words Barb had heard all day. "I've got your tables all set up. And guess what? There are already two ladies waiting for you!" Beth ushered them to the setup.

Barb set down her basket. "Look at the bagel bites and schmears Beth set out!" Barb said to Frank. "Oh, *thank you,* Beth! And ten-percent-off coupons for the next week. How kind. Here," she said, handing Frank a coupon. "Pass it on if you can't use it. Every penny counts." No wonder Barb had returned time and again to the little bagel shop across the street from her job. If she'd told Michelle once, she'd told her ten times this week how excited she was about the

Encouragement Club and how gracious Beth had been. "You have outdone yourself, Beth!"

"I used day-olds, so no biggie. My pleasure."

The two waiting ladies rushed the table. They'd worked in Barb's department—her previous department, she reminded herself—and they'd both been let go in last Monday's first wave of departures. Simultaneously, Sheila and Becky began gushing about how glad they were to see Barb and Frank again, how much they'd been looking forward to this gathering, and how worried they were that something might have changed to cause the club to disband before it even began.

Barb's heart was so happy, she gave them bear hugs. Next she grabbed Frank, who looked like he might faint.

"That felt so good," Becky said.

"Indeedy-do," Frank whispered, which they all ignored.

"I've missed your hugs and your laughter," Becky continued. "I told my mom when I left the house—she's baby-sitting my kids for me—that I felt like I'm hanging on by a thread, but at least I have the Encouragement Club to look forward to this week."

"I'm just excited that we're here for each other," Barb said. "Now, would you two ladies be so kind as to help me set things up? Sheila, I remember how pretty you made the napkins the last time we had a birthday cake at work. How about you do that marvelous and mysterious twirly thing again?"

Sheila's face brightened. "I can't believe you remembered that!"

"How could I forget? I've tried to copy it several times myself, but all I accomplish is twirling napkins onto the floor.

"Becky, how about you measure the coffee. When you make coffee for the lunchroom it always tastes better than mine. Then you can set out the cups for the lemonade and mix up a batch. The can of instant stuff is in that basket over there. It's already got the sugar in it."

For a moment, Barb froze in place and watched the two women as they quickly set to work. She could see a spark of energy bubbling within them. *The smallest things,* she thought. *Everyone needs to know they are valuable and remembered. Thank you, Lord, for helping me be a part of it.*

"What do you want me to do?" Frank asked, tapping her on the shoulder.

She looked around the small room. "How about you fold up all but a few of these chairs and stack them against the wall. What we want here is for attendees to talk and mingle, not sit in little groups. We'll only be here half an hour. Time will fly. Let's keep the energy up and stay on our feet."

"Good idea!" Frank said, snapping his suspenders before getting right on task.

Barb felt a hand on her shoulder. She turned to find Lyle standing behind her. It just about did her in. "Oh, Mr. *Waters,*" she said, her voice cracking.

"We will have none of that today." He put his arm around her waist and pulled her to his side. "We're here to encourage and be encouraged. No whining, remember?" He winked. "No pity parties. No tears. We're in this together. I am grateful for the chance to . . . Well, I am grateful." He glanced at Becky and Sheila, both of whom he'd personally let go, and Barb saw a sudden pang of discomfort cross his face.

Barb threw back her shoulders. "Exactly. And by the way," she said, lowering her voice to a whisper, "everyone knows it was not your decision to get rid of them."

"Is mind reading going to be your new career?" Lyle asked.

"Maybe," Barb said. "Hey, how about you help Frank. I see two more people have arrived!" She nodded toward the door. John and Hef from IT had just walked in. Hef had maintained his job; John had been let go.

John strode straight up to Lyle, hand extended. "Man," he said in his booming voice, "I'm sorry to hear you lost your job too. Honestly, I just couldn't believe it when Hef called to tell me. I hate to say it, but in an odd sort of way, it made me feel better about losing mine. If they canned you—and you were the best boss I've ever worked for—then I shouldn't feel so bad about getting the ax myself."

When Becky overhead that Lyle had been let go, her mouth fell open. She raised her eyebrows and looked at Barb, who nodded. "Did you know this, Sheila?"

Sheila shrugged and whispered, "Wow. Nobody is immune, huh? I haven't spoken with anyone since I left. I've been too busy job hunting, to no avail. But *that*," she said, nodding her head toward Lyle, "is a *real* shocker."

"Amen," Barb said.

Sheila drove her knuckles into the top of the stack of napkins and torqued and retorqued them, as if her hand were a screwdriver, until they fanned out aesthetically to her liking. "If Mr. Waters can lose his job, how is anyone supposed to hold their job—or find one?"

"Hel-LO, EVERYONE!" came a shout from the doorway. All activity stopped as heads turned toward the voice. "My name is Julio, and I'm unemployed. Wait! I'm at the right meeting, aren't I?" Julio Garcia, one of the funniest, if not the funniest, past employee at Diamond Mutual had arrived. A ripple of welcome laughter spread through the room.

He was followed by four more people who'd maintained their jobs, which delighted Barb. The room was suddenly alive with the vigor of those who cared for each other, and the sounds of "How are you hanging in there?" "It's so good to see you!" "I heard Modern Mutual might be hiring." "How about grabbing a coffee with me tomorrow?" "You wouldn't believe the changes at DM! I barely recognize the place when I walk in in the mornings."

Barb smiled. The room was filled with people who needed each other, each filled with their own vulnerabilities and hopes. *Yes, Lord. Wait until I tell Michelle!*

"Please help yourselves to some lemonade, bagels, and cookies," Barb said over the din. "The coffee will be ready in a few minutes. As promised, we're going to start exactly on time, so keep up the visiting until I tell you to stop. After all, this is my last week to boss anyone around— at least here at the Encouragement Club—so I better take full advantage of the opportunity." She chuckled, as did everyone.

"Trouble," Frank said to Barb out of the side of his mouth. "*Buzzzzz* is standing just inside the door. Looks to be scouting the place."

She turned toward Buzz and was instantly both unnerved and mortified. Remarkably, this was the first time she'd set eyes on him. How, she wondered, had she missed him all day in those bright clothes?

"*Buzzzzz?*" Lyle asked, staring that way too.

"What did you tell him about who is welcome

here, Frank?" Barb's voice was harsh. At first, she didn't remember how she'd left their previous conversation on the topic. *Oh, no! That's right! Josie walked up, and we never got back to it!*

"I never actually told him anything, other than what I'd told him before."

"Which was?"

"Which was that you are the person at Diamond Mutual who always makes everyone feel better, and that you like prayer and encouragement. And that you make the best cookies and brownies I've ever tasted."

"Who is *Buzzzzz*?" Lyle asked again.

Barb wrung her hands.

"*Buzzzzz*—Branford—Blinker," Frank said in slow motion, looking Lyle straight in the eye. "Your replacement." He looked down at his right shoe, which he scuffed into the floor.

Barb was relieved the words didn't have to come from her, which made her honor all the more how difficult it surely had been for Lyle to give her the news that she was losing her job. But here was Lyle, needing encouragement too, and now this.

"Let me be the first to tell you," Frank said, clearly reveling in his firstness, "that in my humble and lowly mail clerk opinion—although you know it's not like me to share my opinions—Mr. *Buzzzzzz* Branford Blinker is an unwelcome piece of work. He won't make the grade, he won't last long, he won't be liked—already isn't," he added out of the side of his mouth, "and he's a blow-hard. And I do believe he has just proved my point because anyone with an ounce of sense would know that you don't show up at an Encouragement Club meeting where many of the people in attendance have lost their jobs at the place you just got hired—especially with the guy you replaced in attendance. That's how ignorant he is. I'm sorry to give such a sad report, but I call it the way I see it."

Barb gasped. "Frank! What kind of thing is that to say? He's only been at DM for a day! You can't possibly know that much about him."

"It's the same thing I'm sure you'd *like* to say shortly after you finally meet him, Barb, but which you won't say because you are such a fine lady. I'll tell you, Mr. Waters, he is surely to goodness the polarized opposite of you. And not in a good way."

A murmuring hush had spread throughout the room, most eyes now on the door, word of exactly who had arrived rapidly spread by the few who knew. Barb felt gut-punched. With one quick appearance, the growing positive energy in the room had the life sucked right out of it.

Quietly, Frank said, "Feels like the bad guy just walked through the swinging doors of the Tumbleweed Saloon."

• • •

Lyle's stomach tightened. This was about as awkward as it got, on a number of levels. *How long ago did they start looking to replace me?* Again, the strange conference call popped into his mind.

He didn't know whether to go over and introduce himself, just to break the crackling tension in the room, or to ignore Buzz Blinker, hoping the atmosphere in the room would self-correct. Or to punch the guy's lights out for raining on Barb's parade. So for a moment, he did nothing but stare.

The guy was impossible to miss, wearing those colors. He moved just inside the doorway and leaned up against the wall. Lyle watched as *Buzzzzz*—Branford—Blinker's eyes flicked from here to there as he scanned the room. Lyle stared at his very bright, very blinking, very rude replacement. On second glance, although Buzz's posture was cocky and challenging—arms crossed over his chest, hands under his armpits, one leg crossed over the other, toe down—Lyle, a good people reader, thought Buzz's eyes revealed otherwise. He looked vulnerable, almost. *If the guy wasn't apprehensive, he'd already be in the room passing out business cards. Hmm.*

When the two men made eye contact, Lyle felt protective of Barb's plans. He stared at Blinker, willing him to leave.

"Attention, everyone!" Barb loudly announced,

startling Lyle. "I promised you an on-time start and finish, so I'm going to get the ball rolling. I'll give you another minute, and just a minute, to quickly grab or refill your refreshments." Lyle looked at his wristwatch. She was starting early, obviously just to move them past this speed bump in the road to encouragement. "I see a few more newcomers," she said, giving a happy wave to Marsha, who'd just walked through the doorway with a couple of other people still working at DM. "Welcome, and please ready yourselves to share, and therefore to encourage."

Thankfully, Barb's announcement broke the awkward spell. Although the energy did not quite return to its previous festiveness, chatter and action at the food table once again began to swell.

At exactly 5:10, Barb banged her hand on the table and waited until the room quieted. "Welcome to the *official* opening of the first meeting of the Encouragement Club!" she said in a loud voice. She waited for a round of applause to die down, expressed how delighted she was at the turnout, then began entertaining everyone with her waitressing trials and tribulations. Lyle noticed that Mr. Blinker had disappeared. *Whoa. Either I'm extremely powerful, or Buzz is smarter than he appeared.*

Lyle finally felt himself begin to relax and settle in. When Barb was done with her waitressing story, Frank quickly threw everyone back into stitches by sharing his first job out of high school: assistant to a mortician. "I'll tell you what," he said, grabbing his suspenders and pulling them out a couple of inches, "it didn't take me long to figure out that I had way too much to say to people who were too dead to listen." *Snap.*

"How about you, Mr. Waters?" Frank said, turning toward Lyle. "What was your first job out of school?"

Lyle held up his hands to defer, but Frank's question was quickly followed by a chorus of "Yes!" "Tell us!" "Come on, Mr. Waters!"

"Okay, okay," he said, thinking how strange it was that he'd just been reminiscing about that himself. "But Barb and Frank are hard acts to follow." He composed himself, realizing that sharing his heart's first desire would feel vulnerable. But looking around at the rest of the people in the room, some facing a murky, unknown future, he felt more one with them than ever. He'd already received two calls from executive headhunters. But Barb? Becky? Sheila? The handful of others from the old data entry department who arrived during Barb's talk? They might be out of work for a long time. He hated to think about how long.

Yes, they were all in this together. Who was he to hold back now? He drew a deep breath and exhaled.

Who *was* he now? Was he just an ex-vice president without a title? Or was he Lyle Waters, a man with a sudden opportunity for a do-over?

He decided to spend a few minutes pondering those questions out loud, right here, right now, since maybe, just maybe, they were universal questions that others would benefit from asking as well.

Fifteen

Josie sat at her kitchen table, staring at the snowglobe, touching it, turning it, once even verbally encouraging the water to run. As lovely as the scene was, as much as she willed it to "do something," the water in the creek stayed frozen in time. When she touched the globe, her hands remained outside the glass, achieving nothing more than leaving her fingerprints behind.

The longer she stared at it, the more her frustration glazed over, as if she were striving to make one of those magic eye pictures come into focus, which she never could. ("Don't you see it? Relax your mind and eyes and let the image appear.") The less intent she became on seeing something happen within the globe, the more she longed to once again feel the intense and wondrous quenching that had taken place within herself. She wondered if this was what it felt like after the first time someone tried crack cocaine or shot up with heroin, this overpowering pull for more. The thought gave her a chill.

But this wasn't a drug; it was a simple snowglobe. What was there to fear?

She placed the globe on the table directly in front of her. Resting her hands on the table, thumbs up, she slid her hands toward each other slowly, as if sneaking up on it, until she cradled the glass orb in her palms. She allowed her thumbs to relax onto the top of the globe and closed her eyes. Within moments, she sprouted goose bumps. The memory of how saturated she'd felt, how filled with gratitude and kindness and warmth and love and light resurrected. She'd overflowed with the indescribable joy of being *known*. *Oh, to experience that quenching again!* Her lips, her throat, her entire being longed for those refreshing waters. *Please . . .*

She heard the waters begin to gurgle and instantaneously felt her heart surge with hope.

She opened her eyes and removed her hands from the globe, but as soon as she did, the bubbling stopped, and the creek was no more than a painted scene.

But when she turned her palms upward, they were dripping wet. In desperation, she rubbed her fingers over her parched lips, but the water evaporated before she could swallow.

Barb made everyone take a few cookies home. She nearly had to shoo Frank out the door so she and Marsha could finally talk. Marsha helped her empty the remains of the coffeepot, wash out the lemonade pitcher, and repack her baskets.

Barb shared how glad she was when "the very bright *Buzzzzzzzzzzzzzzzzz* Blinker, who I finally got to lay eyes on," disappeared.

"Seriously, he showed up here?" Marsha asked.

Barb nodded. "He was standing right next to the door when you came in. You didn't notice him?"

"That is totally unbelievable. The nerve! Is the guy clueless? Honestly, some of the questions he asked me today seemed bizarre. I even caught Josie Brooks shaking her head after he walked away from her. I can't decide if he's a genius in a loud disguise or a bozo."

"I hate to say this," Barb said, setting her handbag in the empty basket, "but as much as I'm sad to lose my job, I'm beginning to believe it's for the best."

"Gee, thanks."

"I'm just talking for myself here. When I saw Mr. Waters walk in today, it struck me that if I had to let go of this job—and of course I eventually would have—I'm glad it was him who told me. The whole thing is starting to feel like a divine appointment. Based on some of the terminology I've overheard bantered around, I can already tell the industry is passing me by. Make that *has* passed me by. Trying to keep up with it would stress me to the core. But you, Marsha, are just enough younger and smarter to make a good go of the transitions. You were beyond wise to take all those classes and keep up with what's new. Don't think I didn't notice the collection of technology books you amassed on your desk. I was thinking just last night that since you're the only one from the department they're keeping, these changes might finally open up your chance to really shine. My advice? Give that new boss a fair chance."

Marsha's eyes welled. "How am I ever going to manage at DM without you?"

"Press on," Barb said. "Show 'em your stuff, oh great and beautiful Marshalleon," she said with a wink. "It's not like I'm moving to Dubai. We'll find plenty of time and ways to stay in touch, I promise. Friendships don't end because jobs do. Not when people are determined to keep them intact. We've been at this sisterhood thing too long for it to fall apart over a job disconnect."

"If the new kid who started in IT today— straight out of college, I heard—is any indication of the talented pool of people out there looking for jobs, I can't help but believe my days are numbered."

"How old is he?"

"Probably twenty-three or so. Maybe twenty-five, if he was on the slower college track or took any extra courses or certifications. He looks about fifteen."

"Do you remember being twenty-five?"

Marsha screwed up her face while she thought

about it. "Yes. I was pregnant. I had a husband. I was in love with him. And now I wonder if he ever loved me back, *really.*" She lightly smacked herself in the cheek. "Well, enough of *that.* And you?"

"Ted and I couldn't keep our hands off each other. You'd think being high school sweethearts, we'd have been sick of each other by twenty-five, but just the opposite was true. He was a gentleman in every sense of the word. Every day of our married life, that man drove forty-five minutes to work each way and never once complained about it."

"Did he like his job?"

"Did he like his job? Hmm. The sad truth is, I'll never really know. I hope so. He spent a lot of hours at it." Barb's eyes veered off. "So many things I'd like to ask him . . ."

"I wish I could have met him."

"He was a big flirt," Barb said, her eyes brightening. "You would have loved him, and he sure would have loved your spunky spirit and quirky humor. He always enjoyed the company of the ladies."

Marsha's face tightened.

"Oh, not *that* way. I just mean to say he had a winsome, twinkly way about him, which is how he got me, of course." She smiled, then closed her eyes. "I still miss him. He was a good and faithful man. He used to say, 'As long as I have God, you, and our kids, that's all I need to make me happy.' And I'd say, 'Ditto, ditto, ditto.' And then one day, he was gone. And life marched on, and now twenty-one years after his death, it's time for my next major transition. Wow. Twenty-one years that passed in a finger snap. Not a bad ride; a ride for which to be extremely grateful."

"Interested in grabbing a bite of dinner after we get the baskets to your car?"

Barb looked at her watch. "Quick one. I've got more baking to do tonight for tomorrow's meeting. Maybe a sheet cake. Wonder if I have enough plastic ware for that."

"You should pass the hat tomorrow. Everyone would understand. No one person should be feeding us all week."

"Nah. I can afford it; some in the room can't. No sense embarrassing anyone who doesn't have an extra dime to put in a hat. Cake mixes don't cost much, and I can use a drizzle frosting to keep expenses down." Barb yawned, the stresses of the day catching up with her. "But now that I've had a chance to reconsider, I think I'll pass on the dinner. Let's plan it for tomorrow night, okay?"

"Deal."

Not for the first time on Tuesday, Marsha's mind drifted back to last evening's writing efforts. She'd been too tired to summon the energy to compose the actual combat scene and, instead, headed to bed. But today, all during work, her muse was hyperactive and unrelenting, busy plotting and introducing lines, so that when she got back to her keyboard this evening, she could hammer them out. She could already picture the words appearing on her computer monitor. They would begin Chapter Thirty-Eight.

The high-pitched buzzing sound just about drove everyone out of their minds, so shrill and constant was it. At times the sound even seemed to morph into that of a yapping dog. Yap-yap-yap, right into their brains. Of course, this was the tactic the ornery Buzzing Blinker used to drive his enemies insane. So very unassuming and wily.

But the beautiful Marshalleon was ready for him—and she certainly couldn't miss him. First came the sound, *Zzzzzzzz*, then a yap-yap or two as his mouth spewed forth the sounds of battle, his skinny arm aiming toward her like a saber with what appeared to be a clipboard (but of course she knew it was actually his Rancor Ray Gun) attached to its sneaky tendrils.

And there was the bright light. Always. It radiated from him like a seventies disco ball.

The next time the Buzzing Blinker approached her, saber extended, mouth open, tongue wagging absurd orders, the beautiful Marshalleon would beat him at his own game, for alas, she, thank goodness, had her own means of warding off his attacks. Her gift of Knowitall made it extremely easy for her to do battle with him, for she knew his type. Alas, she would buzz and blink right back at him, only faster (speed of light faster), using the ancient rhythmic blinking code her forefathers had taught her, which was similar to Morse code, but different. It would take her only a moment to do him in.

"Ms. Maggiano. Are you okay?"

The male voice yanked Marsha out of her writing reverie. There, right in front of her, stood the Buzzing Blinker! *YIKES! I've crossed over into the land of fiction!* The dreamlike thought momentarily freaked her out—until she realized the real Buzz Blinker, her new *boss,* stood in front of her, asking if she were okay, a deeply concerned expression on his face.

"Yes, I'm fine," she said. "Why do you ask?"

"You were blinking so rapidly—an odd type of blinking. I thought you might be having a seizure."

"I'm sorry, Mr. Blinker," she said, not knowing what else to say. She dug deep into her creative brain for an explanation of what must have appeared quite a bizarre behavior. "There is a strain of . . . throughout my family's history, we've suffered from these mild blinking . . . *spells.* Nothing serious or harmful, and they don't last long. I assure you, I'm fine now. I'm sorry to have scared you, sir," she said, trying to keep a bout of laughter from erupting.

"I'm glad," he said, sounding genuinely relieved. "I don't recall reading anything about that in your file. Since you're the only person from your old department the previous leadership kept on here at DM, and you've been selected by the new team to play one of the key roles in our immediate future, obviously these spells don't impede your job performance."

"Can I help you with something, sir?" What else could she say? *Key role? What does that mean?*

"Please call me Buzz," he said. Marsha concluded that yesterday's buzzing intro was just so people would remember his name, a tactic that clearly worked. "Last night I spent my evening poring over yesterday's notes and a few of the new manuals. This morning I had a great team meeting with most of management. We concur that . . ." He paused and looked around as if to see if anyone was eavesdropping, causing her to do the same. "You know, I think this would be a better discussion for my office. Come with me."

She picked up a notebook and pen and dutifully followed him as commanded. *The great Marshalleon could* so *do you in right now,* she thought as she followed close behind him. For the first time, she noticed the small bald spot toward the top of the back of his head, not well covered by a minimal comb over. *AHA! Marshalleon has already discovered the soft inroad to your brain.*

It was a sobering act, entering the familiar office of Mr. Waters and watching Buzz Blinker seat himself behind the very same desk, all evidence of the previous vice president gone.

How had this all transpired so quickly? Now, rather than finding Mr. Waters' inspiring and motivational plaques on the wall, there was a single shelf with—*a bowling trophy? You have got to be kidding me.* Even though Marsha enjoyed her ladies' Wednesday night bowling league and an occasional weekend moonlight bowlfest with a few friends, bowling trophies did not belong in managerial offices. They belonged in family rooms next to large screen TVs—or in bedrooms, tucked in drawers, which is where she kept hers. *Is this guy for real?*

"Let me get right to it," he said, snapping her out of her assessment. "Jed McCormick and I have decided to restructure your new department. We'd like to make you the team leader. You'll report directly to Jed, who reports directly to me. I realize things are changing so rapidly that it must be hard for you to keep up, especially since some of the new changes are already being changed again." He grinned, and his face lit up, its friendliness surprising her. "But new management brings new ideas. Although we're of course incorporating the advisement of our consultant"—whom Marsha noticed he did not name, but who was clearly Josie Brooks—"I have a slightly different view of the in-house structure than she. Thus, your new position."

He leaned back in his chair, then flailed his arms as he almost tipped over backward. His face reddened, and he sat up and scribbled a note, likely about the locking device on Mr. Waters' old chair.

Marsha stifled a laugh.

"Go ahead and laugh," he said. "That must have looked crazy funny."

She couldn't help but release a snicker. At least he could laugh at himself.

"So what do you think?" he asked, after he composed himself and set down his pen.

She noticed green flecks in his eyes. Or were

they hazel? "I think," she said, carefully weighing her words, still reeling from the dichotomy of the one-two punch of her "new position" and his comedic chair incident, "I am . . . happy? I think. Although I'll no doubt feel happier after I learn more about what team leadership actually means." *A raise? More responsibility for the same money? Hysterics because I'll have no idea what I'm doing? Insanity because I have to work too closely with you?*

Buzz responded like a mind reader, lining out the answers to all her questions. No raise for now, but a review after three months in her new role. The reminder that she would report directly to Jed, who reported directly to him. It might take a few days for them to get things firmly settled into place. They were in the process of another new hire who would also come under her team leadership. She should not mention this to anyone until formal announcements were made. He wanted her to know that both he and Jed had confidence she was the right person for the job, although, he said, with a look of extreme seriousness, she might want to alert Jed about her spells, so as not to cause him undue concern.

"Sure thing," she said, wondering how often she'd have to produce a spell in order to keep them believable, or if her creative storytelling and writerly self should dream up news of a miraculous new cure that would soon prevent them.

Sixteen

Never in all her working days had Josie felt so disconnected, not only from herself—what was *up* with that snowglobe, the hot flashes, her growing loneliness, and rethinking her absolute benchmarks for living her life?—but from an efficiency and overall job performance standpoint. She couldn't seem to get a solid read on things or overcome the feeling that she was losing control of her best assets.

Yesterday, Buzz just about drove her nuts by delving into every minute detail of her plans and involvement in them, including dozens of things she had no clue about. Today he hadn't come near her. In fact, he seemed to go out of his way to avoid her.

The first rollouts of the new applications went smoothly, yet the new hires pushed back on one of her core procedures and applications upon which the very foundation of her recommendations had been laid. Normally the IT guys functioned as her *she's-right* backup; today it felt like they'd turned on her. The company atmosphere reminded her of the day she'd arrived late, for the first time hopeful that her job might actually conclude on time—only to discover that Lyle Waters had knocked the emotional wheels off her chugging engine.

Why was it always Lyle Waters who seemed somehow related—even if only tangentially—to her duress?

Adding to what felt like a complete undermining of her position on just about everything, including a peculiar and foreign erosion of her confidence, was all the positive chatter she overheard about the Encouragement Club. *"It was wonderful fun last night! Quickest half hour ever. You gotta come tonight. No, it wasn't at all depressing. Mr. Waters was there! Buzzzzzz Blinker showed up, but he didn't stay long. Frank said it looked to him like Mr. Waters had stared him down."*

She wanted to whirl on her heels and say, "Lyle Waters, a newly released vice president, showed up at an 'Encouragement Club' meeting? How pathetic. No wonder they let him go. Executives deal with headhunters, not club meetings. And Buzz Blinker, his replacement, is *that* ignorant? Diamond Mutual needs to get a clue!"

But her mind stuck on one thought: *Lyle Waters stared someone down?* She couldn't begin to picture that. *Unbelievable, and most likely another of Frank's preposterous rumors.*

By the end of the day, rather than reveling in the victory of a job well done—she loved it when rollouts went well—she felt an unnerving crack in her emotional armor. She felt isolated from the reality of what she knew to be true about herself.

She ducked into the ladies' room and stared in the mirror. She looked sad. Or maybe dehydrated. She pulled out her small cosmetic bag and added a few more swipes of blush and lip gloss, then threw back her shoulders. Better. She withdrew the bottled water from her purse and gulped it down, then refilled it from the faucet.

Why am I always so thirsty? As Amelia had suggested, a quick Internet search revealed that thirst was a symptom of diabetes, but that's all she could line up with it—unless the incident with the snowglobe was some result of diabetic shock or something. But she didn't believe that for a minute.

She looked at her watch. Twenty more minutes until this workday was over and she could once again enjoy Amelia's company, a thought that brought such relief her eyes welled with tears.

What is happening *to me?* she wondered, grabbing a paper towel and dabbing at the corners of her eyes. *And Lyle, at the Encouragement Club?* With fervor, she tossed the paper towel in the garbage can. Coinciding with a sudden rush of heat to her face, she wished she could see him again, to at the very least tell him how sorry she was that he'd lost his job to the likes of someone as pretentious as Buzz Blinker, and that she hoped she'd in no way been responsible for his canning. He was a softie, but he got the job done.

Quickly, the heat drained from her. *It wasn't*

another hot flash! At the thought of seeing Lyle—a possibility she didn't know she even cared about—she'd actually blushed. She'd seen it in the mirror! She had no idea how long she stood there staring at herself, first trying to denounce what had happened, then striving to untangle the mystery behind the eyes staring back at her.

When she finally exited the bathroom, she heard Buzz calling her name. She turned just as he caught up to her. "I'd like to see you in my office," he said. "Please follow me."

Mr. Obnoxious Tactlessness strikes again. Now what?

After they were seated across the desk from each other, she couldn't help but steal a glance at the changes in the office. Before she had time to get a second look at the shelf—*Is that a bowling trophy?*—Buzz got right to the point.

He'd had a few weeks to review her calculations, analysis, and set course of actions, and he was impressed by her expertise. Josie was surprised by his professional demeanor once he was behind the desk and made a mental note that replacing Lyle had obviously been in the works for a while.

"We're grateful for what you've accomplished thus far," he said, sounding sincere. "With the board of directors' decision to put a new person at the helm, a shift in emphasis was set in motion. Therefore," he said, with professional authority and resolve, "we have chosen to exercise the early termination clause in our contract with you. As of today, your services have terminated. Per contract details, within five days you will return or delete all proprietary information from your possession, including that which is on your computer or any other electronic devices. Since you have satis- factorily fulfilled the terms of the agreement, you will, again according to contract, be paid the rest of your fee."

And she could, according to Buzz, now go straight to HR and immediately thereafter pick up her belongings at the front door. A security guard was waiting outside his office to escort her.

Josie was in shock. She stood out on the sidewalk near the front door of DM, waiting for her meager box of belongings, which, no matter what Buzz had said, she certainly hoped contained her laptop.

This was a nightmare.

In an attempt to appear disassociated from the guard, she turned her back on him and tried to appear busy and casual by checking her BlackBerry, scrolling through emails, squinting off in the distance as if looking for someone— which, in her dazed state, she'd forgotten she should be. *Amelia!* Suddenly remembering their dinner date, Josie decided to call Amelia and cancel in order to avoid the most humiliating moment of her life. But before she could punch in her number, Amelia arrived, early and all bright smiles.

At the exact same moment, in an enthusiastic mass of chatter, Barb, Frank, and several other DM employees emerged from the building. *Please,* she thought, *let them keep on walking!* But no, the ever cheerful Barb stopped to tell her she'd see her tomorrow, and that she hoped she had a pleasant evening, and that—

The second security guard arrived with her box of belongings.

Like a mindless robot, Josie held out her arms, wishing she could slip through a crack in the sidewalk. It was clear to everyone exactly what had just happened: the woman many deemed responsible for the shakeup at DM had just been given *her* leave.

"Come on!" Barb chirped, her voice way too perky. "You can all help me set up today. From the sounds of things, we might have quite a crowd." Clearly, she was trying to move everyone past this awkward scene. "Feel free to stop by for a piece of cake," she said to Josie, as though everything were perfectly normal.

Cake. That ought to fix the fact that the wheels have just fallen off my life.

Josie caught the horrified look in Amelia's eyes. She, too, had figured out what had just happened. Josie turned her back on Amelia and watched the little posse walk across the street, a few looking back over their shoulders and smiling, obviously talking about her as they went. When they reached the door of Beth's Bagel Haven, she noticed the familiar, easy posture of Lyle Waters striding around the corner. He met up with the group and held the door open until they all disappeared inside. Just before he let the door close, he turned, caught Josie's eye, and waved.

"Bad day, huh?" Amelia finally said, grabbing the box from Josie's arms. "Let me take this from you until you at least have a chance to"—she shrugged, then delivered a half smile—"close your mouth."

When Josie realized her mouth actually hung open, she snapped it shut and tried to swallow, but her throat was so dry, she coughed. "Honestly," she said, finally garnering enough moisture to talk without rasping, "I don't know what to say. In fact, I'm not entirely sure what just happened or why."

"Would you like to come to my apartment to debrief? Under the circumstances, it doesn't seem like sitting in a restaurant is the right thing to do. I don't live too terribly far. We can grab a cab, kick off our shoes, and order takeout."

"I'm not going to be good company," Josie said, a mixed wave of anger and shame washing through her. *Shame? But I've done nothing wrong!* "I just need to go home. But thank you."

She reached for the box, which Amelia would not surrender. "I'm sorry you came all the way here for nothing." Both women clung to the cardboard.

Amelia studied her a moment, then said, "I have a feeling that the last thing you really need right now is to be alone. Just because that's what you're used to doesn't mean that's always what's best or what you *need*. Come on." She firmly snatched the box out of Josie's hands and hiked it onto her hip. Before Josie could object, Amelia stepped to the curb and let out a loud, manlike whistle as she waved her arm to hail a cab.

Neither of them spoke another word until they were inside Amelia's condo.

The atmosphere in the Encouragement Club meeting room crackled with the energy of a robust attendance that was up by nearly a dozen people from yesterday. Thank goodness, Barb thought, for Beth's generous supply of day-old bites and schmears again. Beth told her the coupons she'd set out at the last meeting were already paying off, so Beth was excited too.

The cacophony was comprised of laughter, camaraderie, and "Did you hear about our Ms. Brooks?" Frank had nearly worn the elastic out of his suspenders, popping them with each rendering of that juicy piece of hot-off-the-streets news, especially since Barb was too busy to stop him. From across the room, she kept trying to catch his attention and shoot him the evil eye, but his voice rose louder than usual above the din, attracting more attention to the topic than she deemed necessary or healthy, considering the circumstances—although if she were perfectly honest, at first Josie's circumstances gave her a brief moment of delight too.

While she cut the cake, she uttered a quick, silent prayer to ask forgiveness for her twinge of satisfaction that, perhaps for the first time in her life, Josie Brooks knew what it felt like to be on the receiving end—the end with no power. The truth was that Barb had no idea how much influence Josie had over who stayed and who went or why they'd let her go. With the economy being what it was, cuts might have arrived anyway, even if Josie Brooks hadn't. *After all,* she argued with herself, *she didn't come on her own; Lyle was likely in on the decision to bring her in to start with.* Barb wondered if he had unwittingly set the wheels in motion for his own job loss.

But there was no more time to dwell on any of that. It was 5:10, time to start the meeting. "Hello, everyone, and welcome to the second meeting of the Encouragement Club," she said in her strongest voice.

The majority of people in the room just kept talking, so Frank hollered, "QUIET! A *lady* is speaking!" which brought everyone to attention.

"It's heartwarming to see so many new faces

today, although there is one face we don't see, and that's Becky's. But what a great hopeful sign for all of us, and what a great announcement with which to start our meeting. Becky isn't here because she is *working!*" She waited while a brief round of applause rippled through the room. "Becky accepted a second-shift job on the other end of the city, which is actually closer to where she lives. When she phoned me early this afternoon to tell me her good news, she sounded quite excited. She said although she'd never worked second shift before, when they called this morning and offered her the position—she just applied yesterday—she immediately accepted. She said even baby-sitting arrangements with her mom, who lives with her, work out better with this shift, and that now she'd be able to spend more time with her kids during their waking hours—which she *hoped* she'd like." More laughter. "She told me to tell everyone hello and good luck, so there you have it."

"I've got some good news to share," Ken Detrich said from the back of the room. "After pondering Mr. Waters' questions last night—and Mr. Waters, thank you for your vulnerability yesterday—I've decided to go back to school. Although funds will be tight, my wife agreed that we should use this opportunity to make the best out of a bad situation. She believes this bad situation is really a springboard to launch me back toward my long-lost dream job. I've got an appointment set up for Friday with a counselor at DePaul. We'll see where it takes me. All prayers appreciated." He nodded and took a few steps back.

Barb had no idea Ken was a praying man. She opened her mouth to thank him for sharing, but before she could say a word, Sheila said she hoped everyone was already praying, not only for themselves, but also for all people dealing with unemployment or the threat of it. She had dark circles under her eyes and a fragile tone in her voice. Barb made a mental note to chat with her before their time was over today. She looked to be hanging on by a thread.

Next, Frank spoke. "I just want to say to those of you who are gone from DM: I miss all your pretty faces—some prettier than others," he said, looking right at Ken, which brought a chuckle. "It isn't easy for an old coot like me to get used to so many new procedures, and Mr. *Buzzzzz* Blinker is filled with them."

To shut Frank off before he launched into gossip about the new regime, Barb spoke up. "Thank you, Frank, for sharing with us. It's always nice to be remembered.

"Now, for those of you new here today, yesterday we had a great time sharing a few things about our very first jobs. Could be funny, profound, or just plain crazy. Hey, maybe

Diamond Mutual was—or *is,* for those of you still working there—your first job. Whatever the case, step right on up." Her eyes scanned the room, but nobody came forward. "Don't be shy," she said. "I know Frank is a hard act to follow, but I bet there's somebody out there who can manage."

Eventually a gentleman stepped forward; he'd worked in a pretty isolated area of DM before being laid off, so he wasn't as well known as most of the others. His voice was quiet when he first began sharing a few crazy episodes from his first job as an assistant house painter. But as soon as he received his first laugh, he was off and running, regaling everyone with hysterical tidbits about mis-mixed paint colors. "The owners were surprised to find what they referred to as a Pepto-Bismol trim around their front door."

When he finished, someone shouted that perhaps he should consider becoming a stand-up comic, a job he admitted he had already tried. After appearing on the stage at a few amateur nights at comedy clubs, he quickly realized that the only thing funny about his life was what a terrible painter he'd been. "Once I was done telling those stories to the audience, I just stood on the stage, microphone in hand, watching people wait for what came next, until I finally said, 'I got nothing else.' For whatever reasons, that just about brought the house down."

Barb was about to ask if anyone would like to

share a good memory from their employment at Diamond Mutual, but she looked at her watch and was shocked to see that their time was officially over. "That was a quick half hour! But it's time to call the *official* end to this meeting," she said. "I see there's no cake left, but we have the room a little longer, so feel free to stick around and chat another twenty minutes or so. And don't forget to thank Beth, the owner of Beth's Bagel Haven, on your way out tonight. She's been more than generous."

Speaking of thank-yous, Barb had yet to thank Lyle for the great tone of honesty he'd set yesterday, but he was already gone. She turned her attention to Sheila, who was slipping out the door and looked ready to bust out in tears.

"Sheila!" Barb caught her out on the sidewalk. "How are you doing, honey?" At that, Sheila broke down. "Come on back inside for a moment. Let's have us a talk." Barb put her arm around Sheila and guided her to a quiet corner. "What's going on?"

"I am the least qualified to find another job," she said, sniffling. "I was so lucky to have landed my position at Diamond, but now . . ." Her shoulders shook as she sobbed.

"Look at me, Sheila," Barb said, tilting her chin up. "You have so many talents. Why, you are kind, warm, sincere, clever with napkins." She smiled. "You know, the artful way you arranged not only the napkins but the whole table today was brilliant. Have you ever thought about looking for a job geared more toward the arts, or with direct public contact?"

"Like what?"

"Oh, I don't know. Maybe retail? Or a bakery? Or what about working with kids? I watched the way you interacted with the little ones at the company picnic last year. You were brilliant."

"Funny you should say that." Sheila grabbed a napkin out of her pocket and blew her nose. "My sister just lost her nanny. She's devastated to have to start looking. I almost asked her what she'd think about hiring me, but then . . ."

"Then what?"

"Then it seemed like she might think I was asking her to support me or something. Plus, a little voice in my head said, 'How far backward in your career building can you go?' "

"Backward?"

"Baby-sitting isn't exactly a step forward."

"Caring for our future is not a step backward! Do her kids know you?"

"They adore me, and I them. But I don't know. I have no idea how much she pays, and I wouldn't want her to make an exception for me, but it sure would be wonderful."

"I'll tell you what, since you're a praying woman, let's both pester God for a solid leading. Let's ask that the right opportunity just opens up, or you get the courage, or your sister does. Let's pray, trusting that if it's supposed to be, it will. But you have to promise me that if you feel that nudge again to ask her, you will. Sometimes when we're down and out, I think God whispers in nudges, so pay attention. And sometimes I think that little negative, self-berating voice in our heads is that old devil messing with us, making us feel insecure."

Sheila cocked her head and chewed her bottom lip, then smiled. "Will do," she said, standing. "I'll also keep checking the help-wanted ads. Thanks, Barb. Thanks for the encouragement." She sniffed and smiled. "But then, I guess that's what the club is for, huh? I'm already dreading the end of the week when our meetings end."

"You might have a job by then. Think positive! A lot can change in a few days."

After Sheila left, Barb whisked back to the table. Marsha already had things nearly cleaned up.

"Thanks, toots."

"You are most welcome," Marsha replied. "Not much to it when nearly everything's gone! Think many more will show up tomorrow?"

"I hope not. I mean I hope so. I mean . . . I don't know what I mean right now, other than I feel like I'm both tickled pink and in over my head. So many shocked and hurting people in the world . . ."

"Speaking of shocked people, Ms. Firing Matrix looked nearly ghost-like. I wonder what happened there. Hear anything?"

"I learned about it the same time as Frank and you and everyone else," Barb said, shaking her head, reminding herself that God loved Sheila and Josie Brooks and Buzz Blinker and Marsha and all of His children equally.

"I can't say I'm sad about it, but I'm guessing it has something to do with why Buzz called me into his office today—although you didn't hear this from me."

Barb stopped what she was doing and looked at Marsha. "No! Not you too! I thought you were safe!"

"I am. I'm not only safe, I'm getting promoted. Sort of," she said, nearly whispering now.

Barb looked around the room. Just a few people left, but nonetheless, they were not alone. "Save it for dinner, okay? Too many ears still in the room. But it sounds exciting."

"I'll give you a short preview: Buzz sports a comb-over covering a bald spot, and he has a bowling trophy on display in his office."

"Well now, it just doesn't get more exciting or enticing than that," Barb said.

Seventeen

Lyle looked at his watch. Seven-thirty. He'd been walking along the lakeshore for an hour.

After he left the Encouragement Club meeting, he grabbed a bite to eat, then drove his car to the planetarium and parked. It was a beautiful evening, and he always found that a leisurely stroll provided productive, yet equally relaxing, think time. But tonight, after more than sixty minutes, he still found himself restless.

Everywhere he looked, he saw couples, families, people with tail-wagging dogs—nobody seemingly more alone than he. Twice he thought he'd seen Josie Brooks walking with another man. *What is up with that?* he asked himself, wondering why and how she continued to penetrate his thoughts with such regularity. When they'd worked together, he'd greatly admired her keen mind—and, he had to admit, her physical features—but he was also aware of their polarized natures and a certain antagonism between them. Now that he'd likely never see her again—now that she, too, had been sent to the curb—he felt drawn to her.

That's crazy. Even if you had stayed at DM, in a couple months she would have been long gone anyway. Stop thinking impossible thoughts, which are likely fueled by your current position in life, which is . . . adrift. Put her behind you!

A bright pink sailing Frisbee caught his attention. He stepped off the path and into the grass to watch. Young men tossed the Frisbee from one to the next, twirling, somersaulting, leaping before catching . . . They were really something. Then he noticed their audience: a group of laughing young women, applauding and whispering to each other.

I'm glad Josie didn't have to be alone tonight. He'd noticed through Beth's Bagel Haven window—and yes, he admitted to himself that he'd been spying on her—that she got into a cab with someone. He thought it was the same woman he'd seen her meet once before. Was she a friend of Josie's? He thought Josie was a loner. But what did he really know of her anyway? Maybe she had a dozen friends in Chicago before she even arrived.

Clearly, efforts to stop thinking about Josie are pointless, so just think *about her for now and then be done with her!*

When he first heard that she was terminated before her job was complete, he was stunned. For a moment, he was sure people had misread the episode. Maybe she was just taking some huge box of files home for review and solicited a guard to help her carry it. She often took heavy piles of work home. But the guard, the box—the way people described the ashen and mortified look on her face . . .

No, he and Josie had shared the same humiliating experience. But that's likely where the similarities ended. Although he had no idea what would happen to him next, she'd probably already networked herself to the next place.

Wait a minute! Maybe she gave them her two-week notice, at which point they decided to pack her up. It's possible. And here everyone is spreading that terrible rumor, and most sounding way too happy about it.

He really wanted to know if she was the one who recommended firing him.

He wanted to ask if she'd been in on the hiring of Buzz Blinker. Maybe Buzz was someone she'd worked with before. But that didn't add up, since he'd likely been the one to fire her. Maybe they'd worked together before and didn't get along. Or . . .

He wanted to ask her if the rest of the system switch over went well. If she liked her work.

If she was lonesome too.

He wanted to ask her anything, just to be in her presence again.

Josie sat on Amelia's couch looking at the Chinese takeout menu. Her brain simply could not compute food items.

Time for a quick self-analysis. What are you feeling? What are you thinking?

Okay, the honest truth is that I feel frustrated. Belittled. Angry. Confused. And trapped by Amelia, who thinks she knows me. No wonder I've stayed away from friends! She nearly kidnapped me. How dare she think she knows what I need better than I do!

"What do you think?" Amelia asked. "Maybe an order of chicken chow mein, some hot-and-sour soup, a couple of egg rolls, and—oh! Kung Pao chicken to spice things up a little? I even have a bottle of plum wine in the cabinet."

"No wine, thanks. I already have a headache." Josie rubbed her temple with her index finger. She continued to stare at the menu, avoiding eye contact. She needed to calm down.

"Want some aspirin?"

"No. It'll pass." *What I need is for you to stop mothering me.*

"Did my selections sound okay? Want to add anything or swap something out?"

Josie finally looked at Amelia. "I should have just gone home. Seriously, I am not going to be good company tonight. And I'm not hungry." Her voice bordered on terse. She didn't wish to be mean to Amelia, but this was an impossible situation. All of it. "I should just go," she said, her throat raspy again as if it were parched, which was how she suddenly felt.

As if someone had slowly turned up the volume, she heard the familiar sound of running water, which caused her to sit up straight and cock her head. "Do you hear that?"

"Hear what?" Amelia asked.

"Gurgling. Bubbling. Like the sound of a creek running?"

Josie watched Amelia lift her chin and slowly turn her head from right to left and back again. "Can't say that I do."

Josie closed her eyes. The moment she did, her mind's eye saw nothing but the refreshing creek, luring, beckoning.

That's what she needed: not food or friends or work, but that creek. She wanted to lie down in it and gulp the cool waters until at last, her thirst was quenched. She longed to sit like a carefree child beside the merry brook and listen to the whispering songs of the waters as they wound their freeing melody around her, drawing her closer, closer, until she, too, became one with their song, flowing along with abandon and joy.

When she opened her eyes, Amelia stood before her, a tissue in her outstretched hand. "Just let it out," Amelia said, empathy in her voice.

At first Josie couldn't make any sense of the gesture. Then she realized she was crying. When she put the tissue to her face, she discovered that worse yet, she was crying so hard that she had not only tears but snot. *What on earth is happening to me?* Amelia pulled a second tissue from the box she held in her hand, then set the whole box down next to Josie.

While Josie wiped and blew, Amelia sat in the chair across from her, likely wondering if she should call the loony bin, Josie thought. *Maybe she should.*

"Feeling better now? A good cry always helps me."

"I guess," Josie said, unsure what she felt. What she was supposed to feel.

Amelia laughed. "At least I don't have to wait any longer to ask if you're ready to start securing your next job."

Josie couldn't help but grin. "True. But to tell you the whole truth about my next job," *and why should I, but here goes,* "I've only received a few nibbles, fewer than normal, and none have been very enticing."

No way was she going back to Houston. She didn't enjoy humidity or extreme heat. *What* do *I enjoy?* New York City offered a certain appeal, but due to the ongoing questions about meeting her deadline at Diamond Mutual, the one interesting query she'd received from upstate New York hadn't panned out. Before she could commit to a start time, they hired someone else.

"You okay financially?" Amelia asked. "I mean, can you afford to do nothing until the right job comes along?"

Had it been anyone other than Amelia, who, from the house hunting, already knew the big picture of her financial situation, Josie would have put her in her place. But from Amelia, all she heard was genuine concern. "Yes," she answered.

"That's good. At least you don't have to hit the panic button, like so many I know. My friend Megan just lost her job. Before that, she used to tell me how she was only one paycheck away from disaster. A year ago she was asked to take a pay cut, then they nixed her company bonuses, then they raised her portion of the health insurance to the point where she could barely afford it. She started running up credit-card bills by drawing cash advances on them, using the money to keep up with her mortgage payments. Now, she's completely out of work. Been out for eight months. If she can't find something soon, she might lose it all. I've uttered countless prayers to help me move past what I know is misplaced guilt for selling her that perfect match of a condo, but who knew the bottom would fall out?"

Josie shook her head. So she wasn't alone in feeling guilt pangs about things not under her control. *Amelia finds her friend the perfect house; the market and economy turn south and it's all up for grabs. Guilt won't help her. Period. Why is that so easy to see on behalf of someone else? I did my job, no more or no less. I didn't cause the economy to fail or rip anyone off.*

"It's good to count our blessings," Amelia said, drawing Josie out of her thoughts.

"You sound like my Grandmother Nancy."

"How so?"

"She signed all her letters with 'Count your blessings. Love, Grandma Nancy.' Or, 'Counting you among my blessings. Love, Grandma Nancy.' I recall her singing a little song about blessings. I don't remember how it went. Something about counting your blessings one at a time or something like that."

"I know that one!" Amelia sang a few bars of "Count Your Blessings," swaying her finger back and forth to the beat. " 'When upon life's billows you are tempest tossed, When you are discouraged, thinking all is lost' and so forth." She stopped and giggled at herself. "Now you know why I'm in real estate and not appearing at the Met," she said with a smile.

The tune instantly infused a melancholy ache in Josie's heart. She remembered attending church with Grandmother Nancy one Sunday morning during a visit to the farm. Such a tiny church. Even as a child, she didn't know they made churches that small. It seemed more like a big doll house than a church for regular-sized people.

When she told Victor about it, he bristled and said something like, "Church is for those who can't figure life out on their own. That's another reason you should be glad you weren't born into all that small-town quaintness: you either saw things the church's way and took a swim in their indoor pool—while the pastor held you under—or you were damned to hell. Hell? War is hell. Weakness is hell."

"You go to church much?" Amelia asked.

It took Josie a moment to answer. "No." She made it clear by the tone in her voice that that was all she cared to say on the topic.

"You up for food yet?"

Josie considered her stomach. "Not really, but you're right; I probably should eat something. I'm sorry I've made you wait so long."

"No problem. That's what friends are for. Let me call and get our order in. It usually takes them about forty minutes for delivery. By the time the food arrives, you might be ready for something." Amelia stood to retrieve the phone. "I'm gonna grab a glass of plum wine. Change your mind on that yet?"

"Nah."

"How about a little music? Jazz, I'm thinking. That okay with you?"

"Sounds good. After the day I've had, I'm up for some soothing music. Anything would be great. Well, anything but the blues."

Helmoot, the Reaper Rephotsirch,
Chapter 41

"Reckoning!" Marshalleon heralded triumphantly as she climbed into her winged chariot. Up and away she flew, higher, higher, until the Firing Matrix appeared nothing more than a deflated speck on the sidewalk.

Late into the night, Marshalleon partied with her band of encouraging merrymakers. No matter the Great Barbizone could no longer join Marshalleon for daily encounters in the Land of Sparkling Diamonds; now that the source of their separation had been crushed beneath her own box of foiled plans, what did it matter? Barbizone and Marshalleon were knit together with cosmic fabric that could not be rendered. TAKE THAT!

No doubt Helmoot and his twin partners in crime known as the Big Bazoombas were at this very moment scouting the land for new insidious ways to thwart the beautiful Marshalleon. But alas, even though Marshalleon had recently faltered during the crescent moon of EasterDale, she felt the tides of relentless pursuit once again rising within her.

• • •

Teeth brushed, pajamas on, Josie sat Indian-style on her couch, snowglobe cradled in her palms. She stared straight down into the globe, waiting. She'd been staring for so long her eyes burned, but still, nothing. Neither a sound nor a ripple. It was two in the morning, and she'd been sitting in exactly the same position for an hour.

Slowly, painfully, she eased her tingling legs out from under her and gimped across the living room to put the snowglobe back in the curio cabinet where it belonged, but then changed her mind and took it to the bedroom with her, just in case. Once she'd tucked herself in, she mentally shored herself up for another reality check.

"What do I know to be true?" she said aloud.

Tomorrow was Wednesday. She had nowhere to go. She had no "next place" lined up to live because she had no "next-place" job. She had no next-place job lined up because this job—for which her services were "no longer needed"— was complicated at best and devastating at worst. *I am confused and angry and sad and obsessing over a snowglobe that has a creek in it—one that either does or does not run. And I am hearing gurgling waters.*

She was obsessing to the point where she wanted to know the location of the real creek from which the snowglobe scene was rendered. Never mind her constant thirst; much of her *life* suddenly felt desertlike, and the only thing that seemed to quench her, at least for a moment or two, was a) occasional exchanges with Amelia, when Amelia wasn't prying into her life; b) the globe when the water ran; c) her momentary bouts of insanity when she imagined it running; or d) . . .

There was no d.

There was no sleep.

There was only silence and darkness until the sun came up. Josie pulled a pillow over her head to block out the light and finally dozed off.

At 9:30 a.m. her phone rang. It was Amelia, checking to see how she was doing on her first day off work. Even though Josie cleared her throat and answered with a manufactured energy, Amelia still detected she'd woken her and gently teased her about her new relaxed lifestyle.

Josie first denied sleeping in, but finally she caved. "I *was* sound asleep when the phone rang. But I have a legitimate excuse: I didn't fall asleep until morning."

"Chinese."

"Chinese?" Josie sat up and swung her legs over the edge of the bed. Her eyes landed on the snowglobe. "I don't understand."

"Chinese food. We ate so late last night. Maybe that's what kept you awake. Not to mention the jasmine tea. That stuff's probably got enough caffeine per cup to keep you awake for days. You should have had the plum wine. I slept like a baby."

Josie yawned and stretched. Her inclination was to lie back down, but she knew she should just get up and get on with her day, lest she set her entire sleep cycle off course. She'd stick to her usual routine. "By the way, thank you for last night. I'm sorry I was so out of sorts. I hope I didn't come off too cranky. I'm not used to . . . Well, thank you."

"Under the circumstances, I'd say you behaved like a lady." Amelia laughed, and the sound of her laughter helped Josie lighten up a little. "It's not every day someone's sent packing just before a dinner date. To be honest, I enjoyed the evening maybe a little more than was fitting. But it just felt so good to have a turn at being there for somebody else for a change. Believe me, we all take our turns being the needy one."

The needy one? Is that how Amelia perceives me? Needy? Josie bristled, stood, and headed toward the bathroom. She had no idea how to respond.

"Hey, you there, or did you fall back to sleep?"

"I'm here. But I need to hang up." She offered no explanation as to why.

"Sure. I'm on my way out the door anyway. I'm meeting a client in forty-five minutes. I just wanted to check on you, make sure you're okay. I should be home by six or so. Alfred's going to the gym after work, then out with his buddies. We can catch up later. I'll be anxious to hear what you did

230

with your day. I'm guessing you will make the most of it."

"Good-bye," Josie said. The last thing she'd do tonight would be to call the woman who viewed her as needy. Of all the ways Josie had *ever* viewed herself, that description wasn't even on the charts. And it certainly wasn't acceptable now. *I don't have to explain what I've done with my day to anyone!*

Whatever she'd been thinking about forming a friendship, it was certainly all wrong.

She threw on a set of workout clothes and forced herself through her most rigorous routine. She showered, dressed, made herself a poached egg and dry toast, and poured a glass of orange juice, which she consumed before she even sat down to eat the egg. She poured herself a big glass of water and took it to the table with her.

Do not read more into getting a glass of water than is there. Sweating makes a person thirsty.

Eighteen

Marsha's Thursday morning meeting with Jed McCormick went well. He seemed impressed with her ability to interpret, assess, and contribute to anything he threw at her in terms of software language, concepts, team leadership, and what was now being referred to as the *new* new company vision once the final layer of restructure fell into place. Barb was right: maybe it *was* Marsha's turn to shine.

Barb. Tomorrow was her last day at Diamond Mutual. Even though Marsha didn't see her that often at work now, she at least knew Barb was still in the building.

It hadn't occurred to Marsha how very much she'd miss so many of the other gals too, like Becky and Sheila. Back in the good old days, there'd been a spirit of oneness in their department—a department that no longer existed. Diamond Mutual was now made up of teams.

Gheesh. Sounds like I've moved into the NFL.

Still, the team concept was beginning to take form. Much to her surprise, Marsha didn't feel in over her head. For the first time in her life, she felt like she was stepping into her own power.

Perhaps it had to do with her ability to write her emotions. *Thank you, Marshalleon!* Sure, she was nervous, but Barb had shown her that when you keep your sense of humor, treat people with dignity and respect, and dig deep into yourself to give your best, things go better than when you don't. Their friendship was one thing, but when was the last time she let Barb know what a great boss she'd been? She'd have to remember to tell Barb how she'd influenced her professional life. Showering Barb with kind words might not be much of a bandage to the greater hurts of her job loss, but maybe Barb could take some solace in knowing that what she'd modeled—what she'd left behind—was worthy and would live on with appreciation.

Oh—my—GOSH! We can't let Barb go without a farewell party! She grabbed her Moleskine notebook and wrote "FAREWELL TO BARB" across the top of a new page. *Tomorrow is her last day! Duh!*

In all the shock and change, nobody had uttered a single party peep. Barb had always been the queen of the party organizers. If Mr. Waters was still there, she bet they'd have had a major party lined up for Barb; he'd have set the wheels in motion. In fact, if he'd departed under different circumstances, there'd have been a going-away party for him too. Things simply could not end this way, not with two such vibrant and kind people just slipping away.

But what on earth did you call a party for people who didn't really want to leave? An Exit Party, maybe? Or a Moving On Party, to coin Barb's idea? Maybe a We'll Miss You Gathering? *Boring. Come on, muse. You're smarter than this.*

It struck her that if she scrambled and scouted out a couple of cohorts, they could take advantage of the last Encouragement Club meeting tomorrow. She opened a new Word file and set about lining out the details. If Barb found out about it, she'd try to give it the kibosh, so it had to be top secret.

I know! We can tell her it's a surprise thank-you party for Mr. Waters! She'll love that idea! And we'll tell Mr. Waters it's a . . . Barb's own words popped into Marsha's head, ones she'd mentioned after she learned of Mr. Waters' departure. She'd said it was all beginning to feel like a divine appointment. *A Divine Appointment Party for Barb. Perfect! YES!*

The official "invitations," such as they were, couldn't be posted on the bulletin boards, or Barb might see them—as well as newbies who had no business at their party. Thus Marsha typed up a memo on half sheets of paper for Frank to distribute. If she got them done in time, he'd have at least three mail rounds before tomorrow's meeting to achieve that task. He'd know exactly who should get one. She'd also print a bunch of invitations to stick in her purse. That way she and a few designated others could deftly sneak them to people at today's Encouragement Club meeting and tell them to spread the word to any others who'd lost their jobs and might otherwise not find out.

She decided to order a sheet cake. Once word spread, there might be a larger turnout, and attendance at each Encouragement Club meeting had been growing as it was. Barb shouldn't be expected to cover her own party favors! Plus, she'd call Beth, use her ten-percent-off coupon and order a couple dozen special bagels. She bet Beth could party them up somehow. *Oh, cards!*

She'd go buy cards on her lunch hour—a thank-you for Mr. Waters and a happy retirement for Barb—and start passing them around for signatures. If she kept it simple and Frank kept his mouth shut when he handed out the papers, everything should work out perfectly.

She made sure to put the words SURPRISE and NO GIFTS on the invitations. In the midst of unemployment, one didn't ask others to spend their money. *And I'll have to figure out how to let Mr. Waters know—well, believe, anyway—that the party is for Barb. I'd love it if he would give a speech too.*

She went straight online to search for a home phone number for him. *Darn! Private listing.* Maybe Barb had his number, and since Barb would think the party was for him anyway, she'd ask Barb the next time she saw her that day. If Barb didn't have it, she could corner him at tonight's meeting, and if she couldn't get to him, Frank could act on her behalf.

Right, Frank?!

She looked up just in time to see Jed coming her way. Quickly, she swapped computer screens and launched into a rapid and random "spell" of blinking, which he'd asked her about in their morning meeting. Buzz apparently spared no details.

By the time he reached her desk, thankfully, her spell had passed—"It was just a minor one"—and she greeted him with a smile.

• • •

Marsha and Frank were chatting when Barb walked up. Immediately, Frank headed off with barely a wave over his shoulder. "See you tonight," he said out of the side of his mouth.

"I'm sorry, Barb, but I can't talk right now," Marsha said, gathering up a bunch of papers on her desk. She quickly stacked them and popped them into a drawer. "I don't mean to cut you off before you've even said anything, but this is a crazy day. I had a meeting with Jed McCormick this morning, and things are really heating up. I'll help you carry stuff over for the meeting tonight though, okay?"

"Sure thing," Barb said. "No problem. I was just killing time anyway." She'd just spend a little more time thinking about tonight's gathering.

The Encouragement Club meetings had turned into more than Barb ever hoped or expected. It was hard to believe that tomorrow would be the last meeting; already a few people had suggested they keep them going. She loved the mix of energy and witnessing the benefits. Although she wished more solid job leads were coming in, it gave those out pounding the pavement something to look forward to at the end of the day.

Pound the pavement? You are a dinosaur, Barbara Jean DeWitt. Did anyone still use that expression? Most people no longer put shoes to cement looking for jobs, unless they were fast-food jobs. Even then, they probably filled out applications online. *At least if I decide I do want to apply for another job, I'm computer savvy enough to put in my résumé.*

Barb spent the rest of the day trying to look busy. Killing time. Watching the clock. Determining that in no way was this how she wanted to spend the rest of her days on this earth. She'd have to find a purpose, and soon.

Come Monday, I'll have all the time in the world to figure it out.

"Whatcha got there, Frank?" Buzz asked when he noticed Frank handing out a fistful of fliers.

"Nothing, sir. I mean, nothing you'd be interested in," Frank said, drawing his hand behind his back like a little kid caught with a handful of candy.

"Now Frank, let me see what you got there. I'm assuming it's company business or you wouldn't be involved with it, right?"

Frank hooked his thumb around a suspender. He'd heard others say it, but now he saw it for himself: Buzz had an unnerving way of smiling and talking all nicelike, almost too nice to be believed.

"A bunch of us who've worked with Barb DeWitt *for a long time,*" he said, emphasizing the fact that he was not including Buzz, "are throwing a surprise party for her tomorrow, sir." Since he had the fliers in his hand, there was no sense making anything up. But he also saw no reason to mention Mr. Waters.

Buzz stared at Frank, squinted, cocked his head, and said, "Carry on." Then he walked away.

Frank exhaled, but he wondered if he might have just encountered the final nail in his employment coffin. After all, there were plenty of people out of work and likely all of them could sort and deliver the mail. How had he even held on to his job this long?

On his way home from errands, Lyle picked up a sub sandwich. He ate as he watched the noon news. *Enough of that depressing bout of murder and mayhem.* He flipped through the channels, stopping only once when he thought he saw Josie. Of course it wasn't her. He'd landed on a soap opera. *Perfect. As if I need more drama in my life.* But he watched for a while anyway. Here he was, brand new to the story lines, yet within two commercial breaks, he wondered if that guy really was the father of the blonde's baby. *No wonder people get addicted.* Off the television went.

The last few days, he'd tried to trick himself into believing he was on vacation—vacationing in Chicago.

His dad taught him that when allowed to work in the relaxed subconscious—his dad described the subconscious as "the miracle space that lives in the background of life's noise"—the mind could produce perfect solutions. His dad—and oh, how Lyle still missed him—was a master at coining quirky theories. No matter how discombobulated most of his theories seemed, most still proved true. "The trick," he'd said, "is to keep yourself busy enough to allow that subconscious to be just that, so that it can surprise you after doing its own thing."

With intent and clarity, Lyle had strived to release himself from all pressure to do or achieve or figure things out. He took long walks, watched a matinee, and shot hoops at the Y. He'd also spent nearly four hours in the Museum of Science and Industry, which he hadn't visited for at least a decade and where the coal mine still proved to be his all-time favorite exhibit, and he chowed down an entire eight-ounce bag of The Chicago Mix (cheese and caramel popcorn) from the Garrett Popcorn Shop, something he almost never allowed himself to buy since the stuff was so addicting and likely filled with whatever dreaded deathtraps made it taste so good. That and it turned his fingers yellow for a couple days. But now, who cared? It wasn't like he had to sign reports or shake hands with anyone. He might even get another bag tomorrow.

But the only thing his subconscious mind had brought to the surface was that he'd visit his mother and sister in his hometown near

Oklahoma City. It would feel good to spend *leisurely* time with them for a change—maybe even a week or more—while there wasn't a major crisis brewing with his mom and no set time he had to be back. He'd already fired off e-mails to a few old friends still in the area in hopes of getting together with them, too. He'd drive and take his sweet time getting there.

No time like the present to lay a little groundwork, he thought, tossing the remote control across the counter. Without a secretary to hand him an itinerary, he had time and the Internet to find his own way, so he fired up his laptop.

Both MapQuest.com and RandMcNally.com proved very clever and resourceful tools, including the ability to locate motels and restaurants—even a few quirky touristy exhibits— along a couple of optional routes. Sure, he could hop on the Interstate the way he always did, but after eleven years in Chicago and every trip home feeling like a race down the superslabs, it was time to engage in a little exploring. In fact, maybe he'd pursue as many bits of the old Route 66 as he could find between Chicago and home. He'd talked about doing that for decades but never had the time. If not now, when? His spirits lifted at the mere thought of it.

While prowling around on the Internet, he discovered Wikitravel.org. The site charted a "Historic Route 66" four-day journey from

Chicago to Oklahoma City. He made a few notes, bookmarked the page, then moved on to another link. One link led to the next until he came across an online version of a quirky little magazine called *BackRoads Illinois*, in which an advertisement for the Lamp Post Motel caught his eye. He Googled the town of Partonville and decided it sounded nothing short of a modern-day Mayberry. *Why not?*

The online reservation form for the Lamp Post Motel wasn't working, so he gave them a call to see if they had an opening for next Monday night, the day he planned to leave. Nope. Booked full. But the sweet voice on the other end of the line, accompanied by the sounds of a gurgling baby that must have been hoisted up on her lap, said they did have a room for Tuesday and that they'd be ever so happy to welcome him then, so he booked it.

He was starting to get excited. He clicked back to his overview map and added confirmation notes about his Lamp Post reservation. He hadn't stayed in a family motel since his youth when his family took their annual vacation. With the economy being what it was, it made him feel good to help keep some of the mom-and-pop places afloat. *Enough with the fast-paced corporate life for now.*

Then he remembered a recent television exposé piece. It had to do with unwashed bedspreads and a rise in bedbug bites at hotels and motels. Maybe he'd made a mistake with that first reservation. He could always drive by the place first and cancel, if it didn't look like it lived up to the ad. Then again, what would a drive-by tell anyone about bed bugs at a hometown motel—or at a major chain, for that matter?

Lyle, you're thinking like an old lady. Get over yourself! Whether it be people, places, or motels, you can't judge a book by its cover. He spent the next couple of hours flipping between Web pages and charting several alternative back-road routes, just in case he felt like switching it up or zigzagging for a day.

His thoughts drifted to Josie Brooks again. He wondered what she was up to, if she'd landed her next job yet. If she ever traveled back roads.

He wondered if she ever thought about him or if she might show up at the Encouragement Club meeting tonight.

In your dreams, Waters. She's her own cheer-leader. She likely wouldn't even be welcome. You heard the comments. Come on, subconscious! Is this all you've got?

Encouragement Club. It would be time to head that way pretty soon. Maybe he'd take a little nap before he went. Why not? He stretched out in his leather lounge chair and within a few moments dozed off.

Nineteen

A cacophony of laughter, confessions, fear, information, networking, and clandestine surprise-party strategizing filled the Encouragement Club meeting room. While some told jokes, others shared fears about their gnawing worries regarding the ever-flagging economy, rising unemployment numbers, and the ability to pay the rent and put food on the table. Some confessed to nearly letting tomorrow's secret slip to either Barb, who looked tired, or Lyle, who seemed a little edgy, while others held whispering meetings to decide the best ways to celebrate them.

When Lyle learned they'd be honoring Barb's Divine Appointment, he offered to Marsha to pay for a catered dinner, maybe something like spaghetti, salad, and Italian bread. She shook her head, but he said, "I'll keep it simple. Promise. But at least we'll send her on with a nice dinner. Not another word! I'll handle it, including the tableware." Off he disappeared into the crowd.

When Barb heard they were planning to thank Lyle for his years of service and leadership, she told Marsha she wanted to do something special, like cook up a couple of giant pots of chili so everyone could share in a light dinner. "Don't even *think* about arguing with me! If you want to do something to contribute, pick up some plastic bowls."

Every time Marsha turned around, Frank was stuffing a flier into someone's hands, talking too loudly, and snapping his suspenders so hard, she was surprised he hadn't catapulted himself right out the door. Twice Marsha thought she should just cave in and make the announcement: "PARTY TOMORROW FOR BARB AND LYLE!" Two dinners, farewell speeches, and the last EC meeting rolled into half an hour? She'd better check with Beth to make sure there wasn't another party coming in. This was shaping up to be an all-nighter!

"Attention, everyone," Barb yelled. "Thank you all so much for continuing to spread the word about the Encouragement Club. I think tonight we've reached a new high in sound decibels! We need to get the ball rolling, though. I know it's fun to get together and chat, but since tomorrow is our last meeting, we need to make the most of today. In fact, 'make the most of today' is a good motto as we go our separate ways. Does anyone have any good news they'd like to share?"

A guy from accounting who'd been let go by DM said he'd compiled his own list of job club resources to hand out. He'd attended one of the clubs that afternoon and found it quite helpful and hopeful. "Not as *encouraging* as our club," he added, "but an excellent resource. They think they might have a couple of leads for me."

Barb suggested he put his fliers near the refreshments where they were most likely to be remembered. A round of spontaneous applause broke out, not only for his newfound hopes but also for his efforts to help them all.

"I have something I'd like to say," Marsha said, raising her hand. "I want to share my very best Diamond Mutual experience. I don't think anyone's done that yet. Barb, I need you to come here and stand by me." Marsha took Barb's hand and pulled her up beside her. "This woman—right here—she's it!" Her voice caught in her throat, and she had to stop to collect herself. "Yes, I know she's soon leaving us and I'll still be there at Diamond Mutual—at least as of today, that was the word," she said, everyone chuckling. "And of course I miss *all* of you with whom I've worked. But I've recently learned I'll have a new role to play at DM, and since tomorrow will be kind of crazy, what with so many of you wanting to thank—"

Marsha slammed her mouth shut, and her eyes bugged out. Everyone in the room seemed to suck in their breath. She'd almost let the secret slip about tomorrow's tribute to Lyle and Barb. She lifted their clasped hands and patted Barb's fingers. "Well, tomorrow being the last meeting of our club and all . . . you know what I mean."

Snap! Frank's suspenders were heard throughout the room, causing a quiet ripple of chuckles and camouflage coughing to cover the "Close one!" mutters.

"Barb," Marsha said, turning to face her, "I want to publicly express my gratitude for the way you've mentored me." Barb started to open her mouth, but Marsha held up her hand. "Too often we realize someone has changed us in unassuming ways. And too often, we never get around to letting the person know. So today I want to thank you for not only your personal friendship and your many kindnesses to me over the years, but also the way you've modeled what it means to be a true leader and friend. Just look at this room full of people! We're here on account of *you*. And if it wasn't for Diamond Mutual, I would never have met you. Even though tomorrow might be your last day at DM, it will never be your last day in our hearts. Thank you, Diamond Mutual, for giving us Barb DeWitt, and thank you, Barb DeWitt, for giving us yourself."

While the two women hugged and shed a few tears, the room broke out in an eruption of applause.

In a loud voice, Ben Candor said he'd like to share a story about Barb too.

"Save it for tomorrow!" Frank hollered, then slammed his hand over his mouth.

"Yes, save it for tomorrow," Marsha said, glad she'd had a chance to speak her piece early. "I just wanted to seize this opportunity to finally get in a good Diamond Mutual story, since I remembered that was part of Barb's intent for the Encouragement Club. Due to such short time together, and perhaps still a few too many open wounds, we never got the ball rolling on that one. But now it is."

That's all it took for a few others to step forward. One man shared a story about the false fire alarm in the middle of winter just before lunch, and how everyone tried to cram in right here for warmth, into what was then the newly opened bagel shop. Beth, who'd popped in for a moment, said, "I have to admit that day sure helped my business! But I also want to assure you that I did not set off that alarm as a part of my PR campaign."

Another woman reminded everyone about the few months the pop machine rendered two cans for the price of one. Two people shared stories about the good works Diamond Mutual had accomplished; the son of one was the recipient of a special cancer foundation donation.

And just like that, the half hour was over.

As people filed out, Marsha noticed Lyle standing by the door. He was obviously getting a head count in preparation for his food order for tomorrow. Since tomorrow was Friday, the last meeting, and word was out about the farewells, Marsha had a feeling the group could even double.

"I'm thinking I better make three batches of chili," Barb whispered, as if reading her mind. "I have a feeling that since it's Friday and Mr. Waters was so well liked, we might have quite the turnout."

Marsha stared, her mouth open. Then she busted out laughing. "On all counts, I quite agree. But tell me, where do you plan to keep the chili all day, and how are you going to heat it up once you get it here?" Marsha looked around the room, trying to imagine how this was all going to work. She'd have to talk to Beth to make sure they set up an extra banquet table or two.

"I'm going to leave work around two," Barb said.

Marsha raised her eyebrows. How were they going to surprise Barb if she was in the room when the spaghetti showed up? Marsha never figured she'd leave work *that* early to get to Beth's.

"I overheard a couple of women and Frank murmuring my name," Barb said, "and something about 'tomorrow,' so I suspect there's going to be a party for me in the lunchroom at noon." She stopped and studied Marsha's face, obviously waiting for her to crack with the truth.

"How would I know?" Marsha said, feeling like the cat that ate not only the goldfish but a whole pond of them. The perfect smoke screen!

Barb pursed her lips and nodded. "I knew it!

But I wish they—or is it *you* heading up the party?—wouldn't make such a fuss, since you can already see that your kind words caused me to break out in tears. Once that lunch party is over, I'm sure I'll be an emotional *mess.* That will be as good a time as any to take my quiet leave. After all, what are they going to do to me if I leave early on my last day? Fire me? My computer is long gone, and I've already packed up and taken home all my personal belongings."

Marsha was struck by a pang of guilt over something she'd let slip in a meeting with Buzz this morning, which was that Barb had mentioned several times she'd likely sneak out early on Friday to avoid any last-minute cryathons. Marsha opened her mouth to speak, but Barb continued.

"You know, Marsha, I was sitting there at work today, looking around—what else do I have to do?—and was overcome by a sudden *whoosh* of gratitude. It was remarkable." Her eyes glazed over. "Life isn't always easy. At first, losing my job felt like the worst possible thing that could happen. But today, this extreme moment of clarity and *brightness* arrived." When Barb spoke the word *brightness,* her entire being seemed to glow. "I was flooded by such wonderful memories. God's ongoing hand on my life was so utterly clear. The day I met Ted, our children, the way He led me to this wonderful job when I was so lost and bereft. Suddenly, even the timing of my DM departure felt perfectly orchestrated. I have no idea what's coming next, but I sense God has a wonderful surprise waiting for me. Watching today's Encouragement Club, so alive with energy and sharing and caring, and then you affirming that yes, I *have* accomplished something good in the last twenty years . . . It's just . . . I feel so satisfied. Thank you, Marsha. Thank you."

The women hugged each other, heads on each other's shoulders. Barb was so earnest and filled with upliftment that Marsha thought for a moment their feet actually left the ground.

"Wow," Marsha said when they finally separated. "Thank *you* for sharing *that* with me. I've been so worried about you. Hearing you say that helps my heart." They slipped back into the cleanup, packing up the club supplies.

"So," Marsha said, the complications of tomorrow's party plans resurfacing, "you're going to leave at two, go home, heat up the chili you're likely staying up all night to make, driving it back here, pots smothered in dishtowels to keep them warm, and showing up just in time for it to be piping hot for our last meeting, right?"

"Obviously, the great Marshalleon's gift of Knowitall has once again ignited!"

"Exactly!" *Now hopefully the great Marshalleon can make it through tomorrow without completely erupting with worry. If the bakery delivers the sheet cake, Barb will see the writing on it when she gets here, so I better pick it up myself. But if she stays up all night cooking chili which nobody eats because we have spaghetti . . .*

Come on, Marshalleon! You're made of better stuff than this. Besides, who doesn't eat free food, no matter what it is? This is not a problem. This is a party, and a good time will be had by all.

She rested the pad of her left index finger on the half moon of her right pinky fingernail and silently spoke the words, *MarshaMarshalleon, Mistress of Magic, Maker of Payback to Reaper Rephotsirch, you will survive!* The theme to *Rocky* played full blast in her head.

Even after a rigorous workout and an entire pot of coffee, Josie still felt sluggish. And prickly. Amelia's words—*needy one*—haunted her, followed her around like an ominous shadow poking her in the backbone with a jagged dagger.

But worst of all, as if their constant prodding had finally wheedled their way into her, the words began to ring true. She did feel needy. She *was* needy. She needed to find her next job so she could find her next home. She needed to get a good night's sleep and a handle on her volatile emotions.

She needed to figure out why she was so thirsty

all the time and get rid of that dumb snowglobe, right after she found out the actual location of that haunting creek—an insane quest.

She needed to stop comparing herself to Buzz Blinker! Since the moment she'd thought about the possibility of *his* smoke and mirrors act, it seemed as if a haze lifted from *her* eyes, and she didn't like what she saw.

Perhaps she needed to start believing that no man is an island, for the revelation of her own loneliness tore at her. *No man is an island. Who said that anyway? Is it a book title?* Literature classes were never her strong suit in college, not even when she went for her MBA. Math, calculus—anything engineering related, things that demanded black-and-white answers were more to her liking. Lit majors always seemed so esoteric or overthinking and caught up in their own importance as people who could discuss and debate "the greats." All that pompous chatter.

"The greats." In her opinion, people often possessed warped views of what made someone great. Example: Bruce Springsteen, The Boss, as some referred to him. All the guy did was scream. What was so great about that?

"The greats are those who can fend for themselves." Victor's voice played strong and clear in her head. She went to the window and stared out over the city. "When you said those things, Victor, were you trying to empower

Donovan and me, or simply explain away your own physical and emotional absence?"

Am I now concentrating on your shortcomings so I don't have to dwell on my own neediness?

This was an unacceptable and self-destructive loop.

She showered, vigorously scrubbing her skin as though to rub away the confusion. When she applied a second dose of moisturizer, she realized she'd scrubbed so hard that she'd chafed her calves and forearms. *What is the matter with me?*

As she donned a clean sweat suit, she noticed the snowglobe still sitting on her dresser. She picked it up and returned it to the cabinet. After placing it on the shelf, she stood and pondered how, exactly, it had become so symbolic of her problems, perhaps even a visual metaphor for the current state of her life: frozen in time. Painted. Lifeless. Contained. How and what could she research to find the answers for *that?*

A mild hot flash began to roll through her body, a reminder of her age. Back in her teens, could she ever have imagined she'd be alone in her forties? Never.

Displayed on the top shelf of the cabinet, the large bronze statue of a nude couple holding each other in a soft embrace drew her attention. She'd first seen the statue displayed at a fund-raising auction. The bronze was a masterful work of art, yes, but there was something more that spoke to her. Something she couldn't quite pinpoint.

Several times throughout the evening she circled back and studied it from different angles. Why did it attract her so? Relationships were too complicated. And yet . . . *This is what intimacy looks like,* she thought. They did not embrace with sexual tension in their eyes, but in an utter surrender of themselves, one to the other. "Here I am. I am here for you," they seemed to whisper to each other. Such intimacy. But what did *she* know of intimacy? How could she even pretend to comprehend the meaning of the word if she felt it beneath her to admit to one single person that she needed something?

That she needed someone, anyone.

Amelia had not only reached out but suffered through the outward snarkiness of Josie's pride. Amelia didn't reject her the first time she'd been short with her, as was usually the case back in the days when Josie learned to hoist her protective walls. Amelia even called to check on her afterward, said she was happy to be the one in a position to help, for a change.

And what did Josie give her in return? A brisk brush-off. She didn't even think to ask Amelia what *she* might have needed lately; she only thought about herself and her wounded pride, and how she did not need to report to anyone about her day, which, as it turned out, utterly sucked.

Amelia cared. Amelia cared about her the way Lyle cared about his co-workers.

Lyle? Where did that tangential thought come from?

Did Lyle make her angry because he cared about people and, unlike her father, wasn't too proud to show it?

She stared again at the bronze statue. *Intimacy. What do I really know about you? What do I want to know about you?*

How far am I willing to open myself up to find out? When and how will I ever begin? Soon I am starting over, yet again. What's the point of befriending Amelia when that will just result in me missing her?

But might missing someone be better than never knowing them at all?

At first she heard only a trickle of water. But the more she opened to her desire for intimacy, to allow herself to fall into the depth of what the couple revealed in each other's eyes—unconditional love—the more vibrant became the sounds of the water.

When she diverted her attention back to the snowglobe, the creek was not only running within the globe, it was running out of the glass, filling her cabinet, pouring out onto the floor, engulfing the room with its refreshing rivers of water, lifting her off her feet until she began to float downstream in its wonderful, glorious, freeing relief.

Twenty

Barb tasted, stirred, and added a little more spice to the bubbling chili on her burners. She decided to store two batches—one spicy hot, the other very mild—in her Crockpots and keep the biggest medium-spicy batch in a kettle-like pot. When the kids were young, she used that giant pot for corn on the cob, since it could hold nearly a dozen ears at a time. *Such happy memories. Yes, life has been good to me.* It would be heavy to carry, but since she didn't fill any of the pots too full, she felt sure she could manage the sloshing.

Utterly exhausted, she plopped down at her kitchen table. *What a long day.* By the time she'd arrived home from the Encouragement Club, lugged in the coffeepot and all else from the meeting, cleaned everything up, made a grocery list, gone to the store and shopped, unloaded the car again, and started cooking, it was already nine. Now it was ten-thirty, a half hour past her bedtime.

She was weary, and tomorrow was her last day at work. But since this morning's moment of clarity, that seemed anticlimactic compared to the big doings for the last day of the Encouragement Club. She was so excited to give Lyle Waters the send-off he deserved. For that, she would stay up another hour. By the time she crawled into bed, it was after midnight.

The next thing she knew, her alarm was ringing. Friday morning. *The Big Day,* she thought. *I am ready for it!*

She showered, ate a piece of toast with peanut butter, and went over her list of items to pack when she returned home after work to gather everything for the party. Since there was no parking on the street in front of Beth's, she'd need to plan a few logistics. Maybe a back-alley loading dock? She decided to stop by Beth's between work and home, set a plan, and see if Beth had extra extension cords she could borrow. If not, she might have to buy some. Since some people still had to work till five and most others didn't show up at EC till then, she'd have to manage alone. She hoped her back held up till she got everything carried in.

God will provide. Maybe a good Samaritan customer will step forward and give an old "retired lady" a hand.

Friday morning Marsha woke at 4:30 a.m. Such a big day ahead of her, what with the last Encouragement Club meeting and the surprise celebrations for Mr. Waters and Barb. But since last night's conversation with Barb, she'd been niggled by guilt. How could she so carelessly betray her friend's trust, then fail to mention it to her? No, the offense was hardly over a big thing, and surely nobody would care. Still . . .

A glass of warm water with a fresh lemon wedge in hand, she took her confusion straight to her best mental processing forum.

Helmoot, the Reaper Rephotsirch, Chapter 48

Even with the gift of Knowitall in her mental pocket, Marshalleon found herself in an uncommon state of confusion. For the first time, it dawned on her that the menacing Buzzing Blinker's clipboard was not a Rancor-Inducing Ray Gun, as she was first led to believe. If it was, would she not always feel rancored after he aimed it at her? It seemed a theory worth dissecting.

Aside from her astounding beauty, what did Marshalleon know to be true? 1) She was powerful, more powerful than even she first believed. Her supremacy had been publicly ordained at her official upliftment in the Land of Sparkling Diamonds to Queen Marshalleon Teamopolis. 2) Due to upheaval and changes in the land, the Reaper Rephotsirch had currently taken a backseat to the Buzzing Blinker, who was spreading two bizarre words of dictum throughout the Land of Sparkling Diamonds: Die Mute. He bandied them about as though everyone surely understood their implications. If ever a sinister plot was hatched, this was it! To die mute was unacceptable since no one deserved to be without a voice. The Land of Sparkling Diamonds had to be saved from such a wicked plot. 3) Things were not always what they appeared. Thus, the clipboard/Ray Gun dilemma.

Yesterday, when he boldly approached her without even attempting to hide the gun, she steadied herself lest she once again fall under its rancor-inducing spell. But this encounter of the gun's firing questions produced no potency. This time, she knew all the answers and delighted in firing a few questions right back, each volley fueling her empowerment. This time, she

259

understood the calibrations of his weapon and therefore why he loaded the gun as he did.

And yet, this time, she'd divulged a personal piece of information about the Great Barbizone! She was aghast! What kind of powers *did* this man possess that she, Queen Marshalleon Teamopolis, would let slip Barbizone's early escape from the clutches of dying mute?

This time, she felt kind of sad when he walked away, as if she might miss him.

AHA! It was not a Rancor-Inducing Ray Gun the Buzzing Blinker used to slay his enemy. It was a gun of deception and trickery. In that case, she would have to be extremely careful during all forthcoming encounters of the Buzzing Blinker kind.

The words came slowly, thoughtfully, hesitantly. Yes, she knew it was bad writing. Usually her fingers nearly smoked by the time she quit a session. But this morning, she felt more like she'd dragged them through the quicksand of confessions. How could she have let it slip that Barb would be leaving early today, a piece of information Barb had confidentially shared?

What tactic had Buzz used to cause her to like and trust him?

Just before noon, Barb stepped into the DM ladies' room to freshen her lipstick and read through her notes. While she'd waited for the chili to finish cooking last night, she'd scribbled a few lines about the people she wanted to be sure to thank during her surprise party at lunch today. Just a few thoughts, though, since Marsha was her last close friend left at DM. But of course she wanted to thank Frank too.

She laughed at herself. *How nerve-racking it must be to prepare an Academy Award acceptance speech, just in case. I'm only going to say a few words about getting let go!* She looked in the mirror and practiced a look of surprise for when everyone yelled the word.

When she entered the lunchroom, nobody paid her any attention. In fact, it seemed as though a couple of people went out of their way to avoid her. *Ooh. Tricky. They must be saving it for dessert.*

But by the time she was done eating, there was still no evidence of a cake or anything. Marsha never even made an appearance in the lunchroom. Frank stopped by and said he had to run some errands, that he'd see her tonight.

Hadn't Marsha as much as admitted yesterday that the lunchtime party was on? After further thought, Barb realized that no, she had not. She'd only said she didn't know, likely thinking someone else was planning a party. After all, Marsha was busy with her new position now. But she'd had that mischievous twinkly look in her eye . . .

Then it struck her like thunder. *Of course! Here I am planning a party for Lyle, and they're likely saving my party for tonight too!*

As she folded up her note and packed up her sandwich bag, Buzz Blinker charged into the lunchroom and sat across from her, slamming his clipboard onto the table so hard it caused her to jump.

"I know we haven't had a chance to get to know each other, Ms. DeWitt, but from what I've heard—and from the show of respect Die Mute gave you by keeping you on as their key transition person—I'm sure you'll land on your feet."

The backhanded compliment—at least it sounded like a compliment—caught Barb off guard, but his odd way of opening the conversation left her bewildered. *Die Mute. Die mute? Seriously? Yes, it is time to go!* "Thank you, Mr. Blinker."

He flipped through a pack of papers secured to his clipboard, then slid an envelope out from between the pack. "Twenty years at the same job is a long time. You don't see that kind of loyalty much anymore. It's a few years here or there, then on to the next job up the rung. I admit to living in that fast track myself. But people like you? Well, you're your own breed.

"On behalf of the new management . . . well, me," he said, smiling, "I'd like to thank you not only for helping Die Mute become what it is today, but for helping point us toward what we'll soon become: a lean, mean insurance machine. So thank you, Ms. DeWitt." He slid the envelope across the table.

Barb stared at his hand, which was shaking. He was undeniably uncomfortable in this role. *No social graces, poor guy.* For the first time, it occurred to her how difficult it must be for someone to come in unannounced and take over for a man like Mr. Waters, a much beloved leader and a tough act to follow.

"Thank you, sir," she said, reaching for the envelope.

"You can open it later," he said, more commanding than suggesting. "Marsha advised me that you'd be heading out a little early today. I wanted to make sure you didn't get away without a chance to say goodbye and thank you." He jutted his hand across the table. Barb put her hand in his cold, nervous grip, and he gave it a couple of hearty pumps.

"Thank you back."

It was all she could think to say. She tucked the envelope in her handbag. When she looked up, he was gone.

Friday morning Josie woke feeling more refreshed than she had in months, which was surprising after yesterday's roller coaster of incidents and emotions. First the unwelcome plague of self-doubt and neediness. Then the crazy creek in the snowglobe filling her house and carrying her away—at least in her mind. There was no way that could *really* have happened. And yet, when she'd found herself in the kitchen afterward, she had no idea how she'd arrived there.

But *something* powerful surely happened yesterday, for whatever it was triggered an immediate response. She wanted—no, she *needed*—to call Amelia to report in before Amelia called her. She needed—no, she *wanted*—to honestly share with Amelia how her day had gone: it sucked. It was as if a protective layer of ice, one she didn't know had encased her, melted, and she was finally free to dare to be herself.

At 6:30 last evening, she'd given Amelia a call. She hadn't talked about the snowglobe and likely never would, but she opened up and thanked Amelia for sticking with her. She even admitted that she *was* somewhat needy right now, and that she appreciated Amelia for recognizing that fact before she herself did. It wasn't the epitome of an intimate exchange—at least she didn't think it was—but it was a baby step.

And it felt good.

Josie followed their conversation with a good night's sleep and was determined to engage in something useful today. It would do her no good to sit around moping, beating herself up, or second-guessing every aspect of her life. Maybe this was a new beginning.

She decided to take a long walk to the Newberry Library, which she'd heard was overflowing with topnotch research materials, especially regarding the humanities. It was one of the places she'd been meaning to scope out, having passed it several times during long walks in the Gold Coast district.

It was time to track down the origin of the saying "No man is an island." Sure, she could use the Internet to find out, but how much time would that burn? She'd go to the Newberry and do a little research on the topic, or the author, or whatever the case might be. That would not only kill a few hours, but perhaps further fuel her desire to think outside herself for a change. Famous quotes were famous for a reason. Ignorance was no excuse for ignorance. It was a great day for a walk and an adventure.

Time to up my quotient of research and literary prowess. I'll take the rest of the weekend off too, then Monday I shall aim my energies in the direction of a new job. But for now, no man—nor this woman!—is an island. I shall seat myself among other avid researchers until I feel one with them, a thought which caused her to first smile, then flinch. *That is downright corny.*

But the first thing she did was fire up her computer and do a little research on the Newberry Library. *I am who I am.*

"The Newberry Library provides a home to a world-class collection of books, manuscripts, and maps, and also to a growing community of readers," she read. Maybe she could even find some references or maps or guide books highlighting great creeks in America.

Or something on magical snowglobes.

Or insanity.

Why not?

Lyle closed his eyes and let his head fall back. He was stiff. He'd been at the Newberry Library since it opened, partly scanning reference books for Midwest authors, then perusing maps—their map collection was unrivaled—for tidbits about the inception and ultimate dissemination of Route 66, but mostly tormenting himself.

In the wee early morning hours, he'd been visited by a wild thought: maybe he should join the Peace Corps. Before dawn, he'd actually gone to the Peace Corps Web site and participated in the short "Am I Qualified?" multiple-choice questionnaire. He found he had not aged out, as he thought. The oldest volunteer to ever serve was eighty-six. *But seriously, the Peace Corps, Lyle?* Although he believed in the organization's efforts, his gut told him it wasn't really the right match or choice for him. Shortly after breakfast, he'd headed to the Newberry to distract himself and allow his subconscious space to do its thing.

The Newberry, he thought as he looked around, was full of heady facts and harbored an aristocratic ancient calm. He enjoyed sitting in the Special Collections room on the fourth floor, maps spread before him. And yet, Lyle had observed that his gut, which his mom used to declare was closely related to the Holy Spirit— although his sister occasionally took exception to their mother's sketchy religious claim—was smarter and more reliable than any other resource. He'd have to learn to yield to it more.

As for that subconscious? So much for "vacation mode." All he could think about was what came next for him.

His upcoming road trip was perfect timing, since aside from his mom, his sister knew him better than anyone. She'd be a good sounding board, always had been. He was anxious to glean her perspective on the idea of changing the course of his life in his fifties and to visit his nieces and nephews, two of each. All bright and in their twenties, they'd likely lend an interesting perspective on today's job climate.

Lyle stretched his arms above his head and twisted from the waist to work out a kink. When he turned to the left, he looked through the glass wall in time to see a familiar backside walking down the hall. The woman wore black slacks and a green top, and his heart skipped a beat at the particular sway, but she quickly disappeared.

Not again! It was uncanny the amount of times he thought he'd seen Josie, and from so many angles. He shook his head, then rubbed the left side of his neck with his right hand. It was as if her ghost followed him around, haunted him, nagged him about how pathetic it was that he hadn't tried harder to get to know her better. Taunted him with how *like* him it was to have once again waited too long to trip his trigger. Glimpses of her here, shadows of her there.

Maybe for his next profession he should become a novelist and write a great tome titled *The Torment of Josie Victor Brooks*. Maybe hanging out in the Newberry Library spawned authors simply through osmosis, a thought that made him smile.

There she is again! This time he caught a quick profile view of the woman wearing the same black slacks and green top. He jumped up from the table, causing those around him to turn their heads his way. *Now you're going to chase ghosts? Nice.* He stretched again, as though that's what he'd intended to do. While he was up, he checked his watch and decided he should probably head out anyway. He wanted to get to the Encouragement Club early to make sure the spaghetti dinner arrived and got set up okay.

He also wanted to get Beth a thank-you card for all the generosities she'd extended the club. She'd let them use the room free, supplied day-old bagel bites and fresh schmears, and now was collaborating with him on the surprise party for Barb. When he'd called her that morning to warn her about the spaghetti, she'd seemed really excited about it. She said that although she couldn't afford to supply them for free, she'd extend him a good discount on a few dozen of her sweet muffins to set out for dessert, ones that would "complement the chili, I mean, spaghetti." He quickly gave her the okay and his credit card number.

With carefulness, he closed his materials. He went to the desk to get the page, who came and checked and then collected the resources. He listened to the sound of his own footsteps as he walked down the glass-enclosed marble staircase. Someone wearing heels clacked down the stairs behind him. Just before he got to the second floor, he felt a tap on his shoulder. He turned to find the lady with the black slacks, green top, and . . . deep blue eyes of none other than Josie Brooks, one step up and looking right at him. His heart did a flip-flop.

"Hello," she said. "I saw you in Special Collections. You looked deep into research, and I didn't want to bother you, so I went on down to the third floor reference room. I was just stepping out for some air when I noticed you on the stairway. It's nice to see you."

"Really?" He couldn't believe that came out of his mouth. He sounded like a dumb teenager talking to the popular girl in the class, all tongue-tied.

"You sound surprised."

"I am. To see you, I mean. I thought I saw you earlier. In fact, I guess I did." *Nice.*

"Find what *you* were looking for?"

"Truthfully, I'm not sure what I'm looking for. But I do like this place. You come here often?"

"First time," she said.

"Find what you were looking for?"

"At least one of the things. I can now tell you with confidence that it was English poet John Donne who first said 'No man is an island.' " She smiled.

Lyle was torn. Should he bring up her early dismissal? Ask her how she was doing? Ask her where she was moving next? If she'd recommended his release? Instead he heard himself say, "Do you have time for a coffee?" A group of people came down the stairway. They moved aside to let the group pass. Josie finally stepped down beside him.

"Actually, I . . ." She looked at her watch. Pursed her lips.

"That's okay," he said. "I understand." *Just give her the out, moron.*

"Actually, I was going to say yes. A quick one. But I'd rather have an iced green tea, if there's a place nearby."

"There's an outdoor coffee house just around the corner in Mariano Park. Maybe you know it?"

"Mariano Park?"

"That little triangle of land between Rush, State, and Oak."

"Oh! Whispers Café. I've seen that little hut but never stopped."

"I bet they have green tea. They've got some outdoor seating too, and it's such a nice day." He kept himself from checking his watch again. He didn't want her to think he was in a hurry, even though he was. But he had a little time to spare. The caterer said there'd be no problems with set up and delivery, which he'd paid extra for, so he decided to just trust them. Beth would point them in the right direction. "You don't need to finish something here first?"

"To be honest, I'm not sure what else I'm looking for. As it turns out, I've got plenty of time to both figure it out and find it though. Doesn't need to be right now. Kind of nice, really."

"I hear that," he said. *So there. Seems we've both acknowledged our joblessness. Maybe that's enough. For now.*

Twenty-One

B arb left her last day of work even earlier than planned. What was the point of riding out another twenty minutes? Time to pick up the chili!

As she drove, she considered the grace of her personal circumstances. Every single day, so many people throughout the country lost their jobs. Some had faithfully been at their place of employment for decades, like third-generation auto workers she'd heard about in a television news spot. Others maybe only for a month or less. Still, no matter how long one was on the job, the loss of employment could be devastating: old dreams and new dreams alike, right down the toilet. How many stories had she heard about people in the suburbs losing their homes because they didn't realize they were getting in over their heads, never imagining that they would be next on the employment chopping block?

Unemployment delivered a knock to the psyche, a dent in one's self-esteem, a feeling of utter helplessness when it became clear that no, it wasn't a temporary cutback or layoff; your job was eliminated. The worst part, she thought, was that you had to fend for yourself. Vie against your friends for open jobs, buck the odds, keep a positive spirit so that when an opportunity did come along, you didn't sound like the last person on earth who deserved it. Or you had to reinvent yourself. Be willing to try a new adventure, get more education, maybe even move, if you had to. But how could people afford to move if they still had house payments on a home they couldn't sell?

The thoughts made her even more grateful that in the midst of trials, the Encouragement Club was a success. That at least for one week in her little corner of the world, folks had come together for fellowship and to laugh and help see each other through.

Thank You, Lord! If we can't be here for each other now, when can we?

Before she knew it, she was packed up and bound for Beth's Bagel Haven, singing along to "Great Is Thy Faithfulness," the CD track blaring through her car speakers.

Not until they exited the Newberry Library together did it become clear to Josie that this spontaneous walking-for-coffee situation between her and Lyle was awkward at best and a mistake at worst. Like suddenly shining a spotlight on the dust under a bed covered with a beautiful spread, the outdoor sunshine illuminated the dark side of that which had seemed bright in the heady ambience of resource materials. Sure, she was glad to discover him there, to have a chance to properly say good-bye, or "I'm sorry," or whatever. Yes, it was the right thing to do to say hello, but . . .

She listened as their footsteps hit the sidewalk in syncopated rhythm. She listened to snippets of conversations of passersby. She listened to car horns and background sirens. She listened to the silence in her own head verifying her lack of anything to say.

Lyle was suddenly challenged for sidewalk space by a skateboarder zooming straight at him. When he leaned toward her to get out of the boarder's way, his hand brushed against hers.

She was instantly electrified, her mind no longer filled with silence, but infused with the still, small sound of a brook. She actually scanned the area, looking for nearby running water. *Come on!* She quickly rubbed just in front of her ear canals, hoping to make the sound disappear, which it thankfully did.

"Beautiful day, isn't it?" Lyle said, sniffing the air. "I love spring, although I imagine we're still in for some cold weather."

Weather. We've already sunk to talking about the weather. "Yes. It is," she said, inhaling, only to catch the subtle scent of his cologne. Had he worn cologne at work? If so, how had she missed the earthy fragrance? It dawned on her that this was likely the closest in proximity she'd ever been to him.

They walked up to the window of the coffee shop and studied the menu. "Lucky you," Lyle said. "Looks like they have green tea every which way."

"Can I help you?" the young man asked, looking directly at Lyle.

"I'll have a medium iced green tea," he said, turning to face Josie. "No time like the present to try something new. Which one do you recommend?" he asked the attendant.

"The People's Green is our most popular."

"Is it sweet?"

"Slightly."

"But it's good for you," Josie added. "Lots of antioxidants." *It's good for you? What a doltish thing to say to a grown man.*

"I'll have one too," she said to the attendant. "But make mine a large."

"Antioxidants. One of the buzz words of the decade, huh?" Lyle said.

She nodded.

"For Christmas last year, my sister gave me a wooden box filled with tea samplers. I haven't opened it yet. I've never been much of a tea drinker. I'm more inclined to the manly art of Gatorade and cognac," he said, firing her a playful grin.

"Together?"

"Hmm. Haven't tried that yet. Maybe next week."

She relaxed a little, rather enjoying the lighthearted banter.

"I almost got into the tea a couple of weeks ago, though. I was braising some pork chops, wishing I had a little orange juice to squeeze into the liquid. I wondered if there might be some kind of orange-rind tea in the box, if that would add the flavor."

"Talk yourself out of it?"

"Too hungry. Decided to just stick with the sliced apples. Tasted good."

"Sounds like you like to cook."

"Since I was little. If I do say so myself, and I do, I'm good at it. I've thanked my mom many times for letting me make messes in the kitchen. For a while in junior high, I thought I'd like to become a chef."

"Here you go," the attendant said.

Lyle reached into his front pants pocket and pulled a ten out of his money clip. "My treat," he said to Josie. Josie opened her mouth to object while reaching for her handbag. "You can buy next time," he said, as he passed her the large. "Want to sit over there?" he asked, pointing toward the far corner.

"Sounds good."

After they seated themselves and Lyle took his first sip, Josie waited for his reaction.

He tilted his head and scrunched his eyebrows, then took another long pull on the straw. "Can't say I love it, but it's wet, so it'll do. Libraries and bookstores make a person thirsty. All that paper must absorb every scrap of moisture in the air. Come to think of it, maybe they intentionally keep humidity low. Isn't moisture what turns paper yellow? Never thought about that before. Something else to look up."

He likes to cook and research? I would never have guessed it. It surprised her to notice her drink sitting on the table, untouched. All that talk about thirst and moisture, and she had yet to take even a sip.

She picked it up and played with the straw, then set it down again. "Obviously you didn't become a chef. What happened to change your mind?"

"Wow. There's a loaded question. When I was a freshman in high school, my youth group volunteered to help cook and serve the annual Thanksgiving dinner my little hometown church offered to the folks in our community. I was blown away by the number of homeless people— some with small children, some muttering, others with open sores—who came through the line. People I'd never seen before. I had no idea where they came from, where they stayed at night. After Thanksgiving, I asked the youth pastor about them. Shocking, what I learned. How invisible other human beings can become to everyone, including me. The looks in the kids' eyes really tore at my heart. Dale, the youth pastor, sensed my interest and pointed me toward a few nonprofits in the area, places that ministered to the homeless. I talked to my folks about it, and Noreen and I—Noreen is my older sister, the one who gave me the tea for Christmas—volunteered to pass out sandwiches once a week with a crew of volunteers." He stopped talking and stared at Josie. "You sure you want to hear all of this? I feel like I'm monopolizing the conversation."

"I've got time," she said, smiling. "It's fascinating, really, and sure like nothing I experienced growing up. Please continue." *Interesting, the way career paths unfold, the influence of parents, the moments that define us— or at least how we think they do.*

"Anyway, I began talking with one of the older homeless guys, Marvin. He told me I reminded him of his grandson. You know, you don't think about the *families* of homeless people, or that they even *have* families. That's when I decided— felt utterly compelled, really—that the homeless needed a voice. With the help of my English teacher, who'd encouraged me for some time to get involved with the high school newspaper, I made it on the staff. Marvin's story was my first feature. A boy-meets-homeless-person kind of tale. The story got a good deal of attention, so nearly once a month I told another homeless person's story. The big payoff: my writing upped the number of school kids who volunteered. And that was that. No more chef. I was drawn straight toward social services. One high school volunteer job led to the next; same in college. After I graduated I entered the world of fund-raising for nonprofits." He stopped, staring pensively toward passersby, and took a long drink from his tea. "Thirstier than I thought," he said, sending goose bumps up Josie's arm when she realized she had yet to take a drink.

She fiddled with the straw and picked up the plastic cup, but then set it down again to ask a question. "From nonprofits to Diamond Mutual. How and when did that gigantic transition come about?"

Lyle frowned. "Sometimes life serves up surprises." He looked at his watch. "Whoa! I'm sorry I've prattled on all this time, and now I have to go. Pretty rude on both counts. Time got away from me."

It seemed clear to Josie that whatever those surprises were, he either wasn't happy about them or didn't want to share. At least she understood where the impression he was a bleeding heart came from, since he was. Now that she'd heard part of his story away from the pressures and confines of their working relationship, that heart seemed more like an asset.

"I should get back to my research anyway. Think I'll give the maps a try. Thanks for the tea," she said.

"Doesn't look like you were as thirsty as I was," he said, rising and tossing his empty cup in the garbage.

"Apparently not."

"You gonna stay and finish your tea? Take it with?"

"I'll sit here for a while longer. Watch the people go by," she said. "Go on."

"Seriously, I'm sorry to have to cut out like this, but the last meeting of the Encouragement Club is tonight, and we're turning it into a surprise retirement party of sorts for Barb DeWitt. I need to get there early and set up a few things."

"Oh. That's right. The Encouragement Club. I heard about it."

"Interested in coming along?"

"No," she said a little too emphatically. "No, thank you." She smiled.

"Good-bye then." He started to walk away but turned on his heels. "Hey! You have a business card handy?"

She picked up her handbag and withdrew one from an interior pocket. Without a word, she handed it to him, stunned that he'd asked.

"Thanks!" he said nearly over his shoulder. "I'll give you a call."

She leaned forward and watched his tall, lean

form disappear into the crowd. He looked good in jeans.

She stared at her tea, then drank the entire thing with barely a breath between gulps.

Twenty-Two

Lyle didn't arrive at Beth's Bagel Haven until 4:30. Thankfully Beth had everything under control, at least as far as the spaghetti dinner and the muffins went. Sternos were lit under the two large containers of pasta, and the salad was in place. Beth told Lyle her part-timer was working late at the counter so she could help with the party, and she'd bring out the muffins after dinner was served. Although she was on top of things, she also seemed oddly distracted.

"Have you by chance heard from Barb today?" she asked Lyle.

"No. Were you expecting her this early?" Beth shrugged. Then Lyle said, "Didn't she say she was working part or most of the day? She's likely been waylaid by DM employees bidding her bogus farewells so she doesn't get suspicious about this celebration."

"Maybe that's it," Beth said. But she didn't sound convinced.

"Is there anything I can help you with?"

"At this point, maybe just watch for her. She

said she was bringing a few extra goodies today, so I told her she could pull up in the alley."

"Will do."

"The back door is right through there," Beth said, pointing. "Thanks. I'm sure she'll get here any minute. If I hear from her, or she shows up at the front door, I'll send someone for you."

Lyle exited into the back alley and looked around. A big delivery truck blocked one end of the alley entryway; maybe Barb was stuck waiting on the street. He walked around the truck and looked both ways, but no Barb.

On his way back, he noticed a vagrant digging through the garbage. *What are the odds?* he wondered. He'd just talked about the homeless, and now here he was, back in their shadowy company. He hadn't told Josie that Marvin's life ended in a terribly violent way. The streets were hard.

Lyle, striving to erase the mental image of Marvin's demise, pulled out his money clip, peeled off a twenty, and called out to the vagrant. "Sir. *Sir!*" He knew better than to tap him on the shoulder; one had to stay on guard on the streets. People were jittery.

The old man half-turned and looked over his shoulder, obviously ready to hightail it.

"Here," Lyle said in a softer voice. "God bless you. Buy yourself a hot dinner."

The man's eyes went wide. It was clear he thought it might be a trap.

Lyle set the twenty on the ground and walked several paces away. "There you go, sir. It's yours."

He turned his back and waited until he heard the old man's light footsteps scurry toward the money. He was grateful the guy dared to take it. Aside from the sandwiches, Marvin, a man with mental handicaps, possibly like this gentleman, never accepted a handout. He said he didn't trust money.

The sound of the old man's footsteps echoed down the alley toward the sidewalk. Lyle did not turn around until he was certain he was gone.

"Be well," he whispered. "Lord, keep him safe."

What a remarkable and unanticipated afternoon, Lyle thought. *What were the odds—for any of this?*

He'd been in such a rush since he left Josie at the coffee shop that he barely had time to think through what had happened with *her.* How bizarre that he'd so easily opened up to her like that, all but spilling his guts. When she asked why he left nonprofit work behind, of course thoughts of Miriam rose to the forefront. How could he explain all that to someone he barely knew, especially when he sometimes wasn't sure himself? And if he'd tried to tell Josie? He imagined several scenarios, most of which involved Josie saying, "I've heard enough to last me a lifetime. Good-bye."

And what would happen if he called her? Would she brush him off?

It was one thing to run into someone, to have no time to analyze all the reasons you should *not* spend time together. It was quite another to intentionally seek that someone out. He pulled her card from his pocket, half believing—hoping, maybe—it would be blank, but there was her number. He tucked the card safely into his money clip.

How long should I wait to call her? Maybe Sunday afternoon.

He stepped inside, ordered a large iced tea from Beth's shop, and downed the whole thing before he was out the back door again.

When Marsha arrived at 5:05 for the Encouragement Club meeting, decorated sheet cake in tow, and found out Barb wasn't there, she privately commiserated with Beth, who was worried sick.

Beth said Barb had stopped by earlier that day to work out a few details and told her she'd be back by 4:15 at the latest to set up the chili for Lyle's special party. Beth nodded toward Lyle. "He's worried too. Was she okay when she left work? I know today was going to be hard on her."

Marsha had been busy, but she'd also intentionally avoided Barb most of the day so she wouldn't accidentally give tonight's surprise away, especially since she'd almost blown it at yesterday's EC meeting. "To be honest, I have no idea. I stopped by just before she said she was going to leave, but she was already gone. I'll call her cell."

"Oh, good!" Beth said, relieved. "After all these years of chatting with her on nearly a daily basis, I don't have her number. That's the way it is with customers, even when they feel more like friends."

Marsha called both Barb's cell and her home number, but the calls went straight to voice mail.

As the questions spread to each new arrival, "Have you heard from Barb since she left work today? Did you see her before she left?" and the answer was always no, an unsettling feeling spread throughout. Frank was beside himself. He'd mindlessly popped his suspenders so many times he complained his chest hurt.

Then someone said he'd heard there was a giant traffic jam on the inbound Ike, which Beth, Marsha, and Lyle all knew Barb traveled from the suburbs.

At first the possibility she was stuck in the logjam brought a little relief, but Marsha felt sure Barb would have called from her cell phone, what with the last Encouragement Club in the works. This was a big deal. She had all that chili with her too. Marsha tried both Barb's home and cell numbers again, but to no avail. It was not like Barb to be late. Ever.

Something was seriously wrong.

At 5:10 when the meeting was due to start, Marsha consulted with Frank, Beth, and a few others. Since no beverages were available—Barb always brought her coffeepot—Marsha said she'd pay if Beth could crank up one of her big coffee brewers and bring in a large pitcher of iced tea.

She talked to Lyle about the spaghetti. He told her there was no need to reveal who bought it, just that they should start eating it, so Marsha made the announcement for everyone to begin, if for no other reason than to set the room more at ease.

At 5:20, not knowing what else to do with her nervous energy, and realizing some people might have to leave soon, Marsha asked Lyle to come forward so she could at least set the ball rolling on the Thank-You-Mr.-Waters portion of their gathering.

She handed him the thank-you card full of signatures. Barb had put Marsha and Frank in charge of it. Several people stepped up and shared their personal Lyle stories, but everyone was distracted and kept an eye on the door for Barb.

By the time Lyle's well wishes and farewells were over, it was 5:35, and *still* Barb hadn't arrived. Beth, who'd been peeking out the back door, checking the alley, came in and shrugged. Frank, sweating from anxiety, decided to say a few more words about Lyle.

Just as Frank began talking, Marsha's cell

phone vibrated. She'd held it in her hand the entire time so she wouldn't miss Barb's call. She quickly headed to the back of the room so she wouldn't distract anyone.

"Where *are* you?" she firmly but quietly asked Barb by way of a hello. "We're worried sick!"

But it wasn't Barb. It was Gina, Marsha's daughter.

"Mom, what are you doing right now?"

"I'm at the Encouragement Club. Remember? I told you about the big party today. We're waiting for Barb, who was supposed to be here eons ago. We're worried sick."

"Yes, I remember," she said. She sniffled. "I mean where are you standing right now?"

"I'm in the room. Gina, what's wrong?" No sooner did she ask the question than she knew: this call was about Barb, and it wasn't good. "Hold on a minute," she told her daughter. She noticed several people watching her, so she smiled, waved, and stepped out into the shadow-laden alley, which at any other time would have scared her. "Talk to me."

"Mom. Barb was on her way . . ." She went silent. Marsha realized her daughter was crying. Marsha's kids had both grown close to Barb over the years. "Mom, I don't know how else to say this," she said through shattering sobs. "Barb is . . . gone. She was killed in a terrible car accident. It happened about four on the Eisenhower."

Marsha felt faint.

"From what I understand, they couldn't even get her out of the car until nearly 4:45. She was taken to the hospital, but they declared her dead on arrival. Oh, *Mom!* I am so sorry to have to call you at the party to tell you, but I knew you'd be waiting . . ."

Together they sobbed.

After a long sniffling silence, Marsha asked Gina how she'd heard.

"Michelle called me. She knew her mom had been on her way to the Encouragement Club. She said it's all she'd talked about for a week. She knew I could track you down."

"Everything okay out here?" Lyle stepped into the alley. He must have seen her sneak out the back door with her cell phone to her ear.

When Marsha turned to face him, he went ashen.

Part Two

Twenty-Three

When Lyle and Josie parted at the coffee shop, Josie thought she'd head back to the Newberry. But after sitting and people watching for a while, she'd lost the desire. It was just too nice to go back inside.

As she began a long, leisurely walk home, she dialed Amelia's cell number. Maybe Amelia could meet for dinner. As luck would have it, Alfred was going bowling with his buddies tonight; dinner sounded perfect.

"This time, I'll try not to engage in anything dramatic before we meet. And my treat," Josie said. Amelia laughed and gave her no arguments. They agreed on Greek. Santorini's in Greek Town. Six-thirty. Amelia said she'd call for reservations.

Josie's sense of self-awareness—self-assessment and self-analysis—felt tuned to supersensitive. Because this was the first time she'd seen Amelia since the day she was released from Diamond Mutual—and especially after she'd been so rude, then needy, and later confessional—she wondered if she might feel embarrassed or awkward. Instead, she felt not only at ease but relieved to be in Amelia's company again. It was nice to learn that someone could hear firsthand that the stoic, self-controlled Ms. Josie Victor

Brooks was human and not turn away from her.

Before they were even halfway through their salads, Amelia had Josie in stitches, regaling her with stories about Alfred's family and her own hilarious yet humiliating experience two days ago in a dressing room. They agreed that finding a bra that both fit and was comfortable was an exhausting chore, and they bemoaned the fact that once they did, the manufacturer immediately discontinued that model.

The conversation flowed from shopping to news to wedding plans. Yes, the bridal registry was finally complete and the seating chart was halfway there. They'd decided to set that task aside for a while after bucking up against a family drama: two of Alfred's uncles were in another tiff. Alfred's mother recommended against seating them at the same table, especially since one of their wives was the instigator of the argument. Separating those two couples caused a domino effect of tablemate disasters.

"I'll tell you," Amelia said, "if celebrating my wedding day wasn't the fulfillment of a lifelong dream, I don't think I could survive the planning. But you know how it is: from the time we girls are three years old, we start imagining ourselves in wedding gowns. I bought my first *Brides* when I was nineteen years old. Since then, I've been cutting out pictures of wedding gowns from newspapers and magazines and putting them in a scrapbook. I cracked myself up browsing through it the other night. My taste in fashion has sure changed over the years! The first gown looked like Cinderella at the ball, all billows and hoop-skirty. The next several looked more like explosions at a sequin factory."

"What did you end up with?"

"Chic. Simple. Cream. Low—very low—back. Satin. Sleeveless. My veil is long, down to the bottom of my rear. It has a few tiny silver beads sewn in it to catch the light."

Josie noticed the light in Amelia's eyes as she described more details. She looked so happy, so ready to wear that dress and commit to a lifetime of . . . What? Fulfilled expectations? Fighting over where they'd live? Giving pieces of herself away? Compromise? Gaining a lifelong lover? Dancing in the moonlight like Grandmother Nancy?

". . . and his best man *promised* me he'd keep Alfred out of trouble during the bachelor party. So what about you?" Amelia asked. "What kind of wedding did you picture as a teen? Tell me about the ever-changing dress of your dreams. Oh! Pardon me if you were married before! You know, this is the first it occurred to me you might have been."

"No," Josie said emphatically, "no ex or exes for me out there. I was going to say 'never the bride, always the bridesmaid,' but to be honest,

I've only been in one wedding party: that of my brother and his wife. Their wedding was extremely casual. No marching down the aisle or horrid matching dresses, thank goodness."

Try as she might, Josie could not remember a time she pictured herself in a wedding dress. As a youth, she always had her nose stuck in a book, either studying or researching or lauding the adventures of the likes of Amelia Earhart. When she did daydream, she pictured herself as an astronaut or the dean of a university. Anything short of joining the military—it wasn't for her— that would make her dad proud. Something special that set her apart. It was a happy day when she overheard him tell a family friend that his daughter had "hung out her own shingle. Top-tier ranking in her specialty too. She doesn't need a staff to get the job done. She does it all on her own."

All on her own. No, she didn't need a wedding dress for that.

Still, she'd never pictured herself *alone* at this age either, so how had she ever thought marriage would happen without a wedding gown? Elopement like her parents, who married during her father's short furlough? Las Vegas in a drunken stupor? Internet wedding? Now here she was in her late forties and—hot flashing. *What kind of wedding dress could endure hot flashes and keep a bride looking radiant rather than roasted?* She pictured herself in pit-stained satin, sweat dripping off the end of her nose, and somehow it struck her as funny.

"The truth is, Amelia, I never thought about a wedding dress." She refrained from sharing her disgusting vision. "I imagine that seems hard to believe, even for myself. But there you have it."

"I've always been a bit of a dreamer. Alfred says I'm the most incurable romantic he's ever met. Maybe that comes with a built-in wedding gown fixation, which, to be perfectly honest, is perhaps not mentally healthy. I mean, dreaming about the wedding gown means you need to find and marry the handsome prince who will adore you in it. What good would wearing the gown be if the handsome prince wasn't ogling you coming down the aisle?" Amelia ate another bite of salad while chewing on her thought. "Maybe that's not a good model for teaching young girls to grow up to be independent women, think?"

"I think," Josie said, pausing to chew and swallow, giving herself time to analyze the concept, "that it's possible to both grow up a strong, independent woman *and* fall in love with the handsome prince. Seems to me you've done that, and done it well. I, on the other hand, am apparently just now figuring out who I really am."

"What? You're one of the most successful and self-assured women I've ever met. You know what you want and aren't afraid to ask for it; you're drop-dead, head-turning gorgeous; fit; financially secure. I don't know many women—many people, for that matter—in this economy who are in a position to call their own shots, not only as to who they'll work for, but where they'd like to locate next."

"Drop-dead gorgeous? Hel-LO!" Josie pointed to the crows feet sprouting around her eyes. "I'm hot-flashing ancient and caught in the throes of reexamining the premise of my entire life right now."

Amelia set down her fork. *"What on earth?* You're not letting a little we-no-longer-need-your-services encounter rock your boat, are you? Goodness, from what I understand, you'd already accomplished nearly everything you set out to do on that job anyway. They're paying out your full contract. I see no failures there!"

"It's not that. It's . . . honestly, I don't know exactly how to explain it. When Lyle and I . . ." She tucked her lips in her mouth. She had not meant to open that can of peas.

Too late. With an eyebrow-raising smile, Amelia jumped all over it. "Lyle? Seems I've missed a chapter here. Who is Lyle?"

"Lyle Waters."

"The name sounds vaguely familiar, but I can't place why. Have you talked about him before?"

"Not exactly. Remember the first time we met

for dinner outside Diamond Mutual?" Amelia nodded. "And you mentioned the man who had been studying me? He was standing inside the door watching us?"

"Oh, the handsome one."

Josie felt her cheeks warm.

"Hey, girl, you're blushing. Seems I *have* missed a chapter here."

"I'm not blushing; I'm hot flashing. Told you." But no sooner did she speak the words than she felt her face return to normal. "Okay, so I'm blushing. This is what I'm talking about when I say I'm reexamining: I can't tell a blush from a hot flash."

"Hormones." Amelia set her salad fork on her empty plate and leaned back. "They're enough to drive a person batty. When I'm PMSing, Alfred says he sometimes thinks I *am* insane. I kind of agree with him, but don't ever tell him I admitted that, okay?"

"Promise."

"So you want to talk about the mysterious Mr. Waters or move on to another topic?"

As always, Josie appreciated Amelia's sensitivity. It was, in fact, Amelia's willingness to move on that somehow freed Josie's need to talk. "For one thing, Lyle is not mysterious, really. I didn't realize until earlier today, when we were together for the first time outside a work environment, that he's truly likable. While we worked together at

Diamond Mutual, one of his personality traits appeared as a weakness." She felt oddly protective of him and therefore refrained from using the term *bleeding heart,* which suddenly felt disrespectful. "But today, it struck me that it's likely his greatest strength—although it doesn't always serve him well in business. At least I don't think it does. Maybe it's just that I've never seen a male role model in a position of leadership who cares so much."

"About?"

"About everyone."

"And I'm assuming," Amelia said, a playful singsonginess in her delivery, "that *everyone* includes *you?*"

"Oh, I didn't mean it that way," she said, feeling her cheeks warm again. "For the sake of expediency, I'll just say it: he's the sensitive type. Okay, a major bleeding heart. But it turns out that's a good thing—I think."

"I can tell you this: if you don't like the sensitive type, you'll highly disapprove of Alfred. It's one of my favorite things about him, though. He's so tuned in to the needs of others, which definitely includes me. Don't get me wrong. He's a macho man. All guy and NASCAR and football and biceps," Amelia said while waggling her eyebrows. "But I've never met a man who cares so much, especially for the underdog. You want to see him ready to fight or go all caring and protective? Just let him witness an injustice or pass a homeless man on the street or think someone treated one of his sisters less than respectfully."

Homeless man. How bizarre. Twice in one day. Sounds like Lyle and Alfred are cut out of the same cloth.

"Tell me more about Alfred."

The conversation was interrupted while the waiter cleared their salad plates.

"Well, he's very family oriented, but I think I told you that before. He works in sales. Air freight. His company's a little slow right now, but he's an optimist, a hard worker, and a scrambler. He's very close with his mom, something that at first worried me. But after I met her, my concerns quickly faded because I immediately adored her. Sometimes I think I like his mom more than my own, who is a wee bit—no, make that a whole lot—controlling. It took me a long time to learn how to deal with my mom, where to file her 'opinions.' Alfred helped me negotiate my unhealthy relationship with her. Since he's in sales, he's a good people reader. He knows how to work some of the personality angles and recognize stopgaps. He's a good closer, as they say, and he sure helped me close the gap with Mom."

Their meals were set before them. Josie picked up her fork to dig in, but she wanted to know more about Amelia's relationship with a strong parent. "What do you mean when you say your mother is controlling?"

"Manipulative. Powerful. Power *plays*. Pouting. Fits. Sarcasm. Whatever it takes to make me see things her way or feel guilty for not doing so— although with Alfred's help and a lot of prayer, these days I am far less inclined to succumb to her wily ways, thank goodness." Amelia smiled at her own description. "Curious, you asking. Familiar?"

Josie thought about her own mother. Quiet. Reserved. Cheerful, but sometimes difficult to read. Certainly overpowered by her dad, who called all the shots. If anyone might be considered controlling, it was Victor. But it was odd. She'd never thought of him as controlling really. Just powerful.

She could only remember one time when her mother stood up to him. Maybe that was because her mother philosophically agreed with him. Who knew. But that one time, her mother certainly did not agree with Victor, and it had to do with Josie, who wanted to buy a trendy, expensive outfit, one like all the other girls in her new high school wore. There was nothing inappropriate about it. No cleavage or mini elements. During a casual dinner conversation, Josie brought up the subject of the outfit with her mom, and Victor fervently interjected.

It wasn't the money that set him off; the crux of the confrontation was triggered by the idea she wanted to conform. Why, Victor wanted to know, would she want to dress like all the rest of the girls?

"So I don't always stand out," she tried to explain. "For once in my life," she said, hot tears welling in her eyes, "I want to feel like I actually fit in." She did her best to swallow the tears, which were considered an extreme sign of weakness and melancholy in the Brooks' household.

The combination of tears and caving into peer pressure set Victor off. A lengthy lecture ensued about individuality and leadership, independence and personal integrity. "Haven't I taught you anything? Who cares if you stand out as long as you can stand up on your own?" he wanted to know.

Josie's mother pushed her chair back and stood. She picked up the empty mashed-potatoes bowl, as if she were just clearing the table. But then, with deliberate motion—and in a slow, firm, clear voice—she moved closer to Victor, who remained seated, and spoke.

"Who *cares?* Josephine Victor Brooks, your one and only daughter, cares." Josie heard her brother suck in his breath while she held hers. "She cares about fitting in, about being accepted, about not looking like the only person at her *next* new school—where she still knows absolutely nobody—who does not have an ounce of fashion sense." She leaned toward him, rested her hand on the table right next to his. "There are many ways to be strong, Victor, and sometimes fitting in is one of them. As a military man, you are well aware of *that*. I know the stars on your sleeve set you apart and identify you as a leader, but let us not forget that you are still wearing a military-issued uniform so you can be identified as one with them." Cheeks aflame, she whirled on her heels and left the room.

"May I be excused, sir?" her brother asked.

"Yes," Victor said without taking his eyes off the kitchen doorway, through which his wife had disappeared. Josie sat frozen in her chair, unable to speak.

Shortly after her brother left the room, her mother reentered and remained standing. Although her eyes looked a little red around the rims, her jaw was set, and she stared straight at her husband.

"Well then," Victor said to his wife, then nodded to his daughter, "I'll leave that shopping decision up to the two of you." With the carefulness given to folding the corners of the sheets on a military-made bed, he folded his napkin and placed it in the center of his empty plate.

That was the last word ever uttered by him about Josie's wardrobe.

More than thirty years had passed since that

incident. Josie could hardly believe that not until this very moment, sitting at the table talking with Amelia, did it dawn on her that her mother *did* possess her own power. She *did* know how to stand up to Victor. Josie wondered how many times that same type of scenario took place behind the scenes. It was suddenly so clear, so obvious: her dad wouldn't have married a weak woman. Yes, some men did enjoy overpowering their spouses, and in unthinkably brutal ways. But her father wasn't like *that.* He was strong, strong-willed, and powerful, but he'd never raised a hand to any of them.

In the instant that she reframed her perception of her parents, she knew her father likely fell in love with her mother because she could and *would* stand up to his forceful personality, yet understood him well enough, and was bright enough and strong enough in her own right, to know how to handle him.

Still, this was also true: it was one thing to be Victor's adult wife, but it was quite another to be a young daughter raised under the impression he was the final and right authority on everything and anything, and thinking that the last thing she ever wanted to do was to disappoint him.

"Are you okay, Josie? You look befuddled."

"Yes. And I am befuddled. At my own ignorance. I'm astounded, in fact. This is crazy. Not till this very moment did I realize that yes, my mother was powerful too." She heard her own voice crack at the sound of those words. "But in a good, smart, and unselfish way."

"Interesting,"

"I was so busy with my job, making a name for myself and kicking corporate butt, that I didn't take time off to visit her when I should have. Next thing I knew, it was too late."

"I'm so sorry," Amelia said, reaching across the table and resting her hand on top of Josie's.

"It's okay," Josie said, withdrawing her hand from under Amelia's. "I've worked that guilt through—with the help of a counselor." She smiled. "But seriously, I'm dumbfounded how slow I've been on the uptake. The dynamics of my parents' relationship . . . At least I feel pretty sure about it. I wish my mom was still here—for a lot of reasons. I'd love to talk to her about this. Maybe I'll phone my brother tomorrow, get his take on the topic."

"Why not just talk to your dad?"

"You'd have to know Victor. Victor is what you might refer to as a little buttoned-up. Intense, you could say. My friends used to be afraid of him, and that made him happy," Josie said, with a wicked smile. "Military lifer. Not that everyone in the military is hard-nosed. Certainly not. My Uncle Willard, his brother, was a lifer too. 'Life of the party' would better describe his personality. But Victor? Not exactly your party man."

"You keep talking about Victor. Is Victor your stepdad then?"

"No. Victor is my natural father."

"Why not just call him Dad or Father or Pop, like Alfred calls his dad?"

"It wasn't the rule," Josie said. "It just wasn't the rule."

Twenty-Four

Marsha fell into Lyle's arms and sobbed. Between racking bouts of crying, she shared the facts about the accident. "It's so unbelievable. And it just isn't *fair!*"

Lyle remained silent until Marsha's crying wound down. "Marsha, we have to go back into the meeting and tell everyone. They already know something is up. They're going to come looking for us soon."

"Not yet. I *can't* face anyone right now," she said, falling into more tears.

After another minute, his voice filled with resignation, Lyle said, "Marsha, I don't want to have to do this either. But we have a whole roomful of people in there who are here *because* of Barb."

"I can't," she whispered in a voice so broken and hushed it could barely be heard.

He drew and released a big breath. "I understand," he said, resting his arm on her shoulder. "It's okay. I'll handle it. You go on home. But I won't leave you out here in the alley by yourself. Come on in with me. You can slip into the bagel shop."

"Okay. I'll have Beth retrieve my handbag. I'll be okay getting to the car myself."

"You sure?"

"Yes." They reentered the building and walked down the short hallway. Before Marsha stepped through the back door into Beth's Bagel Haven, Beth stepped out of the meeting room, about to check on them. Marsha broke into tears again, and Lyle shared the news.

"This is unbelievable," Beth said. "Let me clear the store out and lock up before you come in, Marsha. We were only going to be open another few minutes anyway." Beth dabbed at her nose and disappeared into her shop.

"Thank you, Lyle," Marsha whispered. "I'll stay right here till Beth comes for me."

"And you *stay* with Beth until you're ready to drive, okay? I feel like I'm handing you off."

"You have a job to do, one I don't envy. Beth and I can take care of each other. And Lyle, thank you," she said, weeping again as he walked away.

When Lyle stepped into the banquet room, all eyes turned his way and a hush fell over the crowd. It was immediately clear they were about to hear something terrible, and they did.

Frank was the first to break down. Lyle watched

helplessly as Frank retreated out the door and passed by the window, first walking, then running. For a long while, only the sounds of sniffles and nose blowing could be heard, then quiet murmurs as people tried to process the news, make sense of what they'd heard. A few asked Lyle for specifics.

"I've told you everything we know." Lyle felt helpless. The Encouragement Club—the club Barb started—simply could not end like *this*.

Then something struck him. It wouldn't change things, but it might help.

Beth stepped into the room. He asked if she had a tablet of paper and a few pens he could borrow, which she quickly produced from her office. He told everyone to write down their names and contact information, especially e-mail addresses.

"I'm sure funeral arrangements will be listed in the newspapers, so please watch for them and spread the word to anyone who might miss hearing about Barb's passing." His voice sounded strained, even to him.

"It's almost too much to digest." He paused, giving himself a chance to shore up his emotions. "But the fact we are gathered here *because* of Barb does not escape me, as I'm sure it doesn't you either. The last thing we should do during our final Encouragement Club meeting is walk out this door without at least *some* note of encouragement." He swallowed, slowly rubbed his palms together.

"So, here's what I'm thinking. We need to encourage each other to stay strong, to stick together, and to do it for Barb. She started something important here, and in her absence, it's our job to carry it on—in some shape or form. I don't know what that will be, exactly, but I'll at least have contact info for those in attendance today. We need a couple of weeks to just pull ourselves together. But I'll talk to her family and see if we can't come up with something."

"Somebody should pass the hat," Beth said. "The Encouragement Club should send flowers or maybe make a donation in her name."

"That's a great idea, Beth," Lyle said.

Beth grabbed an empty basket and placed it near the food.

"If it's not in your financial realm to spare a buck right now, just give as you can," Lyle said. "We'll make sure her family knows it's from everyone."

As soon as Lyle got home, he searched through his ancient Rolodex. He kept an electronic calendar synched with his BlackBerry, but when he was home—and especially when the tidbits of information he wanted to keep were of a more personal and private nature than business as usual—he still wrote on the old familiar cards. *Pieces of my past,* he thought as he slowly turned the knob and fanned not only the cards, but memories. When he got to the *D*s, he started flipping through one by one until he came to "Barb DeWitt."

He still remembered the day he added her card to the wheel. It was about five months after he started at Diamond Mutual when Barb handed him a thank-you card on which she'd written, "You're doing a fine job. I'm proud to call you boss." That was exactly what he'd copied onto the card, along with her name and a date.

Through the years, he'd added miscellaneous tidbits to Barb's card, including the names of her children. Several years ago Lyle overheard Barb talking about her daughter, Michelle, heading up a committee at her church to collect coats for the homeless. He'd asked Barb for details, and she'd scribbled Michelle's contact info on a piece of scrap paper. Lyle had called Michelle for particulars and instructions, posted a notice on the DM bulletin board, and ultimately delivered a carload of outerwear to her church. Before he tossed the scrap paper, he thought he'd transferred Michelle's number to her mother's card. *Yes.*

As terrible as it would be for them, Barb's kids would likely work on her obituary this evening. If so, he wanted to ask Michelle if she'd mind listing the Encouragement Club among her achievements. It also gave him a chance to express his sympathy directly to Michelle.

Michelle took Lyle's number and said she'd

call him the next day with funeral details. She told Lyle that she appreciated his stepping in to help spread the word, especially among DM employees and the Encouragement Club, which, she said, had meant the world to her mom. "She always spoke so kindly of you, Mr. Waters."

The line went quiet. Lyle heard Michelle blow her nose.

"It might not sound like it right now, but your call is comforting," she said, her voice quiet yet strong. "It's wonderful to think that the last thing Mom did was so in line with her heart and motto. She encouraged . . ." She broke down crying and mumbled she needed to hang up, but that she'd be in touch. "Thank you," she said through a sniffle, before the click.

Lyle hung up and stared at the phone, at the Rolodex, out his window, then back to his Rolodex.

So many stories, he thought, slowly turning the knob. He wondered how many people still in his Rolodex were deceased. More than he'd likely guess. Once in a while he'd run across the name of somebody who'd passed, but he never found the heart to remove the card. Although there were a few cards with names that rang no bells—he didn't remove those either, thinking one day he might remember—most of the cards ushered forth memories, most of them kind. He'd purchased the giant Rolodex in college, back when he first started job hunting. Funny, he thought. In some ways, it was a diary of his entire adult life.

He fingered through until he came to Miriam's card. There were so many notes on both the front and back of her card that he could barely decipher them. The last two entries were dates: one of her wedding, the other her death. No, he could not pluck cards out of the Rolodex and discard them as if the people never existed.

He fanned through a few more, musing how even the rascals left their mark on a life, and not always in a bad way. Sometimes they'd encouraged him to step up, speak his mind, or maybe even unite against them. He smiled, recalling the youthful times he'd marched in this rally or that, gatherings often inspired by the inflammatory words of a politician or policy, each holding a space on his memory wheel.

Even though he loved keeping up with electronic evolutions—and he wouldn't trade his gadgets for anything—he still enjoyed the tactile pleasure of fingering through the cards. With computers and smart phones, all you had to do was start typing someone's name and the name popped right up. Nice for saving time; bad for remembering the impact of so many others in your life, those whose entries you ran across, perhaps in front of the *B*s or *D*s as you fingered your way to someone else on the wheel.

He removed an empty card and wrote "Josie

Victor Brooks" across the top, then pulled her business card out of his money clip, wrote "green tea," and added her number and the day's date. He rifled through the alphabet until he found where she belonged—at least on the wheel. He had no idea if another hand-scrawled entry would ever show up on her card, but there it was. Just in case.

He started to put the business card back in his pocket, but instead he flicked the end of it against the fingertips of his empty hand. He looked at the clock. Eight-thirty. He was tired, hungry—he hadn't had a bite of the spaghetti—and feeling very alone, and his mind flew all over the place. Who would one day write his obituary? His sister? Life was so fragile, so uncertain. No one knew who in their family might go first. Betting folks would put their money on his mom, but in light of today's sudden events, all bets were off.

Maybe I should call Josie—while I'm still breathing. He laughed at his own melodramatic thought. But the truth was that he was too exhausted to repeat all the details of his afternoon, and he figured once he heard her voice, he'd want to. *Look what happened at the coffee shop. I turned into a regular motormouth.*

Just the same, he wondered if Josie would like to know about Barb's death. After all, she'd worked with Barb for many months. *Nah. That wasn't the most comfortable of relationships.* He put the card back in his money clip, disappointed—about a lot of things.

He changed clothes, went to the kitchen, and prowled through the bags of whatever Beth and Marsha had packed up for him after the EC meeting. One bag contained a giant piece of cake, the next three muffins. The largest bag had a plastic plate laden with spaghetti, salad, and a roll, all wrapped in plastic wrap.

He got a fork and started eating. *Nothing like cold spaghetti to warm and soothe the cockles of a bachelor's heart.*

He picked up the phone and pushed one of his speed-dial numbers. "Hello, Sis, it's Lyle. You got a minute? Good. Yes, I'm okay. But it's been a long and ultimately sad day. Barb from my work died. No, a car crash."

Noreen expressed a few words of comfort and sympathy, then they moved on to his upcoming visit. Lyle guessed the funeral would take place on Monday.

"I need to be there, so if it's Tuesday, I'll have to change my travel plans. For now, I'm looking forward to seeing you by Friday, absolute latest, and likely on Thursday." He thought about all the maps and back roads, Route 66 pamphlets and alternative routes he'd gathered and charted. None of them seemed appealing. Right this moment, he needed the love of family. He might even drive straight through and be there by Tuesday night, if the funeral was on Monday.

He decided to leave himself some leeway. As he'd learned earlier, a day—a flash of a moment—could make a world of difference in a person's best laid plans.

Twenty-Five

Marsha cried all the way home. She was relieved to find her daughter sitting in her kitchen when she arrived. They fell into each other's arms.

"Thank you, Gina, for being here."

"I told Rich I'd stay as long as you wanted me to. He'll get Bradley down for bed."

"Have you heard anything else?"

"No. Nothing specific, and nothing about arrangements yet. I imagine that information will come tomorrow. There is one thing though, Mom. Don't watch the news tonight, maybe not in the morning either. They're showing a film clip, an aerial view of the four-car pileup. I didn't realize what it was at first, but after I did, it was really upsetting. Too hard to get that image out of my mind. So just leave the TV off."

"Thank you. I will. Did they say if anyone else . . . died? Honestly, Gina, I still cannot believe I'm saying that word!"

"I know what you mean. And no, there were a few injuries, but only one death, Barb's, which, if you'd seen the wreck, seems like a miracle in itself."

"Now I know what *you* mean. At the same time, it seems crazy to think of an accident that takes even one life as a miracle. Yet even as I hear myself say that, if it was in Barb's power to spare anyone else, she would have done it."

They visited until nine-thirty, moving from the kitchen to the living room, where they sat on the couch, one on each end, feet propped up facing each other. Marsha started yawning and couldn't stop. Hard emotions and buckets of tears drained the life out of a person. Yet, it was clear both were reluctant to part.

"I keep thinking about Michelle," Gina said. "Here you and I are, comforting each other. But poor Michelle. She didn't even have a chance to say good-bye to her mom."

Gina started to slide toward her, so Marsha swung her legs down and patted her lap. It was a familiar gesture from Gina's childhood, and Gina rested her head on her mom's lap. Marsha began raking her fingers through her daughter's thick hair, the texture and color of her dad's. Marsha had to smile—at least Helmoot the Reaper Rephotsirch had left something wonderful behind.

"Your hair is just like your dad's, you know? You're lucky you got his hair instead of my wimpy strands."

They sat in silence a few moments, Marsha parting and twirling her daughter's hair, then combing it with her fingers and massaging her head.

"You never talk about Dad anymore," Gina said in a hushed voice.

"What is there to say?"

"Do you still love him?"

"He will always be the father of my children," Marsha said, giving her daughter's head a light rap with her knuckles.

"That's not what I asked you, Mom." Gina reached up and stopped the motion of Marsha's hand. She sat up and looked her straight in the eye. "Do you love him? If he was suddenly killed in a car wreck, would you be sad, or even care?"

Marsha noted the dead-serious urgency in her daughter's red-rimmed eyes. What was it about death that so quickened the need for hard answers about life? What could she say that would be honest, yet not further rip either of their hearts? Certainly nothing that made it sound like she was talking about the likes of the Reaper Rephotsirch.

Rephotsirch. Christopher. Gina's father. Her father. *This woman sitting before me is still her daddy's girl.*

She pictured Christopher's hands wrapped around Gina's tiny fingers holding the fishing pole. "Feel him tugging? I think you've got a big one!" he'd said. The moment touched Marsha to the core, burned into her memory forever. Such a tender love the two of them shared.

Marsha recalled the first daddy-daughter dance Gina and Christopher attended, Gina so beautiful in her new blue satin dress, so proud to have her handsome daddy at her side, to give him a boutonniere and stand like a princess as he pinned on her very first corsage. Marsha's already swollen eyes teared again.

Marsha stared into Gina's eyes. *Yes, the woman before you is that same little girl who loved—who* loves *her daddy so much.*

But did she, Marsha, still love Christopher? That was the question her daughter had asked. This wasn't a Tevye-from-*Fiddler-on-the-Roof* question with a romantic soundtrack playing in the background. This was real life. This was her daughter, with a husband and children of her own, wanting to know if her mother still loved her father.

Pangs of guilt and grief alternately seared her heart as she searched for the answer. Guilt for spending so much time trash-talking the father of her children. Sure, it was only in a novel, and aside from sharing some of the funnier details with Barb, only she had seen the extent of it. But still, all the anger she continued to lather up within herself by writing about it?

And grief. She still grieved the trust, time, and yes, the love, that was lost between them.

"Gina, I love you. Your father loves you. And sadly, I think we *both* proved to you over Easter—and I'm sure that wasn't the first time—that we aren't perfect." Marsha broke eye contact, rubbed her thumb knuckle, bit her top lip. "That's a hard thing to admit, since sometimes it's easier just to be mad at him, you know?"

Gina nodded and shrugged.

"When I married your dad, I think I loved him more than I loved myself. I gave him everything." Marsha's voice cracked. She swallowed. "But a series of moments—of choices on both our parts—ultimately *changed* my love for him."

She watched as Gina's eyes filled with tears again. This tender-hearted woman deserved complete honesty. With the fragileness of life so close at hand, maybe Marsha could finally reach way down deep inside herself and find it.

"For a long time I was so angry, Gina, and I couldn't even find my voice to express it. With the help of a counselor, I eventually found what I deemed a nondestructive way to vent. Writing has been my sanity. Once I opened the door on the pent-up rage and worked to shore up my self-esteem, the pendulum began to swing. Rather than just drowning in my sorrow and second-guessing myself, I allowed myself to *despise* your father. To loathe him. To villainize him, even. But the truth is—and right this moment, it is suddenly so very clear—we all have our shadowy sides, and here is mine: I've spent far too much time feeding my anger."

Gina tilted her head, and her tears flowed at a new angle, a new bend in their river.

"If your father died today—and from my mouth to God's ears, I do not wish that—I would be sad for you and your brother and our grandbaby." She swallowed hard, already digesting the weight of what she was about to say. "But I would be equally sad for me to have let the chance to forgive your dad slip away. It's time I do something about that while I still have the chance. Will it mean I ever love him again? I doubt it, at least not the way I used to. I couldn't anyway. He's got a new cutesy-pie wife." She smiled. "But by finally allowing myself to release my anger, maybe enough room will open in my heart to at least like him again."

Gina flung herself into her mom's arms. "Thank you, Mom. Thank you."

"Don't thank me yet. I haven't done anything. It'll take an act of God, I'm sure, but I think I'm finally ready."

Josie reminded herself it was Saturday. Since she wasn't working, the days melded together so that nothing set the weekend apart.

Aside from one minimal early-morning hot flash, she'd slept well. She was refreshed and ready for a challenge, the turmoil caused by her early dismissal losing some of its power over her. She felt invigorated by her budding friendship with Amelia, happy she'd enjoyed Lyle's company, and not as thirsty as usual, which was nice.

It was time to give her condo a Josie-do-it cleaning. She chuckled. She hadn't thought about that phrase for years. Both her mom and Victor had, with delight, repeated the Josie-do-it stories from her youth. When she was quite young and they'd try to help Josie with her hat or buttons or lacing her shoes, Josie would knit her eyebrows together, wave them off, and say "Josie do it!" Her mom thought it was cute, but Victor relished his daughter's independence, which fueled it all the more. When she reached teenhood, the Josie-do-it phrase—now a shortcut to describe her determination—occasionally surfaced. By her early twenties, the phrase went the way of many childhood tags. But it didn't escape her that even before Victor's powerful influence, she was a strong-willed child.

While dusting her condo, Josie came to the cabinet in the living room. Softly, gently, she ran a cloth over the face of the woman in the bronze statue. *Such trust in her eyes. Trust and surrender. What strength it takes—perhaps more strength than I possess—to overcome fear of intimacy, to ever give myself like that.*

Josie closed her eyes and wondered if her

parents shared such a personal closeness of mind, body, and spirit. Now that she'd begun to view her mother in a reframed light, it was easier to imagine they did. With her eyes still closed and her hand resting on the woman's head, Josie pictured the way her mother had settled her hand on the table right next to Victor's during their discussion about Josie's new outfit. There'd been no need for that proximity. In retrospect, the placement seemed deliberate, her mother's thumb maybe even touching her father's little finger. Josie quickened with the notion that something powerful might have been exchanged between them during that gesture, something only the two of them recognized. What else could explain her father backing down—something he certainly did not believe in?

She opened her eyes and studied the look on the male statue's face. So tender. Such respect. For such muscular arms, they appeared to hold the woman with feather-light touch, as if she were the most precious and fragile gift, his equal in all things.

Amelia and Alfred popped into her mind. Josie hoped Alfred was everything Amelia said he was. Not all men *were* what they appeared to be. It was possible Alfred might harbor the "gift" of the salesman's BS, which was good in business, but could be terrible in personal relationships. Amelia was a smart cookie though. Surely she knew what she was doing. She was in sales herself! And she was totally in love with her softhearted man. Josie remembered the glow on Amelia's face as she described her wedding gown, spoke of the way Alfred helped her navigate rough waters with her mother, waggled her eyebrows when she mentioned his muscles.

A sudden pang of jealousy flicked through Josie. The rest of Amelia's weekend, hopefully the rest of her life, would be spent with the man she loved. It wasn't that Josie didn't enjoy her singlehood; she did. But at least momentarily, she coveted how nice it would be to have something lined up, someone to spend time with. Someone she felt strong emotions for, as Amelia did for Alfred.

She wondered if Lyle had a busy weekend schedule. He'd sure been jazzed about the Encouragement Club. Josie remembered how she'd privately maligned him for getting involved with such a group. Now that she'd spent personal time with him, his decision to join made perfect sense.

Encouragement was a powerful thing. She'd learned that from Amelia, who had encouraged her to just be whatever it was she needed to be— whatever and however it was she *was*. It gave her pause to think she'd considered herself above such a club, above such a need.

No sense looking back. I am where I am. On to

the next object to dust, the snowglobe. She studied it a long while before cautiously picking it up, as if touching it might incite another bout of craziness. She felt too good today for such nonsense.

She rested the snowglobe on its side in her upturned palm, slowly turning and dusting, watching as the snow and the entire creek scene, tree and all, rotated with it. As the snow turned within, so too did the familiar desire churn within her to find that creek. It had to be somewhere, right? *Right?* She sighed. The way the snowglobe was crafted, it was insane to think that water could run within water, or that the snowglobe had leaked or spouted enough liquid to fill the cabinet, let alone the room.

"Oh, my gosh! I wonder if something strange like this happened with Cassandra Higgins and her snowglobe! Maybe that's what her odd calls were about! How could you not sound crazy trying to describe something like what happened to me?" After all, they did buy them from the same gentleman.

Come on, Josie. What did the guy sell? Magic? Voodoo? Hallucinatory rays? What? Maybe she should give Cassandra a call.

And say what? Ask what?

What did Cassandra say the last time she called? Think, Josie, think. Something about how glad she was, or how crazy something would sound. Yes! How her life had changed. Something to do with the snowglobe. She might have mentioned God.

At the thought of God's possible involvement with the snowglobe, goose bumps ran up Josie's arms and her cheeks flushed. *Surely not. That would be as crazy as thinking the Virgin Mary shows up on a slice of salami. God does not "do things" with snowglobes.*

She started to set the snowglobe back on the shelf, but her fingers would not release it. Try as she might, they would not uncurl. At first she feared she was having a stroke. Then the creek began to run.

The water, carrying gentle waves of whispers, rippled up her fingertips and arm, over her shoulder, up her neck, and into her ear. *Blessed is the man . . . trusts in the Lord . . . extends its roots by a stream . . . will not fear.*

Her breath caught in her throat. The words were from the Bible verse they'd read at her grandmother's funeral! She might normally not have remembered such a thing, but it was printed on her grandmother's memorial card, which she kept in her jewelry box.

She stared at the globe. "Roots by a stream."

Her eyes moved back to the intimate look on the statue faces. The words *will not fear* sank straight to her heart as her fingers uncurled from the snowglobe.

Wasn't I just thinking about my fear of intimacy? Wasn't I?

Breathless, she stood still as a post until her racing heart recovered.

Twenty-Six

M arsha sat on her couch, giant mug of coffee in her hand, banana peel discarded on the newspaper on the coffee table, crumbs of dry Kashi cereal littering the front of her robe. It was nine o'clock Sunday morning. She'd been parked in the same place for two hours.

When she woke that morning, she'd contemplated going to church; her daughter had suggested that it might be good for her. But she'd talked herself out of it. Tonight was Barb's wake and tomorrow, her funeral. She didn't feel like listening to some perky sermon about God's love, and she sure did not want to hear parishioners spew pat words about how her best friend was "in a better place." If anyone was a sure bet for heaven, it was Barb, but she had no business being there now. Not yet.

Marsha cycled through the channels on the television again. This time she held the remote control in front of her like a loaded weapon, determined to fire until she found something interesting. No, she did *not* need another set of anti-aging creams as advertised in an infomercial, her decision made after a brief moment of weakness when she almost picked up her phone. She thrust the remote toward the TV as she hit the channel button, her arm recoiling from the direct hit. No, she did *not* want to listen to the politicians argue or wax poetic about health insurance. No, she certainly did *not* want to watch cartoons or reruns or listen to television preachers, not even if they weren't perky.

She finally switched off the TV and tossed the remote on the coffee table. It hit the banana peel and skidded to the floor. *What are the odds?*

She picked at the cereal bits on her robe and tucked them into her pocket, then pictured the sticky wad they would create in the laundry. She shucked off her robe, carried it to the kitchen, and turned her pocket inside out over the garbage can.

Thoughts of her conversation with her daughter churned her gut. Anxieties about her new team leadership position niggled her brain. Memories of how she'd avoided Barb all day Friday—never to see her alive again—took their toll. Her mind exploded like popping corn without a lid, flying in every direction. She needed to snap out of this useless crazy-making.

She needed to write. She needed to get hold of her chaotic thoughts and string them onto the page.

She donned her robe and refilled her coffee mug, then padded down the hall to her computer room and plunked into the chair. She stared at the cold grey screen, thinking how she should first work on a few notes for Barb's funeral. Michelle had called yesterday and asked if she would be willing to share a story or two at the funeral. Preferably funny stories. Michelle had requested something to help them remember Barb the way she really was: full of life and laughter. Michelle said Pastor Claven, Barb's pastor, believed in celebrating a life.

Celebrate? *Celebrate?*

Marsha planted her elbow on her desk and rested her cheek in her hand. The angle of her fingers and the weight of her head pushed her skin up until it nearly squished her eye closed. *Maybe I should have ordered the face cream.* She lifted her head and began a hand-over-hand movement, pulling her neck skin downward as if she could stretch and unfold all the wrinkles time accrued.

Stop it! Just stop it and do something. Something like . . . .

After a few minutes of mulling, she opened her top desk drawer and stared at the red leather notebook with the bone button and leather strap. She recalled the day she bought it, how she stopped at Barb's on her way home. How long ago was that now? Not even two years, but it felt like a lifetime. She hadn't opened the journal since she started writing fiction.

Carefully, as though its private contents might

327

spill, she removed it from the drawer. Things were dark enough right now without all *that* landing back in her lap. Yet the leather felt so buttery soft in her hand that she couldn't help but unwind the strap.

Drawing a deep breath, she opened to the first page.

"The lying, cheating bastard."

First she gasped, then she chuckled. *For two people who don't swear . . .* "But you were right, Barb," she said, looking up. "Those words sure did get my emotional ball rolling. Thank you, friend." She embraced the diary to her chest. "But now, how to stop that destructive speeding ball?"

After she shored herself up enough to read on, she felt as if she stood outside herself, window peeping on the thoughts of a stranger. Page after page of detailed turmoil delivered a surprising ride. Some of her most damning thoughts—and the angrier she'd been, the less legible her writing—seemed borderline funny in their melodramatics. *Stand back: Fury unleashed!* she mused.

Yet a few of the entries still constricted her throat, especially her earliest questions about herself: her weight, her lack of interest in the bedroom, her whining about all the time Christopher said he spent at "the office," working late into the night. So many pages filled with wondering. If she had only done more of this or less of that, might he have remained faithful? *Scary, looking at my own rock-bottom self-esteem.*

Thanks to counseling, Barb, writing, and time, she'd found her way out of the pit. Hopefully, she'd now find the way to let go of her anger toward Christopher.

She picked up a ballpoint pen and drew two dark lines under her last entry, skipped two pages, and wrote the day's date across the top of the next page.

April 19, 2009
Dear Blood Red Leather Diary,
It's been a long time since I've talked to you. Too long—although I already wish I was writing in pencil because I'd erase that "too long" part, which sounds like a self-indictment, and to be honest, I'm done with that.
I'm done with many things.
I <u>want</u> to be done with many things. But how?

She tapped the page with her pen and waited, as if the diary itself might pour forth sage wisdom.

I'm starting to think I can't do this by myself.
WAIT! Barb, are you still praying for me

and Christopher? Now that you're in heaven, do you have more pull with God? Is that what this turn of heart is about? Because if it is, no fair. You have an advantage.

God, is Barb up there <u>encouraging</u> You to mess with me? If she is, tell her thanks for not forgetting me already, what with all the angels and harps and silver and diamonds and stuff. Tell her I said the beautiful Marshalleon is trying to use her gift of Knowitall to know how to start at least liking her number one enemy.

Maybe Marshalleon just needs a can of attitude-be-gone.

God, tell Barb for me that . . .

She set down her pen.

"Tell her I already miss her," she whispered aloud, "and that . . ." She stopped and sniffled. "I'm doing my best to try to talk to You again."

Marsha closed her diary, strapped it tight, and put it back in the drawer. It was the best she could do for now.

Home from the Monday funeral and the dinner that followed, Lyle unknotted his tie, slid it off his neck, and hung it in his closet, then reconsidered. Maybe he should pack at least one tie for his visit home. Maybe toss his suit and dress shoes in the car too. Yes, he probably should, just in case. Rather than hang his suit back in the closet, he put everything he'd worn to the funeral, including the tie, on a suit hanger and hung it over his closet door.

It felt good to get back into a pair of jeans and a light sweatshirt—*a guy could get used to living like this*—and to have the funeral behind him. Now he could focus on the last of his trip preparations.

He'd stopped by AAA on his way home and picked up a couple of state maps. He tucked them into his briefcase and checked that item off the to-do list he'd scribbled on the back of a junk-mail envelope. *What else?* He'd already gone to USPS online and filled out the form to hold his mail. *Check.* He still needed to put a hold on his newspaper delivery, which was what he did next. He also phoned his neighbor to let her know he'd be gone for a while. They kept an eye on each other's dwellings in case the mail or newspaper folks messed up or something looked fishy.

It struck him that Barb's family would have to go through much more of this type of thing, but for permanent changes. What would her kids do with her house? So many details after a death, so many things people didn't think about.

He stared at his computer monitor. For instance, who knew his passwords for his computer? The amount of business he handled online now was incredible. E-mail bills and online banking made life easier, but how on earth would his sister, since that's who the task would fall to, even begin to tackle that project without a list of passwords? He added another item to his list: "Spend time with Sis outlining emergency procedures."

He tossed a final load of white clothes into the washer. Maybe he'd give Josie a call while they cycled. He'd thought about calling her numerous times over the weekend, but his head wasn't in the right place. He didn't want to sound mopey and morbid when he called or make it sound like he was only phoning to pass along bad news and funeral arrangements. He felt assured Josie wouldn't attend Barb's funeral anyway.

But as tough as the funeral had been, it was also good to be with so many people who knew Barb. And the stories! Thank goodness for Marsha, who helped them laugh.

Yes, he'd give Josie a call now and share a few of the highlights, see what she'd been up to, let her know he'd be leaving town for a while.

"Hello, Lyle," she said, after answering on the third ring.

"Glad to know I passed the test."

"What test would that be?"

"The caller ID test." She chuckled.

He liked the sound of her voice when it wasn't all business. "Did I catch you at a good time?"

"Good as any. In fact, good, period. I put in a pretty full day of work. It's time for a break."

"Work?"

"Job search."

"I figured you'd have something lined up by now."

"I always have my nets cast. Today was the first day I got serious about gathering them up and taking a good look."

"How'd it go?"

"Leaner than I predicted. More like minnows than lunkers. Although I have a couple of potentials, I think I'll cast a few more nets tomorrow and dig a little deeper into the networking. How's it going for you? Oh, but before you answer, first let me say how sorry I was to hear about Barb DeWitt. I know you were fond of her. My friend Amelia called. She saw the obit in the *Chicago Tribune*."

"Did she know Barb?"

"No. But she thought I might, since the obituary mentioned she'd worked at Diamond Mutual for so many years. I don't tend to read the obits, but after Amelia called, I took a look. It was an impressive obituary. Barb certainly accomplished a lot. It's nice they even mentioned the Encouragement Club. It made me wonder, though: when did you learn about the accident? Was she on her way home from her surprise party when the accident occurred?"

"No. She never made it to the party. We were waiting and waiting. Marsha's daughter phoned to tell her about it. It was pretty rough going."

"How awful. Again, I'm sorry."

"Her funeral was incredible. Truly incredible. The church was packed. She would have loved it. I've never been to a service quite like this one. Sure, there was enough sorrow to go around, but it was also pretty upbeat too. Made me really stop and think about the quality of my own life."

"How so?" She sounded skeptical.

"Person after person came forward to share stories about Barb and the influence she had on their lives. It was interesting, really, getting an overview on someone from so many perspectives. She's leaving quite a legacy. Kids, grandkids, people from her church, friends, co-workers, just about everyone who knew her talked about her as the ultimate encourager.

"Do you remember Sheila from Barb's department? She lost her job in the cuts?" He felt a little awkward as soon as he mentioned the cuts. He hoped Josie didn't think he was implying anything about her hand in them.

"Yes."

"Even she got up and spoke, and she's on the shy side. She introduced herself as a member of the Encouragement Club, as did everyone who attended one of the meetings. Over the weekend, Sheila accepted a job as nanny to her sister's kids. She said she would never have had the courage to follow her heart without Barb's cheerleading."

"A *nanny?*"

Lyle wasn't crazy about Josie's tone of voice. "Yes, nanny. She adores her niece and nephew. As Sheila told us, Barb helped her reframe how she perceived the position by asking her, 'What could be more important than caring for our next generation?'"

An awkward silence followed, which he pushed through. "One of Barb's longtime friends said Barb had been so inspiring, that in Barb's honor, she was going to sign up for a computer class through the senior center. And Barb's prayer circle, who from the sounds of it knew her about as well as anyone, had us all in stitches too. I've never heard so much laughter ring throughout a sanctuary."

"How's Marsha doing? She and Barb seemed pretty tight."

"It's tough, but Marsha convinced us all that Barb's up there already encouraging God to pull a few strings for us." He chuckled, then wondered what Barb might say to God about him—and what Josie might think about him saying such a thing about Barb and God. Although he couldn't pinpoint why, he didn't get the feeling Josie was much into religion.

They chatted for a few more minutes as the topics wandered from one thing to the next. He finally told her he was leaving town tomorrow and that he'd likely be gone a week or two. He stopped short of saying he'd call her when he got back, which seemed a little pretentious since she might not want him to. Plus, the conversation wasn't as easy as it had been when they'd been face to face in the coffee shop. She was still a difficult woman to read.

Maybe too difficult, he thought when he hung up. *Too difficult, period.*

Twenty-Seven

*F**riday night again,*** Josie thought as she looked at her calendar. *What have I accomplished in the entire week since dinner with Amelia? Let's see.* She'd managed to sound like a heartless, snobbish ogre when she spoke with Lyle on the phone the day before he left town, so she doubted she'd ever hear from him again. Got hit on at the grocery store by a man who must have been in his eighties. Endured about twenty hot flashes. Cleaned her kitchen cabinets, which didn't need it. Worked out twice a day instead of once and gained half a pound from too much time to snack. Pursued every networking lead in her database and turned up nothing. Found out she priced herself out of the one possibility that felt like a good match. *Nice, Josie.*

But that wasn't the worst of the news: Out of the blue, Victor had phoned early that morning. In an uncommon burst of what could only be described as blathering enthusiasm, he said it had been too long since they'd had a chance to visit face to face and he'd be passing through Chicago on Monday, so he was coming to spend the night with her before she moved on to the next place because wasn't her contract about up? He looked forward to hearing all about where she'd be moving next and how she'd be "whipping them into shape."

Even though she hadn't seen him for nearly two years, it wasn't like Victor to "come for a visit" or prattle nonstop. He was also neither impulsive nor sporadic, so what was with the short notice?

She told him he was of course welcome to spend the night, but when she inquired about the purpose of his trip, he seemed vague. He said they could talk when he got in, which he thought would be about 1700 hours and not to worry if she wasn't home from work yet; he'd wait outside. "Don't make plans for dinner. We'll grab a bite out after I have a chance to freshen up."

Grab a bite? Out? He liked eating at home. Full meals. Meat and potatoes.

It wasn't that she didn't welcome the chance to see Victor. She did. But his timing couldn't be worse. She had two whole days of weekend in front her, which meant no job calls, so no way to have a new plan in place before he got here—unless she landed something Monday, which seemed impossible. Amelia was busy all weekend, so no socializing to pass a few hours speculating with her about Victor's visit, or how he might react to the news his daughter had momentarily displaced her plan for the rest of her life. She had nothing purposeful to do but try to dislodge the growing unease about her future.

It seemed things were tougher than she thought out there, even for the likes of the unstoppable Josie Victor Brooks.

In attempts to burn off some nervous energy, Josie had spit-polished every piece of furniture and eradicated each tiny morsel of dust, including that above the trim over her doorways, by Monday morning. This was more than a determined Josie-do-it frenzy; this was manic behavior, she thought, as sweat dripped off the end of her nose.

At 10 a.m. she put the last of her cleaning supplies away, took a shower, and for about the tenth time that morning checked her e-mail. Nothing. Not one single nibble.

She took inventory of food supplies and decided to stock up on a few things for tomorrow's breakfast, like white potatoes and thick-sliced smoked bacon, neither of which she kept on hand. She remembered the smoky bacon fragrance—nice, in a woodsy kind of way—in the house every morning Victor was home for breakfast, which wasn't that often. But when he was, he ate three eggs over easy; a pile of American potatoes, browned, but not too much; two pieces of toast without butter, just a light smear of raspberry preserves (not jam or jelly); and four strips of thick, smoked bacon, not limp but not too crispy either. Her mom used to blot the cooked bacon in a cotton dishtowel to absorb the extra grease before arranging the strips like good little soldiers in row, never overlapping. Josie still wasn't good at making over-easy eggs without breaking the yolks, something her mother did with masterful ease, but she'd give it her best try.

When she arrived home with the groceries— including a small selection of lunch meats, sliced cheeses, and a hearty loaf of artisan bread, just in case Victor stayed through lunch tomorrow—she checked her e-mail before putting things away. Much to her relief, she'd received two nibbles, which she quickly read.

Are they serious with those pay ranges? She highlighted the e-mails and pushed the delete button, then quickly went to her trash folder and moved them back to her in box. She'd create a "highly unlikely" folder after she put the groceries away. At least she could honestly tell Victor she had a couple of offers to consider.

"Apple," she said, holding the golden delicious in her hand, "should I put you on top of the fruit arrangement or on the bottom?" She turned the wooden bowl, surveying its aesthetic appeal.

Then she remembered Victor once telling her and her brother how he didn't get to eat a whole banana until after he enlisted. Too many mouths to feed with too little money meant sharing everything, including bananas. She took all the fruit out of the bowl and put the apple on the bottom, then rearranged the pears and oranges twice before setting the small bunch of bananas on top.

As she turned the bowl to inspect her final creation, she noticed a small bruise on one of the bananas. She quickly removed the imperfect little soldier and ate it for lunch, along with a container of yogurt and a green salad with walnuts and raspberry vinaigrette dressing. She cleaned up the dishes and wiped down the counter twice, then tossed the yogurt container in her recycle bin.

As it *thunked* against the bottom of the empty bin, her call box buzzed. The doorman said there was a gentleman there to see her. *Lyle?* Then she heard the familiar cadence of the voice in the background.

"Tell her Victor is here." She pictured Victor already waving the large man out of his way.

"Hello!" she said, as she opened the door. "Welcome." Victor stepped inside. Josie placed her hands atop his shoulders, which felt alarming frail, and he gave her a quick peck on the cheek. "You're"—she glanced at her wristwatch—"almost five hours ahead of schedule!"

"I didn't expect you to be home, but the doorman said he'd seen you come in not too long ago."

"Yes. Well . . ." She absolutely was not ready for a conversation about her recent comings and goings. Absolutely not. "I didn't expect you to be here yet either. Change of plans?"

"Caught an earlier flight. Sometimes standby works!" he said with gusto.

Victor looked good, but she couldn't get the feel of his bony shoulders out of her head. Grayer with a few more wrinkles, but otherwise rosy cheeked and as upright, rigid, and slicked back as ever. "I trust it was an uneventful flight?"

"Yes. Rather pleasant. Had a nice young man seated next to me."

"Come on in. We don't need to stand here in the entryway. Did you have lunch?"

"Yes. I grabbed a Chicago hot dog in the airport. Thought about it the whole flight. The last time I was in Chicago, about twenty-five years ago, I said if I ever came back, the first thing I was going to do was to eat another Chicago dog. It was just as tasty as I remember."

"Good. Good. Well, this way, then. Let me give you the grand tour," she said with a smile. "We'll start with the kitchen, then I'll take you to your room. We can grab something to drink before we settle into the living room." Her voice cracked, it was so suddenly dry.

Not the crazy thirst again! The last thing she needed with Victor around was something, anything, with that snowglobe. Maybe she should

341

just steer clear of the living room. "Or maybe you'd rather see some of the city? It's a little cool and windy out, but I'm guessing you still love 'braving the elements.' "

"It's always smart to make good use of time. That's one of the reasons I tried the earlier flight."

"Got a jacket or umbrella?"

"I'll retrieve my jacket out of my bag. Don't need an umbrella. I won't melt. Never have."

She smiled. Same old nonmelting Victor. But in her heart, she was still smarting over his comment about making good use of their time. Wasn't it enough they were together?

Nonetheless, a brisk walk would feel good. They'd always talked better side by side, *marching-along, / ca-dence, / step to the-right, / back to the right.*

Lyle's side hurt from laughing so hard. He, Noreen, Robert, two of their kids, and three of Lyle's high school buddies, along with two of their wives, had gathered at five-thirty Monday night at Ancona's Place, a local hole-in-the-wall pizza joint. It was nine already. Empty wine bottles and spumoni ice cream bowls still littered the table. Lyle couldn't remember when he'd enjoyed himself more. So many memories, and such fun guffawing over them.

Nobody wanted to break up the party, but finally Noreen stood and reminded Lyle that "some people," which she pointed out included everyone at the table but him, had to work tomorrow.

"We'll see you when you get home," she said on her way out, handing him a fistful of cash to cover expenses for her family.

One by one, the others tossed in their share of the bill and headed out the door until only Lyle and Randy remained.

"How long do you think you'll be around?" Randy asked, moving to a chair next to Lyle.

"Not too much longer. Maybe a couple of days."

"Maybe I missed it, but what's the hurry to get back to Chicago if you're unemployed? Maybe you're seeing someone?"

"Nah. No women, no pets to feed or plants to water either. I just don't want to wear out my welcome at my sister's."

"She's a good egg. Always has been," Randy said. The two of them dated in high school for a few months. "My wife was a lot like Noreen. Steady. Lively. Easy to be with. I sure miss her."

"How long has she been gone now?"

"She died eighteen months ago tomorrow. I'm not embarrassed to admit that I don't like being alone. Seems to suit you, though. Got any practical tips?"

"You cook much?"

"Wife did all the cooking. I maybe grill a burger or brat. I'm pretty good at bacon and eggs and

343

boxed macaroni and cheese," Randy said, grabbing the lone piece of garlic bread left in the paper-lined plastic basket. "Why do you ask?"

"Because *you* asked if I had any practical tips for bachelorhood and cooking's the first thing that came to mind. It's enjoyable. Keeps you busy shopping, chopping, and cleaning. House smells good—sure better than dirty socks." They chuckled. "Also healthier for you than eating out all the time or living on frozen dinners. Maybe you could take a cooking class. Hey, come to think of it, when I was in OKC Friday, I saw a notice about cooking classes in a gourmet shop I prowled around in. Or maybe the park district offers classes right here in this neck of the woods. Learn to cook, maybe meet a nice woman." Lyle raised his eyebrows and smiled. "Just a thought."

"What were you doing in Oklahoma City?"

"Remember Chip Reed?"

Randy nodded.

"We've kept in contact too. Well, Christmas cards and an occasional call. I told him I was coming this way, and we arranged to have lunch."

"What's he up to?"

"He owns quite a successful car dealership. You probably knew that, though. Remember how he could talk us into anything?" Both of them nodded and smiled, and Lyle guessed the great streaking adventure sprang to life for Randy too. "He put that natural-born salesmanship to good use. He's really done well for himself. But here's something about him you maybe don't know: he spends most of his time with community charity work. Fund-raising, brainstorming. He's on a couple of boards of directors. He's got a son with MS, which originally spurred his desire to do what he could for research. Then, he said, one thing led to the next, and next thing he knew, he was the king of Oklahoma City charity work."

"Charity work. I thought that was gonna be your lifetime gig. What was it your high school yearbook said next to your picture? 'Most likely to make a difference in the world' or something like that?"

Lyle laughed. "Or something like that. Since I recently lost my job—and a friend in a terrible car accident—I've spent some time pondering how it is that life's surprising twists and turns steer us in new directions."

"You thinking about moving back?"

"What made you ask?"

"I don't know. Maybe the way your eyes lit up when you talked about what Chip was doing. If he's still the same old Chip, I'm guessing he tried to talk you into partnering with him on *something*. And like you said, you got no wife, no girlfriend, no dogs, and no plants to hold you back, so why stay in Chicago? I bet you haven't found one slice of pizza as good as they still serve here. I swear, Angelo's got to be seventy-five if he's a day.

Think slinging pizza dough is the magic elixir for youthfulness?"

Lyle looked around the little restaurant. Angelo's head, donned with a short white paper hat, appeared and disappeared through the serving window as he bent over the dough, tossed the pizza ingredients together, placed bits of sausage just so. Same worn checkerboard vinyl tile on the floor, same tables and chairs and jukebox. Same Angelo and Shirley, his wife, seating people and giving them a playful hard time. The only thing that had changed in all these years was the addition of more duct tape on some of the bench seats. Angelo still broke out in occasional loud choruses of the old song "That's Amore," and everyone in the restaurant still sang along when he did. It was tradition. They'd already been through three cycles of it this evening.

"The older I get," Lyle said, draining his glass of water, which Shirley immediately refilled, "the more I think doing what you love, following your passions, is an elixir for a lot of things. Just look at these two. Still singing, still happy, still living their dream to own their own restaurant. My friend who died? She was gung-ho full of passion."

He sat up and leaned closer to Randy. "Don't tell anyone I said this, not even my sister, okay? But I *am* talking with Chip about some opportunities. Not sure what will come of them, if anything. He doesn't hold the power to make the decisions, and I might not feel either of them is a good fit. But he told me he knows of a couple of nonprofits looking for new leadership. Things are tough out there for everyone, but most nonprofits are really taking the hits. He's contacting a few folks. Maybe I'll be able to get some meetings set up for later this week, before I head back to Chicago."

"My lips are sealed," Randy said. "But I have to admit, I'm hoping! It sure would be great to have you back again. Bachelor friends at our age are few and far between." He laughed. "Maybe you could teach me how to cook then. As I recall, you were already pretty darn good at it way back in junior high. I'd never stayed at any guy's house whose mother didn't make us breakfast, but your waffles were dang good."

"Well, I hate to brag, but . . . I'm bragging. I am an excellent cook. You'd be a lucky man to feast on Lyle's Manly Manicotti. I could probably give Angelo a run for his money if I set up my own pasta shop."

Shirley passed by. "I heard that. Don't even think about it."

They all broke out in a hearty round of laughter, a great lighthearted way to end the evening.

All the way to Noreen's, Lyle thought about how surprisingly and instantly he'd let himself get excited about the possibility of moving back home. He'd heard it in his own voice while talking to Randy. Home to his family and ailing mother, home to his old friends, and maybe even home to his original career passions.

Maybe.

Twenty-Eight

Helga, the Mysterious Matron,
Chapter 1

In a land of milk and mazes, honey and hostages, lived a mysterious matron whose sole purpose was to conquer the evil spirits buried deep in the hearts of fairies and leprechauns, for if there was one thing Helga knew to be true, it was that all good intentions were interwoven with threads of wickedness. Thus it was in the beginning and shall now and forevermore be. At least so believed Helga—at least for the moment.

The most deceptive weapon once used against Helga—and by her own hand—proved to be the "gift" of Knowitall—which, unbeknownst to her, she did not. But who would, who could believe that the beautiful Marshalleon—the powerful and vengeful Marshalleon—would have steered her wrong? Certainly not Helga—until she wisened up.

But let us start from the beginning of this story.

In the land of giants (rather than fairies and leprechauns) there once lived a Rephotsirch named Helmoot. He was a reaper of havoc, to be sure. Alas, of all the creatures in the land, he was the darkest, for Helmoot had betrayed the trust of his people. What could be worse than that? Time and again, he turned the hearts of his followers against him.

But worse yet, sometimes their own self-doubt caused them to turn against themselves.

His followers felt utterly defenseless, beaten down and tromped to an all-time low. They needed a greater power, a higher power, to step in and squelch his march across their well-being.

Thus it was that Marshalleon, summoned by the guttural cries of the people, exploded into the land. Beautiful, cunning, and dripping with power, Marshalleon became the voice of the weak, the hope of the wounded, and the plan for a happy future existence in all the lands, whether those lands consisted of giants, kings, fairies, leprechauns, or beautiful maidens.

For a while, Marshalleon was unstoppable, thwarting this, plowing through that, apprehending and smashing everyone in her path, including the Buzzing Blinker.

But then, something unthinkable took place: the Great Barbizone, co-hero and morale booster to Marshalleon

[MARSHA, NOTE TO SELF: you need to figure out what happens to the Great Barbizone. WHO makes her disappear and why? Or does it matter to this new story?]

In the great silent void left in the wake of Barbizone's disappearance, Marshalleon began to question her quest. Like the bad witch in *The Wizard of Oz*, she sensed her powers melting. She felt snagged around the throat by the hook shape of her own question marks. Not even when she placed the pad of her left index finger on the half moon of her right pinky fingernail and silently spoke the words, "Marsha-Marshalleon, Mistress of Magic, Maker of Payback to Reaper Rephotsirch" did the gift of Knowitall flash forth wisdom. Rather it withered in the knowledge that without the Great Barbizone cheering her on and the surety of another day with her to set things right (great body-snatching episodes arrive in the land without warning!), Marshalleon was forced to turn tail and run.

Who could save them now? Who held the power to fight the shadowy Helmoot—or possibly even join forces with him to save the land?

One day Marshalleon, believing her reign was coming to an end, ran into an older, humbled, and slightly used up woman—but not too used up—who introduced herself as Helga.

Helga said, "My intuition tells me you are troubled, Marshalleon, and that you need a new power, a different kind of power, to contend with a Reaper Rephotsirch, no matter his name. Is this true?"

"Yes," Marshalleon said, feeling herself shrinking smaller by the Infinitone, implement of measurement to keep track of time in the land of both milk and mazes and honey and hostages.

"I see." Helga stroked the foot-long black hair growing from the bottom of her chin, the one she'd obviously become weary of trimming. Since her fingernails were razor sharp, when she let go of the hair, it curled up like a Christmas ribbon into a beautiful bouquet of sparkling silver and mysterious shades of gray.

Marshalleon, mesmerized and unaware, had fallen under Helga's spell, just as Helga planned.

"So, now I must tell you something that you won't like to

hear, and worse yet, you won't want to do," Helga said, her eyes aglow.

"What is it, Helga?" Marshalleon said in a trancelike voice. "I will do anything to regain my power."

"That is just it," Helga said. "If you do the thing I ask, the thing that will give you peace, you will no longer possess any powers of your own."

"It is too much to ask," Marshalleon said. "I see no way to have peace in the land without power."

"Do you trust me?" Helga asked, stretching her long black chin hair until it was straight, then letting it *boing* back into sparkly, mesmerizing wonderment.

"I trusted the Great Barbizone, but she left me. How do I know you won't do the same?"

"You don't." *Boing. Boing.* "Without trust, I am afraid you are not ready," Helga said. "In that case, I will only ask one thing of you now."

"Yes?"

"I ask you to look straight into the eyes of the thick- and wavy-haired Ginalilyoseon, daughter of Planet Uterus, and explain your reasons to her."

With unnecessary force, Marsha pushed the computer key to save her file. How could her own story betray her like this? Next time she started a story, she'd be more disciplined. Write an outline and stick to it.

She brushed her teeth and put on her pajamas, then trimmed the short hair growing from the bottom of her chin. She needed sleep. Tomorrow was another day at work, another day working without Barb or Mr. Waters or anyone else in her old department.

It would also be her first day working with someone she would never again refer to as the evil Buzzing Blinker.

Enough of all that already.

Behind the wild look and bravado of Mr. Buzz Blinker—her *boss,* she reminded herself—lived a kind man. She'd suspected so, but now she knew for sure. Sometimes lacking in social graces? Yes. But every time she was around him, he revealed another piece of himself that helped eradicate what first seemed an almost cartoonish characterization of a man. Instead, Buzz was sincere and smart, a quick learner, and from what she could tell, making solid decisions. For instance, the idea to brand the company with a catchy new modern logo—DīMute—pleased everyone after they saw it. Sure, he was flamboyant, unconventional, and a little bit goofy, but he was also way more tender-hearted than anyone realized. She'd learned about his true heart in a most uncommon way.

The previous Tuesday, Michelle called Marsha and asked if she could drop by after dinner. They chatted for a while, cried a few tears, then determined to encourage each other as they both knew Barb would want them to.

Michelle told Marsha that if she got a chance, to please thank everyone from the Encouragement Club. She asked Marsha if they'd found a way to pull meetings together again, but sadly, all Marsha could do was shake her head. Michelle was so grateful that club members had given her the card they'd all signed for Barb's surprise retirement party. Her family had a few good laughs reading all the notes, and the card would remain a lovely physical reminder of how beloved her mom had been, even by people they'd never meet.

Michelle said their favorite note in the card was from Frank. Frank had told Marsha he'd likely be unable to bring himself to attend Barb's funeral, and indeed, he had not shown up. But in the card, he'd drawn a stick figure picture of himself, complete with suspenders. His little stick arms and fingers were pulling the suspenders away from his little stick body—which wasn't that far off the mark. He'd written a note beneath the picture that said, "Happy MOVING ON. Guess who? If you ever need a hand, let me know." In a very bold gesture, he'd written his home phone number under his name.

"So sweet," Marsha said. "I never saw that note! Frank must have added it after everyone else signed the card. Thank you for coming over to share."

"That's actually not the reason I'm here," Michelle said. She reached into her purse and pulled out another envelope. She hoped Marsha could enlighten her as to who this man was and how he knew her mom.

Before Marsha could get the card out of the envelope, Michelle said, "We found it in her handbag. The envelope was open, so I think Mom had a chance to read it too. I hope so. It's so tender."

The printed front of the card had the words "Thank you" under a picture of a rainbow. The moment Marsha opened the card, she recognized Buzz's terrible handwriting. He must have given it to Barb before she left work on Friday.

"Thank you for so many years of dedicated service to Diamond Mutual, soon to be known as DĪMute." He'd carefully printed the word and drawn the shape of an upside-down jewel-diamond on which the phrase DīMute balanced. "I thought you might like to see some of the changes in store, changes your two decades of dedication helped make possible. For the short while I was in attendance at the first meeting of the Encouragement Club (Hey, new guy in a new town, I thought I could use some encouragement too, then realized I'd made another of my social blunders!), it was clear why you moved up the ranks. You are valued, respected, and know how to take charge—attributes I hope to live up to in my new position. Sincerely, Buzzzzz."

"Do you know him?" Michelle asked.

"Yes," Marsha said, swallowing and brushing back a tear. "He's the man who took Lyle Waters' place. Brand-new on the job. Your mom never mentioned him?"

"That last week, she said she just could not talk about work. All she talked about was the Encouragement Club. This Buzz—or *Buzzzzz* or however you pronounce a name with five *Z*s—sure sounds like a nice person."

"Yes. Nicer than I thought," Marsha said, a little embarrassed. "Thank you *so* much for sharing. It's quite a surprise and honoring thing he did, writing such kind words to someone he barely knew."

Yes, honoring. And *kind,* Marsha thought after Michelle left. She almost picked up the phone, to call Barb to discuss it.

Then she caught herself. Life was going to hurt without Barb. Barb, who would probably say what she'd said after the first time she met Buzz. "You can't judge a man's nature by his terrible lack of fashion sense."

How can a body laugh and cry at the same time?

Twenty-Nine

We might have gone faster if we'd walked," Victor said, as their taxi crept along in rush-hour traffic. "But truthfully—and up till about a year ago, I would *never* have admitted this—I was ready to sit down."

He rested his large palms on his knees and used his arms as leverage to twist and crane his neck to look out the taxi window up toward the top of the buildings. Josie noticed he rubbed his right knee. By the time they left the planetarium, she thought she'd detected a slight limp in that leg. Maybe he was in pain and that's why he hadn't argued about a cab. He'd never admit to that, though. She was dumbfounded he admitted it felt good to sit down.

"You ready for dinner yet?" she asked. "After all the walking we've done, I imagine that hot dog wore off about three hours ago. I know I'm hungry. I'm thinking steak sounds good." Although she would order fish and a salad, her dad enjoyed a good piece of meat. "There's a decent steakhouse a few blocks from my condo. Truthfully, though, I'd like to clean up and relax a little before we head out again."

"Yes, I'm pretty hungry too. But I agree with you. After flying and traipsing around all afternoon, a shower would feel mighty good. Do you happen to have a deli nearby? Maybe we could pick up some lunch meats and a couple of salads on our way back, clean up, and just relax at your place tonight. I've been up since four this morning." He rubbed his knee again, gave a yawn.

Josie felt a pang in her chest. Victor, someone she'd always imagined invincible, was starting to show his age. "You sure that's what you want to eat? Lunch meat?"

"Sounds good to me."

"You're in luck then. I picked some up from the deli today, along with a few nice cheeses, a great loaf of artisan bread, and a quart of vinaigrette coleslaw. I also grabbed a six-pack of Budweiser. Just in case," she said with a smile. "I'll never forget the first time I saw you with a bottle of beer in your hand. Do you remember that?"

"Yes ma'am. I remember saying to your mother, 'Now we can finally keep a little beer in the house.' Your brother had moved out already, and you'd just turned twenty-one. I wish I had a picture of the look on your face when you saw me with it. I guess since you'd never seen me drink before, it never occurred to you that I did. I never was much one for liquor, but every once in a while, a beer just tastes good, and I do believe it'll taste five star tonight."

He laughed and patted her knee, allowing his hand to rest there, and the surprise of it caused her to stiffen. This was a lifetime first. Such a small gesture, yet one that felt so welcome, so intimate. She might have a beer herself, just to celebrate it.

"So did you have the day off, then?" he asked, out of the blue. They'd managed to spend the whole afternoon together without covering any personal ground, which wasn't uncommon. But now, there it was: the question she dreaded.

"Yes." No lie there.

He did not ask for more detail, for which she was thankful.

When they arrived at the condo, the doorman said, "Good evening, sir. I'm glad you found your daughter." He opened the door for them. As they passed through, he said, "Now that I see the two of you together, I believe you share quite the remarkable resemblance."

"Thank you," Victor said, looking pleased.

All the way up the elevator ride Josie turned over one question in her mind: *How did the doorman know Victor is my father?* She distinctly remembered that when Victor arrived and the doorman called, he'd said in the background,

360

"Tell her Victor is here." But it seemed too odd a thing to pursue, so she kept the question to herself.

While Victor was in the shower, Josie checked her e-mail. Two responses from a job board she'd discovered yesterday. The first one read like a form letter, so she clicked to the next.

Hmm. She felt a hot flash beginning to roll in as she scrolled. *Could be something here.* No mention of money, but they'd called her references today and liked what they heard. They wanted to arrange a preliminary conference call if she was equipped for that, which she was. In this day and age of technology, all it took to have a "face time" meeting was a computer and a Webcam, and for her, a Skype account.

She grabbed a file folder and fanned herself with one hand while scrolling with the other. They said if the conference call went well, they'd invite her out for a meeting to show her their operation, then proceed from there—as necessary. No promises, of course.

She clicked on their Web link, thinking the company sounded vaguely familiar. She'd give them this: they put together a slick face forward with their Web site. She opened a new browser window and engaged in a little research. No time to read everything now, but she set up a new bookmark file and added several links. She'd follow through after her father went to bed tonight, or, if they stayed up much past nine, after he left tomorrow. She was pooped.

Even though she was in excellent shape, she'd done more walking that afternoon than she had in a long time. It wasn't until the end of their cab ride that she began to finally relax; now she was fading fast. She yawned and found two more links to miscellaneous information. One included stats about the company, the other information on the city, which she knew nothing about, aside from the bombing that made national headlines back in the nineties.

She closed her eyes and listened. Victor was out of the shower. She wondered how long she'd been sitting there. Time always sped by when she engaged in research. She better start pulling stuff out of the fridge.

When she entered the kitchen, Victor was already seated at the table, eating a banana, which delighted her.

"Think a beer would go with that?" she asked.

"I don't see why not." He popped the last bite in his mouth and asked where she kept her waste basket.

"I'll take that peel," she said, reaching out. "The trash compactor is under the sink." She opened the cabinet, pointed, and tossed in the peel. "While you're here, please feel free to help yourself to anything. Forage, hunt, make yourself at home."

She grabbed a couple of beer bottles from the fridge and screwed off the tops. As she walked toward the table, Victor stood to receive his. As soon as the bottle was in his hand, he raised it and announced he'd like to propose a toast. A rush of joy raced through her.

"Here's to my upcoming wedding." He clinked her bottle and took a quick swig.

Josie was sure she'd misunderstood. She held the beer in front of her open mouth as her mind surfed through words that sound like "upcoming wedding."

"I'm afraid I've rendered you speechless," Victor said.

"I'm afraid I misunderstood what you said."

"I'm not surprised. I can hardly believe it myself. We've only been dating six months, but at our age, why wait?"

Josie set her bottle on the table and pulled out a chair. The two of them sat facing each other.

So this *is why he's here.*

"I'm sure this is quite a shock," Victor said, somewhat slumping. "I didn't mean to blindside you like that. I was going to tell you several times today, but I . . . I couldn't find the gumption. I finally just had to blurt it out, for fear I'd never get to it."

Victor Brooks with a case of nerves? Josie thought for a moment she might faint.

"I'll always love your mother, Jo. But she's

been gone a long time now. Never did I believe another woman on this earth could or would ever want to put up with me." His voice grew hushed. "Her name is Virginia Oldahm, but she goes by Ginny." He took another sip of his beer, picked at the label, set the bottle down.

"She's from my childhood town. Can you believe it? We went to kindergarten together!" he said, his voice both strengthening and lightening. "I hadn't seen her since I enlisted—until last fall after I received an invitation to my fifty-fifth high school reunion. I started to throw the invitation away, then I thought, *What the heck?* Only about twenty people showed up for the event, one of them Ginny. It's hard to believe how many of us are gone already. Ginny had never once left the county, not in all these long years." He smiled, then frowned, then shook his head, obviously still in disbelief. "She volunteers at the nursing home where she spent her career as a nurse. Her husband, whom I didn't know—he moved to town when he opened a feed store—died about the same time as your mother.

"A group of us took a ride out to the cemetery, past our old houses—or where we thought they used to be anyway, since 'progress' has marched through. At first I just kept thinking about all the hard times, how glad and smart I'd been to get out of there. But the way Ginny talked about the people she's spent her whole life loving . . ." His eyes welled, something Josie had only seen one other time, at her mother's funeral. "It's not that I felt a sudden love affair with either my old hometown or Ginny, or regretted leaving for a life in the military. No, sir!" he said, his posture spiking to attention. "The military was not only good for me, but good *to* me. And I wouldn't trade you and your brother and your mother for *anything*. Just the same, something . . . shifted, is the only way I can describe it. Ginny and I have talked about this for hours on end. Seeing my folks' graves and those of my two brothers, viewing the past through her lens . . . A longing took hold of my gut. Maybe for something that had never been? I can't quite say. For the first time, I realized that the trials of my childhood poverty had colored my view of so many, many things."

Josie sat mesmerized. Horrified. Intrigued. Befuddled. She finally found her voice. "Are you telling me you're getting married and moving back?"

He smiled, relaxed his posture, pursed his lips. "The only thing we know for sure is that we want to be together, and I want Ginny to see more of the world."

Josie raised her eyebrows.

"*Ginny* wants to see some of the world too, before we're too feeble to travel," he said. Mindlessly, he rubbed his knee again. "Listening to some of her stories about folks in the nursing home—many she's taken me to meet, some who remembered me from my youth—opened my eyes to the fact that you can't outrun aging. The most you can do is to live life as best you can, while you can, so you have something to talk about when you're stuck in a wheelchair wearing a diaper." He chuckled and gave a slow blink.

"My last visit back, I went to the nursing home to visit Homer Road, a guy I went through high school with. He spent some of our visit telling me what all he wished he'd done. He'd married young. Never had kids. Lost his wife. 'Now look at me,' he said. 'Who'd want me now, sitting here like this?' I tell you, Jo, it was an eyeopener. That very evening I asked Ginny to marry me, she said yes, and the wedding is in two weeks. Mother's Day, to be exact. Just a quiet wedding in her church. The same church your grandmother attended," he said, his voice turning suddenly raspy. He swallowed hard. "We'd be honored if you could attend, and very disappointed if you can't. I am speaking for both of us when I say that. Ginny's heard so much about you and your brother, she said she feels like she already knows you. In fact, she remembers your grandmother introducing you to church members when you came for a visit as a child. She described your grandmother as one of her favorite people in the world. A cornerstone of the town is what I believe she called her."

"You're getting married in the church?" Josie leaned back in her chair. It was all too much to take in. *Victor in a church? Getting married? What kind of woman is this Ginny?*

Victor rested his hands on top the table and laced his fingers together. "I'm sorry, Josie. I should have let you know earlier. It's all been such a whirlwind. Such a surprise to me—to both of us. Ginny's faith—her lifelong church family, as she puts it—is important to her. I'm not going to sit here and tell you *I've* found religion. Of course if Ginny were here with me she'd chime in with, 'At least not yet.'" He broke out in a wide, broad, and warm smile. "But out of respect for something that means so much to her—and because she said she won't marry me anyplace other than in her church—that's where the ceremony will take place. Her son and daughter and their families will be there, one coming in from Virginia. She had another son, but he died when he was only fifteen. We visited his grave site too. He's buried next to her husband."

He paused as if waiting for her to say something, which she didn't. She was reeling just trying to keep up with the story.

"I realize it might be difficult for you to get off work, but I'm sure at your stage of the game you can figure something out. You could come in on Saturday, maybe go to church with us Sunday morning. The ceremony is at three with a reception immediately following in the church basement. I'm told it will just be cookies and punch and that I should wear a suit and do what she says." He chuckled, took a swig of his beer. "She made it clear my old military ranking has nothing whatsoever to do with her.

"I think you're going to like her, Jo. She's a feisty one, like you. More vocal than your mom, and certainly more open, but just as loving. It would be ideal if you could stick around a few days and get to know her, but I told Ginny you might have to head out on Monday. I know how you are about work. I also know it's short notice, but it is for us too." He rubbed the back of his neck with his hand. "I just asked her a few days ago, and as soon as we settled on Mother's Day, I called your brother in France and made my plane reservations to come tell you in person."

"What did Donovan have to say about all of this?" She was surprised her brother hadn't e-mailed her.

"He said he won't be able to get the kids out of school, but that he wishes us well." Victor's voice revealed a mix of formality, disappointment, and resignation. "I told him Ginny and I would come visit him soon, and that I was coming to visit you now. I asked him not to tell you before I got here. From the look on your face, I see he kept his word. So tell me, what are you thinking?"

"What am I thinking?" How could she possibly

answer such a question when what she was thinking was that she had no idea who this man was sitting before her. None.

"Yes, I want to know what you're really thinking. I promised Ginny I would give her your honest reaction. She's been fretting. She said that me just showing up here and breaking this type of news is too much for anyone to take, especially a daughter. I asked her to come with, but she said absolutely not. She finally convinced me that the only thing more shocking than a seventy-three-year-old father springing something like this on his daughter would be if that father showed up with a fiancée on his arm."

"You want honesty?" she asked. "Well, here's what you can tell Ginny. She was absolutely right."

At 1:30 a.m., Josie still had not dozed off. Never in her life had she felt more alone.

Thirty

I have a good idea. Why don't you tell us about your mysterious meetings the last couple of days?" Noreen said to Lyle as she passed him the potatoes.

"I can hardly wait to pop one of these in my mouth," he said, hoping to divert the conversation. "I can't remember the last time I tasted oven-browned potatoes basted with pot-roast drippings." He stabbed one and held it to his nose. "Mmm. I detect a hint of thyme, right?"

"Yes. And it's about *time* that you tell me what you're really up to."

"I don't know what you're talking about."

"Nice try." She raised her eyebrows as she passed the crescent rolls. "I know you too well for that. You've never been a good liar. Your bottom lip goes all stiff when you try to fudge something. Did you know that? Didn't you always wonder how I could be such a clairvoyant tattletale when you were little?"

Lyle frowned, then made a motorboat sound with his lips. "What does that mean?"

"That you need to start taking Beano before you eat?"

"Come on, Uncle Lyle," Nathan said after the laughter settled down. "Even I know when you're fudging. And now I also know how I look when I try to pull one over on Mom because she always says, 'You look just like your Uncle Lyle when you try to snow me.' So what's up with the suit two days in a row?"

Lyle cut a piece of meat, closed his eyes, and moaned. "Wonderful, Sis, just wonderful."

He took his time chewing, swallowing, and wiping his mouth. Finally, he realized there was no point trying to divert the conversation; his sister was highly intuitive and relentless. Plus, there was no one in the world whose opinion he valued more.

"As for the suit, I don't want you to get excited, so hear me out before you start cheering. I've been talking to a couple of people in OKC about nonprofit job opportunities." He watched as everyone drew to attention, then he held his open palm toward them. "Let me finish. One of the places sounds intriguing since it's a newer venture dealing with the homeless. I understand the homeless numbers are rising here, too, even though the economy has held pretty tight in the area. Well, tighter than many places. The other lead shows some potential too, but both are a long way from turning into anything solid yet." He shared a few details, things that excited him along with several issues of concern.

"Look, I know you'd like for me to move back into the area since you've been telling me that for about the last thirty years now," he said with a smile. "Mom's health being what it is, I'd like to be closer, help you handle more of Mom's burden, Noreen. But if you could separate our personal thoughts from the realities of such a *career* move, I'd seriously value your opinions. Have you heard anything about these two organizations?"

"That second group was involved in a scandal a few years back," Robert said. "Made lots of headlines."

"Thanks, Robert. Chip Reed already told me

about it. From what he says, they've weathered the storm and come out the other side, but it took quite a financial toll. They're still digging out of the hole, and with government funding cutbacks, they could be on the verge of possible shutdown. If I did take that job, it's possible the wheels could quickly fall off and I'd be out of work again. On the other hand, getting involved with a new group focusing on the homeless might prove to be even riskier—on a number of levels. Nonprofits always have their issues. But it sounds like both organizations need fresh blood, someone with more business experience. Still, I don't need to step into quicksand at this stage of my life."

"Lyle," Noreen said, setting down her fork, "you asked that we leave our personal feelings out of this, but I can't. I know you too well. I love you too much. I admit," she said with a chuckle, "I'm already secretly hoping you move back. Just talking about these two possibilities caused the passionate fire in your eyes to glow red hot, something I haven't seen for a long, long while.

"Having said all of that, let me ask you this: are you sure you're not running *from* something rather than coming *to* something? You haven't let your Diamond Mutual termination rock your belief in yourself, have you? I mean, you're not tucking tail and running back home, are you?"

"Good question, honey," Robert said. "How about it, Lyle? Where have you filed that whole episode? You haven't talked about it much, at least with me." He looked to Noreen, who shook her head. "Even after twenty-five years, I still remember how long it took me to get over losing my first job."

They waited in silence while Lyle searched his heart.

"The truth is that I couldn't have been more stunned. I thought Josie's plan was a good one. Heck, we'd already moved through the bulk of the transitions. Although it was hard to see so many good employees go, in the end, I thought we were coming out strong."

"Josie the consultant, right?" Noreen asked.

"Yup." Lyle stabbed a piece of meat with his fork, then rested the fork, meat still dangling on the tines, on the edge of his plate. He took a drink of water, realizing his heart felt like it skipped a beat when he mentioned her name. Josie was a mystery and perhaps a bad match, but random thoughts of her continued to fly into his mind and snag his emotions. Then again, what was the use? They were both on the verge of leaving town, likely in opposite directions.

Her head at a tilt, Noreen studied Lyle.

"Is she the one who axed you? That's usually the way it goes when a consultant is brought in." Robert sounded like the voice of experience.

"Couldn't say, but I hope not," Lyle said, avoiding eye contact with Noreen.

"Why is that?" Noreen asked, leaning toward him. He never could hide anything from her. It was as if she possessed hidden antennae that picked up his least little emotional twinge.

"Because," he said, putting the bite of meat into his mouth, giving him time to think while he ate it—and to hide his bottom lip from her view, "if she did recommend my release, I bet she was more surprised than I was when she lost her job too."

"They canned the consultant?" Robert asked.

"My replacement started shortly after they let me go. To be exact, I received my notice on a Friday and *Buzzzzz* started Monday. A few days later, Josie got her walking papers. Like I said, we were almost through with transitions, so I'm not really sure what happened there. The most I could get out of DM management when they let me go was that they'd decided to head in a new direction, whatever that means. I will admit I've wondered if she was the one who recommended my dismissal though. She's a tough cookie, and I think she pegged me as too much of a bleeding heart. Go figure." He smiled. "I ran into her at the library last week, but I didn't have an opportunity, or perhaps the guts, to ask her. We didn't have time at the coffee shop either, though I'm not sure what knowing the answer would gain me."

"Buzzzzz?" Nathan asked. "You got replaced by someone named *Buzzzzz?*"

Lyle's only experience with Buzz was when he showed up at the Encouragement Club meeting. He could still see Buzz standing against the wall, feel how annoyed he'd been at Buzz's presence, hoping he didn't wreck Barb's excitement.

Barb. The fresh reminder of Barb's death caused his heart to sink. That was one piece of unfinished business he *did* have in Chicago: if at all possible, figure out a way to keep the club going in her honor.

"Sorry, Uncle Lyle. I didn't mean to rub something in."

Lyle realized his face must have darkened. "It's not that, Nathan. Not really. Mentioning Buzz's name—Mr. Buzz Blinker, I'm told—reminded me of something else. A couple of somethings, actually. No apology necessary."

"So when do you think you'll know if you're taking a job here and moving back?" Nathan asked.

"Hard to say. But you get your bed back tomorrow night, just in time to celebrate May Day, in case you're all into that," he said, with a teasing smile. "I'm heading to Chicago in the morning. A week is long enough to disrupt your household and the job stuff has to work its way through the system. If anything develops with either of them, I'll keep you posted, likely just fly back in if I need to engage in more interviews. Some things need to take their sweet time to play out. So for now, let's just enjoy the rest of this delicious meal and be thankful for the moment." He picked up his water glass and raised it.

"We'll be sorry to see you go, Lyle," Noreen said, lifting her glass. "But we hope you'll soon be back, for good. For now, I'm quite in agreement about enjoying this wonderful thyme-laden meal before it gets any colder." She tilted her glass toward Lyle. "Then maybe over coffee we can talk more about this Josie Brooks person," she said, waggling her eyebrows.

Lyle lay in bed that night, his mind a whir of thoughts. He was glad his sister hadn't pressed too hard about Josie. It was, he told her, likely a story that was already over.

He turned on his back and stared toward the ceiling. He wasn't looking forward to the twelve-hour drive home. Too much time to get anxious about job possibilities, selling his place, packing up and moving. In a week, he'd grown used to the company of family, which made it harder to leave them behind and would make him feel more disappointed if things did not work out. And his mom . . . his visits with her had been devastating. She was failing fast.

When he arrived last Thursday, he'd been really excited about making plans for everyone to gather at Ancona's Place. He assumed his mom would enjoy the family outing too, the chance to catch up with some of his old friends. Noreen told him he was getting ahead of himself. He brushed her off, saying he'd always been able to "work the magic with Mom."

But this time, there was no magic. It took him nearly twenty minutes to connect with his mother, for her to place him as her son. The connection only lasted a few minutes before he found himself repeating everything he'd already said to identify himself as her flesh and blood.

During the brief time they *were* on the same page, his friendly cajoling to "come out and enjoy the singing" only upset her. She made it clear that "all that noise" was too much for her. People were too loud, she said. Too rude. She just wanted to stay put.

By the time he left her, he had tears in his eyes. His mom used to be the life of the party—any party. And now this. At best, she was often lost in her own ghostlike thoughts, and at worst, she was difficult, sometimes bordering on combative. How did his sister do it every day, sit there and endure that kind of emotional ride? Maybe if the nonprofits didn't work out, he should just commit to moving back into the area and taking any job he could find.

But first things first. *Play it out, Lyle. Patience.* He could use a good dose of Barb and the Encouragement Club about now. *I'm driving home tomorrow. Such a simple and ordinary plan and thought. Wonder if Barb was thinking, "I'm driving to Beth's Bagel Haven" when the impact hit? The simplest plans run amuck. The simplest plans, sometimes the last plans.*

First thing when he got home, he would call Marsha. There had to be a way to keep the Encouragement Club going, even if it was only via a Yahoo! Group or something. Then he'd give Josie a call. Just to check in. Just to say hello.

And maybe good-bye.

His last conscious thought before nodding off was how extremely lonely he would feel on his drive back to Chicago. Family left behind in the suburbs of Oklahoma City, no person or job to greet him when he arrived in Chicago. Maybe before he left in the morning, he'd download a couple more audio books, just to keep his mind off . . . everything.

Thirty-One

Marsha looked at the clock on the office wall. Only fifteen more minutes until the day was over. Now that she was finally settling into the rhythm and stresses of her new position, she couldn't believe how quickly time flew by. Meetings. More meetings. Pass on info from the meetings. Report to the team members. Field a phone call. Listen to the team members. Come up with a team agreement. Go over a checklist.

Another phone call. One more meeting. *Sha-zam!* Time to go home again.

She checked tomorrow's calendar for early morning meetings. *May Day. I can't believe it! Two weeks tomorrow since Barb's death.* Every year Barb brought her and several others on staff, including Frank, a homemade May Day basket. The simple baskets usually contained lilies of the valley from Barb's yard and a few sprigs of houseplant ivy. A knot caught in Marsha's throat.

"See you tomorrow," Buzz said, as he flew by. Then he stopped dead in his tracks and backed up to her desk. "You okay? You look rattled."

"I'm fine. Just a little sad. It'll be two weeks tomorrow since I lost my best friend. She always brought flowers in on May Day."

Marsha never mentioned to Buzz that she'd seen the retirement card he'd given Barb. It wouldn't feel right to let him know it had been passed around, a private moment invaded like that.

It made her think about what all her kids might find if *she* suddenly died. *The diary!* How awful that would make them feel! What if they didn't realize how far she'd come, how much she'd changed and grown from those first angry and bereft pages? But where else could she keep it if not in her desk drawer? Certainly not at work. She needed to make sure she recorded things that were going right in her life: personal growth spurts, signs of hope within the doubt, her new job achievements.

"Okay then. Have a nice evening," Buzz said as he chugged off again.

"You too." No, she would never mention the card, but she would always be grateful for it. It wasn't often one got to peek inside the heart of an acquaintance. Buzz was an okay guy. It made her wonder how many others she'd misjudged by appearances and first impressions throughout the years.

She began packing the black leather briefcase she'd bought now that she was in management. Barb would love that she'd done that for herself.

DīMute had recently issued her a work laptop, which made her feel all corporately. She didn't much care for the teensy keyboard, and she was quickly learning that the ability to take work home was both a blessing and a curse. Nonetheless, at this point in the game, DīMute's faith in her made her feel not only valued but respected.

"Hey! Got a minute, Marsha?" Marsha looked up to find Frank ogling her bowl of Tootsie Rolls. Now that Barb was gone, he hardly ever stopped by to see just her. Another shocker: she missed his quirky ways.

"Frank! I'll always have a minute for you," she said, picking up the bowl of Tootsie Rolls and holding them up in offering. He snagged one and began to unwrap it. "No one can eat just one of these," she said. "You better take a fistful. You'll save me the calories."

He took a few more and stuffed them into his pants pocket, the same pants he'd likely wear tomorrow.

"I don't know about you, but I miss Barb's goodies," she said. It suddenly struck her how odd it was that no one mentioned Barb, as if she'd never existed.

"To be sure," he said. "And I surely do miss Barb. Tomorrow is May Day, you know."

"Funny. I just thought about that myself."

He ate the Tootsie Roll and dropped the wrapper in her wastebasket, then continued to stand there, fiddling with a suspender.

"Can I do something for you, Frank?"

"I'm wondering if the Encouragement Club is done for. I had a few people ask me during my routes this week. I told them I imagined so. But then, I imagine a lot of things," he said, shooting her a halfhearted smile. "Like for instance that I see Barb every now and then."

"Me too. I almost picked up the phone to call her again yesterday. It stinks to have to keep remembering, over and over again, that she's gone."

"Indeed it does. So what should I tell folks about the club?"

"Let me think about it over the weekend. I know at the last meeting, after we heard about Barb,

Mr. Waters collected e-mail addresses. Hey, do you have an e-mail address, Frank?" He shook his head. "Hmm. Well, that's okay. I haven't heard from him since the funeral anyway. Without that list I don't know how to contact many of the people who've lost their jobs—but don't worry, even without an e-mail, Frank, I know how to get ahold of you." She winked and waggled her candy bowl. "For now, just tell people you're not sure. Maybe we'll figure something out. Or maybe we'll just be done with it. It is kind of hard to imagine *any* kind of Encouragement Club without Barb."

"Indeed it is," he said, pulling his suspenders out, then relaxing them back to his chest. "I'll be heading home then. I was just wondering."

"Good night, Frank."

"Night, Marsha." She watched as he quickly high-footed it down the hall. "Frank!" she yelled.

He turned on his heels. "Yes?"

"Thanks for stopping by and telling me people are asking. I appreciate it."

"You bet."

She wondered who would ever appreciate Frank as much as Barb. Likely nobody, but she could swear she felt Barb tapping her on the shoulder. *I guess it's my turn to make sure he gets his sweets and his compliments, and an occasional reining in with the gossip, right? Maybe I'll make him a May Day basket in your honor. Let's see, what do*

I have in my yard? Grass. No lilies. No house-plants since I killed them off again.

She opened her desk drawer and grabbed a blank piece of computer paper, then cut a one-inch strip off the narrow end. She rolled the larger piece of paper into a cone, then stapled on the strip to serve as a handle. Using different color highlighters, she drew a few flowers on the paper and plunked in a fistful of Tootsie Rolls.

"There," she said, hiding it in her drawer. "I'm ready for you tomorrow, Frank." She nodded toward the heavens. "Thanks, friend," she whispered.

You were right. Giving feels good. Encouragement is good.

"Thank goodness that's over," Josie said. She closed her peripherals and gulped the giant glass of water she'd stashed behind her monitor. She wondered if they'd noticed her cheeks reddening, the droplets of sweat sprouting on her upper lip. She wiped her face with a tissue.

As handy as video conferencing was, it also had its downsides. It was one thing to sit around a big corporate conference table laden with pitchers of ice water placed on trivets, a glass at each place; it was quite another to watch a solitary person on a computer monitor tilt her head back and drink. She'd once been on the receiving end of such an action, looking right up a gentleman's nose, which was magnified through the end of the glass and enlarged by its proximity to the built-in camera in his computer. She barely heard a word he said for thinking how much he needed one of those nose hair Roto-Rooter things she'd seen advertised on television. She made a note to steer clear of engaging in such visual mistakes herself.

"Look straight into the monitor. Glance down as little as possible, and then just with your eyes. Never turn your head to look behind you or to the side. Remain seated. Don't lean forward. Smile, even when you don't feel like it. And for goodness sake, keep your hands away from your face."

She'd printed the set of instructions before her first video conference and read it aloud before each one since. She also checked another of her pre-conference-call lists to remind her to turn off all her phones and the call waiting and let the doorman know she was not receiving visitors.

Aside from her dry voice and the untimely hot flash, she felt good about the actual business they'd conducted. The exchange of information between her and the four gentlemen at Bricktown Mutual had been lively, ending with the HR guy saying, "I wish we had more time to talk." Always a good sign. He'd asked smart questions and seemed impressed with her base of knowledge. One of the VPs said he felt encouraged by their conversation, another good sign.

She was glad to have something positive to

talk about with Amelia at dinner tonight, the first time they'd be together since Victor arrived and dropped his bomb. As Josie told Amelia during their two brief phone conversations, "Have I got a story to tell *you!*"

Josie changed into a sweat suit, refilled her water glass, and sat back down in front of her computer. She'd amassed quite the file on Oklahoma City, a place—a possible opportunity? —that grew more interesting by the moment.

The more she'd researched, the more she wondered how the second largest geographical city in the country, an incredible factoid, had thus far escaped her avid attention. Okay, it wasn't Chicago, but still, there looked to be plenty of culture; change in seasons with an average yearly temperature around sixty degrees; the crossroads of major interstate highways; an equal distance from L.A. and New York City, another fun tidbit to discover. The city looked clean; the economy seemed to be holding steady, considering; recent upscale downtown housing; restored warehouse neighborhood, which reminded her of some of the kitschier housing areas she'd discovered in Chicago; Myriad Botanical Gardens . . .

Of course no city was perfect, and tourism bureaus could make the mundane sound miraculous. And there was the whole "tornado alley" thing. But what area of the country wasn't ripe for some kind of disaster?

Her research efforts had whetted her appetite enough to hope she at least got to check the place out during an interview. She located Bricktown Mutual on Google Maps using the satellite view. It looked situated not too far from the heart of Bricktown, Oklahoma City's entertainment district, and a mile-long man-made canal.

The phone rang, startling her. It was Victor.

"Hello, this is your father," he said, as if she wouldn't recognize his voice.

My father. She missed his next few words as she considered yet another of his many startling changes in behavior. *Did finding a new woman bring out the paternal in you, Victor?*

"How go the travel plans?" he asked.

"Good. Since I'm between jobs right now,"— something she'd told him during their last phone conversation, which wasn't a lie yet didn't exactly cover the entire truth—"I've decided to drive in on Thursday. That'll give me more time to spend with Ginny before the flurry of a pre-wedding day." She would never have considered such a thing had she not listened to Amelia talk about her wedding planner's agenda for *her* pre-wedding day.

"How long will you get to stay?"

"It's uncertain right now. I might have to make a trip to Oklahoma City for an interview, but I'm not sure yet."

"Ginny," she heard her father say, his mouth

turned away from the phone, "Josie is coming in on Thursday."

"Wonderful!" the enthusiastic voice in the background said.

"Where are you, Victor?" Josie asked.

"I'm at Ginny's house. I'll be glad when the wedding is over and we're settled in together. Commuting in order to date a lady is for the young. It'll be nice just to be an old married couple, rest up a little before we plan our first vacation. We were thinking Hawaii, but now we're considering France so Ginny can meet Donovan."

For the first time ever, it flew through Josie's mind that perhaps her mom didn't like to travel or move but also wasn't willing to explore. *Hmm.*

"I've been moving some of my stuff into Ginny's home already, but truth is, she has everything we need. We've decided there is no point establishing a new place. I think I'll donate my furniture and household goods to the American Vets, have them bring a truck and just pick everything up. I'm not attached to anything anyway, not the way Ginny is here." Josie noticed he was nearly blathering again. "I bet you'll find this hard to believe, Jo, but at this point in my life, *quaintness* is starting to grow on me." He laughed, as did the voice in the background. *Nervous energy? Lovesickness? Renewed hormones?*

"I told you quaintness was nothing to laugh

about!" Josie heard the lilty female voice say. "Just wait until *religion* starts growing on you!"

Their combined laughter—their inside jokes and upcoming wedding and the whole concept of the "two of them"—left Josie feeling outside their new, blossoming family.

When their laughter died down, Victor said, "We'll see you in a week then, Jo. We're so glad you're coming. Do you think you can find Partonville? It's been a long time since you were in town."

"MapQuest can find anything, and I can follow MapQuest, so I'll be fine." *On my own, which I always am.*

Victor gave her Ginny's address. He said they'd be waiting for her and she should come hungry. "Ginny loves to cook and make sure nobody leaves hungry."

After they hung up, Josie sat deflated. It wasn't like she had a close relationship with her father to begin with, but now this? Now that he was finally retired from the rigors of the military, someone else swooped in to receive his focused attention?

But the sounds of Ginny's happy laughter—the heartiness of their combined laughter—stayed with her. *Who wouldn't want to meet a miracle worker?* she asked herself. *Consider it research.*

For now, Josie went back to vetting Bricktown Mutual's financials, then mapping the greater OKC area using Google's satellite view. She'd read about the canal, which she explored by running the mouse along it, but she was intrigued to discover so many twisty-turny streams of water throughout the city and beyond.

The first time she zoomed in on one of them, she heard the faint sounds of rushing water.

"I'M NOT EVEN GOING TO LOOK AT YOU!" she yelled loud enough that the snowglobe in the living room could hear her. "DON'T EVEN BOTHER!"

No matter which way she moved the mouse, she was stunned to be able to find a lake, or follow a river to a stream, a stream to a creek, the sound of the running water growing louder at each fork until she finally had to put her hands to her ears and start humming to drown it out.

Not until she moved the mouse over the block where Bricktown Mutual was located did the roaring sounds of the water stop.

Thirty-Two

That's incredible. Just incredible," Amelia said. "My friend Suze experienced something similar with her mom. Suze's folks divorced when she was in her teens. Her mom declared to her only daughter that she'd never marry again. But then one day, decades later, Suze's phone rings and her mom starts gushing about this man. *Gushing*. She says they met

389

online at Match.com, which blew Suze's mind to begin with. Her mom told her they e-mailed for a month, then called each other and talked for hours. Even though they only lived about a hundred miles apart, it took them another month of phone calls before they met in person. Two weeks later, she called Suze to say she was getting married, and that she sure hoped Suze could attend. Same exact thing, nearly. Swept off her feet. Giddy crazy in love. Wedding plans made, such that they were, without even consulting her only daughter."

"How did Suze respond?" Josie asked.

The waiter set a giant piece of chocolate cake between them. A mixture of hot fudge and caramel sauce ran down the sides of the mound like lava, nuts flowing in its midst. Amelia had ordered it, asking for two forks and an extra plate. She told Josie that if ever they needed the comfort of a massive sweet-out, it was now. They stopped talking and downed a couple of bites, moaning in the decadent pleasure.

"How *can* you respond?" Amelia said, picking up her story. "She felt betrayed. Left out. Hurt. Angry. But in the end, she couldn't miss her own mother's wedding, so like a dutiful daughter, she went—and fell in love with the guy. Years later, the two of them still live like two happy little love doves. Maybe as you age you learn to let go of things? Or gain a different perspective? Or lose your marbles. Or finally just find the right match, or the next right match, or . . . Who knows. Love does what it does."

"As you age, huh?" Josie said, reminded she was quickly heading toward fifty and was a good deal older than Amelia.

Apparently Amelia read her mind. "I meant nothing personal by that, Josie. I was shocked when I learned you were older than me. You don't seem like it at all. Plus, you haven't hit fifty yet. We're talking sixties and seventies here. *Really* old. Which when we're that age will not seem that way at all. Then *really* old will be nineties, I guess."

They polished off the cake while Amelia shared the latest details about her wedding plans, seating charts, bridesmaids drama.

"By the way," she said between bouts of licking her fork, "we haven't received your RSVP yet, but I assume you're coming."

Josie cocked her head.

"I gave you the invitation, right?"

Josie shook her head.

"What a numbskull! What ever happened to the one with your name on it that I carried in my purse for so long? I was going to hand deliver it last time we met. I am so embarrassed! Seriously, I am aghast. You do know you're *invited* to the wedding, right? You have it on your *calendar,* right?"

Josie's eyebrows raised on their own accord.

"You are kidding me! Please tell me you're available on June 6. *Please.*"

"I, um . . . To tell you the truth, I have no idea. Seriously, I didn't expect an invitation. You haven't known me that long. Guest lists need to have their limits, and I've never even met Alfred."

"Are you serious? I consider you among my top-tier friends! It doesn't take a long relationship to bond people—obviously," she said, chuckling, the implication about Victor and Suze's mom not lost on Josie. "You got your BlackBerry with you, right? Check your calendar. Right now."

Josie did as she was told, feeling like she was horning in on something. She could count on one hand the list of weddings she'd attended. She hoped Amelia wasn't inviting her just because she felt sorry for her about Victor's wedding.

But as quickly as she had the thought, she dismissed it. Deep inside herself, she knew better than that. She was learning that wasn't the way true friends operated. And yes, Saturday night, June 6, was open. What else would she have down for a weekend? "So far, that date is free."

"So far? Write down 'Amelia's wedding. Four o'clock. Wedding reception immediately following.' I'll make sure you get an official invitation STAT. You'll meet Suze there; I have you at her table.

My, won't you two have things to talk about!" She threw her head back and laughed. "But seriously, all this time I thought you had the invitation. I am so sorry and incredibly embarrassed. Blame it on jittery bride syndrome, okay? Why don't you ask Lyle Waters to escort you?"

"Where on earth did that come from?"

"From the land of handsome and possibilities," she said, sprouting a devilish grin.

Josie ignored the comment. "The date is open," she said, "but the only thing is that I could—and here's the next big thing you and I haven't discussed yet—be moving to Oklahoma City."

"What? When did this happen?"

"Nothing has actually happened yet, other than preliminary phone calls and a teleconference. But Oklahoma City intrigues me." She decided to keep her heebie-jeebie events to herself. "Not sure when they'd want me to start, if it's a go. But on the professional front, be prepared to get my house on the market and priced to sell."

"I can't believe you waited through the whole dessert to tell me this breaking news."

"I wanted to hear all the wedding stuff, and we'd already spent enough time on me. Too much time on me, in fact. Only one bomb permitted at a time."

"Nonsense. Utter nonsense. I like hearing about you. How else do you get to know a person if it's not through their stories, and tonight you had a juicy one about your dad. And now a possible new job offer? Double bomb!

"Look, Josie," Amelia said, making it clear she was about to get serious, "I know you're new to this best-buddy thing, and you're always worried about sharing. Just don't forget that I'm a big girl, and I'm adorable." She struck a cheerleader-grin pose and laced her fingers under her chin. "But since this particular story *is* about me, I haven't seen your thumbs entering anything in that BlackBerry yet, so get my wedding down for June 6."

Then her face turned sorrowful. "It's dawning on me that if you do move to Oklahoma City, you'll actually move to Oklahoma City. Out of Chicago. Away from me. Wow," she said, "that thought makes me incredibly sad. Happy for you, of course, but still . . . I've always known you'd be moving one day, but since we've gotten to know each other, I'd miss you something fierce," she finished, her voice barely audible.

Josie stared hard into Amelia's eyes, which began to water. "Seriously? You'd miss me?"

"Of course! Why would you ask such a thing?"

Amelia's tear pool dissipated as quickly as it appeared, but an onslaught of tears blindsided Josie. She tried to swallow them back, hide them behind her napkin, and smile them away, but like the river in the snowglobe, when they decided to run, there was no stopping them.

Amelia pulled the paper cocktail napkin out from under her cola and passed it across the table. "Josie, what is it?"

When Josie collected herself enough to speak, she did so through a fresh onslaught of tears. "Not since years before my mother died have I heard anyone say they'd miss me." She melted into quiet sobs. The waiter cleared the dessert dish and made a quick exit when he realized a distraught woman sat before him.

To help them both recover, and to end the evening on a happy note, once Josie finally pulled herself together, she raised her water glass and said she'd like to propose a toast. Amelia, always ready to celebrate, raised her glass and waited.

"Here's to love," Josie said, "however old or new or confounding it may be." They clinked. "And here's to the fact that I get to attend two weddings within the next month, and that they will be absolutely and utterly nothing alike!"

Clink.

Much to her surprise, Josie slept like a baby that night. No hot flashes, no nightmares, no snowglobe tricks. She didn't wake until her phone rang.

"Josie, it's your father. I didn't wake you, did I?"

What is up with my father suddenly calling all hours of the night and day? "Of course not," she said. "I just haven't spoken to anyone yet today. Is everything okay?" It struck her she was beginning to think of him in terms of *father* rather than *Victor.*

"Couldn't be better. I was just talking about something incredibly coincidental, and Ginny said why don't you just pick up the phone and tell Jo about it, since she's the one it pertains to?"

"What's that?" Josie said, looking at the clock. *Seven-thirty? I thought it was about five.* She had to go to the bathroom, but she doubted the conversation would last very long—and how was it that this woman who didn't remotely know her was already referring to her as Jo?

"Last time I called, you mentioned a job possibility in Oklahoma City. I don't know if you knew this or not, but before I married your mother, I did a stint at Fort Sill, not too far from OKC."

"Huh. No, I don't believe I ever heard that."

"You know that snowglobe you have at your house? The one in your cabinet in the living room?"

A prickle ran up the back of Josie's neck.

"When I first saw it, it reminded me of Oklahoma City, what with so many lakes, creeks and streams, and rivers running through and around that area. Then I got to thinking about how coincidental it was that out of nowhere, you find a job possibility in OKC. I told Ginny, if Jo likes water, I think she'd really enjoy it there. Hear anything more about that job yet?"

Josie sat up in bed, her entire body electrified. Of all the nice pieces of art in her home, that was the thing he noticed? She hadn't pointed it out to him, had in fact steered them both clear of it. "When did you notice the snowglobe?"

"Let's see. I think it was the day I arrived. Yes. After the planetarium but before we ate dinner. When I finished my shower, you were in your office, which puzzled me because I thought you were in the kitchen."

"Why did you think that?" she asked, standing and raking her hand through her hair.

"Because I heard water running in that direction. But when you weren't in the kitchen and I still heard water running, I wandered around a little, thinking maybe you had another restroom."

"*Was* the water running . . . anywhere?" She put her hands over her eyes, as if to shield herself from whatever might come next.

"No. Guess I just imagined it. Or maybe water had been running in the pipes in your building? But that's all beside the point. I called about the peculiar timing of me seeing a snowglobe that reminded me of Oklahoma City, which I hadn't thought about for years, then you right away entertaining a job possibility there. Did you hear any more from the company?"

"No. But I just spoke with them yesterday, Friday. When you called, I'd barely hung up from the teleconference. I don't expect to hear from them until late next week, if even that early. I'm sure I'm not the only consultant they're querying."

Again from the background Josie heard, "Tell her I've been praying about her next job, and that I have a good feeling about Oklahoma City."

"Ginny says to tell you she's been praying for your next job and that she has a good feeling about Oklahoma City."

It prickled Josie to have someone she'd never met offer an opinion about something she knew *nothing* about. "Yes, I heard."

"Well, keep us posted," Victor said, his voice suddenly deflated. Josie realized her negative thought must have affected the tone in her voice. "In the meantime," he said, chippering himself up, "we'll see you in less than a week."

She forced herself to chipper up too. That's what they did in her family: buck up, soldier! Or at least they used to. Now that Victor seemed to be turning sappy and preparing to marry the Queen of Perky, who knew.

"Yes. Less than a week," she said. "I look forward to it."

Oh boy.

Thirty-Three

I am so glad to learn we're on the same wavelength about the Encouragement Club, Mr. Waters," Marsha said. "I've been thinking about it a lot lately, but I didn't have the list."

"Marsha, if you don't start calling me Lyle, I'm going to start calling you Ms. Maggiano."

"That wouldn't be right," she said. "That would make me sound a bazillion years old."

"Exactly."

"I'll try," she said. "But back to the Encouragement Club. Frank asked me just the other day about the club—and you know Frank: if anyone is talking about anything, Frank knows. He said several people asked him about the club, if and when it was coming back. You know, that really speaks to Barb's efforts *and* the economy, doesn't it?"

"I hear what you're saying about Barb, but how so about the economy?"

"Anyone Frank talked to obviously still works at DīMute , so I guess nobody feels secure in their job. Plus, the club meetings were a good time. In this day and age of so many transitions, it's easy to feel adrift, by yourself out there. We all still miss Barb, we all still miss our past coworkers, and we want to know how they're faring."

"Good observation. By the way, I'm glad to learn you're prospering."

They'd spent the earlier part of the conversation catching up. Lyle had shared a few highlights about his recent visit to Oklahoma City, from which he'd just returned that Sunday afternoon, and she'd navigated the tricky waters of sounding pleased with changes at DīMute without making it seem like they were better off without Lyle.

"How is it working for *Buzzzzz*?" Lyle asked.

She hesitated a moment, switched the phone to her other ear. "You know, he's turned out to be surprisingly different from everyone's first impression." She remembered what a terrible start they got off to, the way Buzz dropped by the club, seemingly to spy—and instead he'd just been looking for a little encouragement himself. "I'd say he's doing fine. He's not you, Mr. . . . Lyle. But then he's not the ridiculous monster we first feared either."

"Just goes to show you that you can't judge a book by its cover, or its pants," Lyle said, chuckling. "I'm glad for you and DM or Diamond Mutual, or . . . what are you calling it now?"

"DīMute, but not as in die mute. You'd have to see the new logo. It's pretty slick. We're rebranding, as the saying goes."

He sighed. "Yes, rebranding. Rebuilding.

Remaking. Redoing. We live in the age of *re* now, don't we?"

"I guess so, in which case the question for us is, do we restart the Encouragement Club? And if so, how? Should one of us talk to Beth? I've been thinking about that, and here's what I've come up with." *Huh! All those team meetings are certainly teaching me how to speak up!* "I think the only reason it worked at Beth's before was because of Barb, who was nearly a daily customer of hers for so many years. I'm guessing Beth let us use that room for free because the club was only meeting for a week."

"I agree. To ask Beth for more would feel like an infringement on a friendship that wasn't ours to begin with. Have you come up with an alternative?"

"First of all, daily meetings are too much. When DĪMute was transitioning, that was good. But now, who can make daily meetings, especially among the commuters? I think either a weekly or bi-weekly schedule makes more sense. What about you?"

"Since networking is critical to job hunting, if the club only meets every two weeks, I wonder if we'd serve a purpose beyond socializing. Job opportunities might be gone before anyone gets a chance to share them. Then again, do we care?"

"Hmm. Good question," Marsha said. "Where's Barb when we need her? Hel-LO BARB! You listening?" The line was quiet for a moment, as if they awaited a response. "But we both know what Barb would say, that the point is to encourage one another."

"Exactly. Maybe we should start with weekly meetings, which are easier to remember, and see how it goes. If you can't come one week, you can drop in the next. I hate to say it, but without Barb as the honey pot, I wonder how long the bees will remain interested anyway." He didn't sound very positive.

"We'll just have to see. If they don't, so be it. Let me clarify something, though," Marsha said. "When I said we shouldn't ask Beth, I meant we shouldn't expect anything for free this time. We should go into it as a business deal, pay her for the use of the room. Or maybe she'd let us use it for free if we bought trays of bagel bites and a couple carafes of coffee for the meetings. I'd be willing to pony up for those the first couple of weeks."

"All excellent points, Marsha. No wonder you're doing so well. Barb would be proud," he said, his voice tender.

"Talk about an encouragement," she said. "*Thank* you. You couldn't say anything that would please me more."

"So, you want to talk to Beth then? What night of the week are you thinking?"

She looked at her calendar. "Wednesday, hump day. Same time slot as before, which was 5:10 to

5:40. If Beth could have things set up, that would work for me, unless you want to volunteer to arrive early."

"Can't commit to that."

"Do you have a new job then, or one in the works?"

"I have a little something under consideration, but nothing I'm ready to talk about."

"Do you want to e-mail me the EC list? If you type it up, I can send out a blast. Would that work for you?"

"Yes! I'll get on that tonight. Want me to send it to the work address on the list?" he asked. She could hear him flipping through pages.

"No. Let me give you my home e-mail. I do have a work-issued laptop, but I'll keep this off the official DiMute clock," she said.

"Wow! The new branding program must be doing okay for itself. Well, good for them, and good for you." His voice was sincere.

"Thanks, Lyle. I'll look for your e-mail."

"Check!" Lyle said to himself as he hung up the phone. For the last two hundred miles of his trip he'd missed half of his audio book while obsessing whether or not he'd arrive home in time to call Marsha. However, no sooner did he utter the word *check* than he realized he'd been obsessing about the Encouragement Club so he'd quit obsessing over Josie, because there she was in his thoughts again.

He looked at the clock. He and Marsha talked longer than he thought. Was eight-thirty on a Sunday night too late to call? Maybe Josie wasn't home anyway. Maybe she was out on a date. There was only one way to find out, so he dialed her number.

"Yes, you passed the test again," Josie said with a chuckle, referring to the caller ID. It made him happy she continued to remember their little exchange. "So you're home from your visit then?"

"Yup. Got in a couple of hours ago."

"How was traffic?"

"Moving. Sometimes fast, sometimes slow. How are things with you?"

"Shocking. Surprising. Hopeful. Calamitous. Pending. That about covers it."

"Wow. All that in under two weeks? Is the hopeful and pending part job related?"

"A couple of phone calls, several e-mails, and one teleconference don't quite add up to an offer, but Ginny is hopeful," she said, a note of sarcasm in her voice.

"Ginny?"

"My father's fiancée." Now she sounded annoyed.

"Would this be the shocking and surprising part?"

"Yes. Hopefully it's not the calamitous part as well. Honestly, I'm not even sure why I threw that word in."

"The word 'calamitous' does not seem a good fit for the Josie Brooks superwoman I'm familiar with."

"Superwoman?"

He wondered if that was a little too flippant. He probably shouldn't have called when he was tired. Time to back-pedal. "Strong. Assured. That's all I meant. Nothing derogatory."

"It didn't occur to me you were being derogatory. But superwoman? I think not. Maybe last year, but I've matured since then," she said, chuckling at herself.

He always found it sexy when women laughed at themselves. *All that and more,* he thought, picturing her sashaying down the Newberry Library hall. "Where's the job lead? Anyplace interesting?"

"My father and Ginny seem to think so," she said, then sounding chagrinned, she quickly added, "My apologies. Clearly I'm behaving like a two-year-old about this."

"And you, do you think the job lead is interesting?"

"Could be."

"You're not talking yet?"

"No mystery. Maybe you've been to the area and can shed a little light on it for me. Oklahoma City."

"You're kidding me." He stood up. He felt both electrified and terrified, with no time to sort out the why of either.

"No. Why would I kid you?"

"Maybe Ginny made you do it?" His mind reeled. *Surely this was a . . . what?*

"Can't blame this on Ginny," Josie said. "Honestly, I can't blame anything on her, and in fact I should probably be thanking her. She's obviously done wonders for my father."

"Your pending job offer in OKC wouldn't be with Bricktown Mutual, would it?"

"Okay, you're kidding me now, right? How could you possibly know that? I haven't told anyone."

"I walked right by the place a few days ago."

"You were in Oklahoma City?"

"Yep. I'm from a little town just outside the city. That's where I went when you encouraged me to visit my mom after her first stroke. Remember that? Maybe I didn't mention where she was, though."

"I do remember the conversation about your mom, but I don't recall you saying where she lived. It wouldn't have occurred to me to ask. I hadn't been working at Diamond Mutual very long. I just remember being glad you went. It takes a long time to get over a wrong choice like that. How is your mom doing now?"

"It's difficult. But we don't need to get into that. I'm more interested in this job thing of yours."

"Is Oklahoma City where your homeless guy Marvin lived?"

"Wow. Steel-trap memory you have there. Yes.

Yes, it was. But I never mentioned Oklahoma City then either? Obviously not," he said, answering his own question.

"You like it there then? Or maybe you don't, which is what you're doing in Chicago."

"Hang on to your seat. How unbelievable is this?" He was pacing now. "I like it enough that *I'm* hopeful about a job possibility that might move me back—and it deals with the homeless." He raked his fingers through his hair. "Seriously, this is an unbelievable coincidence."

"Incredible," she said, but he couldn't get a read on the tone in her voice.

"I really enjoy my family, and Sis could use help with Mom. But on the location front, OKC has really upped its presence the last couple of decades. Something for everyone, from canals to cowboys."

"Looks good on the Internet."

"Looks good in person," he said.

"Is a job lead why you went back this visit then?"

"Nope. Went back just to vacation and see my mom." He gave her a short recap of the circumstances that led to his interviews.

"I detect a genuine excitement in your voice, the same enthusiasm I heard in the coffee shop when you talked about Marvin. I hope it works out for you."

"I hope it works out for both of us," he said. "I truly do."

• • •

Josie sat on her couch, staring at the snowglobe in her hands and the phone lying next to her, still warm from Lyle's surprise call. It was all so surreal. Her father's wedding. The kindness of her new friend Amelia, who would miss her if she moved. The ease with which she admitted to Lyle her feelings about her father and Ginny. How naturally their friendly banter sprang to life the moment they no longer worked together.

She turned the snowglobe upside down for a moment, then uprighted it and watched as the snow landed on the still waters. A feeling of utter peacefulness washed through her.

"*When* I move to Oklahoma City, land of many creeks," she said, for just like that, she *knew*. Her job offer there was a done deal. All "coincidences" led directly to Oklahoma City. Her father, Ginny, Lyle, Bricktown Mutual . . . It was meant to be. She laughed out loud when she realized Ginny knew before she did. *How did* that *work?*

Without giving it a second thought, she called Lyle.

"And you, Ms. Brooks, have now passed my caller ID hurdle."

"After I tell you why I'm calling, I hope you're happy with that decision."

"Try me."

"This might seem forward at best and tacky at

worst, but I'm calling to see if you'd like to attend a wedding with me."

"You are definitely full of surprises. Looking for a second opinion about your dad and Ginny?"

"Not that wedding. That one is for family only and it's down in Partonville, Illinois, a little town I'm sure you've never heard of. But a friend of mine is getting married right here in Chicago on June 6. To the best of my knowledge, you haven't met Amelia, but I know you've seen her a couple of times. She and I used to meet just outside the entryway to Diamond Mutual. She remembers seeing you there."

"Does this mean you've been talking about me?"

She opened her mouth to respond, but nothing came out. How embarrassing was this?

"I herewith retract my inappropriate and egotistical question," he said, a playful note in his voice, "and replace it with an affirmative answer: Yes, I would be happy to attend a wedding with you on June 6. And I would be happy to invite you to dinner at my place tomorrow evening. I'm planning on whipping up a batch of Lyle's Manly Manicotti, but I have a feeling you're a strong enough woman to handle it."

Josie looked at the snowglobe. *Still waters,* it seemed to whisper. "I believe I can handle your manly manicotti too," she said, thinking that at the moment, she could handle just about anything. "What can I bring?"

"I can't think of a thing. Just a hearty appetite. By the way, here's something else for you to think about. I *have* heard of Partonville. In fact, I spent the night there on my way to Oklahoma City. At the Lamp Post Motel, which I highly recommend. How's that for another cosmic mind-boggler?"

"I'm speechless."

The bigger cosmic mind-boggler came the next day when she filled out the RSVP card for Amelia's wedding invitation. She could hardly believe her eyes when she saw their names written side by side: Brooks and Waters.

Thirty-Four

Josie thought her stomach might explode. She wasn't used to consuming so much at one meal. But not wanting to disappoint her father, she'd asked for seconds of nearly everything Ginny served, which made him beam.

"I told you Ginny was a good cook and to come hungry. She has a huge garden every year. I got to see the tail end of it during our class reunion last fall when she invited everyone over for cake. She canned those beans too," he said, nodding at the pile on her plate. "A lot of work goes into canning."

Ginny cooed and thanked him for the compliment. She looked at Josie and said, "I heard your mother was a good cook too. Vic said she made the best meat loaf this side of heaven."

Vic? Not even my mother called him Vic.

Josie didn't know what she was supposed to say in response. Not wishing to offend, she kept her mouth shut, nodded, and smiled.

Josie felt like she was riding a bullet train down the unfamiliar rails of surprise and reassessment. As much as she thought she would not like Ginny, she did. She couldn't help herself. Ginny was a sturdier woman than Josie had imagined and thankfully older in appearance than she expected. She was friendly, easygoing, and open, and she put on no airs. It was obvious she went out of her way to pave a road toward Victor's only daughter, and thankfully without patronizing her.

Ginny was so different from Josie's mother, who, although loving, was stiff compared to the earthiness of this lively woman. Ginny was a hugger, a jokester, and a fun person to be around. By comparison, Josie realized her mother was formal, slightly uptight, and always particular. Josie wondered if she'd every really known *either* of her parents. She could see why her dad was attracted to this bubbly, charismatic, and relaxed woman. Who wouldn't be? Ginny seemed sincere and absolutely head over heels in love with her father. Still, it was mind-boggling to understand how the same man could fall in love with two such different women.

After Ginny cleared the dishes and stacked them on the counter—a mess Josie's mother would never have left behind—she announced she was off to the nursing home to check in on two of her longtime friends. "I'll be gone about an hour," she said. "Make yourselves at home and have another piece of pie." She grabbed her bag of knitting and out the door she went.

Before the door had fully closed behind her, Victor said, "So what do you think?" He searched Josie's face, his eyes clearly expectant—and utterly vulnerable.

"I think she's lovely. I see why you like her. I'm happy for both of you and glad I'm here."

He reached out and took her hand, something he'd done twice to Ginny during dinner. Josie stared at her father's fingers curved up around her palm. The moons in her fingernails were the same shape as his. His hand was warm and comfortable, and the feel of it nearly made her weep.

"I see you're surprised at this," he said, lifting their hands. "I caught you staring when I reached for Ginny's hand too. I imagine it's as shocking as catching me with that first beer." He grinned and released her hand. "The thing is, Jo, your mother did not approve of public displays of affection, and from the beginning, she trained me well. She was a fiercely independent, strong, and strong-willed woman. You're a lot like her, you know."

Josie blinked several times, trying to bring a new picture of *herself* into view.

"Until I met Ginny, I forgot how natural I used to be at reaching out," Victor said. "I'm not saying it's better with Ginny, just different."

Different. The word rang in Josie's heart the next few days as she watched her father prepare to marry the woman he loved, then stand, tears in his eyes, and proclaim that love in a small and intimate church he used to make fun of.

Victor—her father—*was* different. Or maybe, just maybe, all these years she'd held a different and incorrect view of him.

Or maybe she was just now looking through her own "different" and more vulnerable eyes, transformed by the snowglobe's rivers of alluring intimacy and fearlessness, a new female friend, and the attention of a bleeding-heart kind of guy.

Different indeed.

Amelia and Alfred's wedding proved to be a giant splashy affair that went off without a hitch.

Josie was glad she and Lyle had a chance to enjoy a couple of double dates with them before the big day. It turned out Lyle and Alfred had played basketball together in a tournament at the Y a year or so ago. The world got smaller and smaller with each "coincidence." And Amelia was correct when she said Josie and Suze would have a good time chatting. They laughed themselves silly exchanging stories about their love-struck parents.

Several times during Amelia's reception, Victor's grinning wedding-day face popped into Josie's mind. Those two "old honeymooners," as Ginny referred to them, were off to Hawaii. Donovan said he'd have more time to visit with them if they came later in the year, so her father declared France would serve as honeymoon number two.

Even near the end of Amelia's wedding, after her veil and shoes were off, she looked stunning in her gown. Perfectly stunning. It warmed Josie's heart to witness Amelia step into what she'd once referred to as a lifelong fantasy: to be the beautiful bride.

It must be wonderful to live your dream.
Now, what is mine?

The Encouragement Club began meeting Wednesdays at Beth's Bagel Haven. Lyle told Josie that the attendance, which was lively and ever-changing, satisfied him a great deal.

Josie's curiosity finally got the best of her, and she stopped by one evening. To her relief, Marsha welcomed her with warmth. Marsha was a hoot and did a great job conducting the meetings. Although the Encouragement Club wasn't Josie's cup of tea, she understood why Lyle participated.

After a few weeks, it was no surprise to Josie that both her job and Lyle's came through in Oklahoma City. Amelia listed and sold both their places in record time and recommended a couple of Realtors in OKC—one who proved just as accomplished as Amelia.

Ultimately—and surprisingly—both Lyle and Josie decided to rent places their first year in OKC, Josie close to Bricktown and Lyle near his family. Amelia and Alfred promised to come visit the first chance they got, speaking as though Lyle and Josie were already a done deal as a couple, which Amelia believed they were.

"Some days," Josie told Amelia, "it feels that way. But we'll see. One day at a time. For now, I'm just glad to finally make a move in my life knowing someone will miss me when I'm gone and that I don't have to *keep* moving to outrun my own fears. You've helped me grow, Amelia, and for that I will always be grateful. It'll be interesting to see what my life looks like at the end of this annual contract. Who knows, I might finally feel I've come home to the place *I* belong and stay put for a change."

"I have a feeling you're right about that," Amelia said. "I bet Ginny has that same feeling too."

The two of them laughed until they cried, which they were both doing when Amelia waved good-bye as Josie pulled away, Oklahoma City bound.

• • •

On a warm, humid, summer evening, Josie walked along a path in the Martin Park Nature Center. Each weekend she charted a different course on one of the OKC's nearby trails. As she stopped to rest a moment in the shade, she slid her sunglasses down her nose and peered over the top of them, past the swaying branches of the massive cottonwood tree she sat beneath. The Oklahoma sky was incredible today.

Azure.

She felt the whisper of her mother's voice deep within her as a memory sprang forth. "Josie, do you even know there *is* a sky?" Madeline asked her swiftly moving daughter.

"Of course, Mother."

"Do you know that today the sky is a beautiful *azure?*"

"Azure, Mother," Josie said, her voice sounding more like an impatient old-maid teacher than the grammar school student she was, "is the blue cyan color on the HSV color wheel."

"Yes, I know, dear. You've told me that before."

Josie shook her head at the memory of her own precocious self, felt the *whish* of her mother's loud sigh. She pushed her sunglasses back up on the bridge of her nose and leaned against the tree.

"But Josie," her mother had said, "don't you want to see that color in the *real* sky, which is up there above you?" While a determined Josie marched on and rolled her eyes, Madeline fruitlessly pointed not just a finger, but her entire arm toward the heavens.

It's a wonder I didn't wear out my eyeballs rolling them around in their sockets so often.

"One day, daughter of mine, you're going to finally notice the sky, and you're going to think, 'Wow!'"

Josie removed her sunglasses, stood, stretched, then tucked them into the pocket of her shorts. Floating on the breath of her mother's sigh, she strolled into the sunshine and stared above the horizon.

Azure.

"I'm looking, Mother," she said in a near whisper. "Wow! is absolutely right."

She drew a deep breath, her lungs expanding with the welcome arrival of discovery and peace. The music of the rippling water in the stream paralleling this area of the trail further quickened her senses. She moved closer, walking down the stream bank, drawn by an escalating desire to take off her shoes and dip her toes into the cool waters. *It's hot. Why not?* She wouldn't be the first she'd witnessed doing so this evening.

Leaning on a bench for balance, she removed her walking shoes and tennis socks. She tucked the socks into the toes of her shoes and set them off to the side, pondering how in the brief time she'd been in Oklahoma, the pace of her entire life felt more in rhythm with the rest of the world. Was it the air? Her job? Postcards from Ginny and her father? Nightly phone chats with Amelia?

Lyle?

She carefully sidestepped down the slight incline to the water's edge. The creek bottom looked like it might drop off fairly quickly, so she decided to sit and stretch her feet into the water rather than to step into it. The moment she sank her toes into the coolness, she felt sated to her core, and in that instant, she knew: whatever she'd been longing for all her life, it was already arriving in subtle and satisfying ways.

She stretched her arms behind her and leaned back on her palms, feeling the nuances of the curls of water run between her toes. The sound of the creek was as happy as the sound of the laughter she'd shared with Lyle last night. *What another unbelievable moment.* For the first time, he'd noticed her snowglobe and picked it up.

"Huh. This kind of looks like it could be from any number of places around here. You had it long?" He turned the globe upside down to stir the snow, but before he could upright it, the globe slipped through his hands. Although he scrambled to catch it, it crashed to the floor.

They both looked on in disbelief as the globe busted to pieces. The water rushed between them, and the tree broke lose from its base and floated right to her feet.

"No! Oh, Josie! I am so sorry," he said, bending to pick up the shards of glass.

"Leave it!" Josie said with such force that he stood, thinking she was angry at his carelessness.

In disbelief, she stared at their feet, the water, until a great bubble of laughter rose up within her and she could do nothing but let it escape, unable to explain, even to herself, what was so funny.

So freeing.

Perplexed, yet caught up in Josie's unstoppable laughter—especially after she laughed so hard she snorted—Lyle busted into guffaws too.

When the laughter began to subside, he wrapped his arms around her, drew her close, and said, "You always manage to surprise me."

They stood in silence for a long time, clinging to each other in the midst of bits of snow, shards of glass, and a spreading stain of water.

Josie closed her eyes. The full-bodied laughter left her feeling *so* good, as if it had jostled something open within her. She felt her shoulders drop as she allowed herself to relax into him.

When he leaned back to look at her, her breath caught in her throat, for in his eyes was the tender and intimate look of the man in the bronze statue—a look she fully returned.

With her bare toes in the creek water and the memory of last evening alive, Josie looked down the bank toward the large tree under which she'd been sitting. If she didn't know better, she'd think she was *in* her snowglobe, floating, sipping, quenching her soul with its goodness.

Epilogue

Josie loved her job at Bricktown Mutual. For the first time ever, rather than feeling like the outside loner soaring in to slay the fat in the land, she sensed a unique synergy between herself and the employees, management, and their mutual goals.

Bricktown Mutual already ran lean. What they needed from Josie were the fresh eyes of a new way, a better way, to stay competitive in the marketplace while upping their game.

A few months after she arrived, the number three man on BM's totem pole left for a new job. They immediately offered the position to Josie, who accepted without batting an eye.

"Are you sure?" Lyle asked her the night she accepted the position and invited him over for dinner to celebrate.

She'd never felt more sure of anything, she told him, a declaration she followed with a shamelessly robust kiss.

Every time Josie spoke with Amelia on the phone, she shared a bit more about her intense and intimate feelings for Lyle, and how quickly their mutual respect and love grew for each other.

"I *never* thought I'd share my shortcomings and confusing pieces of my past the way I do with him. And it's amazing," she told Amelia, "how wonderful it feels to watch the guy I used to refer to as a bleeding heart ignite with passion and dig, head down, into advocacy for the homeless. Powerful, really. Attractive beyond measure."

Josie was ecstatic when Ginny and her father called to say they were coming for a visit, mainly because she couldn't wait for them to meet Lyle and his greater family, whom Josie had grown to appreciate.

The first time they met, Noreen had regaled Josie with stories of how obvious it was Lyle had been attracted to her for a *long* time. When she told Josie about watching for Lyle's "bottom lip syndrome," Lyle feigned foul play, but they all had a good laugh over it.

"No wonder he wanted to come back home," Josie told Amelia.

Home, indeed. Within months, they were inviting Amelia and Alfred, Ginny and her father, and Donovan and his family to their wedding. The reception?

"What till you hear this, Amelia! We've rented out a little pizzeria called Ancona's Place. You're gonna love it. It's a place where the moon hits your eye like a big pizza pie—that delivers lifelong amore."

Helga, the Mysterious Matron,
The Final Chapter

Although things were never perfect in the multicultural land of milk and mazes, honey and hostages, in their hearts the people prospered. Fairies and leprechauns, giants and beautiful maidens learned to live together, encouraging each other as best they could.

Even Helmoot, the Reaper Rephotsirch, lost his sharp corners. The beautiful and cunning Marshalleon, now under what she at long last understood to be the holy and comforting spell of Matron Helga—not only a mysterious matron but a mystical and marvelous one—looked on in wonder as Helmoot's ugly warts began to fall away. Or perhaps, Helga told her, the crusty and vision-blurring spiky scales were at long last lifting from Marshalleon's own eyes, enabling her to witness such a miracle.

Marshalleon still doubted

Helmoot would ever sprout wings and fly, but at least his dark presence no longer towered over her, threatening to inject her with the evil venom poised on the tip of his tongue. He was no more or no less—no darker or lighter— than her equal now. Whereas she used to perceive him as a vampire capable of sucking the life forces right out of her, or sink her into the depths of her own anger and vengeance, now he was nothing more than Helmoot. A man among men, a person among people.

Marshalleon, wonder that she was, reveled in the freedom. For that, the thick- and wavy-haired Ginalilyoseon, daughter of Planet Uterus, gave thanks.

Late one Sunday night during a gathering of Marshalleon's clan, the sky twinkled with an abundance of grace and forgiveness. Even the bright light radiating from the eyes of the Great Barbizone showered down upon Marshalleon. Lost in the awesome wonder of it all, Marshalleon thought she heard the distant rush of running waters, but when she closed her eyes, she realized it was nothing more than the sound of her own river of grateful tears.

The End

READERS GUIDE

1. Josie's identity is centered on her independence. She works for herself, lives alone, and refuses to let anything—including relationships—tie her down. What does Josie see as the benefits to this lifestyle? What drawbacks does she come to recognize as the book progresses?

2. What does the snowglobe represent for Josie? Do you have anything in your life that triggers such an emotional and spiritual response from you?

3. Josie's thirst is directly connected to her desire for intimacy. How do you think she managed to go through so much of life not realizing she needed the intimacy of relationships with friends and family? What did she use to replace them?

4. Josie refers to Lyle as a "bleeding heart." Though Josie thinks this is a flaw, how is it actually an asset for Lyle? Despite their initial antagonism, what things do Lyle and Josie discover they have in common?

5. Marsha works through her pain and bitterness regarding her divorce by writing a novel called *Helmoot, the Reaper Rephotsirch*, in which she is the heroine and her ex-husband is the villain. Have you ever taken up an

activity or project in order to help yourself work through strong emotions? How does writing help Marsha?

6. As the creator of the Encouragement Club, Barb does her best to uplift the spirits of her friends and co-workers. How does she affect each of the characters? What legacy does she leave?

7. After Josie's many descriptions and stories about Victor, were you surprised when he arrived in the story? How did you expect him to be different? Do you think falling in love again has really changed him that much, or are Josie's memories inaccurate?

8. Amelia becomes Josie's first real friend. What qualities do she and Josie share? How is she different from Josie? How big a part do you think she played in Josie's relational awakening?

9. Which character was your favorite? Who did you connect with the most? Why?

10. Several characters are laid off during the course of the book, due to the declining economy and Diamond Mutual's need to streamline operations. What would you do if you were in Barb's or Lyle's situation? It's not uncommon to know someone who has lost their job in recent years. How did you help them through those days?

11. The Diamond Mutual employees' first

impressions of Buzz aren't in his favor. Marsha eventually realizes her initial judgment of him was wrong and grows to appreciate him as a colleague. Do you think this proves the importance of first impressions, or shows that they can always be overpowered with the truth?

12. What role does the Encouragement Club play in the life of each character? If you were to form an encouragement club of your own, what would it look like? What would its purpose be?

ACKNOWLEDGMENTS

How lucky am I to know kind friends and relatives who assist me with just about anything I dream up? EXTREMELY! I extend a special thank you to Paul Harris, Eric Baumbich, and Jim Baumbich who helped me better understand (well, mostly—including all the times I asked the same questions over and over) nuances of corporate life and the way things might go if a systems analyst and/or consultant made a lengthy appearance in a tight-knit office.

With enthusiasm, mission, and incredible networking, several Oklahoma City folks worked together to find Just The Right Spot. Thank you Julane Borth, Debbie Anglin, Laura Kriegel, and Casey Lindo. When I come to OKC, lunch is on me!

Danielle Egan-Miller, Joanna MacKenzie, and Lauren Olson at Browne & Miller Literary Associates LLC, I bow to you for extending such tireless, detailed, smart care and direction. And laughter. And many beverages. Danielle, I cannot imagine my career without you. Period.

To the cast and crew at WaterBrook Press, thank you for synergy, tolerance, eagerness, prayer, understanding, and SALES! Shannon Marchese, your ability to "get me" and set me free to write what I see in my mind's eye, then nudge the story to its best Self, is a gift.

George John Baumbich, your tolerance is beyond measure. I love you. XO

A Note from the Author

Charlene Ann Baumbich is a story chaser. "Something" comes to me (with goose bumps, an a-HA!, a gasp, a sigh, a tear, a laugh . . .) and if it sticks, my curiosity grows until "it" takes over.

These "somethings" arrive via the wind, a friend, a stranger, a movie, a cloud, a vision, an angel, a billboard, a song, my dog, the television, a salami sandwich, a great pair of earrings . . . or any form or object known to mankind, or not. Always, I am grateful.

As "it" begins to grow, I begin to write. With every word, I chase after the story, always running just ahead of me. It's all I can do to keep up with it and often don't. When I lose sight, I must squint real hard to catch the dust of its trail, hear the murmurs of its gifts.

Thus, Josie Victor Brooks, a systems analyst, appeared to me through a muse-y haze. The first thing I asked her was this: Why couldn't you be a writer? I KNOW about them!

Thus, research and listening to life became my guidelines. Thus, the story finished teaching me what I needed to know. Thus, I hope it spoke to you too.

To learn more about my writing—and sometimes I speak too—visit: www.charleneann baumbich.com.

Once there, lean in. Maybe a story is whispering to you too, and next it will be your turn to write.

Center Point Publishing
600 Brooks Road • PO Box 1
Thorndike ME 04986-0001 USA

(207) 568-3717

**US & Canada:
1 800 929-9108**
www.centerpointlargeprint.com